Dear Dave B

This book is a gift from Jen. You, see after all those parties in Yakima, some of that schooling actually stuck. I never would have imagined I would write a book after all that booze, but here is the proof. :)

Tom Lefter

TOM WRIGHT

DEAD RECKONING

This book is a work of fiction. While some of the characters are based on persons or composites of persons known by the author, their characteristics, attitudes, beliefs, and actions are creations of the imagination of the author to fit a purpose within the novel and should not be construed as real. Most of the locations are real or based on real locations. Any other resemblance to actual events, locales, organizations, or persons, living or dead, is purely coincidental.

Copyright © 2013 by Tom Wright

All rights reserved. This book or any portion thereof may not be reproduced or used in any manner whatsoever without the express written permission of the author except for the use of brief quotations in a book review.

Visit http://www.theweatherguru.com to contact author.

Printed in the United States of America

ISBN 978-1482346169

FOR CINDY, CODY, AND KATIE.

ACKNOWLEDGEMENTS

I would like to specifically thank David Seelye, Mike Lundberg, and Trace Fleming, for without the three of you and the long conversations on my deck and Emon Beach, Dead Reckoning might have never happened.

Others who contributed or otherwise helped in some way as the idea for this book hatched: Jane Seelye, Shaunna Neustel Fleming, and Julie Lundberg.

My first editor, Jennifer Provo Joyner, without whom I would have never found Sarah Cypher who helped me turn Dead Reckoning into something much better.

Last but not least, many thanks go out to my final editor, Jennifer Myers Hammer, who found all those elusive errors to which I had become oblivious.

The front cover photo is called "Sailing from the Storm" and was generously contributed by:

Jim Mandeville
Director of Photography
The Nicklaus Companies
Photo copyright © 2009 Jim Mandeville, all rights reserved.

THE END

It took less than two weeks for our entire civilization to collapse. Every life on this planet changed forever. This is how I remember it.

1

2:34 AM, SUNDAY, MAY 27TH – KWAJALEIN, MARSHALL ISLANDS

Slivers of moonlight knifed between the window sill and shade, pierced the ink-black night, and scattered faintly across my room. I felt watched—not alone—and my skin prickled with goose flesh.

I eased carefully out of bed and grabbed the window shade. It slipped from my hand, accelerated upward, and crashed into the top of the windowsill. It flapped around several times before slowing to a rest. I jumped from having given myself away.

Moonlight flooded the room, and I turned and saw nothing. The room changed from hot to cold in an instant; my breath appeared before me. I began to hyperventilate and the frigid air hurt my teeth.

Startled by a ringing sound, I turned and saw my children standing in the distance stolidly ringing bells. I started toward them, but the faster I moved, the further away they got. A telephone appeared before me. I lifted the receiver and said hello, but no one responded. The phone continued to ring as I held the receiver and looked at it.

Suddenly, I found myself rising through the air, as if coming up from some great depth. The ringing grew louder and closer as I approached the top.

When I reached the top, I opened my eyes. My heart thumped like a pounding fist, and the hairs on my clammy skin stood erect. I rolled over to look at the clock, and the wet sheets peeled away from my skin.

The telephone gave me a start when it rang again—twice in quick succession, signifying an off-island call coming in. As I reached for the phone, I looked again at the clock and the blood-red numbers read: 2:34. Panic returned. There was only one reason Kate would wake me in the middle of the night: something was wrong.

I lifted the receiver and said: "hello."

"Have you been watching the news?" Kate said with alarm in her voice.

I tensed as I rolled back onto the uncomfortably cool, damp sheets.

"What?" I asked.

"The news. Are you watching it?"

"It's two-thirty in the morning. Why would I be watching TV?"

I upset the order of my nightstand in an overaggressive reach and sent the remote to the floor. I righted the lamp and adjusted the clock to its proper angle before retrieving the remote. I switched on the television and waited for my eyes to adjust.

When the screen came into focus, it was tuned to what we called "the roller," or a channel displaying a series of informational slides about activities around USAKA. USAKA stood for United States Army Kwajalein Atoll which was home to Reagan Test Site (abbreviated RTS), a missile testing site in the Marshall Islands, about half-way between Hawaii and Australia. It was also our home and had been for seven years.

I quickly switched to the other channel (we had only two) and found a replay of a baseball game I'd seen the previous night. It was my beloved Seattle Mariners, but I felt irritated not to have a news channel when something was going on.

"All I've got is baseball and the roller," I said.

I heard Kate's sigh all the way from Seattle where she and our three children were visiting her parents. "It's the Red Plague. It's gone nuts."

The media had been hungrily covering an outbreak of a new virus for about a week— the Red Plague, they called it. It was some kind of hemorrhagic virus—very lethal and very contagious, but, so far, no one had been infected outside of Florida where it started. And Florida was quarantined. Of course, it was all they could talk about though.

"You know how they are, if it bleeds it leads," I said. "Has it popped up somewhere else?"

"It's worse than that. It's everywhere."

As a lawyer, Kate was quick, hard-nosed, and a great debater, but also prone to exaggeration. Being a scientist, I preferred rational analysis to emotion.

"It can't be *everywhere*," I said. "You don't have it."

"Cases exploded overnight," she replied. "And now it's in Texas, California, Asia, and maybe even Europe. They think it was engineered by terrorists, and the president is already saber-rattling over it. I was watching Fox News and,"

"Stop watching Fox News," I interrupted.

She continued with barely a pause. "And it has an incubation period of up to a week. We could all have it and not even know it."

"I told you, it will be fine. Just stay at your mom's house and don't go out—any of you. Don't come in contact with people. Just lay low and wait for it to blow over."

"They're already talking about shutting down air travel. I think we should come home."

"Get on a plane?" I said. "There is a reason they're thinking about shutting down air travel. If you want the Red Plague, there's no better place than on a plane."

"Well, what are we supposed to do?"

"Just lay low. The virus doesn't walk through walls."

"What if the shit hits the fan?"

We had talked about that before. Kate and the kids spent the entire summer back in the states almost every year. I usually got a few weeks off, but we often wondered what we would do if separated by 5,000 miles of ocean in a crisis scenario.

"It can't be that bad," I said.

"That's easy for you to say. We're here and you're there, safe and secure."

That was true. In a global catastrophe of just about any kind imaginable, there would hardly have been a safer place than Kwajalein. Kwajalein was completely isolated from the outside with a buffer of thousands of miles of ocean in every direction and a comfortably warm, tropical climate. We were also fully self-sufficient with plenty of fish in the sea, coconuts and other crops on land, and probably lots of emergency food in a warehouse somewhere.

"If things get really bad, I'll come over there," I said. "Better just one of us on a plane than all four of you."

"*If* you can," she said pessimistically.

"Listen," I said in an attempt to placate her. "If worse comes to worst, I will come over there. I promise." I knew it would never come to that.

She said nothing, apparently intent on what she was watching.

"I've got to go," I said. "I have to work early."

"Yeah, right," she said, knowing full well that I had a boat trip planned with the boys the next day.

I sat there for a few moments, just listening to her breath on the other end. Beautiful and intelligent beyond description, I often wondered by what karma I had been able to marry so far out of my league.

"All right," she said. "I'll let you go then. I love...."

The line went dead.

Those were the last words she ever said to me.

2

9:19 AM – KWAJALEIN, MARSHALL ISLANDS

As we screamed past a sailboat in our Boston Whaler, I watched a poor kid scramble to the port side of the sailboat and wretch into the sea. He spat into the water, wiped his mouth with the back of his hand, and then slumped to the deck. His left arm flopped over the side, fingers skimming the glassy water with the relentless rocking of the boat.

A thought about the red plague arose from that place in my mind that I cannot control, but I overruled it. He was just sea sick. His parents came over to console him and offered him something – motion sickness pills, no doubt. It was way too late for that.

I can sympathize. I've only been motion sick twice in my life, both on a sailboat. Even a light wind creates a tremendous force against the sum of sail and hull, and when combined with an opposing current, the boat can rock in every direction at the same time. For me — and apparently that boy, too — that is all it takes. No doubt he had found his spot for the rest of the trip.

My name is Matthew Anderssen. I was named after Saint Matthew of the Bible, a fact about which I have never been fond. I won't answer to any name but Matt, so that's what everyone calls me. I was the Chief Meteorologist for RTS, and I was stationed on Kwajalein (or Kwaj, as we called it), which is the main island in the ring of coral islands that make up Kwajalein Atoll.

My friends and I left the sailboat on our starboard side and made for Bigej (pronounced Bee Gee), another island within the atoll. We intended to spend a few hours there lounging in the bathwater-warm lagoon, snorkeling, swilling cold Corona, and then fishing down the east reef on the way back to

Kwaj. It was a great way to spend a Sunday, the beginning of our weekend. At 167 degrees east longitude (13 degrees west of the dateline), we were nearly a full day ahead of the states, and we staggered our weekends to coincide with the stateside work week.

My friend Jeff Riggins skippered. As the Chief Information Officer for the range, he had a geeky, techno side, but he was not a typical computer nerd—he was just as comfortable with an outboard as a motherboard. As a master sailor and one of the few private sailboat owners at Kwaj, he was salty and rugged. Jeff was the kind of guy that could turn an already relaxing weekend boating trip into a day at the spa for the rest of us simply by being so knowledgeable and reliable. No matter what happened, he knew what to do and how to do it.

I watched Jeff as he piloted the boat, hoping to pick up on some of his techniques. His shoulder-length blonde hair whipped in the wind from under his backwards Milwaukee Brewers cap, and his sunglasses clung to the tip of his nose like bifocals. A loose tank top held firm against his chest while the remainder gathered downwind from him, snapping like a flapping flag. He was a touch taller than me, and he had a deep, dark tan from many hours at sea. I watched as he leaned forward to meet every wave and then back as we slid down into the trough; his body remained plumb the entire trip.

Jeff suddenly jerked the wheel to port and then back to starboard again. I snapped my head to starboard just in time to see a sea-turtle happily treading water as we whizzed by just a few feet to his port side. The turtle splashed frantically over the sudden, unexpected wave of our wake, then it paused and craned its neck to look. Seeing nothing, it continued on.

About fifteen minutes later, we entered Bigej Pass which connected Kwajalein Lagoon (the largest enclosed lagoon in the world) with the mighty Pacific Ocean. In the tropics the seasons were virtually indistinguishable from one another. There were no swings in temperature, only degrees of wetness and windiness. Kwaj was a place with sand as soft and white as baby powder and where the coral-tinted water was such a beautiful shade of blue-green that a less than perfect person is apt to feel guilty merely for having set eyes upon it.

Given the light wind, the unusually large swells in the pass that day must have come from a distant storm. The long period of the swells made them easy to traverse, and without a chop from the wind, the ride through the pass was like a slow, gentle roller coaster—one that my kids surely would have enjoyed.

Bigej was our favorite place on the atoll. Just a forty-five minute boat ride from Kwaj, it was as remote as you could get. In contrast to the comparatively urban nature of Kwajalein Island, home to the world's largest missile testing base, there was not a single structure on Bigej—hardly a sign that mankind had ever set foot there, just foliage, long sandy beaches, and a pristine turquoise-blue lagoon.

As we pulled up to our favorite snorkeling spot, we had already started rolling out every floating, lounging, and drinking conveyance known to man. We worked hard and played hard, and the money was good enough that we did not spare much expense on the playing part.

I was a little unsettled at the sight off to our east though. The weather forecast had called for mostly sunny skies, but I noticed the characteristic anvil-shaped tops of cumulonimbus clouds in the not-so-distant eastern sky. Where there are cumulonimbus there may be lightning, and if there is one thing to be feared on the water, it is lightning. Even a short person is the tallest thing around on a flat ocean, and lightning favors the tallest things. However, as always, the flies pestered us incessantly, so a quick shower would give us a little respite from the swatting.

In addition to Jeff and me, our party included my friend, deputy police chief Bill Callaway, a friend of Jeff's named Ed, and a friend common to both Jeff and I: Sonny Sanders.

. . .

We were barely two beers in before the day started to turn sour. The menace in the eastern sky drew closer by the minute.

We piled back into the boat and Jeff radioed harbor control to ask about the weather. They said they had been trying to contact us for fifteen minutes to inform us of a small craft advisory that had been issued. Jeff asked whether it would be safer to shelter in place or to run for home. Harbor control told us to start for home. It should have taken forty-five minutes to get home, and according to them, the storm was an hour and a half out.

I sat next to Sonny and ate pistachio nuts while he drank Corona, an island favorite. I pried one open, flipped the shells overboard, and popped it into my mouth.

"You know," I said to Sonny with a raised eyebrow that I knew he would correctly interpret, "You've reached a certain station in life when you are no longer willing to fight with closed pistachio nuts. I mean, when I was a poor college kid, I don't know how many times I nearly cracked a tooth trying to get into those stubborn little bastards. And even the ones that are just barely cracked; why those things can cut you to the quick or fold over a fingernail if you're not careful."

Sonny carefully considered my comments, kneaded his thought for some time, and then finally deadpanned:

"Pistachios are a very dangerous nut."

I nodded in agreement. "Yep, I'll eat the easy ones, but if they put up the slightest resistance," I held up a perfect, closed-up example and tossed it over the side "over they go!"

"You two are like a frickin' episode of Seinfeld," said Jeff, smiling.

Jeff was aware of the nearly ubiquitous sarcastic undercurrent in conversations between Sonny and me, but to an outside observer, we were just nuts.

Sonny was a Kwaj-kid, meaning that he grew up on Kwaj and graduated from Kwajalein Senior High School. He went on to study engineering at Georgia Tech just like his dad, and as soon as he had his degree, he landed a job on Kwaj and came right back out. He used to tell me: "Hey, I did my time back in the states. It just wasn't for me."

His parents were Anglo, but from looking at him, you would never have guessed. He was as tanned as a piece of leather from living almost his entire life on Kwaj, and despite drinking at least a six-pack a day, there wasn't an ounce of fat on his slight frame. His thick hair was jet black at the scalp but gradually faded to a sun-bleached, whitish-orange at the tips. And, of course, he had a sense of humor much like my own.

Before responding to the Harbor Control's order to return, Jeff turned to me. As Chief Meteorologist for the range, I was expected to be the expert in all things meteorological.

"Remind me of your guys' criteria for a small craft?"

"Twenty sustained or gusts to thirty," I responded, shooing a fly from my face. "But that would be the least of our worries from the looks of those," I said as I turned and pointed to the now towering clouds. Bulbous clouds called mammatus, which is Latin for breast, protruded downward from the underside of the anvils—an ominous sign.

"What's your E.T.A.?" Jeff asked, implying that he preferred my best estimate over the forecast from Harbor Control.

"Well, the gusts will be well out ahead of the actual storm, and we frequently see forward-building convection that moves faster than the complex."

"Was there an E.T.A. in there somewhere, Einstein?" Jeff retorted.

The guys laughed.

"If radar indicated ninety minutes, and they've been trying us for fifteen, I'd say conditions will be going to shit in forty-five to sixty."

Jeff clicked the transmit button on the radio and said: "Harbor Control, this is Kilo-six-five, over."

"Kilo-six-five, Harbor Control, go."

"It's too dangerous, and we don't agree on the timing. We're going to shelter in place. Over."

"Roger that Kilo-six-five. Recommend return to port as soon as the weather clears. Over."

"Roger, wilco. Kilo-six-five clear," Jeff said as he hung up the radio microphone.

There was no argument from Harbor Control. Local boating regulations made the captain of the boat truly the man in charge. The captain was under no obligation to follow any order that he felt endangered his boat or crew. Harbor Control also knew that we were in a spot that was relatively protected from the wind. We were on the lagoon side, or lee of Bigej Island, which was about as good a place as there was to stay out of the wind. That is why it was a favorite spot among divers and snorkelers—little wind to jostle unattended boats from their anchorage and little wave action to stir up visibility-reducing sediment from the bottom.

We weighed anchor and moved in closer to shore and hunkered down to wait out the storm. It would not have been unusual for the storm to miss us altogether. Convection over the open ocean is so susceptible to random processes that it seems to undergo a build, collapse, and reform cycle almost constantly and never holds together on one course for long. But this storm had an angry look to it.

Worry about Kate and our kids crept into my mind. Kate and I had the two daughters she wanted right off the bat. Elaine came first and was followed about as quickly as humanly possible by Kelly. Elaine and Kelly were less than a year apart and looked so similar that most people mistook them for twins. But, despite being nothing of the sort, they definitely acted like it.

Then one of us dried up. We worked at the boy I wanted for over two years, and while I enjoyed the effort, we grew worried by the lack of production. We were about ready to consult a doctor when Charlie finally happened.

I'm told that the fact that newborns usually resemble the father is nature's way of assuring him that it's his and to get him to stick around. I think that's ridiculous. Nevertheless, Charlie looked like me from the day he was born and still does.

He was like me in many other ways too. He was the only ten-year-old I had ever heard of that actually listened to the news. I had to be careful when I watched TV around him, since he absorbed nearly everything. Due to his curious nature he would almost certainly be aware of the plague, and I was sure he'd be scared.

"What do you guys think of the plague?" I asked no one in particular.

"I think it's all overblown," Bill said as instantly as if he'd been watching my thoughts unfold.

There was a general nod of agreement from the group, except Jeff.

As the sky darkened, everyone grew quiet, and Jeff fidgeted at the helm. Even normally cool Sonny stared at the clouds. We'd all seen storms like this before, but not in a boat with nowhere to hide.

Out in the middle of the ocean, you could check a stop watch by the time in between the onset of the wind and the torrential downpour that followed—five minutes was the norm. The wind came up like a runaway truck. We were less than fifty yards from the beach, and our first sign of the wind was the disturbance in the tree tops on the island. Palm fronds bent and twisted and flapped like the wings of a bird as the gale set in. Entire canopies of palm trees, normally shaped like mushrooms, suddenly folded inside out like a cheap umbrella and pointed downwind. Debris began breaking off from the trees and flew in our direction. We still only felt a muted version of the wind in our protected little alcove. But there was no doubt the wind had gone from near calm to a fresh breeze to a strong gale in just a few minutes.

We heard the rain before we saw it—the light sound of distant static as the first drops found their way into the forest canopy and then it opened up into a roar as millions of gallons of water poured onto the island.

Then it swept over us.

We were in the boat as a preventative measure against the threat of lightning, and while the boat offered some protection from electrocution, it offered no shield against the driving rain. We were drenched in seconds, and our beer bottles began to fill with water, like miniature rain gauges. Raindrops the size of nickels roughened the surface of the water, each one creating a brief dimple in the water as it stretched the surface tension to breaking, until the entire lagoon looked like the face of a golf ball.

Then we saw the first flash—just a general flood of light from no particular direction at all. It illuminated the entire scene, but with visibility down to a few meters at best, it seemed to come from everywhere. I started counting but did not even reach two before the thunder barreled into us, shaking the boat violently. We felt the concussion in our organs, and our skin tingled, either from the actual electric field in the air, or merely the thought of it.

"Jesus!" yelled Bill. "That was close."

Born an Inuit Eskimo, Bill grew up above the Arctic Circle, spent time in the marines, and eventually landed on Kwaj after a medical discharge. He stayed in the shape of a marine and was a six-foot-three, two-hundred and forty pound block of muscle. With shoulder length black hair, a full beard and mustache, and a permanent scowl on his darkly complected face, he looked frightening. Bill had one weakness, though: lightning. He had never seen it growing up, and when he found out what I did, he confided in me that it scared him to death.

"About a fifth of a mile," I replied after a quick mental calculation involving the difference in the speeds of light and sound.

"Maybe we should head back," said Bill.

Jeff ignored him, his attention focused at the helm.

"It's ok, Bill," I said. "The odds of it striking us are low."

"Low is a lot higher than zero," Bill said with a sigh. He searched nervously through his pockets as a smoker might search for a cigarette. "And I don't have any toothpicks," he said. Bill was rarely seen without a toothpick in his mouth.

The torrents of rain began to pull the wind down from above, over the tree tops and onto us. The boat rocked and swayed violently as it fought against the anchor. Lightning flashed again, but this time we saw the bolt just to our north. I counted to two, and then the thunder rattled us again. Someone's sunglasses skidded across the deck.

My eyes trained on the storm for some time, but I glanced down and saw Sonny sitting on the deck, back against the gunwale, arms draped over his knees. A half-empty beer dangled from his right hand, and he looked as content as a man could be.

Water ran down his face and dripped from his chin and the crook of his nose. He took a drink and looked up at me. His lips pursed to contain the liquid, but he gave me a cheery little smile and an upward head nod as if to hint at both some enjoyment on his part and ambivalence to any danger. The water ran into his eyes, so he put his head back down and stared at his beer bottle, fearless and seemingly unfazed by the whole thing.

Then the radio crackled to life: "Kilo-six…do…copy?" static breaking the sentence into fragments.

"This is Kilo-six five, please repeat," Jeff said, microphone already in hand.

The static cleared for a second.

"Kilo-six-five. Be advised that weather says the storm now extends back twenty-five clicks and…that…forty to fifty knots…" and then static.

"Harbor Control, please repeat last. Forty to fifty knots, what?"

"Repeat…..knots….clicks. Is….Anderssen….?"

The radio traffic was garbled and broken. Jeff looked at me, and we both shrugged.

"Yes, he's here. Please repeat last."

"….needed…..station."

"Sounds like they need you back at the weather station," Jeff said.

Since we all technically worked for the government, it was fairly easy for them to find us when necessary. I couldn't imagine what was wrong. It was May—near the end of the quiet, dry season. Maybe one of my employees was sick or hurt.

We heard only static in reply after Jeff repeated his request for clarification several more times. Lightning lit up the scene again, and nearly simultaneous thunder broke through the roar of the rain.

"Ok, that's it. Let's go!" Jeff said, barely audible over the sounds of the weather.

"Finally!" exclaimed Bill to no one in particular.

"But Jeff, we're protected right here," said Ed nervously. "If we go out into the pass, it will be ten times worse."

"I know, but I don't like the sound of forty to fifty knots. And I'm not going to sit here and get struck by lightning. It's going to be dark in another hour, and the only thing worse than slogging through this shit in the daylight is doing it in the dark. Trust me."

I trusted Jeff. With decades of sailing under his belt, if anyone knew what to do in that situation, it was Jeff. Ed wasn't so sure though, and he looked to

Sonny knowing that he and Jeff were occasionally at odds about boating techniques.

Sonny didn't respond, but he did take another pull from his beer.

"I think we're safer right here is all," said Ed.

"I'll take my chances with waves over lightning," inserted Bill, as if to tip the scales.

"We're leaving," reiterated Jeff. "Weigh anchor."

I could barely see the surface of the water as I struggled to pull the boat toward the anchor. Ed sat behind me and coiled the rope into the hold. Jeff revved the engine and powered forward to just above the anchor. That freed the anchor from the bottom, and since I no longer had to fight the pull of the boat against the wind and current, it was an effortless dead-weight pull up and over the bow and into the boat.

Lightning continued to flash, and the wind howled at about thirty knots, driving the rain into every nook and cranny of our persons. The only bright spot was that even in stormy weather it was still relatively warm—even in the heaviest rainstorm, it rarely dropped below seventy-five degrees.

After about fifty feet of nylon rope, I came to the chain and then the anchor. I was barely able to maintain my balance with the rocking of the boat, but I hauled the whole thing up and slammed it down into the hold as Ed closed the hatch. I sat down, and Ed fell on top of me.

"Fresh!" I yelled.

Ed laughed.

"How long do you think this is going to last?" Ed asked nervously while trying to pull himself off of my lap.

I shrugged.

As we motored slowly forward, each of us could sense the impending pass by the incrementally increasing height of the swells. The moment we came clear of the protection of the island was unmistakable. The wind suddenly sent the boat lurching to starboard, and it felt as if we were going over. We all instinctively leaned to port. The canvas on the bimini top flapped in the wind, and Jeff's backwards baseball hat broke free and flew off into the squall.

Jeff turned hard to port to put the nose into the wind and then gunned the engine. The largest wave we had seen roiled up and came toward us. It was at least ten feet from trough to crest. The bow of the boat pitched upward hard, and the rest of the boat followed. We quickly shot over the top of the wave, slid down the backside, and plowed head on into the subsequent trough, which sent a river of water through the boat. Designed for rough conditions, the boat was capable of ridding itself of water, but it was being bogged down by the immense amount of rainwater and seawater in its bilge.

Sensing the danger and the shifting of weight, Jeff took advantage of a lull between waves and gunned the engine. The boat struggled forward and then picked up speed as the water poured from the stern drains. Bill stood next to Jeff, and because of the sudden lurch forward, he lost his balance. It appeared as if he might right himself, but just then he lost his hold on the slippery rail and tumbled over the side into the frothing water of the pass. His head hit the gunwale with a dull thud on the way over.

Before I could even think of what to do, there was a flash of orange in front of me. Sonny had grabbed the life ring and was already in the water. As he swam toward Bill, it occurred to me that Sonny could have been an action hero but for a societal size bias.

Also without hesitation, Jeff swung the stern away from both the overboard men so as not to endanger them with the propeller. For an instant, we were abeam to the wind and waves, and the boat lurched to starboard again. We all braced for a flip, but none came. Instead, Jeff brought the boat around, and in one continuous motion guided the craft in, just downwind of Bill and Sonny. Clinging to the life ring and each other, the men bobbed in the water like corks. Bill was conscious but dazed, and Sonny wore his optimistic grin.

Sonny held onto Bill and churned through the remaining few feet to the boat. I grabbed Bill's arm and pulled, but his massive frame barely moved. Ed took hold of Bill's other arm and Jeff stepped to the opposite side to provide counter weight. We heaved with everything we had as Sonny pushed from below. The greater part of Bill's weight finally came over the gunwale and he slipped the rest of the way in and flopped to the deck like a seal.

Bill stared up at the sky. A drop of blood broke free from a small cut on his forehead and entered a rivulet of water running down his scalp and disappeared.

"I found one," said Ed as he placed a toothpick in Bill's mouth. Bill closed his eyes and exhaled.

The maelstrom had abated slightly, but only enough to allow us to get the rest of the way through the channel without any more trouble. Once in the shelter of the islands on the other side, we plowed roughly but safely through the chaotic sea toward home, the ominous clouds hot on our tail all the way.

3

5:30 PM – KWAJALEIN

By the time we got back to the marina, Bill seemed fine. I left Sonny, Jeff and Ed to take Bill to the hospital to be checked out (forcibly, if necessary) and peddled through the driving rain toward the weather station.

It was always warm on Kwaj, so the fact that personal vehicles were not allowed on the island generally didn't bother me. But the policy was a real bummer during the downpours. The phone at the marina had been out—probably another casualty of the salty air—but I fully expected to have to pull the swing shift in lieu of a sick employee. I couldn't imagine what else I would be needed for on a Sunday.

I burst through the door and stood, trying to wipe some of the water from my clothes. I overheard one of my forecasters, Chris, on the phone and immediately knew something was wrong.

"It's hard to say right now, sir."

He poked his head through the door of the forecast office. He cocked his head and widened his eyes as if to say: Help!

"He just walked in. Let me bring him up to speed, and I'll have him call you back." The bells in the old rotary phone tinged as Chris slammed down the receiver.

"What's the matter?" I asked.

"T.D. zero one."

"Tropical depression?" I asked. "You're kidding."

"Nope. Look."

He sent the signal from his computer to the overhead monitor with a key stroke. A zoomed-in visible satellite image of the storm appeared.

"Nice circulation," I said as stepped closer and finally realized what I was seeing. "How long is that loop?"

"Four hours."

"Shit. That developed fast."

"Where is it?" I asked, fully expecting it to be forming to our west or south of Hawaii as usual.

"Eight, one-seventy-two."

"One-seventy-two....*east*?" I asked nervously.

"Yep."

He spun the wheel on his mouse and the image zoomed out one level. The unmistakable outline of Kwajalein Atoll appeared just west of the circulation. My heart jumped. The storm was about 300 miles to our southeast and not moving much.

"What does JTWC think?" I asked.

"Just got off the phone with them about fifteen minutes ago. High water temps; low shear; rapid spin-up. Models blow it into a typhoon within twenty-four. They blew off the models earlier today. So did I. But now they can't find a reason to doubt them."

"What do you think, Chris?"

This wasn't Chris' first tropical storm. As a tropical meteorologist for over ten years and a former navy weather officer, he'd seen his share of foul weather. I valued his opinion.

Chris lowered his glasses and peered over them at the monitor. He flopped down in the chair, and his ample belly folded over his belt and rested on his lap. He let out a sigh.

"I don't like it," he said.

Many thoughts streamed through my mind seemingly at once—thoughts of storm surges, overreactions, wind damage, and missed forecasts. I was paid to make decisions in the face of uncertainty, and a developing tropical cyclone is inherently one of the most uncertain things in meteorology. It doesn't matter if you have good data, bad data, conflicting data, or no data at all. Forecasters must make a forecast with what they've got. I knew what Chris and the JTWC thought. I knew what season it was and what that meant. I knew what I saw and what my experience told me. In a split second, I weighed it all, judged the uncertainty, assessed the risk, and calculated odds. But sometimes the best forecast comes from the gut.

"Ok, I'm declaring TCCOR 2," I said.

"I'll call someone in," Chris offered, knowing that Tropical Cyclone Condition of Readiness 2 required double forecaster coverage around the clock and automatically set in motion numerous standard operating procedures.

"Thanks. And re-work the schedule for the next three days, would you? All days off are canceled."

Chris agreed, so I telephoned the twenty-four hour operations center for Reagan Test Site and asked them to round up the crisis management team. I then telephoned Lieutenant Colonel (LTC) Sam Polian, the range operations officer, to ask him to activate the Emergency Operations Center, or EOC.

6:30 PM – EMERGENCY OPERATIONS CENTER (EOC), KWAJALEIN

When I entered the EOC, the crisis management team was already assembled.

In contrast to the sleek, high-tech missile control center on the range, the EOC on Kwaj looked like an afterthought, which probably was not too far from the truth, since that room was rarely ever used. It had a communications console, a short-wave radio set-up, a small external weather station with wind and temperature information, a few computers, and a single, small window which was above the eye level of most people and contained the distinctive crisscrossed wire of reinforced glass. The conference table was nothing more than four brown, fold-up tables, like you might find at a church potluck, pushed together. The chairs around the tables were all the leftovers from the range—some with torn cushions, others leaning badly, and still others with missing parts—the chairs that nobody wanted to sit in on a daily basis but that the range did not want to throw out. A small alcove off one side held a coffee maker, microwave oven, and sink.

"Well, let's get this started," said LTC Polian. He introduced me, and I relayed what I knew to the team:

"Tropical depression 01-W formed earlier this afternoon approximately 300 miles east-southeast of Kwaj. It is already well on its way to becoming Tropical Storm 'Ele.' The storms we are already seeing today are likely the beginnings of a feeder band which indicates the storm is quickly gathering strength. It will likely reach T.S. strength within the next 12 hours, and within 24 hours, Ele will be near Typhoon strength.

"Isn't May a little early for this sort of thing?" asked one of the other contractors on the island.

"Yes. But it is not unheard of. The El Nino we've had going on for the last year has kept the very warm water parked over the central Pacific, and it is just an unfortunate set of meteorological circumstances that came together in the wrong place. Best guess movement right now is west at 5 knots. Steering flow is not very strong, but her general movement will be west-northwest around a sub-tropical ridge positioned between Johnston and Hawaii."

"So, it's going to go right over us?" asked Sam.

"Forecasting the exact track of tropical storms in the first 24-48 hours after development is very difficult...."

"Cut the bullshit," ordered Range Commander Blaine. "It sounds like we have less than 24 hours to ready this installation for a typhoon. Now is not the time for waffling. You know what happened on Wake!"

He was referring to Super Typhoon Ioke, which struck Wake Atoll, just 500 miles due north of Kwajalein Atoll. Ioke devastated Wake Atoll, and if not for a very fortuitous jog to the north just before landfall, the atoll likely would have been turned into a sand bar.

"Of course I do, sir. But the good news is that all the buildings are still standing. People could have survived there."

He looked at me skeptically over the top of his glasses.

"They had time to evacuate, and you and I both know that they were lucky, Matt. That was a hell of a forecast by the JTWC which gave them five days to get everything ready and then bug out. We don't have that luxury. Give us your no-bull shit best answer."

It was rare for anyone to contradict Colonel Blaine, primarily because he was the Commander, but also because he was a large, black man and quite imposing despite his pronounced limp. His clean-shaven head, crooked nose, penetrating eyes, and deep voice only added to his bad-ass image. He played football at the United States Military Academy at West Point—linebacker. The rumor was that he blew out his knee in the first quarter of the first game of his junior year, and the team didn't find out about it until half time. He made two tackles and one interception in the second quarter with a blown knee. Because of his knee, he never started another game for Army, but he was already legendary. I knew him casually but never dared ask if the rumor was true. The fact that it was within his power to throw anyone off the island for no good reason, didn't put people at ease around him either. But I knew my business.

"Sir. I'm not bullshitting you. I just don't want to give you an inflated sense of the confidence I have in the going forecast. Obviously, we didn't see this coming, and it really is very difficult to predict the exact motion of developing storms. It is hard enough to determine the exact strength and position of a storm at this stage, much less forecast the movement of a storm that is hardly moving at the moment. My best estimate is that it will go very near Kwajalein and that we should prepare as if a direct hit is imminent, because it might be."

It felt as if the air had gone out of the room. I noticed the ticking of the wall clock as we stared at the commander.

"My apologies. I was out of order," he said.

I noticed a few surprised looks around the table.

"Timing?" he questioned, apparently unfazed by the turn of events.

"As I was saying before, steering flow is weak, but I expect it to pick up as the subtropical ridge strengthens and moves further west. Twenty-four to thirty-six hours."

"You sure we don't have more time to prepare? That would be helpful," he asked.

"Actually, we don't want that, sir."

He raised an eyebrow.

"The longer it takes to get here, the more time it will have to strengthen. There is little to inhibit its development at this point. The faster it gets here, the better."

"What should we expect?"

With the momentum on my side, I launched into the specifics. "Best estimate: winds: 70 gusting to 85 knots; seas: 20-30 feet; overwash with severe flooding likely north of the storm track. Much worse if it takes longer."

I heard a few murmured swear words around the table.

"How high will the storm surge be north of the track? I've heard it can be 10-15 feet."

"We won't see anything like that here. The bathymetry of the atoll isn't conducive to large storm surge. The Oceanside parts of the atoll essentially go straight down into the abyss. There is no sloping undersea floor for the surge to build up on. It's essentially the same reason that we don't worry much about tsunamis here. Our surge, if any, will be almost entirely from wind loading."

"So how high?"

"I think we will probably just see some of the larger waves washing onto the island. Maybe a foot at most and that will be north of the track. Even Wake wasn't substantially over-washed with Ioke. But even this amount of water will cause significant flooding."

"Any idea where it will cross the atoll—you know, which assets might be at most risk?"

"Sir, like I...."

"Never mind, I know," he said waving me off.

The commander stared at his hands for a few moments, a noticeable tremor developing in his left.

"Very well then. This base is officially in warning status," said the Commander.

Typhoon warning status was the Range's equivalent to TCCOR 2 and set in motion the entire range to prepare for the onset of damaging winds within 24 hours. A few minutes after this meeting, hundreds of people's quiet weekend would come to an abrupt end.

Commander Blaine looked at LTC Polian.

"Secure assets a.s.a.p. and begin personnel evacuation preparations immediately. And inform SMDC."

SMDC stood for Space and Missile Defense Command, the next agency in the chain of command. SMDC answered to the Department of the Army who reported to the Department of Defense who reported to the President—all of whom had some interest when one of their "assets" was threatened.

Commander Blaine turned to the Public Affairs Officer.

"Prepare a statement for the roller highlighting the need to begin personal preparations immediately. Now I know word travels fast on this rock, but let's sound the sirens, just to get people off the beach and let them know something is going on."

"We will meet here again at midnight. I want a report on the status of preparations from each operational area. Let's get to work."

Myriad conversations broke out around the room. As I rose to leave, Commander Blaine put his hand on my shoulder.

"You have my direct number. Call me if anything changes. This really worries me. I keep thinking about Wake. We're no more above sea level than they were."

"I will be sure to let you know the minute I know anything, sir."

"You just couldn't hold this off until after the change of command in July, huh?" he asked, smiling. "I'd be hunting and fishing back in Missouri by then."

7:15 PM – BASE HOUSING, KWAJALEIN

I decided to check on my quarters before heading back out to the weather station to pull what would likely be an all-nighter. The sun had set, and the showers and thunderstorms had moved on, but just as I rounded the bend onto the road toward home, the siren cut through the air like a knife—three short bursts followed by a long burst. The siren normally sounded the "all clear," which consisted of one long blast, every day at six p.m., except Sundays. Other than the all clear signals, the siren had been silent for our entire stay on the island up to that point. Given the unusual signal, hundreds of people were likely scrambling to find the section of their telephone books that would remind them what it meant.

The thought reminded me of Kate. She had a photographic memory and certainly would have known what the siren meant without having to look it up. To most people, her memory was just a novelty—people loved testing her with trivial questions—but it also was a big part of her success as a lawyer. She could recite any case she had ever read, remember every legal technicality, and she never forgot a name, face, or a statement anybody made. In addition, she was also a great debater—a nearly insurmountable combination in a courtroom. But just because you are good at something, doesn't mean you enjoy it.

I met Kate on a dare in a bar two weeks before I graduated from college. My friends knew she was out of my league and bet me that I couldn't get her number. With little money, no job, and no prospects, I marched over to her table in order to get it over with—so we could all have a good laugh about how pathetic I was and get back to drinking. My plan to win the bet was simple: I just told her about it. She told me that she admired honesty most, and that she'd play along and give me her number if I promised to actually call her. I realized at that moment that I had stumbled onto a great pickup strategy, but I never needed it again —I kept my end of the bargain by calling her, and we've been together ever since. And I won the bet.

We dated for two years as I worked as a weekend meteorologist on a small local television station. On a whim, I applied for a job at RTS and got it. It was twice the money I was making on TV, and it was a chance to live in paradise. On another whim I proposed to Kate and asked her to come with me. Had she said no to either question, I would have refused the job offer—I already knew what I had in her.

I nearly fell over when she said yes to both questions.

I may be the only man in the history of the world who followed up an accepted marriage proposal from the woman of his dreams with the question: why? She made plenty of money, had lots of friends, was destined to be a superstar in her law firm, and I had never heard her utter a single complaint about her job. In retrospect, it was selfish of me to ask her to leave all that.

But she answered me with only four words: "I hate my job." She retired from law at the ripe old age of twenty-seven and has been happily married to me and raising our children ever since.

I walked in the door and the first thing I did was to call Kate. It went to voicemail, but it was after midnight on the west coast, so her not answering didn't worry me. I didn't leave a message; she'd see that I called and call me back in the morning.

As I wandered around our quarters, I marveled at the immaculate condition in which Kate kept it. I realized there was little I could do to protect anything. Either the storm was going to destroy our quarters, or it wasn't. I raised some of the more expensive electronics a little further off the floor and then turned and walked out.

12:00 AM, MONDAY, MAY 28TH – EMERGENCY OPERATIONS CENTER (EOC), KWAJALEIN, MIDNIGHT BRIEFING

"Tropical Storm Ele has picked up speed and is now approximately 250 miles east-southeast of Kwaj," I began my part of the briefing.

"At this rate, I believe typhoon conditions are imminent at Kwajalein Atoll, starting in approximately eighteen hours. While Ele is strengthening faster than expected, I am watching an upper level trough coming down from the northwest which will increase shear and should help to limit the growth of the storm, if it gets here in time. Onset of 35 knot winds now looks to be within 12 hours."

All departments provided their status in turn, and preparations were moving along as expected. My mind, however, was focused on the doubt that I always lived with as a meteorologist. We got kicked around a lot, but most people understand how hard it is to predict the weather. The worst case scenario was that I was wrong, and Ele would continue her rapid intensification and explode into a killer that not only destroyed our paradise, but killed many people I knew. After all, the average elevation of our island was only eight feet, and there were no good places to hide.

I looked around the table and thought about the people sitting there. Some were my friends, but they all depended on my forecast that day, whether they knew it or not. One woman tapped a pencil on her notepad as if annoyed by the whole thing. Another guy appeared to be preoccupied with something in his coffee cup. Most listened intently but without a sense of urgency. I wondered whether people appreciated the danger.

I had considered every piece of available data and provided the best forecast I could. And I tried to instill in people a sense of the worst case scenario. But there is always a fine line between covering your ass and crying wolf too often. I had been wrong before, and I could have been wrong then.

Sometimes I hated my profession because uncertainty was my constant companion. I doubted engineers worried much about whether the equations they used to build bridges were correct. X amount of concrete and Y amount of rebar will support Z amount of traffic, and everyone lives happily ever after. I never enjoyed such certitude in my job. The problem with my job was chaos theory. The saying goes that a butterfly flaps its wings in Africa and sets off a chain of unpredictable, chaotic events that leads to a typhoon in China two weeks later. That's an exaggeration, of course, but it illustrates a point: the weather is subject to so many interactions that range from chemical reactions on the atomic level (that cannot be adequately measured over the globe, much less modeled) to the physical forces of fluid dynamics acting over hundreds or thousands of miles, that a meteorological forecast is most accurately defined as little more than an educated guess. While forecasting continually improves through better methods of estimating that which we cannot explicitly model (we call this parameterization), given the unimaginable complexity of the system, we can still state virtually nothing with certainty. You might say meteorologists suffer from occupational confidence envy!

I noticed some movement on the far side of the room. It looked like a cockroach crawling backward up the wall. Curious, I squinted my eyes to better focus on the object. Ants were carrying a dead cockroach up a wall toward a hole at the top. I wondered if they sensed the impending weather better than I did.

The cockroach was many times bigger than all the ants combined, so the fact that they could transport it up a wall was remarkable enough, but their organization was what truly impressed me.

Most of the ants were common laborers, but a couple of leaders scurried about communicating with the heavy lifters. When they got to the top, they spent a few minutes trying to get the bug turned into the hole. The leaders frantically circled the work party, shooting in and out of the hole and planning out each move, and communicated the plan to the workers. What they could not see was that the roach was too big to be turned into the hole. It had to go in straight, which would have required it to float in midair, a feat that even they could not engineer.

I was so fascinated by the spectacle that I didn't hear another word of the briefing. When the meeting ended, I stood and walked over to the wall. How had they carried the roach up the wall? It seemed to me like the equivalent of a football team carrying a school bus up the side of the Empire State Building.

Guilt overcame me and I pushed the roach into the hole myself. The ants scurried about frantically and then stopped in unison—as if to pay tribute to the invisible, incomprehensible, and apparently benevolent force—and then carried on through the hole. I imagined the day that God reached out and helped them bring home the grand feast as going down in ant lore, the story retold many generations later around little ant campfires.

7:00 AM, KWAJALEIN

After years on the island, I had developed a number of ways to gauge the wind without instruments: the sound it made in the palm trees, the amount of work required to ride my bike into the office, the violence with which the flags over the memorials flapped as I passed. All my senses told me the wind had increased overnight, but when I rounded the turn at the southeast end of the island and found the wind sock standing erect, I knew; it took twenty-five knots of wind to fully inflate it. The uncharacteristically dark sky to the east threatened rain, and with the rising sun obscured behind a gray overcast, the normally turquoise ocean churned black.

Before jumping into the frying pan that would almost certainly cook me until the conclusion of this disaster, I decided to stop and clear my mind at my favorite place on the island: a little turnout near the edge of the golf course at the east end of the runway.

The crumbling, overgrown old landscape reminded me of an ancient ruin. The entrance to the turnout was overgrown with plumeria, pandanus, and breadfruit trees, which during the rainy season, flooded the area with a sweet fragrance. A rock wall gently curved from the entrance toward the back with dense plumeria completing the enclosure on the opposite side. Other than some scattered trash and a fire pit near the rock wall, there was hardly any indication that anyone ever visited the place.

Towering coconut palms normally cast shadows that seemed to converge somehow at the center of the expanse like an ancient time dial. The rest of the area, including the rock wall where I liked to sit, was well shaded from the relentless tropical sun that normally baked the island. Given my Scandinavian heritage and low tolerance for the heat and humidity, shade was a luxury I did not take for granted. But this morning was comfortably cool and cloudy.

The Pacific Ocean rumbled on the reef just behind the rock wall. Seas were a little higher than normal, five to seven feet or so. Even small waves like that packed a lot of energy, and they pounded the reef relentlessly, as they had done for millennia, and sent perceptible vibrations through the ground.

As I climbed awkwardly to the top of the wall, a palm frond dislodged from a tree and crashed to the pavement behind me giving me a start. The wind had picked up. From atop the rock wall I could feel the vastness of the ocean. On Kwaj in general, and in that spot in particular, one's own insignificance was palpable. I am but a tiny, insignificant organism on an immense, water-covered world.

As I had on so many other mornings, I sat and stared out over the ocean, my mind adrift. In summers past, I sat in that exact spot and took comfort in the fact that this very body of water extended uninterrupted to where Kate and the kids were on Whidbey Island, WA, north of Seattle. I took comfort in that fact again that morning.

I was surprised Kate hadn't returned my call. She liked to talk and called me nearly every day whether she had anything to say or not. I had watched about ten minutes of news before I left. Deaths from the red plague continued to rise at an alarming rate, according to the news anyway. I continued to think it was all just hyperbole.

Charlie had not wanted to leave on vacation at all, which was weird; normally he was bouncing off the walls weeks before going to Grandpa's house. But he told me about a nightmare he had the night before they left. He couldn't remember the specifics—people rarely can—but it scared him stiff. And then I remembered the nightmare I had before the last time I spoke to Kate.

I wondered if our nightmares had been prescient. Of course, we sometimes have dreams that are bizarre and not necessarily reflective of anything that has ever happened or ever will. But I rarely ignore dreams, since I believe that they are often instances where we tap into what I call "the stream," or the unconscious, sub-atomic current of intelligence that I believe is present everywhere and connects all things. The stream, I believe, is what nudges a person into consciousness just before she steps in front of a bus, cautions one not to accept a ride from *that guy*, and tells you that she is the one.

I had awakened from many dreams where I felt as if I had actually interacted with other people. I came to believe that sometimes during dreams (whether we are asleep or not) we literally cross streams with other real people having similar dreams at the same moment. We interact on a subconscious level that is as real as if we'd bumped shoulders on the street. I believe this to be true whether it is simply thinking of a person you know just before they call, or a dreamed interaction with a complete stranger.

My occasional connections to the stream were where I derived my notion that there is more to this world than meets the eye. I despise religions, but I am not an atheist. Rather, I believe that if God was to be found, it was almost certainly within the stream.

Having procrastinated long enough, I peddled out to the weather station and spent the rest of the day deluged by data and slammed by a whirlwind of briefings. Everybody wanted a piece of me that day, and by the time Typhoon Ele got really close, I was glad to make the final deployment to the EOC to ride out the storm with the rest of the crisis management team.

The weather station had been prepared as well as could be expected, my forecast staff manned their posts, and the rest of the island's residents had evacuated to their designated shelters. All there was to do at that point was wait and hope for the best.

7:45 PM — EMERGENCY OPERATIONS CENTER (EOC), KWAJALEIN

Communications to the outside world had gone down hours before. I was no longer receiving any data on the storm other than radar. The Kwajalein radar was designed to withstand 120 knots, and the anemometer inside the EOC was still peaking below 100 knots. As long as the radar held, I had all the information I needed. The eye of Typhoon Ele was less than 20 miles to our southeast and would arrive within the hour. Unfortunately, my hunch was right and it looked as if Kwajalein Island was going to take a direct hit. The upper trough was going to arrive a little too late to suppress the storm.

Pressures continued to fall, and the wind increased—now 75 mph gusting to around 90 mph. We would certainly see a spike in wind as the eye wall came ashore. Reports of damage streamed in around the island—windows blown in at base housing; barges and sailboats breaking loose; minor wash over on the north end of the island. All these things would increase, but so far all the shelters were safe.

I ran to the little porthole of a window and looked out. I could see nothing but black. I jumped as something smacked into the window and cracked it. I thanked the little embedded wires for the fact I didn't have to pick glass out of my eyes, or worse.

8:33 PM — EMERGENCY OPERATIONS CENTER (EOC), KWAJALEIN

Winds howled as I sat at my terminal and watched the dial. Northeast at 90 mph gusting as high as 115 mph—by far the highest winds I had ever observed in person. The building groaned, and a constant whistle echoed through the room as wind accelerated around an obstruction somewhere just outside. The radar stopped updating, most likely due to water infiltration into the fiber-optic lines crisscrossing the island. I looked at the barometer: 979.5

millibars. I had expected a lower pressure with such strong winds. Of course, the eye hadn't reached us yet.

Then suddenly the barometer went into free fall as I watched: 977, 975, 972, and then all went quiet. The wind speed dial on the anemometer dropped to almost nothing and the pressure bottomed at 970 millibars. The wind direction indicator spun around randomly. My ears popped as they tried to equalize with the free-falling atmospheric pressure. I looked around as others rubbed their ears.

I jumped up and began to run to the door. I was stopped by LTC Polian.

"What are you doing?"

"It's over!" someone exclaimed.

"No it's not, this is the eye," I yelled. "We've still got the backside to go."

"Other people will think that it's over," someone shouted.

LTC Polian jumped on the radio.

"Everyone remain in shelter. The storm is not over. Repeat: REMAIN IN SHELTER!"

The commander, now standing next to me, asked almost rhetorically: "The back side will be weaker, right?" I leaned in to hear as the pressure inside my ears built.

The commander also leaned closer as I replied, "Should be. The forward motion of the storm adds to the winds on the north side and subtracts from them on the south side. Sir, have you ever been in the eye of a typhoon?"

He shook his head.

"Me either. I've got to see it. Let's go."

"Sir, I don't recommend…"

The commander cut off LTC Polian: "Stand down, Sam. I'm with a professional." The colonel winked at me, and we bolted out the door and down the stairs.

I opened the main door to the EOC and stepped confidently outside into the calm. A single light flickering above the door provided the only illumination. Ankle-deep, debris-choked water covered the parking lot. Ripples fluttered through the pools as wisps of wind nudged at the water. We could hear the ocean churning violently just beyond the breakwater. I looked up, and stars were out. Lightning fractured the darkness and revealed one of the most beautiful things I had ever seen.

"Oh my gosh, that was incredible," said the Colonel. "Was that the eye wall?"

I stood slack-jawed and unable to respond.

The colonel laughed. "I'll take that as a yes."

The wall of smooth, solid cloud extended up to the tropopause—the top of the layer of atmosphere in which weather occurred—ten miles, straight up. The wall enclosed a circle of twenty miles in diameter, and we saw the entire thing—a fleeting but magical glimpse inside of one of nature's most powerful entities. It was as if we stood at the bottom of a white, five-gallon bucket.

"Is this safe? Hello, Matt, are you still with me?"

"Yes. Yes sir. It will be a few more minutes before the backside of the eye wall gets here. Let's back up under the shelter, though. The wind will come from behind the building this time."

I walked slowly backwards, unable to avert my eyes from the darkness in the hope that lightning would flicker again. Suddenly, as the storm slid west, a sliver of moon appeared and faint, pale light poured into the hole in the center of the cyclone.

"It's far more incredible than I ever imagined," I said. "I wish everyone could experience this."

The Colonel laughed loudly. "Most people would avoid this like the plague! No, I think this is just for you."

As suddenly as it abated, the storm roared to life again. The moon vanished in a wall of water and darkness. Torrents of rain poured over the roof above us and off into the distance. As the wind accelerated over and around the building, the ground water pulled away, leaving debris beached on the concrete. Even under shelter, a breeze tugged at us from behind as the air was sucked out of the structure.

The light above us went out. We sensed the danger and felt our way back up the stairs toward the EOC, ears popping again.

I rushed to my workstation and found the barometer rising quickly. When the pressure and wind finally stabilized a few minutes later, we had 988 millibars and south winds of 70 mph gusting to 85 mph—much lower than the front side of the storm.

I let out a cautiously optimistic sigh of relief.

The commander came over and looked at the instruments.

"That's it, right? That's the worst of it?"

"Yes, but....."

"But? What's the matter?"

"I don't know. I have a feeling. Something isn't right."

I sat back and stared at the stale data on my radar screen.

Colonel Blaine walked to the center of the room and began directing his personnel.

"I want security to begin checking on assets and survey the damage as soon as the wind drops below 50 mph. Get me the status of the shelters. And let's find out how housing fared. Let's see if we can get people back in their quarters when the winds subside, or if they will have to stay sheltered."

I anxiously tapped at my keyboard. I glanced at the wind again. The direction indicator wobbled between 190 and 200 degrees—slightly west of due south. The winds were coming around.

Then it dawned on me.

"Wait!" I exclaimed.

Everyone turned.

"The winds....they're becoming more westerly."

"So?" Someone questioned.

"A few more degrees and they'll be blowing directly across the lagoon."

"Sir!"

It was LTC Polian.

"What is it Sam?"

"I'm getting reports of water in town. The guard at the library says half a foot of water is coming in the door."

Everyone looked nervously in my direction again.

"Storm surge," I said nervously.

"I thought you said we wouldn't have much storm surge!" said Commander Blaine angrily.

"It didn't occur to me at the time, but if the wind is just right it comes through the southern passes and across the lagoon. Since the lagoon is much shallower and sloped, water could build up. I think that is what's happening now."

There was nothing we could do at that point. It wasn't safe for anyone to venture out into the storm. I reminded myself that all the shelters were on the second floor of concrete buildings, so as long as the buildings held and the surge remained below five or six feet (an almost unimaginable amount given the situation), everyone should be fine.

Water made it most of the way across the island over the next hour. I listened carefully as reports came in from the shelters. Two feet of water entered the first floor of the library, but the building and all its inhabitants were fine. All the other shelters reported in safe as well.

Winds quickly abated as the storm pulled away, and about three hours after Ele's eye went across Kwajalein, security and safety personnel began to venture out. Indications were that the island fared well except for the flooding, but the decision was made to keep everyone in shelter until dawn. That meant a long night in the EOC for me.

4

5:13 AM, TUESDAY, MAY 29ᵀᴴ – EMERGENCY OPERATIONS CENTER (EOC)

I awakened to the smell of burnt coffee and a commotion. I lifted my head off my arm and tried to gather my wits. The skin on my arm peeled away from the keyboard it had been resting on. My eyes focused just in time to see Jeff walking briskly in my direction.

"Did you hear?" he said.

"I've been asleep here for hours."

"The satellites have gone down. The commander's having a briefing right now."

I wasn't surprised. 100-mph winds could easily knock satellite dishes out of alignment, if not knock them over completely. I took a quick look at the radar and satellite images. Our data were flowing again. Satisfied that Ele was no longer a threat, I poured myself a cup of burnt coffee and headed to the conference room.

As I approached the door to the conference room, Commander Blaine rounded the corner with a serious look on his face. He passed me without so much as a nod, entered the room, and yelled "At ease!"

The commander sat in his chair and collected his thoughts. He looked at LTC Polian and said: "Sam, why don't you bring us up to speed."

I sensed tension in the air; this seemed like more than just some askew satellite dishes.

"At approximately oh three hundred, SATCOM went down. We assumed it had something to do with the typhoon, but tech control has evaluated the systems, and it's not on our end. Uplink is solid, there's just nothing coming from the other end."

Colonel Blaine broke in: "As many of you probably already know, we have a crisis developing, not only in our own country, but around the world. The Red Plague is erupting across the globe, and I am told the virus is extremely contagious and has a high probability of lethality once contracted. Before SATCOM went down, I was in contact with General Whitehead who has been receiving direction from the Joint Chiefs, and they directed us to prepare to raise our level of readiness to DEFCON 3. DEFCON 3 gives me the authority to act independently of and without direction from the pentagon to protect my personnel and assets if it becomes necessary to do so.

"We have no idea what is going on back in CONUS, but we have to assume the worst. Given the nature of this crisis, I have directed that there will be no inbound aircraft or watercraft allowed at this base until further notice. When Continental arrives this morning, only residents will be allowed off. And they will be quarantined. Until we get a handle on this situation, I'm not letting any outsiders onto this base. As of close-of-business tomorrow, that will also include Marshallese personnel from Ebeye."

A gasp went out across the room. The Marshallese workers provided all the basic services to the range: food, janitorial, mechanical, and grounds-keeping—you name it, they did it. The Americans performed the technical jobs, and the Marshallese did everything else.

"I know, this won't be easy," continued the Commander, "but it's necessary. We'll all just have to chip in and do our part and hope this doesn't last very long. We have enough Marshallese personnel here already who will be asked to stay to continue working. As an incentive, I have directed the logistics contractor to offer them pay for twenty-four hours a day as long as they remain. They are, of course, free to go back to Ebeye at any time, but they won't be allowed to return until the threat condition is decreased to four or better. Are there any questions?"

I raised my hand and was acknowledged by the Commander.

"Sir, I know you said until further notice, but what is the worst-case scenario?"

"I don't have any idea. I've been told that if this evolves into a full-blow pandemic, it could be unsafe to allow anyone in for as long as three months. That doesn't leave this room, understood?"

My heart dropped.

Finally, the Logistics Manager, Tom Delaney, broke the stunned silence: "We have emergency provisions for six months if needed. We collect our own water, and we have enough fuel for even longer than that. We'll be just fine out here."

"Yes, but some of us have families back in the states right now," someone interjected from the back of the room.

"I am aware of the fact that it's summer, and many of you have spouses and children back in the states. But I cannot allow any unnecessary aircraft or watercraft to come here at this time. It is simply too risky. There is no way to be sure it is not contaminated."

"Furthermore," he continued after a short pause for effect. "Lest any of you think you'll hop in those remaining seats out of here, I'm not letting anyone leave either. I have a base to run and you're all an essential part of it." He had obviously realized that no one would take their families off the island into a world that could be breaking down, and so the only people likely to try to leave were essential people, people like me.

Several people began to object when Commander Blaine raised his hand to stop them. The room grew quiet. He was nearing the end of his tour on Kwaj, and after almost two years of dealing with a mostly civilian workforce, he had learned how to tend to our needs. A newer commander who had spent a career sternly ordering his troops around wouldn't have taken any questions. He rubbed his clean shaven chin as he thought. I noticed the tremor in his left hand again.

There was a knock at the door, and the Commander shot an annoyed look at his security officer. The beefy, bald security officer got up and answered the door. There was a minor argument at the door that I couldn't hear, but a skinny engineer named Ned was allowed into the room. He rushed over to the communications manager and whispered in his ear.

The communications manager, a chubby, balding, 60-something man called Sal said: "Sir, please excuse me," and he hurriedly followed Ned out of the room.

The Commander retained an air of irritation as he continued. "My decision is final! When Continental arrives, we'll find out what the hell is going on."

The lone woman in the room, sitting across from the Commander, was the only one who had the courage to break the ensuing silence:

"But if it's true about the thirty days, there could already be infected people here."

"Understood," said the commander, visibly pleased that the meeting had returned to useful business. "But we'll have to hope that isn't the case and deal with it if it is. I have instructed the Chief Medical Officer to examine any personnel who have been off island within the last two weeks and, if necessary, quarantine them as well." The commander looked at his Chief Medical Officer, Dr. Frank Pepperdine, as he spoke, and the Doctor nodded back in agreement.

"As a further precaution, I have canceled all community events, and I recommend personnel stay in their quarters and away from other people until we determine if the virus has been able to infiltrate the base."

We all knew he was right. At times like those it fell squarely on his shoulders to protect the personnel and assets of his base from all invaders, whatever the origin, and completely closing the base off to the outside was his only sure way to isolate us from the threat.

"Any other questions?" continued the Commander.

There was no response.

"Good. We will be meeting here every morning at oh-eight-hundred for a situation report. Leads from each area will brief me. Dismissed."

I was fully with Kate on this one now—I was becoming very concerned. There was no way I could get off the island, nor could they get home, and with comms down, I couldn't even talk to her. Furthermore, from the response of the Commander, maybe the virus was actually worse than the media had portrayed it.

After I exited the room, I walked halfway down the hall and stepped into a little alcove to wait for Jeff. As a contractor, the information I received was limited to "need to know," but as an employee of the government and one of the range's senior managers, Jeff heard everything.

I leaned my head against the wall and took a few deep breaths to try to calm the panic I felt rising in me.

As Jeff hurried by, I reached out and grabbed him. It gave him a start, but he immediately anticipated my line of questioning.

"It's worse than you think," Jeff whispered. "He laid it on soft with that three months thing. Brass has been really talking more like six. He says they've been watching this simmer under the surface for about a week now, trying to head it off and hoping it wouldn't explode. That's why they are so quick to react, shut everything down. They've been collecting intel from around the world and planning a strategy. I think all our bases are doing this. It's much worse overseas where they are right in the middle of millions of potential carriers. You know the last time we went to DEFCON 3?"

I shrugged.

"9/11. This is serious shit."

"Why didn't you tell me this shit a week ago? We could have gotten on a plane," I responded in a tone somewhere just above whisper and sounding more irritated than I meant to. "Or never let them go in the first place."

"I didn't know it would happen this fast. Don't you think I would have done something if I knew?"

"Yeah, I guess so," I said with remorse, remembering that, like me, Jeff's wife and kids were off island too. "I'm sorry about that. I'm just getting jumpy, that's all."

"I get it, believe me."

Jeff shot quick looks both ways down the hall in which we were standing, and then he whispered: "Come with me. Something's going on in Comms."

. . .

We descended a flight of stairs and wound our way through myriad hallways and switchbacks. Finally we arrived at a fortified door. Numerous placards warned the unauthorized against attempted entry. There was another placard on the door which said "non-ionizing radiation hazard." The symbol on it resembled those that indicated available Wi-Fi.

Jeff reached down to enter the code to the cypher lock and then stopped and looked at me. "Turn around," he said.

"Oh for Christ's sake!" I said angrily as I turned away.

Eight or ten clicks later, the door opened and cool air wafted out. Jeff held his finger up to me and then stepped through the door and closed it without latching. I heard muffled conversation, and then the door cracked open again.

"So nothing classified," Jeff said as he opened the door the rest of the way and motioned me in.

"I have a top secret clearance anyway, probably higher than yours," I complained as I stepped into the darkened room.

"Not for this area," Jeff replied. "This area is SCI." That stood for Secret Compartmentalized Information, which was indeed higher than my clearance.

Ned and Sal sat at consoles that provided the vast majority of light to the room and listened to something with large headphones.

Jeff tapped Sal on the shoulder and said: "Put it on speaker."

Jeff's job was closely related to Sal's, and I knew that they were well acquainted. I had always thought Sal was a weirdo, so I have never spoken to him.

Sal pulled down his headphones and they settled down around the back of his neck. He pulled the cord from the console and beeping poured from the speaker. I immediately recognized it as Morse code, but I had no idea what it meant. At that moment, I noticed Ned furiously scribbling on a notepad.

"What's being transmitted?" Jeff asked.

"We don't know. It's not English," said Sal.

Ned set his pencil down and slid his headphones down onto his neck. "That's it, it's repeating now."

Sal reached over and tuned to a different frequency. "Listen to this shit," he said.

A computerized voice came into focus as he tuned.

This is K6AB9, transmitting from Phoenix, Arizona, on 101.75 megahertz. We have vacated the city and will begin transmitting from our bugout location a.s.a.p. Conditions are dire. Red plague running rampant. All public systems are down...assumed EMP. Strong static burst detected on all channels at 28May 1409 Zulu. This is K6AB9....."

"Jesus Christ!" Jeff exclaimed. "Is that for real?"

"We don't know," said Ned. "Something has definitely happened, and it brought out all the whackos. It's hard to tell what's real from what's not."

"That sounds legit. Who would know that?" Jeff replied.

"Know what?" I asked. "Wouldn't our radars have detected that?"

All three of them turned to me and gave a look of disgust that seemed to ask: don't you work on this range?

Apparently remembering that I was not among the 90% of range workers with engineering backgrounds, Jeff said: "No they wouldn't. The EMP signals that our radars can receive would be line-of-sight using a four-thirds earth model."

I had no idea what the four-thirds earth model was, but I understood line of sight. Weather radars, for example, couldn't "see" over the horizon unless the beam was being bent by a temperature inversion in the atmosphere.

"And most people wouldn't know that you'd hear a burst of static on the lower frequencies." "Have you actually talked with anyone?" Jeff asked, turning to Ned.

"We haven't been able to get anyone to respond," he replied. "Everything we've heard so far has either been a recorded message, the ramblings of religious nutjobs, or not English."

"What about bases outside CONUS?"

"None so far. Some of the messages indicated that there may have been multiple pulses. Perhaps in many locations worldwide. We just don't know. We're listening for more now."

Sal tuned the radio to another frequency to give us an example of one of the kooks. The guy slowly and steadily read the Bible. At the moment we tuned in, it sounded like he was in the middle of the book of Ezekiel.

I was shell shocked. I began to feel dizzy.

"Hey," Sal exclaimed. "At least nobody's talking about Nukes."

"Nukes?" I repeated to nobody in particular. I sat down in an empty chair.

"Come on, let's go," Jeff said to me. He turned to Sal and Ned, "Are you guys going to keep at this?"

"Yeah," Sal said with an incredulous look. "I wouldn't know what else to do."

Jeff and I rode silently to the housing area. It was a little out of his way, but Jeff escorted me to my quarters. I felt like I should make some parting comment as we approached my quarters, but just as I began to formulate a statement, Jeff peeled off and road quickly away.

5

10:30 A.M., TUESDAY MAY 29ᵀᴴ, BASE HOUSING, KWAJALEIN

After a few hours of fitful, practically useless sleep, I awakened feeling just as tense and restless as when I had gone to bed. I grabbed the phone and dialed 99 in hopes of getting a line off island. Nothing happened. I clicked on the TV and found nothing but the roller, and it looked like nothing new had been posted.

I grabbed a dirty shirt from the floor and pulled it on along with a pair of shorts that didn't match. I ran my fingers through my hair and wiggled my toes into my flip-flops as I hurried out the door.

At only 10:30 am, it was already sweltering under the tropical sun. In the tropics, day and night were almost evenly split year round, and since the sun was highest at noon, the period from late morning through early afternoon was always the hottest. That was the time when you'd usually find the Marshallese waiting out the heat under the shade of a palm tree. With our air conditioning and important jobs, we Americans hadn't learned to appreciate a siesta like much of the rest of the world.

I was already sweating profusely (a rolling boil, as I called it) as I peddled furiously past Jeff's quarters; since his bike wasn't in its rack, I didn't even slow down. I blew by the EOC and made my way to the weather station. By the time I arrived, my shirt was soaked through.

A couple of forecasters and an electronics technician were sitting around chatting in the operations area when I walked in. They informed me that all of our equipment was running fine; satellite images continued to come in (meaning the satellites were operating normally), our radar was fine, and all of our observational equipment was working nominally. We hadn't received any weather model data from the national centers though, and the technicians had conducted tests on the communication lines and found them to be fine with the exception that no data flowed in from outside. Our data flowed out, to where we didn't know, but nothing came back.

Satisfied that everything was fine at work, I headed back toward the EOC. The route from the weather station back to the EOC took me headlong into the stiff trade winds. Winds blow from high pressure over the mid-latitudes toward low pressure near the equator, and thanks to the spin of the earth, the winds turn toward the right in the northern hemisphere. This creates a nearly constant belt of easterly trade winds, so-called because early traders sought to ride these favorable winds to far-away lands. While the wind had a cooling effect, the effort required to overcome the extra resistance more than canceled any benefit.

I struggled slowly past a couple of women stopped on the roadside looking out over the ocean. I recognized one woman as the wife of the island chaplain, but I didn't know the other. I overheard the chaplain's wife comment about the need for prayer in times like these, how we need to pray for the plague to pass and spare our loved ones and how we also need to pray for the souls of those who've already died.

I had a brief argument with her in which I asked why a god who doesn't already know that I would wish for the safety of my loved ones is worthy of being prayed to, and why we shouldn't be overjoyed by all that had been happening, since it's all that god's plan and, therefore, obviously perfect. We pissants are certainly not qualified to object to her god's plan are we? Although the imaginary argument made me even more upset, I won, which I always do.

I arrived at the EOC at the same moment as the Medical Officer, Dr. Frank Pepperdine, or Doctor Pepper, as we called him. He was my personal physician, and while we frequently played basketball together, we maintained a relationship more likened to acquaintances than friends. For it always seemed to me inappropriate to be friends with your doctor. A person simply does not want a friend to know his cholesterol number, weight, or what his colon looks like.

In his mid-fifties, Dr. Pepper was a fine physical specimen and did not look a day over thirty. He could be seen running around the island every evening, and he obviously ate right. He had a full head of medium-length brown hair that would have been otherwise unbelievable in fullness and color at his age, were it not for his tight, wrinkle-free, bronze skin and perfect complexion. He had the enviable tall, slender body that allowed him to jog, play basketball, or engage in any other activity outside shirtless, without making other people uncomfortable.

He went to UCLA, which, as part of my beloved Pac10, made him ok with me. After his wife died in a climbing accident, he took a job as a physician on Kwaj. Other than that, the only thing I knew about his career was that he had briefly worked at the CDC. He and his thirteen-year-old daughter arrived on the island on the same flight as Kate, the kids, and I had.

I timed it so that we would arrive at the door at the same time, and, after the obligatory cordial greeting, I jumped right to what was on my mind.

"Have you heard anything new about the plague? Any idea what's going on?"

"I don't have any magical lines of communication in my office. I know the same as you, Matt."

"But what did you hear before?" I asked as we began to ascend the stairs. "Maybe all this is overblown."

"I don't think so," he said, to my dismay. "I think this is the big one—the one we've always feared in the medical world—an extinction event—Armageddon."

Normally, I appreciated his matter-of-fact approach. I could have used better bedside manner at that moment.

"It has long been feared that some sort of 'super bug' would come along and wipe out mankind," he continued. "I mean think about it. You're a scientist, so you must know that it's just a matter of time before natural evolution brings us something we can't deal with. Viruses are constantly combining in nature via re-assortment and creating new viruses, most of which are no worse than their predecessors and die without causing any harm. And we've generally been able to stay ahead of the ones that survive, thanks to the wonders of modern chemistry. We figured that a superbug would happen naturally all by itself one day, but we didn't count on somebody intentionally speeding the process up."

"What do you mean speeding up the process?" I asked as we reached the top of the stairs.

He held his hand on the door but didn't open it. "I'm pretty sure it was engineered. Somebody created it."

That bombshell left me speechless, so he answered a follow-up question that he must have come to expect. "I'm sure you've heard that it appears to be a combination of different viruses, one hemorrhagic and the other something like bird flu. We already knew that viruses can combine, and so this is not, in and of itself, exceptional. But what was not being said is that the Red Plague managed to retain the worst attributes of the component viruses. It is highly unlikely to have occurred naturally."

I stepped back as someone opened the door, nearly hitting me with it. Obviously uninterested in our conversation, the man scampered down the stairs. Dr. Pepper grabbed the door before it closed, but we remained in the doorway to finish our conversation.

"What do you mean 'worst attributes'?" I asked.

"I never learned the exact particulars of the disease before we were cut off," he said. "But let's imagine that the component viruses were Ebola and bird flu. Either of those would be sufficient to kill the host long before there could be sufficient recombinations to produce a viable second supervirus. In other words, it's practically unimaginable for any host to survive long enough with both viruses for them to be able to produce a third virus with the ability to spread. The Red Plague is as lethal and contagious as Ebola, but worst of all, it's airborne like bird flu. It is just thought to be very unlikely to have occurred naturally. It must have been done in a laboratory."

"By who, though?" I asked.

He shrugged. "Take your pick."

He slipped through the door and began walking briskly down the hall.

"So how long do you think it will take before this thing runs its course?" I asked, following closely behind. He slowed so that I came nearly level with him.

"The bubonic plague took years to peter out, and we have many times the population now. We've also got the means to get from one place to anywhere else on the planet in less than a day. The incubation period of the Red Plague may be up to thirty days. Can you imagine how far this could have gotten in thirty days just by random encounters? Imagine that somebody has been planting it in order to speed up that process, and it could easily be everywhere by now. It's probably going to test the immunities of each and every one of us. Well, with the possible exception of us. Assuming it isn't already here, we are so isolated that we might be able to avoid it altogether."

"Yes, that's wonderful," I said sarcastically as he turned a corner and walked away from me.

I found neither Commander Blaine nor Jeff at the EOC nor at their respective offices, so I decided to go down to the terminal and wait for Continental to arrive with answers. I rounded the corner to the waiting area and found what seemed like half the island waiting there. Some people talked quietly, but most just sat in the grandstand and waited. Except for the large crowd, everything seemed normal. The ground crew busily finished their preparations by moving luggage carts, testing the generator, and repositioning the stair truck. The ubiquitous trades tugged on palm fronds, and waves breaking on the reef sent a fine, briny mist across the area. A small child of a couple I knew in passing darted from the grandstand toward the perimeter road only to be snatched up by his brother in mid stride.

I looked at my watch and it read 11:15 am, arrival time. I stood in the shade of a lone palm tree and leaned against its trunk to wait.

I monitored my watch as it advanced through 11:30 and 11:45, and the crowd grew increasingly restless. At noon I sat down and leaned back against the tree. At 12:10, a breathless young guy announced to the crowd that his friend in the control tower told him that Continental wasn't even on radar yet and they hadn't been able to raise them on radio. The crowd began to trickle away.

At 12:30 a man began to sob loudly. By that time, the crowd had halved. I leaned back against the palm and closed my eyes. Continental never came.

6

5 A.M., WEDNESDAY MAY 30TH, BASE HOUSING, KWAJALEIN

I had not spoken to Kate in three days, I didn't know if they were all right, and I had no way to find out. A plague was sweeping the planet. Our country may have been attacked. We couldn't communicate with the outside world, I couldn't leave, and I had no idea what to do.

I tossed and turned for hours as my subconscious worked noisily on the problem. In that fog between sleep and wakefulness, where the mind attempts to access the stream, wisps of thought float by like leaves in a breeze. It moves rapidly from one to another, constantly evaluating, landing on some, but bypassing most, like a honey bee across a field of flowers. Most of the time, we can sleep through the effort, but great problems, apparently, require our presence.

Suddenly, my mind landed on a promising thought and summoned me. I just stared at it at first, like a person you know but can't quite recognize. Finally, consciousness stepped forward and lunged at the answer and took hold of it before it could slip by. Once in my grasp it felt heavy, but I recognized it as obvious—I don't know what took me so long to think of it.

I snapped fully awake and sat up. I had to see Jeff.

. . .

I peddled furiously down the well-lit streets, and, not surprisingly given the time of morning, found them empty. A heavy, moisture-laden, head wind whipped down the street, probably in advance of some rain. It resisted my progress, made me pedal harder than I would have liked, and, despite the comfortable night-time temperature, caused me to perspire lightly. I found that annoying.

I pulled up to Jeff's quarters, and after several failed attempts at deploying the kickstand, I cursed at the inanimate bicycle and threw it over onto its side as if to teach it a lesson. I looked around to see if anyone had seen.

I started for the front door when I was startled by the sound of someone coming through the bushes.

"Oh! I almost slipped," the person grunted to no one in particular.

It was Randy, Jeff's neighbor, and easily the most obnoxious person I had ever known.

I hurried up the sidewalk in an effort to avoid catching his attention. Randy was what we called "fluff" or an unemployed spouse on Kwaj. There was a lot of fluff on the island, but since most were women raising children, no one looked down on them. But a man who lived off the labors of his wife, especially an older, childless one like Randy, was widely disliked. This fact, however, had little to do with why no one liked Randy.

Dressed in a shiny, new jogging suit that was at least one size too small, he ran over and intercepted me on my way to the door.

"Did you see that? I almost slipped," Randy said.

"Technically, you did slip," I said, as Randy straightened his hair.

"What?"

He frowned and threw me a puzzled look. Even in the dark, his mustache looked fake, and his facelifts were noticeable. That's what happens when an aging man tries to hold onto the only asset he had ever possessed—looks—even though it drained away naturally decades prior.

"Didn't you actually slip on those wet leaves?" I pressed.

"Yeah," he smirked.

"Then you didn't almost slip. You did slip. What you almost did was fall."

"Whatever!" Randy said, which was how he put an end to any conversation he didn't understand—the percentage of which was likely large.

"I'm in a hurry," I continued.

"At this hour?"

"I'll see you later, Randy."

Ever the pest, Randy took a step with me and put out his hand to block my way. "Hey, one more thing. Have you heard anything about the weather lately? I'm going fishing tomorrow."

I could have ignored him and forced my way past, but Randy would just follow, and the last person I wanted around when I talked with Jeff was Randy.

"Randy, I don't *hear* about the weather."

"So what is it supposed to do?" he continued.

I didn't even try to mask my annoyance any more.

"The weather is not *supposed* to do any…." I trailed off. "Look, I don't want to talk about the weather. It will most likely do tomorrow what it does every day out here. How long have you lived here?"

"Well?" he bellered. "Aren't you a weatherman?"

"I am a me-te-or-ol-o-gist…" I said, pronouncing each syllable slowly for his benefit, "…not a weather-*man*!"

"I'm just trying to make conversation."

"It's going to be mostly sunny with a chance of showers tomorrow," I bluffed. "Now, do you mind?"

"Whatever," he said as he turned and jogged off.

I banged on Jeff's door, but he didn't answer. I tried the knob, and it was unlocked. Few people locked their doors on Kwaj. I check his quarters, and he wasn't there. His bed hadn't even been slept in.

I rode past his office, which was dark, and then I searched the EOC and failed to find him. As a last resort, I thought I'd try the only other place I ever saw him: his boathouse.

Boat owners on Kwaj were allowed to have boathouses near the marina, which theoretically served as shops in which to work on their boats. What they turned into in practice, however, were private lagoon-side villas.

The Riggins' boathouse was a veritable tropical paradise. It had a prime view, and rows of palm trees on the north and south sides provided ample shade from the intense afternoon sun. The primary structure was an old, white trailer, but the numerous additions that had been built over the years made the parent structure hardly discernible. Attached on the lagoon side was a sitting porch made almost entirely of driftwood and adorned with a variety of tropical-themed elements. A pair of flip flops, the quintessential footwear of the Marshall Islands, had been nailed over the entrance. Strings of little pineapple lights that crisscrossed the sitting area provided just enough light to function at night while not disrupting the starry views. A fan with blades in the shape of palm fronds rattled continuously overhead as it probably had since its installation. No one ever turned off anything with moving parts in such a corrosive environment; otherwise, the humid, salty air would quickly ruin the device. The work area of the boathouse was on the upwind side, which provided the added benefit of a cool breeze by which to work.

Jeff did not hear me approach over the whine of metal grinding on metal. The wire knotted wheel attached to his drill scattered small bits of debris to the wind. Fragments of castoff stuck to his hair and grimy clothing, and sparks flickered through the dark and went out. As I dismounted my bike, he stepped back and lifted his face mask to inspect his work. Half the small propeller gleamed as if brand new. Jeff touched the fresh metal with a finger and then quickly withdrew it and stuck it in his mouth to cool. Seeing movement on his periphery, he turned and looked toward me.

Knowing he couldn't see me through the dark, I announced myself.

"Couldn't sleep either?" he asked.

"Nope. What are you doing?"

Jeff looked at all the parts on the workbench then to me and then away again.

"Oh, nothing. Just blowing off some steam…cleaning out the parts bin."

"So, what's up with you?" he asked nervously.

I suddenly had no idea what to say. I thought it would be easy. I was sure Jeff would be thinking the same thing as me, but I hadn't thought it through at all.

"I, uh, just had something to ask you."

"What is it?"

I suddenly felt uneasy with what I was about to ask him. He had family in the states too, so he was in the same boat as me. I settled on just coming straight out with it.

"I need to get off this island. No, *we* need to get off this island."

Jeff turned and with a furrowed brow, looked me square in the eye. His expression—a mixture of concern, skepticism, and perhaps even a bit of relief—spoke volumes. His face softened, and he sighed as he turned back to his work.

"I know," he muttered under his breath.

I paused to let the obvious sink in as I moved in closer.

"Jeff, we need to get to the states. Your sailboat is the only way."

He blinked and pinched off a tear that rolled half-way down his cheek. My emotions remained raw, and with the appearance of that tear, I felt myself nearing the point of no return. I desperately hoped he would hold it together because I knew if he melted down, so would I. He wiped his eyes with his dirty arm, leaving a gray smudge across his face. Then, as if a switch had been thrown, he cleared his throat, swallowed hard, and spoke without any hint of sorrow in his voice.

"I know. You're right," he said.

"So what do we need to do?" I asked.

"I've been thinking about this for days," he said. "I didn't want to admit to myself that things are really this bad, but there really is no other way."

"I just can't sit here while God knows what is happening to Kate and the kids." I said, sensing the opportunity to seal the deal. "It's driving me crazy."

"This won't be easy," he said, his voice unsteady again. "There is no guarantee we'll even make it. Crossing the Pacific is a hard trip under optimal circumstances with all the right gear. People spend months outfitting and training for this."

"I don't care." I replied. "I would try to row across the ocean if I had to."

"Me too." Jeff squeaked.

We knew that things might fix themselves the second we left. We'd have felt awfully stupid if they had. But we both sensed that things were not right and not just because of the stuff we knew about. Sure, the plague was bad. But not being able to communicate at all, the bits of information Jeff's friends in comms had been able to gather, Continental not arriving; it all added up to a deep sense of dread. We held out hope that once we got back to the closest point of civilization, we could just hop a plane from there, or at least call our families.

Jeff and I spent the next hour hashing out a plan to cross the ocean on his sailboat. We talked about fuel, gear, food, and the weather. We worried what would happen if we got caught. We planned a route and decided no one should know about it unless it was absolutely necessary. But we realized that we couldn't do it alone, and we agreed to ask Sonny to come with us. We trusted few people more.

Jeff had one last thing on his mind.

"You know Bill pretty well, right?"

I nodded recognizing the rhetorical question.

"Do you trust him?"

I nodded.

"He's the only one with access to guns, and we need one," Jeff said. "I mean, chances are we won't see a soul all the way to the CONUS, but we can't take a chance. There will surely be pirates out. As soon as anything goes wrong those types come out. And God knows what we will find when we get there."

I agreed, obviously. But I would be taking a real chance asking Bill to get me a gun.

"I'll see what I can do." I said, tentatively.

"Again, don't say anything to anyone else," Jeff said. "You haven't talked with anyone about this, have you?"

I shook my head.

"Good. Oh, and although it's summer, I don't have to tell you that the North Pacific is still quite cold. You've got a coat, right? Rain gear?"

"Coat? I don't have...." my statement trailed off.

I felt like an idiot. Over my objection, Kate had brought winter clothes with us when we moved to Kwaj saying: "You never know when you'll need this."

"Actually, I do have a coat," I continued.

"Good. Me too. Wives, huh?" Jeff said with a smile.

Jeff ticked through a final list of things that needed to be accomplished and I wrote them down, divvying the list up between Jeff, Sonny, and I.

Satisfied that we had a workable plan, Jeff turned back to his workbench.

"It will probably take us until tomorrow night, to accumulate everything we need and be ready to go. I'll talk to Sonny this morning. Let's plan on bugging out middle of tomorrow night. If we slip away in the dark, nobody will see us."

DEAD RECKONING

. . .

10 A.M., WEDNESDAY MAY 30TH, KWAJALEIN

I only intended to stop by my quarters briefly on the way to see Bill, but I woke up on the couch two hours later. It was the best sleep I'd had in days. It's funny how much of a relief it can be to simply make a decision.

I checked my watch and decided that I would wait until lunch, since I knew exactly where Bill would be then. I chose instead to begin collecting the items I would need for the trip. Once I'd checked the essentials off my list, I rifled through drawers and cabinets in search of useful items that we hadn't thought of. You could never have too many flashlights or batteries. Who knew when I might need that small pocket knife I found in a kitchen drawer? I emptied drawers on the floor and ripped out the contents of entire shelves in one pull, the way a burglar might have.

By the time I had searched nearly everywhere, a multitude of things lay strewn across the floor. Suddenly it struck me how useless most of our possessions really were. My house contained so much expensive stuff that it likely came to many multiples of the average lifetime wage for most people on earth. But when it came right down to it, almost none of it mattered. It was all junk.

I moved to the last closet and pulled out a box. I opened the lid and stopped cold. I sat back in amongst the garbage and opened the cover of a picture album. The first page held a photo of Kate, beaming from ear to ear, cuddling our newborn Elaine. After twenty-four hours of grueling labor, she still lit up the room. She only seemed more beautiful to me as time went on. On the next page was a picture of Charlie, on the brand new bike he got for his fourth birthday—the bike that freed him from the "baby trailer" that Kate pulled behind her bike—the bike that years later he refused to give up for a "big-boy-bike" despite its size and condition, because it was his first bike and he "loved it."

Tears streamed down my face as I closed the album and set it carefully back in the box. I got up and began to walk away, then stopped, then started, then stopped again—the tears coming faster each time. I finally raced back to the box and ripped it open. I tore the photos of Kate and the girls and Charlie and his bike from the album and stuffed them in my pocket.

I checked my watch again. It was time. I moved toward the door, turned and took another look at all our stuff. The house was a disaster, but everything I really needed was in a single duffel bag in the middle of the floor—and in my pocket—and five thousand miles away. I stepped through the back door, and there sat Charlie's little bike, rusting against a pole, lonely and waiting for him to return. If we never returned, I knew the fate of that little bike that Charlie loved. The humid, salty air would slowly melt it into the ground. I craned my neck to choke back the tears and set off toward the chow hall.

. . .

Deputy police chief Bill Callaway looked nothing like what one might expect from someone in his position. His shoulder length hair and beard were totally out of character for a cop and even more so on a military base. His imposing figure along with a badge and gun frightened most people. But after four years as his friend and teammate in league basketball, I knew him to be a nice, gentle person—off the court that was. On the court he was a beast, a whirlwind of flying elbows and knees, and I was convinced that he could have boxed out a Sherman tank for a rebound.

I knew I would find him heading to the chow hall for lunch at eleven a.m. sharp. He liked to get there right at opening so he could beat the lines. It seemed lost on him that he probably could have walked right to the front of any line unchallenged. I just hoped his partner Tim wouldn't be with him as he was about half the time. Tim was a nice guy, but a very straight-laced, military type. He sported a crew cut, spit-shined his boots, and always walked as if marching in formation. He was the opposite of Bill in many ways. I didn't expect Tim to be sympathetic to my plight, and I definitely didn't want him to know anything about our plan.

When I rolled up to the police station at 10:58, Bill was just coming out, Tim right on his heels. I cursed under my breath. I could have just waited until later to get him alone, but I decided time was of the essence. I had to think fast.

I caught Bill's eye and nodded and he returned the gesture. He and Tim waited for me to park my bike and join them for the hundred yard walk to the chow hall.

"Hey buddy!" Bill said, slapping me on the back as he always did—his form of a handshake. Tim nodded.

"To what do we owe this pleasure?"

"Thought I might buy you lunch."

Bill and Tim both laughed at my joke since chow on the island was free to all residents—just part of the perks.

I scanned my brain for some way to get rid of Tim and quickly settled on the only thread that surfaced. Tim was not only a deputy in the police department, but the island locksmith.

"Tim, we've been having some problems with the cipher lock on the east end of the weather station after Ele. I was wondering if you would take a look at it."

"Sure, right after lunch."

"Could you do it right now? We're not supposed to have those doors unlocked, and it's been that way for days. I know it's not that big of a deal, but it is SOP." I cursed myself for having just given him a way to put off my request.

"It will be fine until after lunch," he said. "We're the ones who'd write you up anyway," he said looking at me curiously. "And we won't."

I stood there searching for another idea and quickly became uncomfortable. I sensed that they were already becoming suspicious. Cops are not easily fooled. I could have just asked to speak to Bill alone, but surely Tim would ask what it was about, and I didn't know if Bill would rat me out. It's harder to keep a secret when someone else knows you are trying to. So I gave in and decided to have lunch with both of them.

After showing our resident ID to the cashier (nonresidents visiting Kwaj had to pay), the three of us filed through the buffet line like so many cattle on the way into the slaughter house. The only consistently good thing about the chow hall food was the variety. Even if any particular item wasn't very good, at least one could usually find a couple of tolerable foods.

As fire and police personnel always did, Bill and Tim gravitated to a table close to the exit. We made mostly idle chitchat through the meal. I was eager to get to my point with Bill, but I thought better than to push my luck any further with Tim present.

As I chattered about a trivial matter, Tim's eyes suddenly slewed to my left and focused on something behind me.

"Oh God. Look who's coming," Tim said.

Tim and Bill both averted their eyes downward to their plates.

"Holy Cow! What are you guys doing?"

It was Randy.

"Same thing everyone else is in here: having lunch," said Bill.

"Is someone sitting here?" Randy asked, pointing to the fourth unoccupied chair at the table.

Tim verified the emptiness of the chair by waving his hand over it. "Nope. Nobody there."

I couldn't help but smile. Bill laughed out loud.

"Actually, we're waiting for someone." I lied.

"Not a problem," Randy said in his whiny, nasally voice. He walked over to the next table and said something. A guy waved his hand over an empty chair, and everyone at the table laughed. Randy dragged the chair over to our table, its legs screeching obnoxiously across the floor.

After making himself comfortable and the rest of us less so, Randy asked: "This is some disease going around huh?"

"Sounds like it." I said, noticing that, like me, both Tim and Bill were eating faster.

Randy's wife, Joyce, was the Commander's secretary, which by osmosis afforded Randy a level of respect he did not deserve. This fact alone generally kept people from telling Randy what they really thought of him. It was still quite easy to make him the butt of jokes, since he rarely understood any of it.

"Anyway, I should be good. I've got plenty of antibiotics," he continued.

"How do you have plenty of antibiotics?" asked Bill.

"I always keep the leftovers from my prescriptions. I've got a couple of bottles."

"Sounds like you are part of the problem," Tim said as he shoveled in another fork full of food. "You're supposed to take the whole prescription every time."

"Well, once I get better, what's the point?"

Tim rolled his eyes and shook his head.

"Besides, this is a virus going around," I said. "Antibiotics only work against bacterial infections."

"Whatever." Randy said. He then smoothed his obviously restored and unnaturally dark hair and rubbed his absurdly white, capped teeth with his finger. Randy's vanity was unmatched.

He turned to Bill: "Anyway, so, what's new in the cop shop?"

Bill quickly took one last fork full of food, dropped his fork and napkin on his plate and said through a mouthful of food: "Nothing. Time for me to go."

Tim and I followed suit and began to get up.

"Hey, I thought you guys were waiting for someone."

"Doesn't look like he's going to show," I said.

Randy shrugged, got up, and dragged his chair noisily back to the table from which he got it. He sat down. They all began to eat quickly.

We emerged from the hall into the sticky, hot air. Bill removed a toothpick from his pocket, peeled back the wrapper, and stuck it in his mouth, letting it settle into the corner. Satisfied, he exhaled.

As we stood in front of the building, I struggled for a plan to separate Bill from Tim without further arousing their already heightened suspicion. Before I could completely embarrass myself, Bill turned to Tim.

"Tim, why don't you go check out those locks? I'll see you back in the office later."

Tim agreed and turned to walk back to the police station. He then broke into a trot as he attempted to catch up with someone else walking his way.

"Now, are you going to tell me what this was all about?" Bill asked, toothpick bobbing up and down like a Maestro's baton.

I was caught off guard.

"Can you do it right now?" Bill mocked. "We're not supposed to have those doors unlocked." Bill chuckled. "Give me a break."

"You know me too well."

Bill turned square to me, locked out his knees, and placed his left hand on his belt and his gun hand on top of his sidearm—purely habit, but unnerving nonetheless. Then he gave me the thousand yard stare. I realized at that moment that I could have never withstood an interrogation by Bill.

"It's not a crime to ask to speak to somebody in private," he said. "So, what is it?"

Partly to break my nerves and partly to ensure that no one could hear our conversation, I asked him to walk with me across the ball fields toward the air terminal.

"Do you promise not to repeat what I'm about to tell you?" I asked as we reached a quiet, shady spot and stopped walking.

"No," he responded, to my surprise.

"What do you mean no?"

"Well, I'm not your lawyer or doctor, so there is no privilege with me. If you tell me that you've committed a crime, I cannot keep it to myself."

"It's nothing like that."

"I'll keep your secret if I can."

I started with the least objectionable part first.

"I'm leaving."

Bill didn't even flinch. He just stared at me, his face expressionless.

"Can the Commander really stop me?" I asked.

"You're a civilian, so technically no."

Bill reminded me that the base was essentially shut down, and the Commander had closed all forms of transport to and from the island.

"He's closed all the ones he controls." I corrected as we began walking again.

Bill thought for a moment and then just as I could tell that our plan was unfolding in his mind, I continued.

"Private boat owners can come and go. Maybe we forget to file a float plan and just keep on going?"

"Then we'd be out looking for you, eventually, when you turned up missing. We would be obligated to do S&R (he meant Search and Rescue) until we confirmed your safety, or"—he paused—"let's say whereabouts." He meant our bodies.

"So you don't find us and we're presumed dead? Big deal."

"I guess you could get away with that, but I'm sure you'd become persona-non-grata here."

"Oh well. I couldn't care less at this point."

Bill conceded that point with a nod.

As we neared the air terminal, we stopped under a particularly dense grove of palm trees. The shade and breeze off the ocean less than twenty yards away felt refreshing. Nevertheless, I began to perspire. A knot formed in the pit of my stomach. I feared opening Pandora's Box. Was Bill my friend more than a cop? I doubted it. I considered what it would be like never to see my family again. I glanced at Bill's gun and wondered if after he put me in jail he'd let me borrow it to put myself out of my misery. Bill noticed as I glanced at his gun.

Suddenly confronted with a feeling of fight or flight, I chose flight.

"This was a bad idea," I said as I turned to leave. "I'll see you later."

"Hey, hold on. I know we're all freaked out about all this shit, but you've got me worried about you. Just tell me. Maybe I can help."

Sensing my vulnerability, Bill softened his stare and put his hand on my shoulder.

"We need weapons," I stated bluntly.

I scanned Bill's face for any hint of a reaction and found none.

"I see. And obviously you think I can get them for you."

"I was hoping so, yes."

"Well, I'm afraid not. There aren't any personal firearms on this base—at least that they know about. And a person could get in a heap of trouble if anyone found out that there were."

"I know that. I'd never say where I got it....them."

My eyes continued to bore into Bill, searching nervously for any sign that the jig was up. Only a few seconds had passed, but I could stand the silence no longer. "You're not going to turn me in, are you?"

The wind suddenly kicked up, and the sky to the east darkened as a shower approached. The air cooled as the sun ducked behind the looming cloud. Bill furiously worked his toothpick back and forth as he considered my question. Then his face brightened.

"No. Your secret is safe with me." Bill slapped me on the back.

"So there is nothing you can do for us? No stockpiles of weapons anywhere that could come up a couple short without anyone noticing?"

"Not really. We do an inventory of issued weapons and ammunition on every shift. We have to sign off on it along with another officer. I'd have to get half the force to go along with me in order to pull that off. The rest of our shit is locked away in the armory. No way to get at that without raising all kinds of flags."

"Any idea who might have personal firearms and might be wanting to sell them around here?"

"Have them, yes. Sell them? I don't know. In this situation? Yeah, I suppose I know a few, but..."

"So?" I interrupted.

"I can't say. I swore I'd never say, and I'd get shit canned just for knowing and not telling."

I sighed, nothing much left to say. "You were our only hope. I guess we'll just have to wing it."

"You guys don't have anything?"

"No."

"Damn," Bill muttered, noticeably disturbed by the thought—the first negative emotion he'd shown during the conversation.

"You might be able to come up with something on Ebeye. But ask the wrong person and you could end up in their jail. You know what that means."

I sure did. In the Marshallese culture, it was the responsibility of the inmate's family to take care of the incarcerated. If you didn't have family there, you would have to persuade the jailers or fellow inmates to give you food. As is typically the case in jails the world over, that meant sexual favors. The jails were bad enough in and of themselves, but to add further humiliation to the process, inmates were stripped naked before being thrown in—to remove any remaining vestiges of personal defense.

Several years earlier, a bunch of Greenpeace activists managed to breach security and delay a local missile test. They landed in zodiacs, walked right up to the launch silo, and looked down in. Everyone was stunned by their audacity, but much more so at how easily they did it.

The Range was none too happy about it, and because they knew it would be much worse and thus more of a deterrent to any future ambitions of a repeat, they let the Marshallese police deal with the violation. Months later, the activists blogged about their experiences in the Ebeye jail and worse, their transfer to the jail on Majuro, the capital of the Marshall Islands. One described spending weeks naked in the jail cell with little to no food, surrounded by violent offenders, and having to sleep sitting up against a wall—to protect his backside.

"I might rather take my chances out there," I said, pointing toward the ocean. Even though I said that, I already knew I was heading for Ebeye as soon as possible after I finished talking to Bill. I had a Marshallese friend on Ebeye that I thought I could count on. Nobody knew when the Commander would shut them down, and I suspected that time was short.

"I would ask around, see what you can dig up. People know things, especially the old-timers," Bill continued.

"I don't know about that. The fewer people that know about my plan the better. You are the first we've told. And time is not on our side."

We walked back to the police station without any further discussion. Before I rode off, Bill said one last thing:

"Don't worry. You never know how things are going to turn out. I'll poke around. Check back with me before you leave, and I'll let you know if I come up with anything."

7

2 P.M., WEDNESDAY MAY 30ᵀᴴ, EBEYE ISLAND, KWAJALEIN ATOLL, MARSHALL ISLANDS

"The miserable have no other medicine but only hope." - William Shakespeare

The boat ride had been rough, and my stomach quivered—not from the motion alone but rather a combination of motion, heat, and the smell of diesel exhaust. My stomach's emptiness and the ubiquitous body odor of dozens of natives didn't help either.

As I rode the Landing Craft Mechanized (or LCM)—the Army's vehicle of choice to ferry personnel and equipment around the range—I thought about the true purpose of the vehicle. I imagined myself as one of the troops aboard such a boat as it landed at Omaha Beach. How must it have felt to hear the rapping of bullets on the steel hull as the craft beached and the ramp in front lowered and they stepped off that ramp with no defense beyond their rifle, helmet, and luck? How were they able to get men to do it? Or rather, how were men able to summon the courage to step forward?

I once heard it said that courage is simply the willingness to be terrified and act anyway. Living on a WWII battlefield supplied ample reminders that I had never had the opportunity to discover if I possessed such virtue. Mostly I was grateful that such personal sacrifice had never been required of me, but in another way, it made me feel empty.

The procession off the LCM was slow because, in rough seas, you had to time your step onto the pier to coincide with the peak of the upward heave of the vessel. In the trough between waves, the pier was chest high. A steward stood by to help women and children, but men were on their own. Now that the boat had docked, the flies settled in again, buzzing people's eyes and slowing the procession further.

At the end of the pier in front of the ferry, several dilapidated fishing trawlers bobbed up and down. Loitering on their decks were young, surly-looking crew members who, apparently having nothing better to do, menacingly scanned the disembarking passengers through squinting, suspicious eyes. Between the boats, a miscellany of Styrofoam cups, plastic grocery bags and other anthropogenic detritus floated among a putrid surface film, flies buzzing just above the surface.

As I picked my way through the crowd toward the end of the pier, I scanned the faces hoping to locate a Marshallese friend of mine called Denver who lived there. He was the only person I knew on Ebeye and, really, my only hope to find a gun since I knew virtually nothing about the island other than where to find food.

I was a good four inches taller than the average local, which made it easy to scan the crowd but harder to see the variety of coolers, shopping bags, and other makeshift luggage scattered about on the concrete surface.

The main street ran perpendicular to the pier. A hot, gusty breeze flowed straight down the road and kicked up dust clouds from the uneven surface. Bits of trash skittered and tumbled along. Other than the dirt, sand, and debris that had settled into low spots as the water retreated, there was hardly any sign of the typhoon that ravaged the island just a few days prior.

I stepped to the curb as the crowd in the street parted and a rundown black Mitsubishi pickup filled with young men whizzed by. Then the crowd closed up again. Had the youths in the pickup been wielding machetes or machine guns, the scene could have been straight out of the Congo. But this was Ebeye Island, a veritable Villa Miseria in its own right, just a short three mile ferry ride from my utopian home on Kwajalein Island.

What the two islands lacked in spatial separation they more than made up for in socioeconomic disparity. The contrast between the two places was so stark that it was literally like boarding a ferry in Beverly Hills and finding yourself in Bangladesh fifteen minutes later. And the flies, my God, the flies! What was a significant nuisance on Kwaj was torturous on Ebeye. It was so bad on Ebeye that we referred to the flies as the "Ebeye Air Force."

Ebeye Island was home to the vast majority of the Marshallese population on Kwajalein Atoll. The island was a mere one-tenth of a square mile and home to approximately fourteen thousand people, making it was one the most densely populated places on earth. With no industry and virtually nothing to export, the conditions were squalid. It hadn't always been that way on Ebeye, and it wasn't really like that around the rest of the Marshalls. It was the presence of the American government on neighboring Kwajalein Island, and the associated jobs, that brought ever increasing peoples to Ebeye. After the initial migration to the island, natural processes soon took over, and the population increased exponentially. Over half the population on Ebeye was under age eighteen.

I crossed the street, and with Denver nowhere in sight, I headed toward the fish market. Denver was a fisherman, and I thought that someone in there might know where to find him. The Ebeye fish market was in an old, light blue concrete building. A wooden sign that read 'Fish Market' hung precariously over the door by a single wire on one side. The eye screw on the other side of the sign had long since rusted through in the heavy, salt-laden air, and its wire dangled uselessly above. The sign squeaked as it rocked in the breeze, and I kept one eye on it as I passed beneath.

As I entered the building, the rush of heat and humidity typically found in unconditioned buildings on Ebeye curiously failed to materialize. The market was uncharacteristically well stocked with fish, all packed in ice. In addition to chilling the fish, the ice served to keep the room cool and discourage bugs. The incorrigible obviously existed in the insect world as well, evidenced by the many that struggled to free themselves from strips of fly paper dangling from beams and doorways.

The market segregated fish by grade—highly prized Yellowfin, Mahi Mahi, and Ono on one row and all manner of lower grade fish and edible sea creatures on another row. Marshallese peoples jammed the lower grade row, bargaining for the cheaper foodstuffs, while the high-grade row sat empty waiting for Americans to arrive.

Americans frequented the high-grade row more often not due to a lack of delicacies on the other side—on the contrary, some of the strange looking tropical fishes were said to be quite delicious—but because the fish from the tuna family were the ones least likely to infect the diner with a nasty case of ciguatera. Ciguatera is a flu-like poisoning that comes from eating tropical reef fish contaminated with ciguatoxin. The Marshallese, who were mostly immune to its effects, called ciguatera "beep beep" which was almost certainly onomatopoeic given the fact that diarrhea and other gastrointestinal disturbances were the most common symptoms.

I approached the person who seemed to be in charge of the market and asked him if he knew Denver. He stared at me blankly. I asked the men assembled behind him if they spoke English and they too just stared.

The higher than normal stocks of fish produced a higher than normal odor, and my stomach had not yet settled from the boat ride over, so I headed back out into the street. I passed the security booth and then turned back remembering that, as a noncitizen, I was supposed to sign into at the booth. I was, after all, technically on foreign soil as soon as I set foot on the island.

When I stepped up to the window, the startled guard jumped to his feet.

"Yokwe," he said. Then, realizing he was staring at an American, repeated in English: "Hello."

He grabbed a clipboard and a pen and pretended to have something important to write down all of a sudden. Then he asked: "May I help you?"

"I just wanted to sign in, and I'm looking for Denver," I said, suddenly realizing that I didn't know his last name.

"Ok, just fill this out and sign here."

I penciled in a fake name and social security number. They never checked ID, and in the age of identity theft, I had no intention of putting down my actual social security number. The guard studied my inputs and then said: "Komol tata. And please remember to check out when you leave."

"Denver?" I questioned.

"Yes, Denver. Maybe church," he said pointing down the street.

I walked along the main street toward Lagoon Road, which did not run along the lagoon. Its name derived from the fact that, of the two roads that ran the length of the island, it was simply the closest to the lagoon. Ocean road, by contrast, did actually run right along the ocean. I walked past the only grocery store on the island with its barred windows and chain-adorned doors. I passed a makeshift restaurant with women lined up to buy entrees. Their children milled about the candy case, a longing look on their faces, green sleepers in the corners of their eyes, and fluid oozing from their noses and down their upper lips. It was all I could do not to swat at the flies that crawled, seemingly unnoticed, over their faces.

I passed a blue building labeled with the word "school." A poorly dressed Marshallese kid of maybe eighteen studied me carefully as I passed. I greeted him, but he responded with a frown.

I reached Lagoon Road and turned right. I walked past dozens of plywood and cinder-block houses, some with corrugated metal roofs, others with plastic covered plywood, others a combination of the two, and still others with something altogether unidentifiable making up the roof—or even some with no roof at all, its rafters having rotted through and its occupants, too poor to replace it, having moved on. I found it amazing how fast they were able to resurrect the tenements after Typhoon Ele. There was hardly any indication that anything had happened.

DEAD RECKONING

The gutters in front of the residences contained a visually offensive fluid—not exactly water but containing water and not exactly sewage but containing sewage. I couldn't smell it, but its appearance strongly deterred me from stepping in it. The odors emanating from the structures were generally offensive but were interspersed with the occasional sweet smell—laundry soap or Pine-Sol—and one house even gave off a pleasant smell of wood smoke and barbecuing chicken. A pang of hunger rose in my belly but quickly gave way to the thought of the flies that probably crawled all over the meat, or at the very least, hovered patiently just above, waiting for it to be removed from the fire. It never ceased to amaze me how uninterested flies were in fire or smoke until a piece of dead flesh appeared. They'd come from miles around just to throw up on it.

I stopped at the intersection of Lagoon road and a side street and looked up the length of the side street. Mid way up the street, several children stood in line next to a blank plywood wall along the sidewalk. The first child in line stood on a wooden box and waited. Shortly, a hand holding a can of soda extended from a small hole in the wall. The child took the soda and placed an amount of money in the hand. He stepped down, and the next child stepped up to the hand. The hand provided the next child with some sort of candy. And on it continued—a human vending machine.

I walked a little further and came to the church that I thought the guard must have been pointing toward.

The church was the tallest and most well maintained structure around. It was painted entirely white and had ocean blue trim. The windows contained no glass but were framed in with approximately three-foot squares of wood stacked three high and two wide. Each square was divided further by wood slats from top to bottom and side to side in the middle, as well as from corner to corner, forming eight right triangles within each square in an obvious attempt to make it difficult to see in, but at the same time allowing free flow of air. Above the windows sat half-circle-shaped wooden awnings painted in the likeness of a rising sun. There was a steeple on top with a cross on top of that. A large main door in the middle, supplemented by two subordinate doors on each side, provided entrance to the building. The courtyard before the church was level and covered in coral gravel, some pieces large enough to cause an ankle to roll over if stepped on askew.

In the courtyard, hundreds of Marshallese stood in lines waiting quietly. A sea of white dresses, shirts, and slacks was punctuated only by the thin, red ties on the men and red ribbons in the hair of the females. Most stood stoically, but a few of the younger performers swayed back and forth as if thinking through their moves or humming in their heads the tune of the song to which they would soon dance. One boy leaned over to rub a spot on his shoes and was immediately admonished by the boys in his vicinity and erected himself. None of them looked the least bit uncomfortable despite the blaring heat and lack of wind in the protected courtyard.

I had apparently arrived just in time for the start of some event. I made my way through the crowd of white and into a seating area off to the side of the church. Inside the church, thousands of mostly women parishioners sat respectfully stiff-backed in the pews. Young women held infants while old and fat women sat fanning themselves with any contrivance capable of moving air. Men, dressed in their best, sat in the back of the church or stood against the wall as if they had just happened in. Perhaps they were unsure of what to expect and desired an easy escape should they find whatever was to come unpleasant.

I scanned the back rows and walls and did not notice Denver. Although a lot of people thought it a sign of racism to say so, I had a hard time distinguishing among the Marshallese—the truth is what it is. I took a seat so that I could search the hundreds of faces without being obvious about it.

A preacher took the pulpit and began to speak in Marshallese. I recognized it as a prayer only because of the sudden bowing of heads. I did not bow my head because I already knew no one was listening. My own beliefs notwithstanding, one didn't have to spend much time in the deprivation, squalor, and suffering of Ebeye to recognize that the prayers of all those people went largely unanswered. But I understood that religion offered such people a ray of hope in spite of the obvious hopelessness. Ignorance is bliss, as they say. As usual, I felt self-conscious about not bowing, but only until the prayer ended.

The preacher then told a story that went on for some time. I scanned the faces. No one made a sound. When the preacher stopped talking everyone looked to the door. An explosion followed causing a banner to unfurl from the ceiling. To the delight of the crowd, it came down backwards and upside down. The Marshallese words written on the other side were barely visible through the fabric. Everyone laughed. This remained a distraction for some time among the parishioners, especially the children, whose attention could only be drawn from the banner with much prodding. Even well after the event, people nudged their neighbors, pointed to the sign, and recounted what had happened—as if the neighbor had somehow since forgotten. I watched one man scowl and nod impatiently, annoyed at his neighbor for telling him that which he already knew.

Everyone clapped as music began and the dancers in white streamed into the church. As they entered, the dancers performed a routine that consisted of a forward shuffle followed by a slightly shorter backward shuffle. At the pace of three steps forward and two steps back, it took them the better part of ten minutes to assemble entirely in the church. In unison, the performers shouted a word and stomped their feet, which signaled the end of the song.

I became very hot and began to perspire, but I knew that leaving in the middle of a performance, especially a sacred one as this appeared to be, would be offensive nearly anywhere. I thought it better to try to leave than to pass out, so I attempted to extricate myself from the church without drawing attention. But as does naturally occur in those situations, I bumped into a small planter that refused to give way quietly. No one looked at me but rather remained fixed on the performers, as if afraid to look away lest they miss the very thing for which they waited. I managed to withdraw to an exterior foyer that gave me a different angle from which to search and also provided access to a light breeze. Hot air moving is always better than hot air standing still.

I was now seated in the front row of a posterior section where the faithful with less dependably quiet children and those wishing to freely come and go were seated. In front of me was a walkway between the sections. Children skittered up and down aisle to the disapproving looks of adults. The ancillary activity provided an interesting diversion since I had no idea what was going on.

I stood out in the crowd, and nearly every child who passed looked at me curiously. Some smiled, some frowned, and some looked away feigning ambivalence, as I looked at them. I decided that children are the same in every culture.

Suddenly, the performers broke into a more vigorous dance and song. I could not understand the song, but it was obviously well known as many of the onlookers sang along. Separated by sex, men on one side, and women on the other, the performers danced in unison. The men made a rowing motion as they danced and sang. At periodic intervals, they shouted a word at which point the women stopped dancing and swooned while the crowd laughed. This performance continued until the group made three complete circles around the church.

For all I knew, perhaps Denver was among the performers. So I sat through a few songs and observed.

For the next performance, the sexes intermingled. It was a much more somber sounding song, and no one laughed. The sea of white swayed to and fro, singing in unison, acting like a single organism, much like a school of fish. Two rows of people shuffled slowly in one direction while a single row of men moved swiftly between them in the opposite direction, much like a current on the open sea opposes the water surrounding it. Denver was not among the people.

A girl of not more than sixteen walked in front of me, carrying one infant child with three others of increasing age in tow. The youngest child ignored me, but the two older boys held up a hand for me to slap as they went by. I obliged, and they smiled. Another girl saw this and began to walk my way. She stared at me as she approached but began to look apprehensive as she drew nearer. I considered that my squinting in the bright light might have made me look angry, so I forced a smile. She sat down next to me and tapped my hand as one's own child might when wishing to ask a question in a quiet place.

She was no more than eight years old and dressed in a thin yellow dress with white flowers printed on it. She wore only flip flops on her feet, but she was clean, and her hair was tied up with a bow. Her teeth were unusually white and straight, although she was too young to have had braces.

"Do you live on Kwaj?" she asked, in perfect English.

"Yes I do."

"Why?"

"Because I work there, so I have to live there."

"My daddy works on Kwaj, but they won't let him live there."

"Hmm," was the only response I could manage.

"Why?" she asked.

"I don't know," I replied.

She got up and walked back to where she had been sitting. I felt a sudden pang of sadness that my new friend had already left—a sort of regret that I now had no one to talk to and, once again, stood out as the American with no friends.

She picked up her backpack and came back and sat down next to me again. Relieved, I smiled.

"Do you understand Marshallese?" she asked.

"No."

"Why are you sitting here if you don't know what they are saying?"

"I was looking for a friend. I thought I might find him here."

"Who is your friend?"

"Denver. Do you know him?"

"Yes. He does not go to this church. Do you want me to tell you what they are saying? What these dances mean?"

"Please," I said, curious to find out why such an elaborate ceremony took place on a Wednesday.

"Today is Gospel Day," she informed me. "This is our celebration of when the missionaries brought the Bible and Christianity to the Marshall Islands."

She proceeded to explain each of three consecutive dances to me. One was about the importance of community, another about the significance of fishing, and yet another was a tribute to the wind, swells, and currents that provided them with abundance. The girl spoke so rapidly that I couldn't get a word in.

Just as I began to grow impatient, she asked me if I wanted her to show me to Denver's church.

"Shouldn't you stay here with your family?" I said. "Just tell me the way."

"What do you mean?" she asked.

"Aren't your parents here?"

"No. My uncle and auntie are here. My parents go to another church."

I didn't bother to continue the line of questioning.

I followed her out of the church and up the street to Ocean Road. We walked a quarter mile to a large, two-story, blue, cinderblock building. A courtyard on the north side of the building held a basketball court enclosed by chain link fence. I heard music inside.

She led me through a side door, and into a foyer next to the large room in which services were being conducted. We walked to the entrance to the room and looked in. Everyone turned to look. Denver, seated across the room, smiled and gave me the standard Marshallese upward head nod and got up to make his way over. Several men suddenly noticed Denver's importance and patted him on the back as he passed. He smiled and nodded to the men as if to confirm that he was indeed, suddenly, very important.

I thanked the girl and offered her a dollar for her trouble. She initially refused but acquiesced, possibly in embarrassment, as nearby children looked jealously at her, then me, then the dollar, then her again.

"Yokwe, my friend!" Denver exclaimed with great excitement.

I turned to say good bye to the girl, but she was gone.

"Who was that girl?" I asked.

"A cousin," replied Denver. "Do you want something to drink?"

"No, I'm fine."

"Why are you here, Matt?"

"I need a favor," I said, knowing that it was beyond him to refuse. He would do anything for me by nature.

"I will be pleased to help. Can you wait? It will only be a few minutes more. Here, sit down," Denver said rapidly.

Before I could refuse, he had pushed a small boy out of a cafeteria style chair and pulled it over in front of me. The boy looked hesitantly at me as he stood next to his mother and rubbed his pride. His mother seemed not to notice, or perhaps found it a perfectly normal way to treat a child. Denver subsequently found a can of some sort of fruit juice, so I sat in a chair I didn't wish for and drank juice I neither liked nor wanted. At least the juice was cold.

Afraid to offend anyone by not appearing to enjoy the proceedings, I feigned interest. Luckily, some natural type of break in the service coincided with my finishing the juice, and I got up and walked toward the door. Denver had managed to slip out unnoticed and was already outside talking to some men.

As I entered the group, Denver proudly introduced me as his good friend.

The men all nodded in unison and then stood silently as if waiting for me to say something profound. I failed them.

"I need to speak to you in private, Denver."

"Yes, yes, ok. Let's go."

Denver hurried me out onto the street.

"Can you come to my house? I have something important to do."

There were still people around within earshot, and I knew it was going to be very difficult to change his mind. So I agreed.

We passed a restaurant called Litake Fast Food. During my first trip to Ebeye, I saw the mayor eat there and reasoned that it must be ok. I had never eaten anywhere else since. Incidentally, it actually had good food, food that was different than what we had on Kwaj, and given the lack of choice on Kwaj, different was good.

We passed in front of the Hospital and Denver stopped. He asked if I could wait a minute as he needed to get something from inside. While I waited out front, I watched people come and go from the building across the street. High plywood fences surrounded the complex, much like what you might find at a lumber yard. People came and went through a single gate, carrying sacks of rice. I moved over a few feet so I could see inside as the gate opened and closed.

The spot was sheltered from the wind, and the sun beat down, so I began to perspire heavily again. The gate opened, and I saw hundreds of identical bags of rice stored inside. The writing on the bags was not English. I thought it might be Filipino. The place reminded me of a feed store, but for people.

Just as I was about to go over and look around in the feed store, some children ambled by, distracting me. Then, Denver came up behind me.

"Ok, let's go. I've got it," he said as held up a brown bag, apparently thinking its contents were obvious to me.

Denver was six inches shorter than me, but his stocky little legs moved quickly. I had to work to stay up with him. People were everywhere. Of the people we passed on our side of the road, Denver greeted more by name than he ignored. We walked into a neighborhood of silver trailers—single wide—which, anywhere else, would have been a sign of poverty. But on Ebeye, such trailers were excellent accommodations. I immediately recognized them as old Army trailers that had been donated to the Marshallese—the government, that is—free to the mayor and almost certainly re-sold or rented to the people at a handsome profit.

Children gathered around as we approached Denver's trailer. Ebeye's children had grown used to Americans passing out candy when they visited, which almost certainly contributed to the Diabetes epidemic on the island. Denver said something to them in Marshallese, and they all stepped back and began milling around as if that was what they had intended all along—all, except for a little boy with no legs who slipped out from under the trailer. He moved by using his arms as legs to swing his body forward, much like a monkey. He stopped in front of us and blocked the path to Denver's trailer. Denver said something to him too, something which I only recognized as different from his order to the other children. The boy refused to move. Denver picked him up and placed him out of the way. A girl came over to comfort the boy. I smiled at them on passing, and the girl reciprocated. The boy simply stared blankly.

The trailer was as clean as could have been expected on Ebeye, but it was, of course, not well appointed. Upside down buckets served as chairs around a very old, steel-legged, orange-vinyl-topped table. A window-unit air conditioner held open a window, but otherwise sat idle.

I heard voices and a child crying from a back room.

"Just a minute. You can come if you like," he motioned me toward the back.

We entered what apparently served as the master bedroom at the end of the trailer. A woman and an ancient Marshallese man sat on a bed consoling a young girl. Denver handed the bag to the old man. The old man opened the bag and withdrew some sort of plant and began to mash it into a bowl. When the plant became a paste, the woman drew back the covers. The girl's right arm was black and blue and swollen between the wrist and elbow. The girl began screaming again, although no one had yet touched her. The woman shooshed her, and I realized that the sound for quiet was the same in any language.

The woman grabbed the injured arm and began to massage it. The girl howled in pain. The old man scooped up a large portion of the plant paste and spread it over the girl's arm. She screamed again.

Despite the tears and snot streaming down her face, the girl was adorable. I took her to be about six. She looked at me with pleading eyes.

"What is the matter with her arm?" I asked Denver.

"It is broken," he said.

"Broken?" I asked, surprised.

"Yes," said Denver, pointing to the old man. "This is Ollie. He is a doctor."

"Why are you rubbing her arm?" I asked the woman. She looked as if she had no idea what I asked. "And what is the plant stuff?"

"That is a mixture of Kadjo leaves and Kaido roots," Denver responded. "Good for pain."

The woman continued to rub the girl's arm as she squealed with pain.

"Tell her to stop touching her arm." I told Denver.

"No, that is the treatment that Ollie recommends."

I looked at Ollie. "Is that right?"

He obviously did not speak English either.

"Denver," I said. "If her arm is broken it needs to be set and put in a cast—not rubbed. Rubbing will do no good. It only hurts worse."

"This is what we always do," Denver said. "They always get better."

"They don't get better because of the rubbing, but in spite of it. It just heals on its own, and the pain eventually stops. But it won't heal right unless it is put in a cast."

"We cannot afford a cast," Denver said. "We cannot afford to go to the hospital, especially for a cousin."

"She is not your daughter?" I asked.

"No, she is a cousin."

I learned that cousin is a designation that the Marshallese apply to any relation not part of the immediate family.

"Why is she here?" I asked.

"My cousin, her father, cannot afford these treatments," he said.

"You can't be serious!" I said. "These are not treatments. He is some kind of witch doctor."

"You may be surprised what our plants can do," said Ollie.

Ollie was extremely old. I would have assumed him to be well up into the hundreds anywhere else, but Ebeye had a way of putting extra years on people really quickly. In fact, Denver was five years my junior, but he looked much older than me. Ollie wore some sort of robe and a number of shell necklaces. His cloudy, unseeing eyes were spooky when they looked at you.

"This is ridiculous," I said, as I stepped over to stop the "treatments." "I'm taking her to the hospital." I grabbed the girl and pulled her over to me, careful to avoid disturbing her arm any more than necessary.

"No, you can't!" exclaimed Denver. "No money!"

"I will pay for it," I said.

Silence filled the room

Ollie shrugged and got up to leave. He spoke to the woman in Marshallese, and she got up too, and they both walked out. The girl whimpered, but clung to me, apparently thankful for the pain relief, even if she had no idea what we were talking about.

"Is this really what you do with broken bones?" I asked. I didn't intend to be as dismissive as I was, but it was hard to believe things like that were still done.

"Yes," he said. "When we can't afford to do anything else."

"Doing nothing would be better," I said as I carried the girl out of the room.

I carried the girl all the way to the hospital and walked in through the front door. To my surprise, it smelled and looked like a real hospital, if not quite as clean.

I approached the counter and placed the girl on it.

"Do you speak English?" I asked the receptionist.

"Yes."

"This girl has a broken arm," I said.

The woman stood and began looking at the little girl's arm. Noticing the stethoscope that dangled from her neck, I took her for a nurse.

"I would say so," she said. "But…."

"Don't worry about it," I said. I took out my envelope of gun money, pulled out two hundred dollars, and placed it on the counter. I saw Denver looking curiously at the fat envelop. I placed it back in my shirt pocket.

"Is that enough money to set her arm and put it in a cast?" I asked the nurse.

"Yes," she stated matter-of-factly.

"Good. Please make sure you give her something when you set it. She's already been through enough pain."

"I will," said the nurse ambivalently.

I held the nurses eyes for a few seconds and saw no emotion. She lifted the girl off the counter and set her on a gurney. I sighed and turned to walk out.

I approached the door trailed closely by Denver, when someone latched on to my side. It was the girl in the yellow dress, from the church—Denver's other "cousin." She hugged me.

"What is this?" I asked.

"Komol Tata," she said, tears streaming down her face.

She let go and ran over to the nurse and the girl with the broken arm.

Denver and I walked out.

"What was that all about?" I asked.

"That is her also cousin," he said in broken English. "Did you not see her following us?"

I hadn't. The Marshallese were like ghosts sometimes.

We stood on the curb in silence. I was unsure how to broach the topic that brought me to Ebeye.

"Our cures have helped for thousands of years," Denver said, breaking the uncomfortable silence. "What if you did not have a hospital to go to? Maybe you would need these cures."

"I don't know, Denver. I hope to God that never happens," I said.

"This is a very nice thing you have done," Denver continued.

I turned and faced him.

"Look, I know you guys don't have much money over here. But there has got to be a better way to live than this. Why don't you all rise up and do something about your conditions? Christ, Denver. That girl was suffering and that so-called doctor was making it worse."

"We don't have the…"

"I know, money." I cut in. "But not everything is about money. And even so, this country gets a shit load of money from my government. Do you have any idea how much money my government pours into this country? Where does it go? Condos in Honolulu for the landowners? The mayor? The King?"

"What can we do?" he lamented.

"Rise up. Refuse to work. Demand better."

"But they will put us in jail."

"Look around! You are already in jail. What do you have to lose? They can't resist if you all rise up. How many police are there over here? Twenty? There are fourteen-thousand of you, for Christ's sake!"

I realized that those were easy things for me to say, but the treatment of the girl really bothered me, as did the thought of how many other children suffered on that island every day. It wasn't Denver's fault, or my fault, or even America's fault. It was the fault of their corrupt government—a government that took the millions given to it by the U.S. and squandered it. It was the fault of universal human greed.

"You shouldn't use the Lord's name in vain, especially not today," he said. He lowered his head embarrassed—I felt like he was always embarrassed in my presence. His flower-print shirt flapped in the breeze, and I noticed his cheap cologne for the first time.

"People all over the world rebel against much less than this," I said. "I'm sorry I hurt your feelings, but I don't understand why you just take it."

Denver didn't know what to say. I knew it wasn't sinking in, and it would make no difference. The savage spirit of the ancient Marshallese people—fierce warriors who used to be feared across the Pacific—has long since been worn out of those people. No work ethic, no spirit, a virtually dead people—at least on Ebeye.

"Listen Denver. I didn't come here to lecture you. I came here for something very important. I need your help."

Denver looked up, his spirit suddenly restored. "I will do anything for you, my friend."

I knew he meant it. And I trusted him, but it was very difficult to know where my request would lead. I doubted he had a gun himself, but he would surely know somebody. He always knew somebody. It was that somebody that worried me. I was definitely paranoid, but I felt certain that anybody on that island other than Denver would throw me under a bus for a small fee—and the police would certainly love to catch an American doing anything illegal for the revenue it could produce. But I was desperate.

"What I am about to ask you, you can never tell anyone."

"You can trust me, Matt. You are my best friend."

I reflected for a moment on his comment and then blurted out my purpose.

"I need to buy a gun."

He briefly looked at me like a stranger. I suddenly worried that I'd scared him off.

"But Matt, why would you want a gun?"

"I can't tell you. But I promise you that I'm not going to hurt anyone. It is very important. Do you know anyone who has a gun?"

"Yes," he said nervously. "But this is very dangerous, what you are asking."

I told him that I would pay him well and immediately felt cheapened by it. I knew he didn't need money to help me. I treated him with as much real respect as I believed he deserved, not the veiled condescension the Marshallese usually endured at the hands of the rich, guilt-ridden American visitors. I treated him like I wanted to be treated, and because of this, he probably did consider me his best friend.

Denver stared at me as if trying to force me to change my mind. I didn't waver. Finally, he motioned for me to follow him.

We walked a few blocks, and Denver stopped at the blue school that I had passed by earlier. The kid was still there guarding the door. Denver said something to him in Marshallese. The kid looked at me again, laughed, and then motioned us in. I worried about what Denver had said to him.

We entered through a side door and immediately descended a dark stairway. The humidity hung in the air of the stairwell, and I noticed a mixture of cigarette smoke and Pine-Sol. As we reached the bottom of the stairs, a fat, smelly man squeezed by us and ascended the stairs.

The dimly lit hallway connected a series of rooms. A sudden argument in Marshallese startled me, and as we passed the room, I glanced in and saw a man stand up and slam playing cards down on the table. A half dozen other men stared nervously through the smoky light.

Denver raced past the next door, and a burly Marshallese man emerged in front of me. He began to yell at me, but I couldn't understand what he was saying. Denver grabbed his shoulder from behind and yelled back. The man slapped Denver's hand away, but stepped back into the doorway.

"This way, my friend," Denver said calmly. I noticed music in the background.

As we passed a succession of rooms, I saw a lingerie-clad woman lying on a bed alone, smoking; two children played in another room; and a uniformed police officer emerged from the final room as I passed. He buckled his belt around his ample stomach. Two young girls stood behind him. They couldn't have been much older than my own daughters. A sickening feeling crept inside me. I felt very out of place.

Suddenly, we emerged into a larger room. A half-dozen young men sat around on a variety of furniture. Some were shirtless, others wore hoodies, but all wore long pants and had bandanas wrapped around their heads. The room was better lit than the rest. Smoke hung in the air, and rap music thundered through the room. A nude woman danced in the middle of the floor. Neither attractive nor unattractive, at least she appeared to be an adult, I thought bitterly.

I had heard of gangs on Ebeye, and although I had been to the island many times, I had never seen any—until now, it seemed.

I stood by Denver's side, unsure what to do. Denver waited until the man in the middle of the room—the apparent leader and the one, I suddenly realized, for whom the woman danced—waved him over. Denver leaned in and spoke to the man. The man looked at the guy by the stereo and drew his finger across his throat like a knife. The music suddenly stopped. He spoke tersely to the woman and gave her a start. She scrambled from the room, her saggy breasts and flabby rear bouncing all the way.

The leader stood up and walked toward me. I became very afraid. He stopped just in front of me and stared into my face. I figured him to be eighteen or twenty at the most. I could smell the styling gel in his hair, and his feeble attempt at a mustache would have made me laugh at nearly any other time. His hollow eyes contained little sign of humanity.

He looked me up and down. He noticed the envelope in my shirt pocket and reached for it. I covered my pocket defensively, and all the men jumped to defend him. I withdrew my hand and allowed him to take the envelope. He opened it, thumbed through the bills, and stepped back. He nodded to a kid across the room who disappeared through a door.

The leader withdrew a couple of the hundred dollar bills, walked over the Denver, and placed them in his shirt pocket. He patted Denver's cheek and then spoke loudly in Marshallese. Denver jumped and hurried to leave, which unnerved me greatly.

Denver stopped at my side and said: "It is ok my friend. They have agreed to your offer." I didn't remember making an offer.

The man yelled at Denver again. Denver patted my shoulder and he left the way we had come.

My apprehension grew as the seconds passed. The men just stared at me. Finally, one of the men said something, and they all laughed. This further agitated my already frayed nerves. I wondered if anyone would come to my aid as these men—kids really—beat me to death. How long would it take for the Range to notice my absence and come looking for me? The skin around my testicles tightened as I remembered telling Bill that I was leaving. He might think I left and never come to look for me on Ebeye. Even if he knew, what could he do? Ebeye was sovereign Marshallese soil. Those kids could kill me, dump me in the ocean, and go back to their strip show. I reassured myself that all would be fine—Denver said so. I didn't think he would put me in danger for two hundred bucks. Actually, I knew he wouldn't do so intentionally, but he didn't always have the best common sense.

Finally the kid re-emerged from the door with a gun. Two uniformed Marshallese police officers filed in behind him—the fat one from before and another skinny one.

The kid walked over and offered the gun to me. Everyone watched as I hesitated. I looked at the police officers, and they stared back. The fat one smiled, and his gold front tooth gleamed in the light. He nodded his head as if to encourage me.

"Go on, all you have to do is take it," the leader said, in perfect English.

I pictured the mud floor of the Ebeye jail. I thought about men like this waiting for me there, all naked, and deprived. I knew Denver would bring me food and water in the jail, but that was the least of my concern.

I turned and ran.

I had barely made it to the hallway before someone got hold of my shirt and nearly tore it from me. It would take more than that to stop me.

I bolted down the hallway and pulled over a shelf as I neared the mid-way point. The man immediately on my tail fell, and the others tumbled over him.

I reached the stairs and bounded them three at a time. As I neared the top, another hand got hold of me. I burst through the door and ducked as a metal pipe swung toward me. The pipe went over my head and hit the man behind me square in the face. He sprawled backward down the stairwell, taking all the others with him.

I turned and watched as Denver dropped the pipe and took off down the alley way.

I suddenly realized that I had nowhere to go. It would take them about ten minutes to find a white guy anywhere on Ebeye.

I had only one hope. I sprinted toward the pier.

Half-way down the road, I snuck a peek behind me. The men were less than fifty yards back and closing.

I made a wide turn onto the main road and caught sight of the pier. An LCM was just beginning to pull away. Marshallese children pointed and laughed as I rumbled down the street at my top speed, three-quarters of my shift flapping behind me.

Just as I was nearing the pier, three security guards stepped out in front of me. I looked back, and my pursuers had yet to round the corner. The guard I had spoken to earlier yelled for me to sign out. I ignored him. Another guard laughed as I passed and yelled: "You'll never make it."

The LCM edged away from the dock as I scampered onto the boards of the pier. The guards, who suddenly noticed that I was being pursued, set out after me as well. Now beginning to tire, I ambled along the pier and felt the boards shaking under me as the guards closed. I reached the edge of the pier, and with one last thought about the Ebeye jail, leapt toward the LCM.

The tide was lower, and the drop felt like a hundred feet. In reality, it was about ten. I cleared the rail of the departing LCM and landed face-first among the assembled luggage—to the shock of the people onboard. The captain in the wheelhouse didn't notice the commotion until all the men came to a screeching halt at the edge of the pier and began yelling. The English-speaking, schedule-conscious captain pointed to his watch, waved, honked, and gunned the throttle for Kwaj.

The gang leader stood and watched us pull away. He smiled mockingly as he held up my envelope. He opened it and began counting. It contained over a thousand dollars.

8

8 P.M., WEDNESDAY MAY 30TH - KWAJALEIN, MARSHALL ISLANDS

When I got back to Kwaj, I rode straight to Jeff's quarters so we could brainstorm some other way to get a gun.

A note stuck to his door read: "Matt, We're ready to play, so meet us at the usual spot a.s.a.p. Jeff."

My mind raced. When did this happen? What's wrong now? I was suddenly sick with the thought of them leaving without me. I told myself that they wouldn't.

I rode as fast as I could to my quarters, avoiding eye contact with anyone I encountered. I raced to the door and found an identical note from Jeff taped to my door. I raced inside, grabbed my duffle bag, and took one last look at our quarters. I knew we would never return. Even if things worked out, we'd probably not be allowed back. The girls would never laugh and play with their friends in our living room again. I'd never tuck Lee into his bed in his room again. Kate and I would never hold hands and watch another sunset over the rocks behind our quarters again. We'd never make love to the pitter-patter of tropical rain on our fiberglass dome again. Kate loved Kwaj and I hated making that decision without her. Tears welled in my eyes.

Just as I was about to leave, I rushed back over to the box on the floor and retrieved the photo album. I decided that there had to be room on the boat for one photo album.

I bolted through the door and turned to lock it out of habit. In the hesitation, I spotted Lee's bike again. It was still leaning against a pole. I noticed rust forming on the wheel. I could not hold back the real tears. I sobbed for a few seconds, and then stopped immediately as someone rode by. The finality and emotion of the situation was suddenly offset by its immediacy. I collected myself and left in a rush.

It took only a few minutes to reach Bill's quarters. He lived in one of the many bachelor's quarters on Kwaj—which amounted to a glorified hotel room. I bounded up the steps to the second floor and found Bill's door. I knocked quietly at first, then more loudly, and finally I pounded on the door. Bill did not answer. I waited, pounded again, and then jiggled the handle. It was unlocked.

I walked into Bill's darkened quarters and flipped on the light switch. He was not there. His quarters were tidy, almost clinical. Except for the boxes of toothpicks stacked on a desk, there was hardly a sign that he lived there. A thought crossed my mind, but I quickly dismissed it knowing that no cop, especially not Bill, would ever leave an unsecured gun in an unlocked room.

I left Bill's quarters as I had found it and took a less than direct route to the boathouse so I could go past the police station one last time. The lights were on at the station, so I slowed as I passed and scanned the bike rack. Bill's green and yellow huffy was not in the part of the rack labeled "Deputy Chief." I sighed and rode on knowing it was over—I had failed and we would have no gun.

I arrived at the boathouse and found Jeff and Sonny loading the last of a pile of supplies into the dinghy.

"What's going on?" I asked. "Has something else happened?"

"The commander is going to close the base at midnight," Sonny whispered.

"Did you get anything from Bill?" Jeff asked.

"No."

"Fuck."

I slung my bag into the boat and grabbed my corner as we began to carry it toward the water. I glanced over my shoulder at the weather station across the runway. Even though I knew they would understand, terrible pangs of guilt erupted in my gut at the thought of abandoning my employees without so much as a word. I knew that they would be all right though.

We ambled quietly across the dirt road that ran along the lagoon. Just then a pair of headlights came around the corner about a half mile down the road. We scrambled up over the rocks and onto the beach. We dropped the dinghy on the sand and hid as best as we could.

A searchlight beamed out through the trees onto the water. We were almost certainly going to be seen.

"It's the police van," I whispered to Jeff.

"If he spots the dinghy, you guys stay where you are. I'll make up a story," Jeff said.

The van slowly crunched along the gravel road, its radiator fan whirring away. The light scanned out onto the water, just inches above our heads. The light flickered on by without touching us, and just as the glare receded, I saw a toothpick bobbing up and down in the driver's side window.

I stood up.

"Get down," Jeff pleaded. "He's almost gone."

"Bill!" I shouted.

The van lurched to a stop. The light swung around to me, then down to the dingy, and then back to me again. Then the light went out with a clink.

I climbed up the rocks as Bill got out of the van.

"Have you found anything yet?" I asked.

"I talked to a couple of guys, but, of course, they aren't willing to part with their guns now—at any price."

I glanced at the sidearm on Bill's belt.

"Come on Matt. I might as well just go with you if I did that."

"I know," I said. "I just got back from Ebeye."

"No luck?"

"Worse than that. I almost got myself killed."

The bob of Bill's toothpick increased, and he rubbed his forehead as he grappled with the gravity of our predicament.

"Speaking of running out of time, you had better get the hell out of here," Bill said. "The commander has doubled our patrols. The shit is about to hit the fan around here."

I extended my hand to Bill. He grabbed it and pulled me to him in a half hug.

"God damn it," he whispered. "I'm really sorry."

I nodded and punched him in the chest. "I'm gonna beat your ass at hoops when I get back," I said.

Bill started to say something but couldn't.

Jeff, Sonny, and I slipped into the dingy and paddled quietly out into the lagoon toward Jeff's boat. Bill resumed his patrol. The light beamed back and forth across the lagoon, carefully avoiding us.

Suddenly, someone dashed across the road through Bill's headlights. Bill barely avoided hitting him. The van's lights reflected off the shiny new jogging suit. Randy stood next to the driver's side door and looked out over the lagoon in our direction.

Randy's annoying voice carried across the water. "What's that out there?"

We froze in place.

"Nothing. Just a stingray," Bill said. "It's ok, I already checked it out."

"Are you sure?"

Bill turned the spotlight into Randy's face, causing him to shield his eyes.

"Why don't you get in, Randy? I've been wanting to talk to you."

His ego suddenly massaged, Randy happily complied. Bill kept the light on him until he got in the passenger's side and then he drove off in a hurry. I considered Randy's luck at being in the only place on earth a person like him could hope to survive given the kind of adversity our species suddenly faced. Survival of the fittest did not always hold true.

We quickly transferred our supplies from the dinghy to the sailboat. Once aboard, Jeff began issuing orders which we obeyed without question. Within a few minutes, we had untied from the buoy and began sputtering quietly northward through Kwajalein lagoon. We cruised silently past the north end of Kwajalein Island and watched a couple of lights flick off as people retired for the night. A woman jogged down lagoon road. All looked normal.

Much of the rest of our trip to Bigej Pass entailed a furious race to organize and stow all the supplies and pull gasoline tanks out of the hold and lash them to the deck before we hit the open ocean. Jeff gave Sonny and me quick, basic sailing lessons. We tied knots, learned the names of various ropes and sails, and were told over and over again to walk on the high side of the deck.

At 2:00 am we crossed Bigej pass into the Pacific Ocean. Half an hour later, we lost sight of land—no more lights, just pitch black. I was already becoming desensitized to the emotion of leaving, but as the adrenaline wore off, I noticed a fear of the unknown creeping up on me. The constant movement of the boat wasn't helping either. I immediately fell into a restless sleep on the hard deck.

I awakened to the sound of a siren. I sat up and rubbed away the confusion. The sun was up, but it was still early. A siren sounded again, and I stood up to take a look.

The police boat roared up from behind us, blue lights flashing. Bill stood on deck with two other officers that I recognized but didn't know well. Bill rested his right hand on his gun and nervously worked a toothpick around in his mouth.

A voice belted from the loudspeaker: "Prepare to be boarded!"

Jeff hesitated. "What do we do now?"

"It's Bill. Take it easy," I replied.

"Maybe they've been ordered to bring us back," Jeff worried.

"What purpose would that serve?" asked Sonny as he emerged from below decks. "It's just three more mouths to feed."

In less than a minute, the police boat was alongside the RY. Bill jumped aboard and landed awkwardly on the slippery, wet, rocking deck. I grabbed hold of his vest to steady him.

"You're a little far out for a day sail, aren't you?" asked Bill, smiling.

"Don't tell me it's time to come home already!" I replied.

Bill drew two handguns, one a standard police issue Glock 19 9mm and the other I couldn't identify, and held them at his side.

I flinched involuntarily, startled by the normally undesirable action by a police officer.

With a flick of his wrists, Bill flipped the guns over and held them by the barrels and extended the handles toward me.

"I changed my mind," he said.

I took the guns.

I glanced at the other two officers—both young, slender, and tan. They shielded their eyes from the rising sun but said nothing. The wind pushed at the boats, and the tide pulled which drew them ever closer. One of the young officers shifted the police boat into reverse and goosed the engine to avoid a bump.

"The thought crossed my mind that you had come out to bring us back," I said, looking back at Bill.

He considered his answer as he took off a black backpack and lowered it to the deck.

"We did. But it's a big ocean, and we couldn't find you," Bill said as he winked at us. "If I didn't think this was the safest place on earth, I'd have come out here to force my way aboard so I could go with you!"

"Thanks, man," was all I could muster.

"I just hope everything is cleared up by the time you get home, but I am not holding my breath. Say hello to Kate and the kids for me, would you?"

"I sure will," I said.

"What about the daily inventory," I asked, motioning to the Glock.

"Already filled out the paperwork this morning," Bill said. "The safety strap on my holster must have come unbuckled somehow, 'cause when I got out of the van on the dock last night, it slipped out and went into the drink. Probably divers down there looking for it right now. I don't guess they'll find anything. "

Bill smiled.

"What about the other one?" I asked.

"It's the darndest thing. I'm driving Randy home this morning, and I start grilling him over this story I heard a while back about how he has a gun he got from Ebeye. It didn't take five minutes and he's singing like a canary. That son of a bitch practically begged me to take it from him."

Everybody laughed.

"Couldn't have happened to a nicer guy," said one of the officers.

"You're a life saver," I said to Bill, not realizing at the time how true that was.

Our boat lurched as a large wave crashed against the bow and passed. A briny mist spread over us on the stiffening breeze. Bill lowered his head to steel himself against the cool spray and then brushed the droplets from his white police shirt. He turned to Sonny and Jeff and said: "I wish you guys the best of luck, and make sure he gets where he's going or I'm coming after the both of you."

"You know, we didn't file a float plan," Jeff said.

"Yes, I know. That's why we're out here. Someone said he saw a boat heading out Bigej Pass, and the marina had no plans on file."

Bill pulled the toothpick out of his mouth and considered it as he rolled it between his fingers. Satisfied that it was spent, he tossed it over. He selected another from his pocket and stuck it in his mouth, letting it settle into the corner.

He looked at us, squinted in the sun, and said: "You know, we'll be out here all day looking for your sorry asses?"

"Don't worry," Jeff said. "I thought of that. I left a signed letter in my quarters. Tells you all that we are gone and not to bother looking for us. Sorry that you've got to be out here in the meantime."

"It's ok. We brought fishing poles!"

Everyone laughed.

"We'll call off the search after the morning bite is over," Bill said. "Commander's got more pressing needs for his police force."

"Like finding missing guns?" I quipped.

"The Chief will probably take it out of my check but, at this point, who cares?"

"If you ever see that gang leader on Ebeye, take it from him. He's got about a thousand bucks of my money."

Jeff and Sonny looked perplexed.

"I see," said Bill. "I know that little shit. One of these days, I'll tell him you said hi."

Everyone smiled as Bill jumped back over to the police boat.

"Hey, your backpack!" I yelled.

Bill shouted back over the engines: "Keep it. You're going to need it."

Bill and the other two men aboard raised their hands and gave us the thumbs up as they gunned the engine and started back toward Kwajalein Atoll.

I dropped to one knee and opened the backpack. Inside were three extra clips for the guns, five boxes of 9 millimeter ammunition, several of Bill's patented fishing lures, a bag of something called Celox, and a box of toothpicks. In addition, was a note from Bill that read: "Good luck. Send us a postcard. –B"

It was 6:45 a.m. on day 1.

. . .

Sonny and I spent the rest of day one stowing cargo and preparing the boat for a long haul at sea, and getting more in-depth sailing lessons from Jeff. I noticed a building friction between Jeff and Sonny, which, although not caused by the lessons, was made worse by them. Sonny had taken sailing classes from another well-known sailor on Kwaj by the name of Marsten Wilcox, or Mars. Mars and Jeff always came in numbers one and two in Kwaj's sailing regattas. Jeff once called Mars a "danger to himself, his crew, and everybody on the water with him," but I was never sure if that animosity came from a dislike of his methods, sour grapes, or both. Whatever the case, Sonny thought he knew something about sailing and Jeff didn't. The RY was Jeff's boat, though, so he made the rules.

Jeff gave us an in depth tour of the RY, showed us where all the important things were, and told us about its history. We called it the RY, but its official name was Romeo Yankee. RY were the initials of Jeff's childhood hero Robin Yount. Yount led Jeff's beloved Milwaukee Brewers to their first and only World Series appearance in 1982, hitting a remarkable .414 for the series with four doubles and six runs scored, and he earned the first of his two league's most valuable player awards.

The RY was what Jeff referred to as a cruiser, which indicated what it was used for rather than being any sort of technical specification. A cruiser is used for cruising rather than living on or racing, and with the cruiser's philosophy being rather minimalist, it is normally outfitted with the least amount of gear and supplies possible. Of course, with our intention being more than your typical day cruise, the RY was loaded for bear.

Technically, the RY was a 40-foot Bristol, single-hulled, sloop (which meant it had a single mast), with a 35 horsepower gasoline engine for those lovely days with no wind. Jeff had retrofitted the fuel tank to hold 100 gallons, and with the inclusion of twenty-six five-gallon fuel cans, we had enough fuel to conservatively motor for about two-hundred and thirty hours. In perfect conditions, the RY was capable of sailing at 8 knots, but the engine was only able to propel the boat at about 6 knots. Jeff calculated that we had enough fuel to motor for about 1,600 miles. This was a very important consideration because it would allow us to take a much more direct route to the U.S. than if we had to sail by wind alone.

To sail by wind all the way to Seattle, we would have had to go west and then north to avoid the doldrums (which normally hung out between 20° and 30° north latitude) possibly as far as Japan where we could catch the mid-latitude westerlies that would take us home. The great circle route (shortest route on a sphere) from Kwaj to Seattle was about 4,800 miles, but if we had to go by sail alone, it could have nearly doubled our trip. By powering through the doldrums, picking up the westerlies due north of Kwaj, and with a lot of luck, we could arrive in Hawaii in a couple of weeks. Maybe we'd catch a plane there, but if not, it we should be able to make Seattle in just over a month. We all knew that everything would have to be perfect for that result, but we held out hope.

The deep trades extended north to approximately 25° north latitude after which the dreaded doldrums existed north to approximately 32° north latitude. North of that point, weak westerlies kicked in. The last time I had checked the weather models they showed that pattern holding for several days, beyond which the models were worthless out over the open ocean. The boat was capable of sailing up to 50° toward the wind so with easterly trades we could set a course of 030 and cross our fingers. If the weather held, we'd only have to motor for about 500 miles to break into the westerlies, and we would be home free after that. At least that was the plan.

As I stood at the galley sink that evening, I noticed the little stow-away. A fly buzzed between the blind and the window above the sink. I poked my finger at him but missed. He buzzed my face, and I swatted again and got nothing but air. Little bastard! This far from land and the things were still annoying the hell out of me.

On the second day, he landed on a sandwich I was making. I grunted as I took a swipe at the bugger. He evaded me again, but I made contact with my plate and knocked it to the floor, my sandwich coming apart and naturally landing mayonnaise side down on the floor. I ate my new sandwich topside, because I knew the fly would not come up into the wind.

I asked Jeff: "Have you seen that fly?"

"What fly?"

"There's a freaking fly still on board."

"Oh, leave him alone. Maybe he has family stateside too."

I spotted the fly twice on the third day and again on the fourth day. I tried to get him each time, but he was living a charmed life. I got close on day four. I actually hit him with my hand, but he was moving in the same direction as my hand, so he actually got a boost. Must be getting weaker what with no feces on board, I thought.

9

DAY 5 AT SEA, 30 MILES ESE OF WAKE ATOLL (GPS POSITION: 19.1°N, 167.1°E)

Ferdinand Magellan was not the first man to sail the Pacific Ocean. In fact, he was not even the first European to do so. But he was the man who bestowed upon the world's largest ocean the name of *Mare Pacificum*, or *Peaceful Sea*. It must have been an unusually nice day when he crossed through the Straits of Magellan and into the Pacific Ocean, otherwise I can't imagine where he got the idea that the Pacific was peaceful. My experience during our first five days at sea, as well as that of the thousands of captains whose ships lie at the bottom of the merciless beast of an ocean, was that it was anything but peaceful.

The trade winds blew at a constant and fairly typical 15-20 knots the entire time, which when combined with chaotic and shifting currents, churned the sea into a frothy 8-10 feet combined. Although I spent much of the first four days feeding my insides to the sharks over the gunwale the hard way, the work of preparing the boat for the long journey helped take my mind off the seasickness, which finally waned significantly on day five.

Late on day five, a tremendous squall blew through, and the wind shifted to the northwest and howled at better than forty knots for three hours and then stopped—dead calm—the doldrums. When we got up the next morning, Jeff had bad news.

"There is something wrong with the rudder."

"I told you I didn't think we should tie the wheel down," said Sonny.

Sonny was referring to Jeff's practice of literally tying the wheel in a certain position rather than engaging the auto-steering mechanism. Jeff believed there was too much drift in the auto steering system.

"It had nothing to do with that!" Jeff snapped back.

"Then, what happened?" I asked, cutting off the argument.

"Feel it," he said.

I took hold of the wheel, and it was vibrating.

"I think it's bent. We must have hit something in the water. It will create drag and slow us down. Not to mention that it will deteriorate over time like that."

Now in the doldrums, the seas were flattening out quickly. Jeff decided to go into the water and check it out. He tied a rope around his waist and jumped over the side. Sonny and I watched for sharks while Jeff inspected the underside of the RY. The rudder had been knocked slightly out of whack, bending the shear pin which held it in place in the process. Not keen on trying to fix the rudder in the open sea, we decided to make for the harbor of Wake Atoll where we could more easily affect the repair.

It took five hours to reach Wake Atoll, which consists of three long, narrow islands in the shape of a horseshoe. Peale Island on the northwest side of the atoll, Wake Island on the east side, and Wilkes Island on the south side encircled a harbor of approximately three square miles. Having been to Wake Atoll myself, I knew the harbor was too shallow to accommodate the RY but that a little alcove on the lee side of the atoll would offer nearly the same protection. The winds were calm, so our only concern was protecting ourselves from the east-northeast swell.

Having already reinstalled the radar reflector on the mast to make sure we were visible to large ships at night, we expected contact from Wake Island security at around ten miles out. I knew they did not have an "Over-The-Horizon" radar on Wake Island, so ten miles was the maximum practical range of their conventional radar on a boat of our size. However, contact did not come until we were within visual range.

"This is U.S. Air Force Station, Wake Island to unknown vessel. Identify yourself. Over."

Not wanting to be fired upon but at the same time wanting to remain as anonymous as possible, Jeff responded:

"This is Whiskey November One Nine Six Eight Alpha with three souls aboard, requesting safe harbor to complete repairs. Over."

Despite having been in the Marshall Islands for many years, the RY was still registered in Washington State, thus the WN call sign.

"Are you in distress? Over."

"Negative. Over."

"This is a United States military installation, and we are under a high threat condition. You may anchor no closer than one hundred meters from the low-water line on the southwest side of the atoll. You may not, repeat NOT, come ashore. You have forty-eight, repeat four-eight hours to make your repairs and get underway, and you will be monitored. Do you understand? Over."

We knew that we could probably get ashore if we truly identified ourselves. But we also knew that we may be arrested or detained for having left Kwaj in direct contravention of the Commander's standing orders, so we agreed. They notified us that they would contact us every six hours to determine our status.

As we pulled around the southern tip of Wilkes Island, we saw another sailboat at anchor. Although it was dark by that time, the boat was a well-lit, magnificent yacht of a sailboat that looked as if it measured a good eighty feet in length. We were all exhausted and glad for some rest after five days of thrashing by the "peaceful sea" and it would have been difficult, if not dangerous, to make repairs in the dark, so we decided to bed down for the night. I slept topside as a security measure and gave Jeff, our tireless skipper and coach, a much-deserved full night in one of the bunks below.

• • •

DAY 6 - WAKE ISLAND, CENTRAL PACIFIC OCEAN

The only interruption that night came from Wake Island security, five hours and fifty-nine minutes after we'd arrived, but I otherwise slept like a baby. I awoke the next morning sweating in the full sunshine to the shouts of: "Ahoy there!"

I sat up, rubbed the sleep out of my eyes, and tried to focus in the brilliant sunshine. I could have sworn that Thurston Howell III from Gilligan's Island was bobbing up and down in the ten-foot Zodiac yacht tender next to us. Despite the tropical heat and humidity, the man wore long pants and a sport coat. His hard-brimmed captain's hat cast a shadow across his pasty-white face which added depth to his chiseled facial features. Wiry, coarse, salt and pepper hair bushed out from under the hat.

"Mind if I come aboard, chap?" the man said in a thick British accent.

"Actually, I do—the Red Plague and all," I responded.

"Whatever are you talking about man? We've been on the high seas for nearly three months now and haven't seen another living soul since my ship mate drove the remaining crew off in Kiribati, or what you might know as the Gilberts, over a month ago. We're in dreadful need of help—our engine is broken down. These blinkered military types won't even allow us ashore, much less help us. Thus, here we sit. Whatever illness you think we might have young man, you can rest assured that we have no such thing."

"You don't know?" I questioned, ignoring the fact that I knew Kiribati quite well and would not have referred to them as "The Gilberts."

"Know about what, young man?"

"So you haven't seen anyone in over a month?"

"Quite right."

"How many are there aboard your ship?" I asked.

"Just two of us. Yours truly, Alastair Campbell and my partner, Rowland Finlay the fourth. I would extend my hand like a gentleman, but alas I am here and you are there."

Ignoring his comment and motioning toward the yacht that dwarfed our own, I asked: "You are sailing *that* boat with just two of you?"

"Trying to, but I'm afraid not succeeding."

"You said you need help. What's the matter?"

"We're simply broken down. The engine won't run."

"Why don't you sail from here?"

"A full crew puts out a fair bit of effort to sail Horatio, and even though I earned my stripes in her Majesty's Royal Navy, I am but one man. And my ship mate is no help whatsoever."

He sat bobbing up and down, waiting for a response.

"I'll discuss it with my shipmates when they get up," I said.

"I can assure you that you will be well compensated if you're able to fix the old tub."

Of that, I had little doubt.

Our discussion must have roused Jeff and Sonny because they came topside just as Alastair arrived back at the Horatio. We decided that out of a sense of common decency, Jeff would at least take a look at their engine. We wouldn't waste any time, but perhaps it was something simple. We didn't need or want anything from them, but we could use the karma that helping someone out could conceivably bring.

It took Jeff about two hours to work the RY's rudder off the shaft, pound the shear pin back into form, and refit all the pieces. As Jeff worked, Sonny and I took turns watching the Horatio. Alastair and the man we presumed to be Rowland sat topside much of the time watching us as well. Rowland seemed to be drinking, but otherwise there was nothing out of the ordinary.

Jeff reinstalled the rudder and re-boarded. This prompted Alastair to return in his zodiac to repeat his plea for help. Rowland remained aboard the Horatio.

Jeff questioned Alastair about the symptoms of boat trouble and thought that it might be something he could fix. The three of us talked privately once more and decided they were probably safe, but as a precaution, I would accompany Jeff, we would go armed, and Sonny would stay aboard the RY.

Alastair pulled up alongside the RY. Jeff jumped aboard the zodiac with a small set of tools, and I followed.

Alastair motioned to Sonny and said: "Well, come along then."

"I'll stay," Sonny responded.

"Oh nonsense! We've got plenty of food and drink. It's the least we can do."

I sensed something odd about Alastair and began to reconsider agreeing to his request. But with this being our first encounter with strangers since the calamity began, my tendency to suppress the wisdom of the stream out of courtesy had yet to be beaten out of me by experience.

"We'll bring some back for him," I said.

"Very well then," Alastair said nervously as he gunned the engine and whipped us around toward the Horatio.

The sea had begun to roughen and salty mist sprayed over us during the short trip over.

"Where are you two headed?" Jeff yelled over the noise of the engine.

"The Philippines," Alastair replied. "Rowland and I retired last year and decided to sail around the world on Horatio. We got as far as Kiribati before the crew took their fill of Rowland's antics and abandoned ship. I attempted to sail on, but it took us over a month to get here and now we up the river without a paddle. We should have hired another bloody crew in Kiribati, but we thought we could make it that far."

The closer we got to the Horatio, the larger it seemed. It was obviously old but in fantastic repair and clearly well kept. As we pulled around the stern of the yacht, we saw the name Horatio stenciled on the stern with its homeport of Portsmouth, U.K. written underneath.

We boarded Horatio via the after-market dive platform and Alistair invited us inside with a simple hand gesture pointing the way and a robot-like bow from the waist. Clearly proud of the ship, Alastair insisted on taking us on a guided tour before Jeff began work. We begrudgingly agreed.

As Alastair strolled stiff legged through boat, heels clicking across the hardwood floors, he explained that the Horatio was twenty-six meters in length (or eight-six feet, making my original guess close enough to bolster my ego) and was a Stow and Sons Classic Yawl built in 1904. It had a wooden hull, slept eight with additional quarters for a crew of four, and sported a supplemental diesel engine. He further explained that a yawl was similar to a ketch in that it had two masts, but that on a yawl, the smaller mizzen mast was aft of the rudder. Whereas Jeff could apparently already differentiate between a yawl and a ketch, I found the information enlightening.

"Where did it get the name Horatio?" I asked. "I thought all boats were named after women."

"I thought you would never ask!" said Alastair. "She was originally purchased by Lord Victor Earl Wathen, whom you might know was a wealthy British writer and oilman. He was also very old at the time of the purchase and held to the convention of naming vessels after men, which was common in the 1800s, don't you know. Lord Wathen was an heir to the British war hero, Lord Nelson."

Jeff and I stared blankly at Alastair.

"Lord *Horatio* Nelson?" Alastair repeated, insulted that we didn't recognize the name.

Alastair recovered from the shock and then continued with an air of great pride: "Lord Nelson, despite being very slight in stature, won many battles against the Spanish, Danish, and those bloody French as an Admiral in the British navy. However, no victory was greater than the battle of Trafalgar where Admiral Nelson's fleet lost not a single ship while destroying twenty-two French and Spanish ships. It was Britain's finest moment at sea and cemented Lord Nelson as one of our greatest heroes."

"A number of wealthy but rather unknown chaps subsequently owned Horatio until my father purchased it in 1955. It came into my possession upon his death in 1983."

As we walked around the topside, I stopped to admire a large bank of solar panels and two medium sized wind turbines.

Alastair noticed my interest. "Keeps the lights on and the wine room cool but it is not much for propulsion."

We entered the galley, the final stop on our tour, and made the acquaintance of Alastair's shipmate as he sat at a table, sipping a tumbler of some sort of doubtlessly expensive liquor.

"May I present to you, Mister Rowland Finlay the third, Esquire?"

Jeff and I introduced ourselves, after which he nodded and replied: "Charmed, I'm sure." He conspicuously refrained from extending his hand for a shake, which was fine by us.

Rowland Finlay was a short, pudgy, balding man in his late fifties. He wore wire-rimmed glasses, which fit so tightly against his face that the skin around his ears closed up over them, nearly to the point of obscuration. He had a penetrating air of superiority about him.

"I suppose Alastair has told you quite a bit about me," said Rowland. "Did he say that I drink too much?"

"Rowland, bloody please!" shouted Alastair. "Are you already buggered up?"

"Such a foul mouth for a man with your breeding, Alastair."

Jeff and I stared cautiously at the two. They sounded like husband and wife.

"Rowland was my attorney and subsequently became my business partner. We splashed out in your American stock exchanges during the internet craze and let us just say that we overstayed our welcome. We exited too late and really fagged our investors. It was time to get out of town as neither of us was welcome there any longer. We decided to retire and sail the seven seas, and now you've found us here in sea number two."

"That's putting it mildly," Rowland deadpanned, as he hiccupped and chuckled to himself. He took another pull from his tumbler, hiccupped again, and then excused himself. "Dreadfully sorry," he said.

"Now that we've gotten the pleasantries behind us, what's all this talk of a virus?" Alastair asked.

We told them what we knew of world events. Alastair was shaken by the news, but Rowland seemed unfazed.

"Well, let's have a look at your engine," Jeff said, hurrying things along.

"I'll show you to the engine room," Alastair said.

"Actually, let's start at the bridge," Jeff said. "I'll need a quick look at the gauges first."

Alastair looked nervously at Rowland and then back to us.

"Very well then. This way."

He led us up to the main deck and then through a narrow doorway which lead to the main bridge. Jeff turned the key, and the engine rumbled as it turned over. I turned and watched as exhaust and bubbled sputter out the stern. After about a half dozen cranks, Jeff stopped. He tapped at a gauge.

Jeff turned to Alastair and began: "Have you...." then he trailed off.

Jeff looked at me, and I saw the fear in his eyes. He immediately spun, drew his gun and pointed it at Alastair. Alastair jumped.

"You're just out of fuel," Jeff said.

Just as I began to go for my own gun, I felt steel press against the base of my skull. Even in the tropical heat, it felt cool.

"Indeed we are," Rowland said from behind me, holding his gun to me. Jeff spun and pointed the gun at Rowland.

"Ah ah ah," said Rowland, clicking back the hammer.

Jeff spun back to Alastair. "I'll shoot him."

"I don't bloody care!" shouted Rowland. "But I'll bet you care if I shoot your friend."

"Rowland, please!" said Alastair. "I knew this was a terrible idea. Just let them go."

"Shut up!" replied Rowland. "All we want is your fuel."

"But the RY runs on gas. The Horatio is diesel," Jeff said.

"Excellent point!" said Rowland. He pressed the gun into far enough into my skull that it hurt. "We'll take your vessel then."

"Lower your gun or I'll shoot him," Rowland said through gritted teeth.

We were at a stalemate, but the house usually wins in the end. Jeff stared at me. I tried to signal him with my eyes. I wanted to drop to the deck and have him shoot Rowland. I didn't think Rowland could act fast enough, but I couldn't be sure Jeff understood. If he didn't, I could get myself or Jeff killed. I shook my head to indicate that I did not want him to lower his weapon.

I felt Rowland readjust his grip on me and then switch hands on the gun. It was now in his left hand. He used his right hand to frisk my right side. I suddenly realized that he was right handed and acknowledged the moment with the gun in his weak hand as my chance—perhaps my last chance. I thought about my family and the jeopardy Rowland was putting them in. I instantly hated him more than I imagined possible. Realization, terror, and resolve swept through my mind in a split second. Time slowed, and I saw everything with great clarity. Colors brightened and sounds separated into their component frequencies, as if to allow me to process each individually. The stream opened to me, and I acted.

I lowered my head slightly away from the gun and grabbed his right hand with my left. With my strong arm free and his strong arm subdued, I wheeled around, swinging my elbow with every ounce of energy I had.

The gun went off. I felt a blast of heat on the back of my head, but knew immediately that it had missed. My elbow landing squarely in the middle of Rowland's mushy face. I focused on the sensation as his cartilage ground and popped under the force of my elbow. His glasses shattered on his face and splintered into his eyes. Rowland tumbled back against the bulkhead. I grabbed his gun hand with my right hand and directed it away from me. It went off again, harmlessly over our heads and through the roof of the Horatio.

I marveled at how much time had slowed. I turned square to Rowland as blood began to spurt from his mangled nose. I pounded Rowland's face with my left fist, and blood spurted and splashed across the controls of the bridge. I heard the crack of his cheek bone. I hammered away on him until he slumped to the floor in a bloody pile of fat and silk. He lay motionless.

Time sped back up; sound recombined; the present returned to normal. I turned, ready to repeat the feat on Alastair, if required.

Alastair stood shocked, Jeff's gun still trained on him.

"Jesus!" Jeff said.

I took Rowland's gun out of his limp hand and stuck it in my waistband.

Sonny ran in, gun drawn and soaking wet. "I heard shots!" he yelled. He looked at the pile of flesh known as Rowland lying on the floor. "Christ! What is going on?"

"Back out," Jeff said calmly to Sonny.

"Please, I beg of you," said Alastair. "Take me with you."

"We came over here to help you, and this is what we get?" said Jeff. "I should shoot you dead. But then I'd be no better than you. We'll just leave you here to suffer alone."

I went over and checked Alastair for weapons. He flinched in fear as I began to frisk him. He had a gun in his jacket pocket. I took it.

Sonny backed out, followed by me and then Jeff.

Alastair tried to follow us out, begging for help. Jeff shoved him back down the stairs.

We rode their zodiac back the RY. Alastair slumped into a chair on the deck.

Once aboard the RY, Jeff shot through the rubber of the zodiac and set it adrift, as air squealed out. Sonny and I watched the Horatio as Jeff pulled us away from Wake Island. Alastair never moved from the deck, but sat with his head bowed.

My left hand began to hurt, and I held it up. Blood ran from my knuckles onto my forearm. I picked a shard of glass from one knuckle and threw it over the side.

"When did you start taking martial arts training?" Jeff asked me.

"I don't know where that came from," I replied. Actually, I did, but no one would believe it.

10

DAY 7 AT SEA, 183 MILES NE OF WAKE ATOLL (GPS POSITION: 21.0°N, 168.7°E)

Being on the ocean during the doldrums is a very strange sensation. The sea is like glass. If left to its own devices, the boat barely moves, which is great for sleeping, but terrible for making headway. Large cumulonimbus clouds grow in all directions, their mirror images reflecting in the still water. The clouds spew drenching downpours and occasional lightning whilst they live and die in virtually the same spot, no prevailing wind to drive them elsewhere. As each storm collapses, it sends out a brief gust of wind in all directions, a faint ghost representing the energy it once contained. Where the gusts from storms collide—an outflow boundary intersection it is called—new storms form. And so goes the cycle of convection in the doldrums. Many survivors adrift at sea have told stories of rain showers taunting them as they drop their life-giving, fresh water within sight but usually just out of reach of the withered, dying spectators.

We must have been in an unfavorable current because in the two days after we left Wake Island, we averaged just over three knots. We should have been able to motor at nearly twice that. At that agonizing pace, it would have taken another two months to reach the Pacific Northwest.

Our inability to contact our families was tantamount to psychological torture. Under such duress, the mind can conjure up all kinds of horrible thoughts. As I observed my mind in action, I wondered if I should be concerned at how easily I could imagine the abduction of my children, the rape of my wife, and murdering the people that did those things. I had had fleeting thoughts in the past which I found offensive, but they were becoming more frequent. I wondered where such thoughts came from and whether they should worry me.

I sat on the bow of the RY, my legs dangling but too short to touch the water, and I watched the reflections of the various cloud formations in the placid water. There were no winds to roughen the surface of the ocean, but the bow of the boat bobbed rhythmically as it cut through the gentle swells from distant storms. My eyes observed the scene, and some part of my brain appreciated the beauty, but the majority of my consciousness worked on other problems.

An ominous storm bubbled dead ahead. Small ripples in the water occasionally distracted me, but the convection was so intense that even through the reflection, I could sense the upward motion. Certain things will draw a person out of a thoughtful trance. Lightning is one for a meteorologist—for most people, maybe. This time it was a rainbow that made me look up, its reflection almost certainly not as good as the real thing. It was a big, beautiful double-rainbow, and while not far ahead, I knew that due to the physics, or rather optics of it, we would never reach it. Sometimes science just takes the fun out of things.

I thought about my grandfather. He grew up during world war one and endured the great depression and he knew hard times. He was a slender but strong man with poor Scandinavian Farmer arms that looked like long levers operated by thin elastic bands under the skin. The skin on his leathery, gaunt face hung and waddled in places but otherwise concealed no fat underneath. He ate well and despite his tireless labor—or perhaps because of it—he was still fully capable of working his farm even in his late 80s when he died.

He was smart but entirely uneducated in an ivory tower sense. A whiz with all things mechanical—out of necessity most likely—he could take apart a motor and put it back together in a few hours. I had helped him do such things many times. "There ain't nothin' what can't be solved with a little good old American engine-uity," he frequently told me.

Despite his deep religious devotion, I credited him with sparking my interest in science. I found it fascinating how a man with such little education could know so much about the world. He inspired in me an obsession with understanding things, especially the world around me.

While he was proud of my interest and ability in science, he worried about the negative effect it was having on my "spiritual learnin'." Of course, as a good Christian he felt obliged to impart his divinely inspired wisdom on me whenever he got the chance.

"I know from readin' the old testament that God sounds like a mean sum bitch!" he'd say. "I just wants ya to keep looking for him is all, boy. Even when he don't seem to be around nowheres, keep looking. Cause I spoze that a man can stand before God and at least say he looked best he could and still come up with nothing. That's got to be better'n not having looked a'tall. A man's just gotta do his best. If he done his best, what else could he a done?"

Truth be told: I never stopped looking for God because of science, but it forced me to look in different places. I resisted my Grandfather's religion, preferring instead the methods I learned in science courses. Grandpa knew all about that too. "Them scientists cain't splain how your dad knowed you was lying in the ditch stung by bees just in time to get ya to old Doc Taylor when you was four, or how I know the rain is coming without any a them fancy computers, or how sometimes I'm thinking of an old friend I ain't seen in twenty years, and then he all of a sudden shows up at my door. Now can they?"

A bolt of lightning brought me back to the present again. I automatically began counting: one-one-thousand, two-one-thousand, three-one-thousand, four-one-thousand—boom! Four-fifths of one mile. The flash reaches us instantaneously, but the thunder takes five seconds for every mile. Once again, we were the tallest thing on the open ocean during a thunderstorm. Just then, the bow swung to starboard as Jeff turned to avoid the storm.

"No thanks! Not again!" Jeff yelled to me.

"Agreed," I said.

Observing that the storm was several miles wide and that we would likely be unable to avoid it unless we turned completely around, I continued: "We're still too close. It's less than a mile."

I started to move back toward the helm when I felt my skin tingle and the hair on my neck stand up—both signs that I was near one of the storm's leaders. A leader is one of the many channels a thunderstorm opens between the cloud and ground over which current can travel. The lightning that we see is just current traveling over whichever of those leaders is the path of least resistance.

"Did you see that?" Jeff yelled.

"No, but it was close."

"Close? No, not that. The main bolt was to port, but a spark went up from the mast about a thousand feet into the air."

"St. Elmo's Fire!" I yelled back.

"What is?" Jeff asked, looking around frantically.

"A coronal discharge created by the electric field," I replied.

"Oh, St. Elmo's Fire. Yeah, I know."

"What did you think I said?"

"Something's on fire."

We continued to try to motor around the storm, but it was no use as the rain closed in around us. We set up the tarps designed to catch fresh water and divert it to the storage tanks. We had to bring them out each time it rained rather than leave them out, because we didn't want salt building up and tainting the catch.

There were several more strikes nearby, but the lightning abated as the storm started to rain itself out. In the world of meteorological observing, a thunderstorm technically ends fifteen minutes after thunder was last heard. To real people in the real world, a thunderstorm is over when it, or the cell that produced it, gets the hell away from you.

Twenty minutes had passed and our fresh water tanks were overflowing, so I started to fold up the tarps. That was when the storm delivered its parting shot, directly to our mast. The flash blinded me for an instant, and while I did not see the actual strike, I did see tendrils of current crawl along the deck radially away from the center of the boat. I jumped to avoid the current, which was ridiculous in hindsight, since I could have never reacted fast enough to make any difference.

It took about ten seconds for my eyesight to return and my brain to begin processing external stimuli again. Curiously, I do not remember hearing any thunder from the direct hit, but I do remember wafts of hot air—like when you open an oven door—as well as the smell of fresh photocopies—the ozone created by the strike. The air was completely silent except for the falling rain. I realized that the engine had stopped running. Then I smelled smoke followed by the sound of a discharging fire extinguisher. When the smoke cleared and all of my senses returned, I saw Jeff standing dazed over the engine compartment holding a spent extinguisher. Sonny who had been sleeping below, was at his side, equally stunned.

I had never been struck by lightning before, but I assumed it would entail a great deal of pain. I took inventory of my body and noted nothing of concern. Jeff had already emerged from his daze and was trying to restart the motor. I asked Sonny if he was all right, and he indicated in the affirmative.

"Most of the electronics are fried," Jeff said. "In fact, so far, *all* the electronics are fried. I can't get any response from the motor."

"Oh shit!" Jeff exclaimed, suddenly remembering something. He hastily descended the stairs into the cabin.

Sonny went in right behind Jeff, and I followed.

Once below, we saw what worried Jeff—water entering the boat from somewhere in the galley—probably under the sink—and from the head.

Jeff ripped past us and grabbed his swim goggles from the counter. He entered the storage area in the bow and proceeded to rifle through a metal box. He pulled out a couple of what looked like small fittings and a hammer and went topside. Before Sonny or I could determine what went wrong, or even ask, we heard the splash as Jeff entered the water.

We heard some muffled tapping on the port underside of the boat and after about thirty seconds, Jeff surfaced, swam around the stern to the starboard side, gulped some air and plunged under again. More muffled tapping and then Jeff surfaced and started treading water, gasping for air.

Through the driving rain, Jeff yelled: "I think I got them all. Go below and see if you can see or hear any water running—any leaks."

Sonny and I both went below. Having realized that the lightning either blew out or melted some or all of the plastic drain cocks, we quickly checked all the places where they might be found.

After we told Jeff that the boat was no longer technically sinking, he tried to climb back aboard, but he was exhausted. Sonny and I pulled him over the gunwale, and he slumped to the deck. After a few seconds of panting, he sat up and threw the hammer, and it skittered across the deck. He cursed.

Sonny moved to the helm and tried to start the engine. It didn't even make a sound. He picked up the radio mic and held down the button. Nothing happened. He flipped the switch to the flood light. Darkness.

"Don't bother. We're fucked," Jeff said, with the calm voice of a madman.

"It's just a short," Sonny said. "We'll figure it out."

"Yep. We only have to go through a thousand components and about five miles of wire," Jeff replied.

I sure as hell didn't know what to do. I felt like crying. Sonny leaned back against the bulkhead and stared out over the ocean.

Jeff looked at me, then Sonny, then back at me. His face changed from anger and fear to worry. Then his face changed back to normal. He stood up and proclaimed: "Well, the compass will still work—it's not electronic. Anybody know which way North America is? If we can get some damned wind, everything will be fine."

I was glad to see our captain return, but we were in the doldrums and I knew it could be weeks before the wind came up again.

Jeff moved to the helm and began fiddling with wires.

I went below to lie down on my bunk. I felt defeated. After a few seconds, the fly landed lazily on my belly. I raised my hand, sure that I finally had him, and began to swing, but then I stopped. He just sat there, facing me, hundreds of little eyes locked onto mine. He looked like a little violinist as he rubbed his front legs together. I wondered if that made a sound that only he could hear. Maybe he's playing Beethoven, but only he can hear it. I wished I could hear it.

"You know, you don't have much longer to live either way," I said to the fly, wondering if I had already gone crazy. "I know that you only live about a month."

I raised my hand again and stopped again.

"All right fine!" I said aloud as I shooed him away gently. "Just stay off my face and my food," he lumbered slowly into the air, barely avoiding my hand. I could have killed him easily.

My grandfather popped back into my head. For some strange reason, a particular conversation with him pressed forward in my mind—a tirade against technology. He was incensed when the bank teller told him that he didn't need his bankbooks anymore because everything was electronic. He wondered out loud: "what if the 'lectricity goes out? How the hell is they spozed to know how much money I had in 'ere if'n it weren't written in my bankbook and stamped by the teller? Why, they might tell me I had none and whose ta say differnt?" Then he went on to rail against that "crooked sumbitch Wilson" and how it used to be that our money was backed by gold and "a fell coulda gone down to Fort Knox and turn in that paper for real gold." "Nowadays," he lamented, "when you got a dollar alls you got is a promise from the government and, why, if you put a cracker (his word for a cow pile) in one hand and a dollar in the other, I'd take the cracker, cause at least it'll fertilize the garden!"

But why was I thinking of that now? Then I suddenly remembered what he was doing when he told me that story. He was working on a tractor engine, and I could suddenly recall every detail of how he got that motor started—the meticulous way he tested the electronic components, isolated the problem, and then fixed it. "Engines seem like something, but they's really simple once you boil 'em down," he told me. "Everything's cause and effect. When somepin don't work, there's a good reason. All's you got to do is narrow it down. Everything can be fixed somehow."

I jumped to my feet, grabbed the toolbox, and headed for the door. I stopped half-way and opened the refrigerator. I found a sour, old grape in the produce drawer, smashed it and left it on the counter. Then I started up the stairs.

"What are you doing?" Jeff asked as I bolted up the stairs and toward the engine compartment.

"I'm going to get that motor started."

"Good luck," he said.

"By the way, his name is Shithead," I said.

"Who's name?"

"The fly."

"What? It's still onboard?"

"Yep. And I've decided to let him live. He's my pet now."

"I think you're losing it."

"Probably," I said.

I opened the engine compartment and stared at the small Volvo engine. It was covered in a gray film, which was a combination of soot, smoke, and fire extinguisher fluid. I inspected the various lines and hoses for fire damage, and there was none that I could see. It looked as if the fire had originated at the point where the fuel line entered the fuel filter. Perhaps it had a small leak which was ignited by the current. The fuel filter casing was warped from the heat but still intact, and the line leading into it had melted away, revealing its inside. I did not see any fuel in the line, and when I turned it over, none came out. Using wire clippers, I removed the melted end of the fuel line and slid it back onto the filter casing.

I needed a way to turn the engine over, which is another way of saying that I needed to rotate the crankshaft to operate the pistons. I grabbed the belt attached to the center-most wheel, the one most likely attached directly to the crankshaft, and pulled. It strongly resisted at first, but then gave way and moved easily through a small motion. It grabbed again, coming to a firm stop after about one-quarter turn and then oscillated back and forth a few times like a car lurching to a stop between successive speed bumps. I wondered if that should have created a spark in all the cylinders, just one, or maybe none.

I reasoned that since the engine had four cylinders and that a one-quarter turn seemed to have completed some sort of cycle in the engine, that a full turn should operate all the pistons and therefore, all of the spark plugs. I removed a spark plug at random, and like I had seen my Grandfather do, placed it against the engine block. I pulled the belt again and on the third quarter turn, I saw a tiny spark at the base of the plug. I performed the same test on all the spark plugs and each one eventually sparked. I found that it took only one complete turn to make each plug fire at least once. The results made me think that the main electrical components of the engine were fine and that perhaps the problem was just in the ignition, starter, or battery.

Theoretically, the engine would run if we could start it. Of course, we could not simply roll it down a hill to compression start it like I had seen my Grandfather do many times with his old '45 Willy's.

Jeff sat down next to me.

"The radio is screwed. How's the engine looking?" he asked.

"I think the engine is fine. I can get a spark manually in all the plugs so I guess that means the wiring and distributor and so forth are ok."

"Really?" said Jeff, surprised and suddenly more upbeat.

"But I don't know how we are going to start it without the ignition system."

"Easy," Jeff said. "We'll hot wire it."

He grabbed a wrench and slid around toward the controls at the helm. He opened the cabinet revealing the ignition switch and wiring. He removed some wires, stripped them, and then asked me if I was ready.

"I hope the battery is ok," he said. "If not, we're really screwed."

He touched the wires together, and the engine turned over several times.

"Yes!" we both exclaimed in unison.

The flood light flickered to life. Jeff reached over and flipped its switch to off.

"Fuel?" Jeff asked.

"Hold on," I said. I pulled the tubing off the fuel filter and began sucking at it. Eventually some gas spilled into my mouth, which I held there as I placed my thumb over the end of the tube. I held the tube upside down as low as I could while I attached it to the filter again. A little fuel spilled into the filter. I spit over the side, swished with a little salt water and said: "Go ahead."

The wires sparked as Jeff touched them together and the engine turned over. I watched as fuel surged into the filter in spurts much like blood pulses through the needle and into the tube when drawn by a nurse. After about ten seconds, the filter was full, and after another five seconds, the engine sputtered to life. Black smoke belched from the stern, and the smell of half-spent fuel filled the air, but then the exhaust cleared as the engine regulated itself.

Jeff twisted the two wires together and we shook each other's hand. We resumed our journey through the doldrums, blind and deaf, but not dead in the water.

I went below to find Sonny, and as I passed the counter, I saw Shithead sitting on the grape, playing the violin. I didn't have the time or the heart to tell him that I thought he should gotten off at Wake where the wind was calm and the decaying matter plentiful. Maybe he wasn't strong enough even to get to shore. I should have given him the grape earlier.

I found Sonny in one of the bunks.

"Are you all right?" I asked.

He did not move. I turned him over, and he edged up out of sleep.

"What's the matter with you?"

"I don't feel so well," he said, dazed. "My ear hurts," he said as he held his hand up to the ear opposite of my position. When he drew back his left hand, there was blood on it.

"Hey, your ear is bleeding. Let me see that."

I rolled him over and found out what I already knew: that blood was seeping out of his ear. There was a small red spot on his pillow.

I had heard of lightning striking people and blowing their eardrums before. It also could have been the concussion from the thunder, but again, I did not hear any thunder.

"Did the lightning strike you?" I asked.

"I don't think so," he replied. "I didn't feel anything."

"Did you fall and hit your head?"

He didn't respond, but just laid there.

I checked him over and found small burn marks on his left foot and elbow. I felt his pulse, and it seemed ok. I put my ear to his chest and listened to his breathing, which also sounded normal to me. I looked in his eyes, nose and mouth and did not see any blood or other abnormalities. I rubbed his fingers and toes and he indicated that he felt it. He was able to move all his limbs with no weakness. He could follow my finger with his eyes and touch his nose with any of his fingers. I shined a light in his eyes and his pupils dilated. That was the extent of my medical diagnostic abilities.

"I'll get you some water. I think you should stay in bed for a while," I said.

After finishing the exam and administering a treatment consisting of a drink of water, I went topside and informed Jeff of my diagnosis.

"What are we supposed to do about his ear?" Jeff asked.

"I had a ruptured eardrum from an ear infection as a kid," I replied. "They didn't do anything for it. He also may be delirious. He was saying something about lesbian vampire hooker pirates when he went out again."

"I don't think that means anything," Jeff said. "I bunk next to him and he's always talking about lesbian vampire hooker pirates in his dreams."

"In that case, I think he'll be ok. It was probably just an indirect strike."

"Indirect? Well, that makes me feel a whole lot better," replied Jeff.

11

DAY 12 AT SEA (DEAD RECKONED POSITION: 25.2°N, 180°E)

"I am become death. Destroyer of worlds." – J. Robert Oppenheimer, Director of the Manhattan Project, which developed the world's first nuclear weapons.

We crossed the Tropic Of Cancer several days ago and then the wind picked up, curiously from the south. That was all right because it gave us a nice tailwind by which to sail and kept us sailing before the seas, which is much more comfortable. We could have gone more directly toward Seattle by sailing more easterly, but there was usually an upper level trough northwest of Hawaii, called the Kona Low, that we could catch and ride to North America. The wind was heading that way anyway, so we didn't fight it.

We sailed at a heading of seventy degrees (or east-northeast), and the wind was at a perfect two-hundred degrees (or south-southwest) between ten and twelve knots. The physics of sailing is such that a tailwind is, counter intuitively, not optimal—at least if speed is your goal. Sailboats attain their maximum hull speed when the sails are correctly trimmed and the wind blows approximately perpendicular to the keel. In that condition, the air attains its greatest acceleration as it passes the sail, and as any first-year physics student will tell you, force equals mass times acceleration. The more that mass of air is accelerated, the more the force on the sails. If the wind is right and the sailor knows what he is doing, the majority of that force can be transferred from the wind to the sails and then into forward motion of the sailboat.

DEAD RECKONING

We had made approximately 770 miles from our previously known position in five days. Our average speed over the last five days had been almost 6 knots which was a marked improvement over the beginning of the trip. We had picked up speed in the last 24 hours or so, and we were finally pushing close to the maximum hull speed of 8 knots. If we had been able to maintain that speed on the great circle path, we would have needed just over two weeks to reach the North American coast.

Truth be told: since our GPS was fried, we were not *exactly* sure where we were. But a sailor always has another trick up his sleeve. Since land is sharp to the hull of a boat, knowing where you are is of paramount importance, and so sailors have more than one way to get a fix on their position. If we had just been on a simple day sail around our favorite body of water, we would have made a few measurements to known points of land, done some high school trigonometry, and had our position in no time. With last land 770 miles behind us, that option was out. We could have whipped out the sextant. Finding your position with a sextant is not much different than using points of land. You need star charts (which we had) and the calculations are a little more difficult—not to mention that it is not easy to hold yourself steady enough to take a measurement on a small point of light on a boat—but we were all college graduates. We just lacked the essential element: stars. Overcast skies will do that.

Since all else had failed, we fell back to the last resort: dead reckoning. I've often wondered if it is called dead reckoning because in the event you need it, it is reckoned that you are as good as dead. Nevertheless, we knew how fast we had been going, how long we had been traveling, and where we had been. Any algebra student could have taken it from there: distance equals speed times time. Plot that distance line on your heading from your last known position and you've got it, give or take the width of your pencil lead. And that's what we had done, every hour, for five days straight. The problem was that you are supposed to use dead reckoning from a known position and ours was 770 miles ago. Errors creep in and multiply every time you base your current position on your last position which was a dead reckoning position.

I reckoned in the logbook that we were at twenty-five-point-two degrees north and right at the international dateline. I arbitrarily picked a moment on my watch and stood up to pay tribute to our crossing the international dateline. It was now technically a day earlier, and I set my watch back. The bad news was that it was just imaginary, and it was still day 12 of our trip. I wished that instead of being just a made-up, arbitrary line that would not lessen the actual time it took to get to our families by a single second, the dateline was a portal that could take me back to before the crisis began. It made me feel better that we were at least in the right hemisphere now.

Darkness fell as I stood third shift at the wheel. The air cooled, but south winds continued to pump tropical moisture over us, making the nights sticky and uncomfortable. The wind was nature's air conditioning though. Temperatures could feel twenty degrees cooler by virtue of a strong breeze.

We had reached a point in the journey when there was nothing much left to do. We were as prepared as we could be for whatever lie ahead. We had already read every book we had aboard and retold all the stories from our history together in the islands. We told stories from our youthful conquests which, for men, regardless of the topic on which it started, always seemed to devolve to the lowest common denominator: sex. Stories of first lovers, strangest lovers, and numbers of lovers, and other things about lovers.

With nothing much left to talk about, we began to get on each other's nerves—especially Sonny and Jeff. I watched the animosity between them percolate like a distant storm. Each little argument developed, billowed for a while, and then died without producing any damage—some fireworks, a big gust of cool wind, and then that was it. The two main points of contention between them—sailing and ideology—were like differing air masses; each was capable of producing its own kind of storms. What worried me was what would happen if the two collided. As with nature, the worst weather of human emotion generally occurs along the boundary between two opposing currents—especially when things are already unstable.

There hadn't been any major arguments yet, but I felt something coming. Like when an old farmer says "Rain's a coming. I can feel it in my bones."

The argument started off innocent enough. Jeff didn't like the way Sonny tied off the mainsail and called him out on it. Jeff and Sonny were usually able to discuss their differences calmly and respectfully, but everybody has a point beyond which reason goes out the window. I didn't really care how the mainsail was tied off as long as it was safe, so I found it amusing at first. But it didn't take long for the argument to devolve into the usual liberal versus conservative talking points.

"What makes you think you can tell a woman what to do with her body?" Sonny asked snidely.

"Why do you think society shouldn't be able to tell her what to do with her body if they deem it to be in society's best interest?" Jeff asked.

"How can anything be in society's best interest when it only affects her life?"

"Because we are not talking about just her life. Most of us believe there is a life inside her that is every bit as valuable as hers."

"That is where we differ," Sonny said. "I don't think a clump of cells four or five or six weeks old is as valuable as her."

"When is it as valuable as her?" Jeff asked. "At birth? Two weeks before birth? Six weeks? When?"

"Well, I don't know, maybe..." Sonny started before Jeff cut him off.

"That's exactly the point. You don't know. Only the far left-wing, Ivy-league or Berkeley crackpots would argue that it isn't a person, worthy of protection *after* birth, and there is fundamentally no difference between a two-minute-old baby and one two minutes before birth, and by extension, ten minutes before birth, or one day, or two weeks. There is no way to know for sure at any time so, you must go back to the only point during the process at which you know there is not a human being there."

"And I suppose you know when that is?"

"Conception!" Jeff snapped.

They were starting to get mad, and I might have stepped in, but there was clearly more to the argument than abortion. Nobody really cared about abortion any more.

"I don't understand most of what you think," Jeff continued. "I mean look at the current situation. I can go through the list and show how it was really the liberal positions that got us here."

"Is that right?" Sonny asked angrily.

"Yes. Appeasement. Let's understand the terrorists rather than kill them. Brilliant."

"Constantly killing people in their own countries was what pissed them off so much." Sonny cut in. "How would you feel if some Middle Eastern country kept interfering in our business?"

"The 9/11 terrorists didn't come from our country, they came from theirs! If we were sending out terrorists to attack other countries, I'd expect that to come back to us."

"They think we are terrorists," Sonny returned.

"Ridiculous!" Jeff yelled.

"Are you seriously saying that if soldiers from some Middle Eastern country were patrolling our streets and killing our citizens, for whatever reason, you wouldn't fight back? Jeff, that's bullshit, and you know it!"

I always enjoy a good debate, but since this was counterproductive to our goals, I wasn't really enjoying this one. However, I thought Sonny had made an excellent point there—one I hadn't thought of before. He was right: there were no circumstances under which I would not want to fight back against some other country patrolling our soil. I waited anxiously for Jeff's reply.

But Jeff diverted: "That's just the tip of the iceberg of what I don't understand about you."

"Really?" Sonny said, chuckling.

"Well, let me just tick through the list. Number one…."

"Don't bother!" Sonny yelled.

"Number one…" Jeff continued unfazed. "Gun control. We wouldn't even be able to defend ourselves right now if you liberals had your way."

"Stop right there!" Sonny barked. "Maybe if we were able to control all these guns the world wouldn't be so damned dangerous right now!"

"Yeah right! All that would have happened is that law abiding citizens wouldn't have guns. Criminals don't obey laws, even gun laws. Remember?"

"Just stop," Sonny said.

"Number two: the environment!" Jeff persisted.

"I said stop," Sonny said in a quiet, angry, monotone.

"The environment is king! We might as well just kill ourselves, for the good of the earth!" Jeff was becoming angrily dismissive and starting to sound irrational. "Even if it meant limitations on where people could live, play, or even where we could get our energy from—which, by the way, is a big reason we got into all this shit in the first place."

Sonny stood up and confronted Jeff. "I said shut up."

Jeff yelled right in Sonny's face: "If we could have just used our own fucking energy, energy right under our own soil, instead of pissing away trillions of dollars in the turd world, we would have never had to set foot in that cesspool, they wouldn't have been so pissed off at us, they wouldn't have had the resources to terrorize us, and we'd probably be sitting fat, dumb, and happy right back on Kwaj right now—our families safe!"

There it was; the real reason for this argument. Sonny stopped and softened, realizing it too.

"Both of you stop," I said, stepping between them. "How do any of these old political arguments matter anymore? No woman is out looking for an abortion now. Only an idiot could argue for gun control now. These are the kinds of theoretical things people sit around and discuss when everything is fine. The rules have changed."

"The bottom line is that I just look at the world differently than liberals," Jeff said calmly. "Liberals think that people are basically ok, and that all we need is just a little bit more government oversight here and there to keep them in line, whereas I think that people are basically no damned good."

"Really?" Sonny asked. "People are no damned good? What makes you say such a thing?"

"Experience. Put twenty-five toddlers in a room and see if most of them are disposed to being good or being bad. That will show you the true nature of humankind, like Lord of the Flies. Look at what happened in New Orleans after Hurricane Katrina. That is what a good proportion of people are really like when all restraint is thrown off. Look around now!"

"And so you think that is an argument in favor of *less* government regulation of people?" Sonny said in a laughing tone. "It sounds to me like we need more government regulation!"

"Stop it!" I demanded. "We all have our opinions about these things, but what difference does it make now?" I had my opinions about these things, but, as a scientist, I based mine on evidence, reason, and intuition. I came in with no preconceived notions about how things were or how they should be. I tended to agree with Jeff on gun control and abortion and with Sonny on government regulation and terrorism, but it was irrelevant. I knew what the argument was really about and didn't want it to get out of control because of things that didn't matter.

"We're all scared," I said. "We all feel like crap. We have to work together, or we're screwed. Arguing about these abstract, irrelevant concepts doesn't help."

Jeff and Sonny continued to glare at each other.

"Seriously!" I yelled. "Does this shit matter?"

They didn't reply.

I turned to Jeff. "Do you really think there is any woman looking for an abortion right now? You can't honestly say you wouldn't fight back against an army occupying our country!"

Then I turned to Sonny. "You don't really believe in gun control now. We'd be slaves on the Horatio right now if we didn't have guns."

Jeff and Sonny went angrily but silently back to what they had been doing before the argument. Neither said another word for over an hour, probably replaying the argument over and over in their minds to see where they could have won.

• • •

I sat in silence for two more hours thinking about liberals and conservatives, my family, the world. I sat until long after Sonny and Jeff retired to their bunks.

Through the moonless, pitch-black sky, I heard a dull thud followed by another a few seconds later. The flying fish are back. I began to smell something strange, offensive, like rotten oranges, but I dismissed it as a random vapor in a sea teaming, inevitably, with dead stuff. Then I heard several thuds in a row—too loud to be flying fish, maybe sharks.

The sound stopped, and my thoughts returned. A few minutes later another dull thud, and another, and two more. Ok, fine. I will catch some of you guys for dinner then. I fished around in the cabinet under the wheel for the flashlight. Once in hand, I grabbed the net behind the seat. Flying fish were so mesmerized by the flashlight that all I needed to do was hold it over the net, and they would swim or jump right in. I had done it before, and they were easy pickings. We had grown tired of eating them, but it was better than eating our portable rations.

Even though it wasn't particularly rough, I put on my harness and clipped myself onto the safety line. We made this our rule when venturing away from the helm, especially when no one else was topside. Jeff and Sonny were both sleeping, and if I had gone over the side, they likely wouldn't have heard my screams and probably wouldn't even know I was gone for hours. I was also careful to walk on the high, upwind side, so that if I did slip, gravity would force me toward the boat and not toward the water.

I scanned the water with the flashlight as I walked along the rail. I saw no fish, but the water was strangely murky, and the smell choked me. It smelled like low tide but, of course, that made no sense out there in the middle of the ocean. Then I saw something round and dark, bobbing in the water a few yards away. I lowered the net, but the object swept around the stern and out of sight before I could get the net on it. Buoys adrift, I guessed. As the boat advanced, it came closer and I spotted another one, further away and lighter in color. I focused on the one that was in position to be netted, and I noticed a frothing of the water around it. "Fish, screwing with a buoy?" I wondered out loud.

One came close, and as I leaned over to net it, the flashlight slipped out of my hand and rolled around on the deck. I felt the net heave as the object entered and began to fight the force of the current. I lifted the net, and it was heavy. As I gained my balance, I retrieved the flashlight and trained it on the net to see what sort of thing I had snagged. I expected to see a buoy, and so my mind failed to register what I saw immediately. My emotion changed from curious to shocked to horrified as my brain processed the image. The mass rolled over, and the empty eye sockets, *human* eye sockets, stared back at me like a ghost, the rest of the skin on its face either missing or riddled with small, toothy pockmarks.

I jumped back, shocked and terrified. I stumbled and fell against the cabin window. My safety line tightened, and I dropped the net. I quickly flipped the net over and emptied the human remains back into the sea. I swished the net around to rinse off the residue, but another mound tried to wiggle in and soiled the net with more slime.

I gathered myself and began scanning more of the ocean. There were a lot of them. My mind scrambled to make sense of what I saw. I went back to the helm and hit the floodlight switch. It illuminated a scene of horror: hundreds of round, fleshy mounds, some attached to the remnants of bodies, some not. Some being fed on and others ignored. A few of them seemed to catch the gentle swells and ride them, like little ghastly surfers, roiling over in the whitewash of the breaking wave. The soup of humanity stretched off toward the east—toward Hawaii—or perhaps more aptly stated: *from* Hawaii. Dozens—maybe hundreds or thousands—of heads and bodies dumped in the ocean, corralled in a current, and driven here like so many willing cattle—little varmints of the sea nipping at them the whole way.

I leaned over the rail and vomited.

Unable to stand another second of the scene, I went below hoping for it to pass quickly. Thud, thud, thud they marched on. Things that go bump in the night, only real this time. With each bump a shock of adrenaline surged through me, and the hairs on the back of my neck stood erect. I sat trembling wishing for the sound to stop.

I did not wake the others, but the bumping did, eventually. I warned them not to go up to look, but they did anyway. They returned white as sheets.

An hour and thousands of bumps later, the horror stopped and the smell dissipated. No one had said a word during the carnage.

I broke the silence: "What do you think happened."

"I saw a life ring. Some cruise line," Sonny said.

"Sunk?" I wondered aloud.

"Or they were all murdered and thrown over," Jeff said, looking at Sonny. "Poor cruise passengers, all unarmed and defenseless. I wonder how it might have turned out if even one of them had been armed."

Sonny stormed up the stairs and retook the helm.

"Was that really necessary?" I asked Jeff.

"Maybe not, but it's true."

. . .

At some point during the night, I awakened to the sound of thunder and pelting rain on the deck. I noticed a drastic increase in the heave of the boat. I heard the mast come around and snap into position on the opposite side of the deck as Sonny tacked. I had noticed a falling pressure and an increase in the southeasterly winds on my previous shift and passed along my suspicion of an approaching cold front to Sonny. I rolled over, satisfied that my forecast had verified and that he had handled the change properly.

I had third shift at the helm again the following day. Third shift started in the late afternoon and continued until after midnight. I awakened in the early afternoon, grabbed some water and a couple of pieces of bread—I hadn't eaten, or been able to, since before the previous night's gruesome discovery—and headed topside. As I emerged, I noticed that the temperature and humidity were way down. It was not cold, but definitely cooler.

"Look at that," Jeff said, beckoning to the sky.

The sky was the strangest, most beautiful color of orange I had ever seen. Red skies at night, sailor's delight was my first thought, even though that adage failed in the tropics since, unlike the mid-latitudes, the weather moved from east to west. The orange sky was not a weather phenomenon because, save for the high overcast and a few fair-weather cumulus on the horizon, nothing was going on—certainly not an advancing or departing storm that would normally be associated with such a sunset. Whatever the cause, it bathed us in an eerie orange glow, as if we were looking at everything through that transparent orange film we played with as children.

"What is it?" I questioned.

"I don't know. I hoped you would," Jeff said.

"I think I do," Sonny said, walking back from the bow with one hand outstretched and the other cupped around it as if cradling something precious and fragile.

We looked into his hand and saw what looked like a tiny cast off from a cigarette. Jeff and I deliberated on the clue and its meaning. Sonny said nothing.

"Is that...ash?" I asked.

"Yes," Sonny said. He smudged the particle against his palm with his index finger, creating a small black streak that followed the lifeline in his palm.

Jeff and I sat back and looked up toward the sky. Jeff snapped upright, put his hand to his face and leaned over, attempting to clear something from his eye. A piece of ash landed on my leg. It was not hot. In fact, it felt like nothing. I flicked it off as tears welled up in my eyes.

. . .

Ash fell for two days and darkened the sky, air, and ocean. If not for the wind, it likely would have amounted to many inches on the deck. On the third day, the ash storm stopped. Visibility improved to the horizon, but the ocean was slate gray and choked with sludge. There were no low clouds, in fact, no discernible clouds at any level. Nevertheless, the sky was gray—the highest, most uniform gray overcast I had ever seen. The sun shone through as a mere silhouette. It was a bit colder, and I was terrified. We all were.

. . .

We stayed below decks just in case the ash was radioactive. Jeff passed out some potassium iodide (or KI) tablets he had. We didn't ask where he got them. They were supposed to keep radioactive crap from accumulating in our thyroid glands, as Jeff explained. We were too numb to care. We just hoped the ash wasn't radioactive since it was all around us, and while we had closed every hatch and vent on the boat, the hull provided no protection from the radiation itself.

"I can't believe this!" exclaimed Sonny, holding up a cell phone as he emerged from his berth.

"There was just a nuclear war, and you are worried about your cell phone coverage?" I asked sarcastically.

"Not the coverage, the battery."

"What about it?" Jeff asked.

"It's dead."

"So?" Jeff and I said in unison.

"So, it's brand new, and I just charged it before the lightning strike. I haven't turned it on since."

"Whatever," I said.

12

DAY 18 AT SEA, APPROXIMATELY 560 MILES NORTH-NORTHWEST OF HONOLULU, HAWAII (DEAD-RECKONED POSITION: 23.8°N, 166.2°W)

"The existence of the sea means the existence of pirates." –Mayan Proverb

We had taken more of an easterly course over the last several days to try to stay out of the ash. We made an educated guess as to the best course based on weather and, well, guessing. We knew this course would bring us closer to Hawaii than we liked, but when the ash became more intermittent and then stopped, we decided it had been worth it. We continued to pop KI tablets just in case.

The weather became jacket cool—an encouraging sign that we could be getting into the Kona Low. Unfortunately, there wasn't even a silhouette of the sun in the sky any longer. It was just gone—obscured behind a veil of debris from, we hoped, an isolated nuclear exchange, rather than an all-out nuclear war. Of course, we did not know. It could have been a volcano or other natural disaster blotting out the sun, but given the world situation last we heard, we feared the worst. I felt odd hoping that the Yellowstone Super Volcano had gone off, but it was better than the alternative. Whatever the cause, the day incorporated a lot more twilight than usual, and the nights were pitch-black.

I hadn't seen shithead in several days. I wondered if he got off and hitched a ride on one of the heads. That was certainly more his style than hanging out with us. Then I saw him, dried and still, next to the head. I picked him up and studied his eyes and wings and little violin bows.

"Seventeen days at sea," I said. "Pretty impressive."

I went topside and buried him at sea. I hoped he was not simply preceding us in a soon to be realized fate. Maybe he had been a she and had laid some eggs somewhere. The thought sparked a brief twinge of hope, until I realized that it was probably too cold for any flies to live.

. . .

I awoke from an evening nap to the sound of Sonny yelling topside. I rolled over to go back to sleep, but a pot clanking ever so quietly in the sink ended my chance for more sleep for the time being. Sonny's voice came down from above once more—something about a boat. I climbed up the stairs and out onto the deck. Sonny pointed to starboard and said: "Out there."

I could barely make out a boat on the horizon. The land immediately behind the boat surprised me more.

"There's land," I said.

Jeff emerged from the helm with a small sailing telescope. He extended the scope and peered through the eyepiece. "I think it's FFS."

I went to the helm and studied our nautical charts. French Frigate Shoals (FFS) was one of the tiny land masses of the Leeward Hawaiian Islands. Most people were aware of the main Hawaiian Islands between the Big Island and Kauai, but few knew that the Hawaiian archipelago extended northwestward for almost two thousand miles.

We were several miles away but decided to lower the sails to avoid being seen. Darkness would overtake us in the next hour, and we could put the sails back up. As we puttered along, we took turns watching the activity near the atoll. We were able to see the U.S. Fish and Wildlife station signs on the island, which confirmed that it was indeed FFS. While we wanted to avoid land and other people, we were glad to be able to get a firm fix on our position. We observed no activity on the island itself which wasn't really surprising—the federal workers had probably bugged out long ago.

There were two boats sheltered in the lee of the atoll, one motored yacht and another more dilapidated looking catamaran. There were at least a half dozen people moving back and forth between the vessels and taking turns at several bottles. I watched a large dark-skinned man emerge from below decks on the yacht. He grabbed a bottle from another smaller man and took a long pull. He held his arm up, and a small flame flickered in his hand. He blew out the contents of his mouth and it erupted into a giant fireball. The man laughed. It looked like a fun party. In any other situation, we might have gone over to join them. At the very least, it was a sign that not all was wrong in the world—some people were still having a good time.

It was sort of weird watching people go about their daily lives without any idea that they were being watched. But it had been ten days since we'd seen another person and I enjoyed the company. The yacht shifted in the current and showed us its stern. Its name was Hawaii 5 Oh!, home port: Honolulu, Hawaii.

I suddenly wished we didn't have to lower the sails since it was costing us time. I didn't need anything to remind me of Kate—hardly a minute passed without me thinking of her and the children—but watching those people having such a good time reminded me of how much she loved boating and parties. She would have loved to be there at that moment.

I took a turn at the helm, and Sonny took up the telescope.

"Oh, baby!" Sonny exclaimed. "There's a woman. She's topless. Looks hot."

"What? It's a little cold for that," I said, jumping up and grabbing for scope. "Give me that back."

After some begging, Sonny gave me a turn. It was hard to make out detail at that range, but as I watched the woman on the deck of the boat, it became apparent she was not just topless, but naked. The titillation was only fleeting as I got a strange feeling from the scene. I gave the scope back to Sonny. "Have at it," I said.

Sonny watched for a few minutes, and then his expression changed from one of lust to one of surprise. "What the hell are they doing?"

Sonny handed me the scope. The big, dark guy held the naked woman by the hair and appeared to be yelling at her. She slapped at him, but he dodged it. He threw her down to the deck, and she buried her face in her hands.

By this time, Sonny had emerged from below with binoculars and Jeff stared through the sextant. Two other men wrestled a fourth man onto the deck. The big man grabbed him by the back of the neck and forced him to watch as he fondled the woman's breast. The man struggled, and the woman lunged toward him. The big man kicked her in the chest, and she fell back.

Sonny was the only one who spoke. "Oh God, no," he said calmly.

Just then, the big man pulled a gun from his waistband. He held it to the woman's head. The other men dragged the fourth man to the edge of the deck and released him. He stood up. The big man pointed the gun at him and then back at the woman. The man jumped into the water. The big man walked over to the edge, pointed the gun toward the water, but did not fire. Suddenly the man disappeared under the surface. The big man leaned back, laughing and slapping his thighs. The woman scrambled to the rail and collapsed on it, her hands outstretched toward the water.

The two men grabbed the woman, dragged her to the bow of the boat and held her. The big man began to undo his pants.

We all lowered our instruments and stood silently. I looked at Jeff and then Sonny. Sonny looked at me and then back to Jeff. Our minds reeled. An anger rose in my stomach. I rubbed my forehead, a migraine suddenly brewing. The idiots on Wake were bad, but we made it; the heads were gruesome but abstract; the ash could have been anything; but a man being murdered and a woman being raped in our very presence was too real.

"We can't save the world," Jeff said, stoically.

"But we can save her!" Sonny snapped.

They both looked to me to break the tie.

My anger melted into fear and then guilt. I thought that if there were a God, it would be a great time for it to say something. I looked out over the bow at the magnificent nothing beyond and waited a second for something to happen. As usual, nothing did. I raised the telescope and peered through for a moment and then quickly lowered it in disgust. I sighed and looked at Jeff. "Would you want someone to ignore this on your account?"

Jeff lowered his head and answered immediately: "No."

"Neither would our wives or children."

. . .

Darkness settled in from the east over the next half hour. It would be pitch black at night, so we could probably get right up to them before they saw us. We knew for sure that there were three bad guys aboard and at least one gun. We knew of only one remaining victim, but we allowed for the possibility of more. We weren't master tacticians, so we planned to get close enough to take a full survey of the situation, but without putting ourselves in too much danger.

The RY engine was very quiet and when in idle emitted almost no sound. We motored to within about a hundred yards downwind of the boats. We occasionally heard laughter but hadn't seen any activity on deck since the rape. The light from within both boats illuminated a circle of at most twenty feet. Everything beyond was vague, so we quietly motored in to the edge of the light.

We heard the muffled scream from within the yacht which was followed by laughter. I felt a sudden burst of pride that we didn't sail on. At the same time, anger seethed inside me.

"Now what are we going to do?" I whispered.

Just then three of the men emerged from below—the two smaller men from earlier (we could now see that they were oriental) and a gangly black man that we hadn't seen before. Two of the men carried another man as he sang some terribly slurred song. He made the men stop and then threw up on the deck. They loaded the man onto the adjacent catamaran and took him below.

The big man stumbled out onto the deck and yelled: "Where the fuck did everyone go?" He slipped on the vomit and fell and then laughed at himself. He looked Hawaiian and had a goatee and Mohawk. He weighed at least three hundred pounds—mostly muscle. His tattooed arms bulged as he lifted himself up. I didn't like our odds if one—or even all three of us—had to fight him. He went back inside.

"He's drunk as a skunk. Maybe we can take him," Sonny said.

"At least one of the others is out of commission, maybe both," Jeff replied.

I motioned to the back of the yacht. "We could swim over and easily get up on the back there. Will the guns still work if they get wet?"

"I think so," said Jeff.

We decided that Jeff would stay on the RY since we might need to make a quick getaway, and he was the best at maneuvering it in tight spaces. Sonny and I would go. We couldn't be sure that there weren't others on board, but the element of surprise was on our side.

Sonny and I checked that our guns were loaded and the safeties off. We took one extra clip each and stuck it all in our pockets. We removed our shoes and slipped silently into the water. As we neared the yacht, I started shaking violently, but not from the cold. The water was still much warmer than the air. No, I was scared shitless. I swam around to the stern and lifted myself carefully onto the dive platform. Then I helped Sonny aboard.

Sonny pointed to his eyes and then made some hand motions. Apparently thinking that I knew what he meant, Sonny took off around one side of the boat. I went around the other.

I peered in the first window I came to. It was the galley, and it had been ransacked. I tiptoed further along and came to another window. My heart jumped as I saw the woman, still naked, tied to a table. She was much worse than I imagined. She had been beaten, cut up, tortured. She bled from the nose and mouth and had bruises all over. The ropes that bound her were tainted with the rusty color of dried blood where she had struggled against them. As she lay motionless, part of me hoped she was still alive, but another part of me knew that she was probably better off dead.

I shifted my angle and noticed the Hawaiian passed out on the couch next to the table.

I tiptoed around to the front of the boat and met Sonny there.

"What did you see?"

"The woman."

He paused for a moment and wiped his eyes. "I swear to God if I get the chance I'm going to gut that mother fucker."

I agreed.

"He's passed out," I said. "Do you think they'd hear it over there if we just went in a shot him?"

"Probably. I wish I had a big knife. We could easily sneak up and put it through his heart."

Just then, the black and the oriental came out of the catamaran and jumped over to the yacht. We ducked, but they had seen movement. The black man stood watching while the oriental yelled the name "Spike" and raced into the yacht. Within seconds, Spike popped out on the port side, and the oriental came out on starboard. They both walked forward guns drawn. We were trapped.

I already knew that we were no Navy Seals, but I expected us to do better than that. We were also not gunfighters. "Stick your gun back in your pants and get ready to jump," I whispered to Sonny. We concealed our guns.

Spike came around the corner and started laughing.

"Well, well. What do we have here? More fisheries people? I thought we got you all the first time."

We said nothing. Desperation rose within me. I smelled the vomit and heard the waves bouncing off the hull. My mind scrambled for an idea. Every thought that occurred to me was more dangerous and less likely to succeed than the previous. My original thought—which was to jump and swim for it—still seemed like the best idea.

"So, how do you like my new boat? Beautiful, eh?"

We just stared at him. I thought of Kate and the kids and knew that they were doomed. I screwed up.

"Would you like to meet my new wife?" Spike asked. "Her name is fuck you. At least that's what she says every time I ask her name." He laughed. "I found papers though. Her name is Jill."

"Of course, maybe you already know her. Maybe she is why you have come."

Spike waited for our response, and none came.

"Chang. Where is Sulu?" Spike asked, looking toward the other man.

"He fucked up. No good," Chang replied.

The black man walked up behind Chang. Spike motioned at him to come over to him.

"Sundance. What do you think we can do with these two, huh? Be a good boy and go check them for weapons."

Sundance hesitated, and Spike raised his hand to backhand him. Sundance cowered and then scrambled over to us to frisk us.

I turned to Sonny and said "Go."

We both sprinted for the rail. Spike fired in front of us, stopping us cold.

"Yes, by all means, do that," he said. "But first I would like to warn you: these waters are infested with sharks. We've been feeding them for days." Spike turned to Chang, and they both laughed. I shuddered at the thought of sharks circling below us as we swam to the yacht.

Sundance checked us over. He ran his hand over the gun in my pants, but he said nothing. His frightened eyes tried to tell me something, but I couldn't understand. He walked back and heeled at Spike's hip.

"How did you get here, anyway?" Spike asked, squinting out over the water through the ink-black night. "I'm surprised you made it all the way from the island. The sharks are usually very hungry."

I studied Spike's face for any hint of humanity. I found none. His right eye looked at me, and the other looked up and left. His taut, weathered face showed no hint of emotion except desire—a desire to watch me die. I imagined little difference between him and the sharks circling below. At that moment, I knew our only chance was to fight it out. I would have rather died with guns blazing than in whatever sadistic way Spike could dream up. It's better to die on your feet than to live on your knees, as they say. As I prepared to go for my gun, I hoped that Sonny saw the same thing I did.

I looked at Sundance. He stared oddly at me, as if he were trying to look through me. He shook his head as if to discourage me from what I was about to do. He shifted his eyes to the right and tilted his head, motioning. I casually glanced that way and saw a triangle emerging from the darkness and heard a puttering engine.

Spike turned to fire and got off one round before the bow of the RY crashed into the side of the yacht. The yacht lurched heavily to port. At that same moment, Sundance punched Chang and sent him tumbling. Spike stumbled and fired up into the black. I fumbled for my gun and drew it, but it slipped from my grasp and skittered away along the tilted deck. As Spike righted himself and took aim again at the RY, the football player inside me kicked in. I sprinted toward Spike and drove my shoulder into his mid-section with every bit of force I could muster. Spike was just as solid as I imagined, but he went down hard and in the process, hit his head on the railing.

As I got to my knees and knelt over Spike and prepared to finish the job with my fists, I heard two gunshots in rapid succession from the other side of the boat. I looked over just as Sonny fell backwards. My heart sank. I scrambled over to Sonny and began to pat at his torso. He stared at me, stunned but all right. I looked at the other two men. A dark pool formed between Chang and the rail. He was dead. Sundance stared straight ahead, clutching his chest.

Sonny leaned in toward Sundance and said: "Thank you." Then he moved toward Spike.

I grabbed him. "We don't have time for that, and we don't know who's on the other boat. Let's get the woman and get out of here."

Sonny and I retrieved our guns and then scrambled into the yacht. I untied the woman and told Sonny to check the rest of the cabin for other victims. I checked for a pulse and breathing and found both.

Sonny came back. "No one. How do we know they don't have hostages on the other boat?"

I slapped lightly at the woman's face. "Jill. Wake up. Are there other hostages?" She moaned. Her injuries were terrible. I repeated the question twice. She finally managed to say no.

"Let's get out of here before the other one wakes up," I said.

Sonny hoisted Jill onto his back and ran from the cabin. I followed, keeping my eye on the other boat and in the direction where we left Spike. I had seen enough movies to know that I should go back and kill him. But I had already done the fight part and was now focused solely on flight.

Jeff had already put the RY in position at the stern of the yacht. We carefully transferred Jill onto the RY and hopped aboard. Jeff gunned the engine, and we pulled away at a break-neck eight knots.

We took her below and laid her on one of the bunks. Sonny prepared an IV for her, and I began to clean and dress her wounds the best I could. I applied some alcohol to a small pad and dabbed it on one of her leg wounds. She winced and moaned in pain. It became obvious that she would not be able to tolerate the pain of our touching her.

"We will probably need to dope her up to get through this," I said to Sonny. "We've got to clean these. And she'll need stitches here and here." I pointed to a spot on her chest and another on her abdomen. "What do we have in there?"

Sonny fumbled through the various medications in our first aid kit and came up with a bottle of liquid morphine.

"Look at this," he said as he held up the bottle. The name of the drug was written across the bottle in big letters.

"Good!" I said. "Do we have any syringes?"

"Yes," said Sonny. "But we might as well put it right in the IV," he pointed to the little injection port on the IV tube that was used for administering additional medications.

"While you're at it, don't you think we should put some antibiotics in that IV?" I asked. "Some of these are starting to look infected."

"I don't see any liquid antibiotics in here. Just pills."

"How much of this do you think we should use?" asked Sonny, holding up the morphine.

"What does it say on the bottle?"

"Morphine. Single-use Vial. 10 milligrams per milliliter."

"Well, single use vial would mean just that, wouldn't it?"

"I don't know."

"Neither do I."

Jill drifted into consciousness and mumbled: "Three milligrams."

"How do you know that?" I asked. "Are you sure?"

But she was already out again.

"She sure sounded like she knew what she was talking about," said Sonny.

Jeff stuck his head in from above. "We've got company."

I rushed topside to see the yacht bearing down on us from behind, Spike at the helm. I drew my weapon and began to fire at him. Spike was a hundred yards and closing, but in rough seas, I was lucky to hit the boat, much less anything meaningful.

As the boat drew nearer, Spike began to fire at us, which sent me under cover. He was going to ram us, and at a top speed of eight knots, there was little we could do about it. That was when I noticed Sundance, still on deck and propped up against the rail in the position we'd left him. His face was calm and unflinching. Blood soaked his shirt. He had Chang's gun and fired rhythmically at something. He fired one round, then rested, took aim, and fired again. Sundance made a half dozen such attempts, and for attempt number seven, we hit a patch of smooth water. This steadied him just enough—he squeezed the trigger and the yacht erupted into a fireball. Even at some distance, the concussion from the explosion nearly knocked me over. An intense heat wafted over us and then subsided. Flaming debris rained down behind us.

Finally safe, Sonny and I went back to tending to Jill. We gave her the three milligrams of morphine as she suggested and then another dose as she began to arouse before we were finished. I stitched her larger wounds as best as I could from the memory of watching my own finger being stitched after losing a battle with a soup can. We cleaned and dressed her smaller abrasions. We checked her for broken bones. It looked to our untrained eyes as if most of the damage had been done on the outside; time would tell about the inside. We decided she would probably heal physically, but we had no idea how she would be mentally.

. . .

Two days later, she awoke screaming. Jeff and I raced below to see if she was all right. We had placed her in the forward berth, and by the time we entered, she had backed well up into the cubby hole of the bow. She looked like a frightened animal. She ripped the IV needle from her arm and pointed it at us. "What do you want?" she asked frantically. "Who are you? Where am I?"

"Jill, it's ok," I said. "You're aboard the RY, and you've been here for two days. We rescued you from your yacht, the Hawaii 5 oh."

Her eyes flitted back and forth between Jeff and me.

"It's ok. We are not going to hurt you. We know what you've been through."

"Just let me out of here," she said.

Jeff and I backed up. "Ok, you can get out, but we're in the middle of the Pacific," Jeff told her. "There is nowhere to go."

She began to shake and cry. "Where is my boat? Where is my..." She lowered her head and sobbed in her hands. The memories were starting to come back. I felt terrible for her.

We weren't sure what to do for her, so we told her we'd be topside if she needed anything and left her alone.

It was at least an hour before she came up. She emerged tentatively at first. Her head poked through the deck and she looked around. She reminded me of a wary cat on the first day in its new home. She didn't say anything and we went about our tasks without speaking.

After a few minutes she came all the way up and stood on the deck. She began to cry and said: "Can somebody please tell me what's going on?"

She sobbed through my entire explanation. Without saying a word, she went below again.

Several hours later, she came topside again. She sat next to me as I wound some rope. The cool breeze flowed through her hair.

"Thank you for all that you did," she said.

I nodded.

She looked at Jeff and Sonny and said: "Thank you all."

She ran her fingers through her hair, looked at her hands, and then felt her hair again. She shook her head back and forth allowing her hair to whip around as she might have after releasing it from a pony tail.

"Who washed my hair?" she asked.

"I did," I said.

"Thank you so much. You don't know how much that means to me."

"Yes I do," I said. "That's why I did it."

She looked at me, puzzled.

"Fifteen years of marriage," I said smiling. "I've learned that women only really want three things in this world: someone to talk to, massages, and clean hair."

"I don't know if that's all, but those are high on the list," she said.

"Where are we going?" she asked.

"Seattle," I said. "If it's still there, that is. Is that ok?"

"Good as any other place, I guess," she said, staring straight ahead.

She pulled down on the sweatshirt we had put her in and looked at the stitches on her chest.

"Who did these stitches?" she asked.

I looked away embarrassed. "It's a disaster, isn't it?"

"Technically speaking, yes. But the wound is closed and not infected which is what really matters," Jill replied.

She put her hand on my arm. "I really appreciate that you tried. Some time I'll show you how to do it properly."

I looked at her questioningly.

"I am a doctor," she said.

13

DAY 31 AT SEA, APPROXIMATELY 500 MILES SOUTH-SOUTHEAST OF KODIAK ISLAND, ALASKA (DEAD RECKONED POSITION: 49.9°N, 150.9°W)

"Die religion ist das opium des volkes." - Karl Marx

It took us two weeks to make the next nineteen-hundred miles. We finally picked up the Kona Low, but, despite favorable wind direction nearly the entire time, we averaged less than six knots, barely seventy-five percent of the maximum hull speed. We were slowed down considerably by rough seas and having to deploy the sea anchor a half-dozen times in severe storms. A sea anchor is a big parachute that goes into the water to which the bow of the boat is tethered. It keeps the boat headed into the wind and seas, limits backward drift, and allows the sailor to take down the sails. Throw out the sea anchor, put up your feet, and ride out the storm. You do not gain ground, but neither do you lose much ground, and, most importantly, you don't find yourself on the rocks, or upside down, or upside down on the rocks. It felt like we spent more time with the sea anchor out than sailing.

Really, by any honest measure, we were making great time though. Jeff told us about a guy who sailed from the Marshalls to California, and it took him sixty days. Here we were, only thirty-one days in, and we were already within striking range of North America.

Now a part of the crew of the RY for two weeks, Jill began to help out more and more. But we could tell she was just going through the motions.

She remained distant and cried a lot. Of course we understood, but we worried about her.

After a while she told us about herself and what happened on French Frigate Shoals. She had been a doctor at a family practice in Honolulu. When things began to go downhill in Honolulu, she and her husband Mark had set sail on their yacht to escape the danger. Along with their son Zach, they cruised to FFS to weather the storm there. Mark was friends with one of the biologists at the fish and wildlife station on FFS, and it seemed like as safe a place as any. All went well until Spike and his men showed up. They killed the three biologists at the station and took Jill and her family hostage. Zach had been killed by sharks while trying to escape the day before we arrived. What we had witnessed was Mark being fed to the sharks by Spike.

As we compared stories, it turned out that Sundance had been on our side all along. Jill told us how Sundance was also a hostage of Spike and the gang. Sundance had worked as a deckhand on a much bigger yacht owned by some Hollywood big shot. When Spike and his men overwhelmed that boat, Sundance was the only one that made it out alive. Jill credited Sundance with her still being alive when we got there. He brought her food and water in between the drunken escapades of the captors. He tended to her when he could—all at the risk of his own life. It saddened us that we didn't know that ahead of time—we might have been able to save him too. Of course, in hindsight we all owed our lives to him.

We were now in the southern Gulf of Alaska, and the weather was frightful for summer. You can never count on nice weather in the Gulf, or anywhere in the Pacific for that matter, but we did not expect such bitterly cold weather. Temperatures dropped steadily as we moved north, which was normal in the northern hemisphere, but with water temperatures in the fifties and air temperatures closer to forty, something was wrong—very wrong. The constant battering by storms began to take a toll on us, one right after the other, which was more reminiscent of late fall or winter than summer.

Clearly, the climate was changing, and we were quite certain it was because the worst had happened.

I pulled the hood over my head in defense against the advancing rain and the bite of the southwest wind. I looked at the barometer, and it had not changed since I reset it an hour earlier. Just to be sure, I tapped the glass and the needle freed itself and lurched down a couple of millibars. Another storm. And with that kind of pressure fall, it was likely to be a big one.

As we drew nearer to the coast, I worried more about what I would find. A sense of foreboding gnawed at me, much like a death row inmate must feel as the clock nears twelve.

"God! What have they been doing all this time?" I wondered out loud. Were they even still alive? Did they stay put, or panic and leave? For where?

Kate's dad, Frank, had been in the military. Even in his sixties he still sported the high and tight haircut and spoke phonetically as a matter of habit. He never said no, always negative; never yes, always affirmative; never dinner at six o'clock, always chow at "eighteen hunnerd."

He was a non-commissioned officer in the U.S. Army's third infantry division, stationed at Fort Stewart, Georgia. He frequently recited his favorite part of his division's fighting song: "I'm just a dog-faced soldier with a rifle on my shoulder," he received SERE training (Survival, Evasion, Resistance, and Escape) at level C (then the highest level available) due to his rank and, apparently, because he was frequently in harm's way. He never talked about exactly what he did in the Army, but given that he was Level C, it was likely something dangerous. He fought in Vietnam, and while he was not an elite fighter on the order of a Navy Seal or Army Ranger, he knew how to get by.

. . .

Unable to sleep, Jill came topside and sat down next to me. She lit a cigarette, inhaled deeply and held it for some time, then released the toxic cloud in a long drawn out fashion as if finishing a huge sigh.

"Where did you get those?"

"Sonny."

"As a doctor, you of all people should know better," I said.

I tried joking with her from time to time, but it hadn't work. I had never seen her even crack a smile. I came to wonder if she would ever recover from what she'd been through. How could she? Hell, I didn't even know if I would recover from what I'd seen her go through.

"I know better," she said. "But I don't really care."

As we sat there, I noticed for the first time that Jill was a very beautiful woman. I thought that she was pretty before, but it was more than that—she had a deep down, no makeup kind of beauty. Her sandy, blond, shoulder-length hair was tied back in a ponytail. Her bangs were just long enough to be tucked behind her left ear, and on bad hair days they hung down over half of her face. Other than a few blemishes from Spike and his crew's handiwork, the skin on her face was flawless. She had the slender and tall physique of a long distance runner, but with a little more meat.

In a way, I was curious how Jill managed to carry on at all. I imagined myself in the same situation—a situation I could actually have yet to face—and didn't think I could manage. She was obviously strong just from the fact that she didn't slip over the side when we weren't looking. In fact, we watched her for any sign of just such a thing. I wondered if she had been sent there to set an example for us. What an awful thought.

"Are you religious?" Jill blurted out. "Never mind, you wouldn't be," she continued before I could answer. "I used to be very religious," she continued nervously.

I took this as a good sign but treaded lightly.

"You're not anymore?" I asked.

"I don't know how I could be…now."

"Me neither," I said honestly. Then I suddenly regretted my sincerity.

"Do you ever wonder about it? God, I mean?" she asked.

I thought about it all the time. Next to weather, the idea of a higher power was, perhaps, the topic that interested me most.

"All the time. But if you are looking for someone to restore your faith in religion, I'm not him."

"So you are an atheist?" she asked.

"No, I just don't believe in religion is all."

Jill took another drag of her cigarette, held it, and stared out over the ocean. I desperately wanted to help her out of her nightmare. I think in some weird way she was an emotional stand-in for Kate until I could get back to her. There was absolutely nothing sexual about it, but I would have done nearly anything to help Jill—even lie to her about my religious beliefs—if I thought that would help. I knew she'd see through it though. She slowly exhaled a streamer of smoke that whipped off toward the stern.

I watched the barometer nervously. I tapped at it, but it didn't move. The wind shifted slightly more toward the west. I untied the wheel and adjusted our course to make optimum use of the new wind direction and then retied it. I wanted to get every knot possible out of the wind.

"How do you think a preacher would explain all this…what I've been through?" she asked.

"I think he'd probably say something like it's all part of God's master plan. God is so much greater than us that we can't understand how this is all for our own good."

"What do you think about that?" she asked.

"My grandfather once used the analogy of how we do things to our pets—give them shots or whatever—things that are definitely for their own good, but that they can't possibly understand. To them it seems like we're just being assholes. My Grandpa said it's the same with God and us. I guess that's at least plausible—assuming there is a God."

"But you believe in some sort of God?"

"Yes. But not like the one religions believe in."

I told Jill about the first experience I'd had that I was certain was an encounter with God. My mother died when I was twelve years old. It was my first experience with death, and given that it was my parent, and I was just a child, it was exceedingly difficult. Of course, I was a tough guy and had to put up a front for my friends, but I was crushed.

At the urging of my friends, I agreed to play in the city all-star baseball game just two days after her death. I was part of the team solely for my fielding ability. I was a terrible hitter. My dad said I was afraid of the ball. He was right.

My second turn to bat came in the sixth inning with two men on, and we trailed by two runs. As always, I took strike one—a dreaded curve ball that backed me off the plate. The curve ball starts out as if it's coming right for your head, which causes a hesitation as you consider bailing out. But the ball breaks over the plate at the end. By the time you realize it's a curve ball, it's too late to recover. I stepped back up to the plate, tapped it twice like always, and took my half-hearted preparation swings.

Then someone spoke to me as plain as day: "This will be a fastball, right down the middle." Startled, I stepped out of the batter's box, which prompted the umpire to call time out. I didn't feel as if I had imagined it. I knew the pitcher but had never faced him before, so what would make me think that he would throw a fastball? I felt a sudden twinge of fear.

"Matt?" The catcher asked, giving me a start.

I popped back to reality. I looked around, and everyone was staring silently at me. I wondered how long I'd been standing there.

I stepped back into the box and took a couple of swings.

"Are you ready, son?" the umpire asked.

I nodded.

"Play ball!" he yelled.

I stared at the pitcher's eyes. He nodded in agreement with whatever sign he'd just received from the catcher. I didn't bother to speculate as to what the sign had been – I already knew.

The pitcher kicked his leg and delivered the pitch. Suddenly time seemed to slow. I watched as the ball spun backward off his index and middle finger – a four-seam fastball. I knew there would be no break. It was right down the middle and that's where it would stay.

I stepped into it and swung with everything I had. I hardly felt the ball hit the bat as it jumped off the sweet spot. I stood and watched as the ball flew high and far. Time sped back up to normal as I heard my teammates explode in the dugout. I began to run, but although I had never experienced a homerun from quite that vantage point, I knew the ball wasn't coming back.

The outfielders barely moved, they just turned and watched it go. When the ball finally landed, some four hundred and fifteen feet from home plate, it bounced across the running track and dribbled out into the football field. It was the longest homerun anyone could remember on that field.

Knowing full well what I had been through, every member of the opposing team gave me a high-five or a pat on the back on my way around the bases. Even the outfielders ran in to pay tribute. My entire team greeted me at the plate. It was exactly the thing I needed at exactly the moment I needed it. It was one of only two times in my life that I am certain something like God spoke directly to me.

When I finished my story, I looked up and Jill was crying.

"Now, I didn't mean to do that," I said.

"That is beautiful," Jill squeaked between tears.

"Anyway, so that's my belief about God," I said quickly in order to distract myself from the emotion I suddenly felt. "I think it generally leaves us alone except in those circumstances where we really need something. And even then, it doesn't directly intervene in the world. It just gives a hint that we still have act on."

"So you've never been religious?" she asked, composing herself.

I had grown up religious. My mother took me to a Baptist church as a child. I never liked the fire and brimstone nor the idea that I was born a horrible sinner in need of salvation. I took issue with that early on. As I got older and learned how to look at things critically, I only got more suspicious. Finally, I realized that the whole of religion was a silly fairy tale. My objections to religion were too numerous to count—from the supposed divine origin of the demonstrably fallible Bible to the immoral idea of someone else paying the price for my sins to the exclusivity of all religions to the depictions of such a bloodthirsty, vengeful, evil God in many faiths. I just didn't buy any of it. But I didn't feel safe telling Jill those things at that moment.

"I was as a kid. I grew out of it."

"When you became a scientist?" Jill asked.

"Before that. Science has actually gotten me closer to God than religion ever did. I think nature is amazing enough all by itself. From the vastness of the universe all the way down to what goes on inside our cells, it is just astonishing. We don't need to make up things about a God to amaze ourselves—we just need to look around."

Jill slumped further into the seat and sat quietly. The look on her face was painful as she fought back tears.

"Jill," I said. "Is there anything I can do for you?"

She let out an audible sob, more like a gasp, and then swallowed the emotion. "You're doing it now," she said.

I sat and watched her struggle for some time. Normally, it would be uncomfortable to just stare at someone, but it seemed as if she just wanted someone to acknowledge, to observe, what she was going through. I wondered if that was how women comforted one another. Maybe I had finally discovered how to deal with women. Finally, she spoke: "I don't know what I'm going to do. I don't have anyone any more. I've lost everything."

"I know it's not the same, but you have us now. We care about you." I slid over to her and put my arm around her. I thought that the fact that someone in that God-forsaken world still cared might help.

"Thank you," she said. "But I've never felt like this before. Nothing really helps."

I was at a total loss as to what to say or do, so I just tried to take her back to somewhere familiar.

"You said you used to be religious. Tell me about that."

"I was raised religious too. But it's more than that. I've had experiences that make me believe in God. A lot of them. Is that silly?"

"Not at all. Not only are your personal experiences a good reason to believe in anything, it is the only legitimate reason—or should be, in my opinion, anyway. Like my story. To me, that is the only real evidence."

The wind barked again and punched at the mainsail. The sail tried to get away as it whipped and struggled against the mast and boom that restrained it. Temperatures cooled, and the pressure dropped another two millibars. A serious storm was knocking at the door. Rain fell in sheets and began to work its way under the bimini top.

Jill tightened her jacket collar against her neck to ward off the rain. She yawned, stood up, and stepped to the stern. Large raindrops began to tap on her jacket. As she stared out over the dark ocean, she lifted one leg and leaned out over the water. Only her grip on the rail kept her from falling in.

"You know our rule Jill. When you go anywhere above decks but the helm, you have to tie off."

She ignored me and continued to dangle out over the water. I held my breath and watched her, certain that I could never turn the RY around in time to save her again and equally certain that she knew it.

"As bad as all this is," she said with tears welling her eyes, "as bad as what we've been through was, what's worse in some ways is that I have lost the one thing I always believed I could count on to pull me through difficult things in life: my faith in God. No god that cares about me, no god worthy of being worshipped would do this."

I lunged toward her and grabbed her arm. She leaned further out. I tightened my grasp on her arm and grabbed a handful of jacket. She let go of the rail just as I leaned back and dug my heels into the deck. Desperation filled her eyes as we balanced precariously over the gunwale.

"I'm not tied off either," I said. "If you go in, I go in."

Rain began to pound down. One wrong move, a big wave, or sudden gust of wind and we'd have been in the drink.

"You risked your life to save me once, and now you're doing it again. Why?"

"Some of us still care about right and wrong," I yelled over the roar of the wind and rain. "With all that's going on, there are still some good people around. In this situation, I think that argues as strongly for a God as anything."

Jill stared at me, fighting against the tears. Finally, a tear broke through and bounced down her cheek. She took hold of the rail again, and we both stepped fully back onto the RY. She lowered her head to my shoulder and cried. I put my arms around her and held her. She returned the embrace.

"Many times I have wished you would have let me die at French," she said.

She stared into my eyes. I both feared she would try to kiss me and hoped that she would. I reminded myself that she was not Kate and that my feelings were purely a longing for my wife. Thankfully, she looked away and I released my grip.

"Please don't give up," I said. "You matter to us."

A wave crashed into the bow, and I stumbled forward. I lost my footing and began to fall toward the railing. She grabbed me.

"Now we're even," I said as I regained my balance.

"Not by a long shot," she replied.

14

DAY 33 AT SEA, APPROXIMATELY 593 MILES WEST OF THE QUEEN CHARLOTTE ISLANDS IN BRITISH COLUMBIA, CANADA (DEAD RECKONED POSITION: 51.4°N, 146.3°W)

"Experience is the name we give to our mistakes." - Oscar Wilde

I knew I should have deployed the sea anchor in that storm, but as my Grandfather used to say: "Shoulda, woulda, coulda."

It was just that we were finally pulling a full eight knots and then some. I was anxious, that's all. I knew the danger, but thirty-three days at sea without knowing whether your family was alive or dead will make you push the envelope. The wind blew forty knots from the south, and it was perfect—we were headed straight for land. If only I could have gotten a few more hours of nine knots, we would have made up a lot of ground.

I knew a cold front was coming. The signs were there, and I figured I would recognize the actual frontal passage before it happened and be able to adjust. I had spent many hours marveling at the ferocity of the storms over the north Pacific from the safety of a forecast office, and I thought I understood their nature. No, I had never been through one at sea. Sure, there were abrupt wind shifts during frontal passages over land, but I obviously did not appreciate what goes on over an open ocean. Maybe it was just an anomalously strong front, or maybe it was a rogue wind.

Whatever the reason, the fact was that the wind did shift far more quickly than I could have imagined and certainly faster than I could react to. In a few seconds, it switched by a hundred and twenty degrees and increased from forty to sixty knots. I was not ready for that, and neither was the boat. The

RY, leaning heavily to port, moved harmoniously with the starboard wind like a shark's fin cutting through the surface water. It did not know what loomed and could not brace for an impact—it relied on its captain for that. Its captain failed.

The first sign of the shift was when I became weightless. In contrast to the boat, I was leaning heavily to starboard, and as the wind suddenly came from port, my side of the boat dipped and the opposite side rose. The boom swung wildly across the boat, and despite the tremendous force, the control lines snapped taut and held as the mainsail began to pull the boat over. The boat certainly could have handled sixty knots from the northwest, but there was that relentless old variable in physics known as momentum, which she could not overcome. The RY went over, and I dangled helplessly for a few seconds, my legs three-quarters into the Pacific. The only thing between me and the abyss was a safety line no thicker than a drinking straw and that wonderful friend known as the counterbalance.

Although we, I, dipped the mast and damaged it badly, we did not roll over. The heavy, lead keel did its job and righted the ship after I failed to do mine. I will never forget that hunk of lead. I owe my life to it—and my conscience, for it most likely would have also cost my shipmates their lives and our families their husbands, brothers, and fathers.

The others were asleep below when I failed to do my job, and they were shaken about like so many die in a felt-lined Yatzee! cup. But somehow they came up only bruised—nothing broken.

When the boat righted itself, I stared up through a tangle of wires with the same bewilderment, the same detached disbelief of an accident victim as he stares at his own protruding femur. The mast was broken a quarter of the way up, the upper three-quarters extending at a right angle over top of me. In my state of shock, I wondered if that was really the mast on our boat or some other mast. I must have been imagining it; the mast could not be broken, because masts don't break.

Except that masts do break, especially when they dip the full area of all their sails into the water and try to come up again. Masts are designed to withstand tremendous wind forces, but as even the casual observer may note, water weighs a lot more than air. Like a femur subjected to hundreds of times the normal force in a head-on collision, the mast wasn't designed for that, and it just could not take it. The weight in the keel guarantees that the boat will right itself, and the foreign water-weight on the sails guarantees they will resist. The aluminum mast buckled and bent over like a chain-link fence post that had been run over by a truck.

With much struggle, we managed to deploy the sea anchor in hurricane force winds. We gathered all the sails, battened down the hatches, re-secured all of our gear, and settled in below deck to ride out the storm.

Unable to sleep or even talk over the roar of the storm, we just lay in our bunks and wished for it to abate. Most of all, I anguished over my mistake. To dip the sail and break the mast was such a colossal blunder that I felt like I should just jump over the side. There was no excuse, and we were just lucky to be alive.

My life slowly flashed in front of my eyes as I considered how dire our straits had become. We were at an unknown distance from land, presumably in the middle of the raging Gulf of Alaska, with no instrumentation, and now our range was limited by the amount of fuel we had. To euphemize, we were in a sailboat without a sail.

The rise and fall of the sea was the worst we had seen. I began counting, and we averaged six seconds up a wave and eight seconds down the back side. I couldn't see outside, but I estimated the seas at over thirty feet. Thirty foot waves with a fourteen second period—that wouldn't be much fun in a cruise ship, much less a forty foot sailboat. The bigger the seas got and the shorter their period became, the more we submarined.

I could feel the action of the sea anchor. Each time we accelerated down the back side of a swell we would run up on the anchor, causing the line to go slack. Then we plowed into the wave trough and began the immediate rise over the next monster. Finally, the line snapped taut and pulled us through the oncoming crest, and the process repeated again—the same terrifying ride every 14 seconds.

The forces were unbelievable. With every snap of the anchor line, I knew what was on everybody's mind: If that line failed we were all done for. We would have had no way to stay pointed into the wind and seas and would have eventually become broadside to the waves. The waves would roll us over and over like a plastic bag tumbling down a windy alley. It could be minutes or hours, but finally the sea would rip a door off or break a porthole and then the water would come. Being completely disabled in such a storm, there would have been no way to survive.

One, two, three, four, five, six, seven, eight, nine, ten, what the fu...? I clung to my bunk for dear life. I heard Jill's muffled scream.

"Oh Shit!" exclaimed Jeff. "Hold on!"

Eleven, twelve.

Water rushed over the boat. Gear came loose as the RY's became nearly vertical. Gravity forced my body toward the head of my bed. Gear clanged around me and on me. I fell onto the ceiling of my bunk and became aware that I had no concept of up. I instinctively wrapped my arms around my head as I tumbled around in my berth like a lottery ball.

I thought about Sonny, Jeff, and Jill. I thought about Kate and my children. I knew it was over.

The few more seconds of chaos seemed like forever, but finally the distinctive twang of the taut anchor line echoed through the cabin. The boat lurched forward and to starboard. The gear fell to the floor and we all fell to our bunks—right-side-up, finally.

I scanned my body looking for pain and found none. I moved my hands and feet, and they worked. I got up.

Sonny was already up. We accelerated down again, and he fell forward toward Jill's bunk. We plowed into the next wave and Sonny crashed into the forward bulk head. I held on.

"Jeff! Are you all right?"

He didn't respond, so I stepped forward. My foot caught some gear and slid as the anchor lined snapped, and we plowed upward toward a fresh crest.

Jeff's head poked out from his bunk.

"I think I'm all right," he said. "You had better get back in your bunk."

"What the hell was that?" I yelled.

"I don't know. Rogue wave?"

"We're ok up here!" Sonny yelled.

I returned to my bunk.

• • •

Jeff awakened me some hours later with a shake. The seas had subsided to a more reasonable ten feet or so. I stood up and felt as stable as if I were on dry land.

"How are we doing?" I asked Jeff.

"Not well," he said. "Come top side."

I poked my head out of the main hatch. The mast was gone. Wires draped across the deck and dangled into the sea. The bimini top was gone. The deck of the RY had essentially been scraped clean.

I climbed through the hatch and took a seat around the helm next to Jill. Sonny pulled wires from the water and coiled them. Jeff returned from the bow and sat next to me.

"Look guys, I'm so sorry," I said, my voice cracking and tears welling in my eyes. "I should have deployed the anchor sooner."

"Save it," Jeff said tersely.

I looked around the group and prepared for the tongue lashing I deserved. Hell, I deserved to walk the plank.

"It probably wouldn't have made a bit of difference," Jeff consoled.

"What do you mean, I broke the mast," I said.

"That mast would have come off anyway, when we rolled," said Sonny.

"We rolled several times," Jeff said. "The only thing that saved us is that the hatches and main cabin door were all closed. If you hadn't dipped the mast, we probably wouldn't have closed the main door and we would all be fish food."

"So I saved us all," I said sarcastically.

"Maybe sometimes God does interfere," Jill said.

Jeff and Sonny looked at Jill and then stared at me in confusion.

"Maybe so," I said smiling.

Jill cracked a smile in return, and that made me feel better.

"You said something about a rogue wave last night," I said to Jeff.

"Yeah. There have been lots of stories about ships getting hit by waves up to a hundred feet high. I saw something on cable that showed data from satellites confirming the existence of waves of ninety to a hundred-and-five feet."

"They must be some sort of standing waves," I said as my inner scientist kicked in.

"Whatever they are, I don't want to ever see one again," said Jill.

Jeff quickly told us the story of the Edmund Fitzgerald. It sunk on Lake Michigan in 1975, allegedly due to a rogue wave. The Coast Guard found it broken in half on the bottom. It sank, killing all twenty-nine aboard, so quickly that they never even issued a distress signal. The only thing that could have done that to a ship of the size of the Edmund Fitgerald that quickly was a wave of epic proportions.

"I heard that some cruise ships have reported having their bridge windows blown out by waves," I said. "The bridges of cruise ships are as high as eighty feet above the surface."

"I would guess that's what hit us last night," Jeff said. "How high do you think that wave was?" he asked to no one in particular.

"I was counting around six seconds of rise on average," I said. "I got to twelve seconds before we got tossed upside down with that wave."

"So if we were getting thirty to forty feet in the storm, that wave could have been seventy, eighty feet," calculated Jeff.

"Thank God for the sea anchor," Jill said.

"I think that blessed sea anchor kept us from rolling all the way to the coast," Jeff said. "Thank God indeed!"

. . .

DAY 36 AT SEA, SOMEWHERE IN THE GULF OF ALASKA (DEAD RECKONED POSITION: 52.8°N, 140.3°W)

In the ensuing days, we motored some, but we discovered that because the currents and wind were in our favor, we made just about as good time drifting. We had little idea how far we had drifted off course during the storm and only a slightly better idea which direction we'd been pushed. The errors in our dead reckoning position were growing, and we figured we could be many hundreds of miles off in any direction. The only good thing was that the compass still worked, and we knew which way North America should be.

We conserved our fuel, let the wind push us, and just tried to stay perpendicular to the seas. The wind blew at twenty knots or greater for the entire time. We put out the sea anchor two more times over the next week. We were lost, but as best we could tell, nature was pushing us in the right direction.

. . .

DAY 42 AT SEA, SOMEWHERE IN THE GULF OF ALASKA (DEAD RECKONED POSITION: UNKNOWN)

We gave up dead reckoning several days ago, since we couldn't even estimate the basic inputs. Desperation grew as we became more and more disoriented. We dared not waste fuel motoring anymore, since it could be a thousand miles to the closest land, and we would need that fuel once we got there—*if* we got there.

However, on the night of day forty two, I made a startling observation: stars! They were still hazy, but a couple of bright ones could easily be seen. Not wanting to waste the opportunity with a novice taking our position, I scrambled below to wake Jeff. The seas were relatively calm, and he took quick measurements of Polaris and Saturn. He consulted star charts and then triangulated. He took the measurements again fifteen minutes later, averaged the two, consulted star charts, and triangulated again. He rubbed his scruffy two-week beard and chuckled a little.

"I'll be damned!" he said, as he showed me the coordinates and the plot of our position on the chart.

54.7°N, 134.5°W.

We had averaged only two knots while drifting over nine days but it had been in the right direction. We were just sixty miles from the southeast Alaska coast. We decided to motor in from there.

15

DAY 43 AT SEA, 8 MILES WEST-SOUTHWEST OF FORRESTER ISLAND, ALASKA (DEAD RECKONED POSITION: 54.7°N, 133.7°W)

At 7:17 pm on day forty-three, we sighted North America.

Forrester Island, Alaska rose from the sea like a beacon of hope, and its thousand foot peaks knifed into the low overcast. At a misty thirty-five degrees, with a northwest wind of twenty-two knots, and seas upwards of fifteen feet, the damp, gray scene at any other time and by almost anyone else would have been described as ugly and cold—perhaps not fit for man nor beast. But after a month and a half at sea, it was one of the most beautiful sights I had ever seen.

. . .

During the night we motored past Dall Island and rounded Cape Chicon and turned north toward Ketchikan. We saw no lights, but we were not sure if we would have seen lights in that isolated section of Alaska anyway. At dawn, we headed into Clarence Strait, which led to Nichols Channel, which led through Tongass Narrows to Ketchikan. We had our doubts about approaching a populated area through such a constriction, but we needed to repair badly. We felt—or hoped—that maybe this part of Alaska had not yet descended into chaos.

Sonny played with his cell phone again and continued to complain about the battery going dead. That was when he and Jill spotted something on a small island to port: smoke.

I scrambled across the top of the boat to get a better look at the smoke. I caught my foot on a loose cable and lost my balance. I fell, face-forward, toward the railing of the boat. In that instant between losing my balance and hitting something, my brain made thousands of calculations, determined that I could not avoid hitting my head on the railing, and came up with a course of action—the only course of action that it could imagine which provided a chance to miss the railing. I involuntarily thrust myself up and forward in an attempt to clear the railing. As time slowed and my head seemingly inched toward the railing, the realization set in, and I prepared for the pain, hoping it wouldn't be that bad. As I cart-wheeled into an upside down position, I looked at the gray sky.

Then everything went dark—and cold, very cold.

. . .

DAY 46, GILLIGAN'S ISLAND, ALASKA

It remained black for some time, but the cold eventually faded. I awakened to a crushing pain in my head and the vision of being on the inside of a cone. Curved sides sloped upward above me to a spot of light at the top. Strange music echoed around in my head. The unmistakable smell of marijuana smoke wafted on the air. It smells like burnt sage, I am told, but although I never had an occasional smell burnt sage, I know marijuana when I smell it.

Very foggy-headed, I groped for some sense of the present, like when you awake from a particularly realistic dream and cannot determine if that was the dream or this is the dream.

I reached for the back of my head near the origin of an awakening pain and felt a bald spot and a ribbed area, like a zipper. What the hell? Swollen and mushy, it felt like a very ripe avocado. Hunger ripped at my gut. I tried to get up but could not. My atrophied limbs refused to move despite my synaptic commands.

I called out and produced only a squeak, but it was enough to roust someone near me.

"He lives!" the man shrieked as he leapt to his feet.

"Hey dude!" he said. "We didn't know if you were ever going to wake up!"

The man came into the light. A long, scraggly beard hung from his haggard face. His eyes were bright but bloodshot, and he smiled at me toothily. His breath smelled awful—and suddenly I knew where the marijuana smell came from. He wore a dirty tie-died poncho—one of those woven woolen kind from the seventies. Darkness prohibited me from seeing below his poncho, but I prayed he was wearing pants.

"Peace man. Take it easy," he said. "I am Jonathan, but my friends call me Jonathan," he laughed.

"Where am I? And what am I doing here?" I asked.

"You're in heaven, man!"

"Seems more like hell to me."

"Whoa!" Jonathan said trailing off, as if he had just discovered something earth shaking. "She was right."

"Who? What are you talking about?"

"Jill, man. She said you would say that. You just blew my mind!"

"I'll bet it didn't have far to go."

I tried again to sit up, but Jonathan held me down by the shoulders with little effort.

"Whoa there, fella. I wouldn't do that just yet."

"What happened? My voice was gravelly and barely perceptible, even to me."

"You almost died, man."

"How? Where am I?"

"I don't know man, but when you guys pulled up you were all limp. Blood everywhere. It was a freak show, man!"

Jonathan hovered over me and stared into my eyes. I couldn't escape the stink of his breath, and I gasped for air.

"Jesus! Get the hell off me!" I yelled, my voice returning.

The throbbing in my head kept me from being able to force my way free.

"Hey, Victor!" he said to the darkness. "Get the other dudes. He's awake!"

"Take it easy, man. They're all here, your crew. Jill fixed you up good, man. She's something else. You're all cool, man!"

I relaxed and hoped he was right. I was sure I would wake up at any moment and be back on the RY, all of it just a bad dream. There had been so many bad dreams that, while this was definitely up there on the strangeness scale, it was not surprising.

Jill was the first one in. She walked over to me and gave me a kiss on the cheek and grasped my head with both hands. She stared into my eyes, just inches from my face.

"Do you know who I am?"

"Of course. What the hell is this?"

Jill followed up with a cacophony of questions. "What year is it? Who is the president? What is your name? Where do you live?"

I must have answered them to her satisfaction because she let out a relieved sigh.

Sonny scrambled in, followed by Jeff.

"Hey, I think he's going to be ok," Jill said.

"Oh man, you gave us a scare," said Sonny.

"It's nice to see your eyes open," said Jeff.

"Well, now that the gang's all here, would you mind telling me what happened? Where are we?" It hurt to talk, and I winced. I lifted my hand up to shield my face from the light above. "What's the matter with my head?"

They proceeded to tell me how I hit my head on the railing on my way over the side. How I nearly drowned.

"How did I get back aboard?" I asked.

"How do you think?" Jeff asked, motioning to Sonny.

"My hero," I squeaked lamely.

Everyone laughed. I tried to laugh too, but it hurt.

"You really went in after me?"

"Yeah, but don't look forward to that again. That water is freakin-assed cold!"

Jonathan walked back in and whispered something in Sonny's ear. They slapped right hands, clasped them, and then made that half-hug thing than guys do.

"I'm pretty sure you have a cracked skull," Jill informed me as I looked back to her. "We stitched you up—well, I did—and it looks like it's healing up without any infection. I think saltwater is a good disinfectant. You had a bad concussion, and I was worried about a brain injury. You were unconscious, but as far as I could tell, the light was still on. Sometimes it just takes time for the body to respond and heal up."

"Jill has been quite an attraction around here," Jeff said with a smile. "They have medics, but she is their first real doctor."

"I don't think she's sat down for five minutes since we've been here," Sonny interjected.

Jill couldn't suppress a radiant smile.

Sonny jumped in again: "She wasn't worried about pressure on your brain from swelling, you know, because of your cracked head. Relieves the pressure I guess. I didn't believe you had a cracked skull. Too thick, I told them."

Everyone laughed but me—it still hurt too much.

Jill put her fingers on my left eyelids and forced them apart. Then she checked the right eye. I couldn't help but notice a spark in her eyes. It was beautiful.

"Looks good. Feeling dizzy?"

"A little."

"I suppose so. When that goes away, you can get up. But make sure one of us is here when you stand up for the first time."

"Yes, ma'am."

"Where are we?" I asked.

They explained to me that we'd landed on an island along the coast of Alaska. A large group of people lived there and they called it Gilligan's Island. They were working on fixing up the RY.

My surroundings began to come into focus as my senses returned. The cone shape I noticed when I first awakened was now obviously the top of a teepee. Smoke from a fire rose out through the opening. I was warm and save for the pain in my head, quite comfortable.

Some smart looking fellow rushed in and whispered something to Jeff. Jeff turned to Sonny and said: "Come on. We need your cell phone."

I drifted back to sleep.

When I woke the next time, it was either still light or light again. I was immediately able to focus this time, and my head felt better. I called out, but no one answered. Just as I was about to get myself upright, the flap in the teepee opened, and a girl walked in. She was skinny as a rail and had a rather homely, freckled face. Her long red hair hung wildly, and she wore the same poncho as Jonathan. Her hair was a little cleaner and she didn't smell like anything. It is funny how some people always stink and others are able to smell utterly like nothing.

"I'm Krystal. Let me help you."

She grabbed my arm to steady me.

We stepped out into the light, and it was raining lightly. Occasionally, a fat snowflake survived all the way to the ground. A line of females, perhaps thirty in all, stood waiting for us. They ranged from young girls all the way up to old women. Their skirts varied in length and color, but each wore that same poncho. Krystal led me to one of many campfires and sat me down in a wooden Adirondack-style chair. Hewn from fir, as far as I could tell, and the chair had obviously been built on site.

One-by-one, they filed past and hugged my head from behind, careful not to touch my wound. Then they went back to whatever it was they were doing before I woke up.

A young girl approached me from behind and handed me a bowl of soup.

"Fish stew," she said. "With herbs."

"What kind of herbs?" I asked skeptically, thinking back to my encounter with Jonathan.

"Black Cohosh," she said. "Squawroot for pain. We have other medicines, but Miss Jill thought we should try this first. Don't take pills if you don't need them. That is what she said."

I appreciated that Jill would say that, since I had the same philosophy about synthetic pharmaceuticals, but yet I hesitated.

"It's all natural!" she exclaimed in a bubbly voice. I thought about how arsenic is also all natural, but Denver and his natural cures popped into my mind, so I just thanked her instead. I took a heaping spoonful, and just as I was about to shove it in my mouth, she stopped me.

"Miss Jill said that you should sip the broth first, before eating the rest."

"Well, whatever Miss Jill says," I said, smiling to the little girl.

As I sipped the broth, I looked around at the variety of teepees and other haphazard structures that constituted the encampment. The rain came a little steadier and more snowflakes mixed in. I noticed the cold and looked down and saw that, to my shock, I was wearing one of their ponchos!

"Do you like it?" asked an old woman. "I made that one, just for you."

"It's lovely. Thank you," I said, trying desperately to hide my insincerity. The ponchos were ugly as sin, but I had to admit it was warm, and somehow waterproof. "Where are my clothes?"

"They're sitting in the teepee. We cleaned and dried them."

I thanked them again. Some of the women got up and moved into other teepees, out of the rain.

"You don't have to be scared, mister," a little girl said as she peeled potatoes.

"I'm not scared sweetheart. I'm just a little confused. Where are my friends?"

"They are down at your boat," said yet another woman. "It's almost done." This woman was heavier than the others but still fairly petite by most standards. I realized that all these people were very skinny. This woman had very clean hair and was an earthy sort of beautiful, the sort of beautiful that most women would die to have as their starting point. To her, it was the end point.

"What are you people? What is all this?"

The old woman explained how they had gotten there. They came from all walks of life, but collectively decided that they wanted a better life. They had been preparing to move away from civilization for a long time, but the Red Plague gave them just the push they needed. They sold off all their belongings and moved out to this island. There were 179 of them—soon to be 180 according to Krystal. They all seemed very nice.

It suddenly became more snow than rain, but the fire was making my shins hot. So I pushed my chair back from the fire. The effort sent a spike of pain through my brain, and I winced.

"Where are the others?" I asked.

"Hunting, fishing, gathering. A work party is building a lodge about a half mile that way." The old woman pointed to what I thought was north.

"Do you want to live here mister?" the girl asked.

"It seems very nice," I said. "But, I am trying to find my family. I lived overseas when all this happened, and they were in Seattle. I am trying to get back to them."

"Do you think they are alive?" she asked before being shushed by her sister.

"That's ok," I said to the sister. "I hope they're ok but I have no way to know. I have to go find out."

The little girl got up, came over, and sat in my lap.

"I hope they're ok too," she said, putting her head to my chest.

"We all do," the old woman said. "But you know, you would be safer here by the sound of things."

"In some ways, but not others," I replied.

The woman asked me what I meant. I told her that I thought the climate was going to grow much colder. I pointed out that it was already snowing on that coastal island in the middle of the summer. They all seemed completely unfazed by the news.

"Frank will take care of us," the woman said.

Frank was a scientist and their leader.

I grew tired again as the natural medicinal cocktail began to work. With my pain gone, my face felt flush. I suddenly felt less in control than minutes earlier. I wanted to say more about the climate, but I wasn't sure if I could speak without slurring. I yawned and tried to get up—I needed to lie down again. My legs felt like noodles. Krystal held my hand to steady me and led the way into the teepee.

"It's the cohosh," she whispered with a giggle. With any other people, I would have been concerned.

When I awakened the third time, it was dark and I was alone. The smell of wood smoke hung thickly in the air. I generally felt better, albeit slightly hung over from the soup.

The fire inside my teepee had died to coals, but I remained toasty warm. I stood up and stepped outside on still wobbly legs. I considered calling out for someone, but large bonfires raged nearby and I thought I could make it. I heard music from the fire to my right and chose to go that way. As I approached, I noticed large skewers with fish splayed out on them like fans, ringing the fire. I had seen that before at a touristy Indian salmon bake at Blake Island State Park near Seattle. Steam rose from the fillets and a sweet, smoky fish smell filled the air. I noticed the faint aroma of marijuana again.

I hesitated to move into the fray due to an irrational phobia of mine: fear of groups of strangers. I always worried about what strangers thought as I walked amongst them and searched for somewhere to sit or people I knew. I reassured myself that, so far, everyone had been more than nice, and I just walked straight in. As I entered the light, a man sitting at the first table greeted me by name and jumped up to hold my arm. He led me to a table.

I found my three friends seated with two other strangers. I sat next to Sonny, and after the greetings, he offered me some fish. It was salmon, and it was delicious. Jill handed me some sort of cooked or boiled plant—seaweed maybe.

"I don't think so," I said.

"Eat it!" she exclaimed.

Startled by her tone, I did so, and it was horribly bitter. They asked me how I was feeling, and I lied that I was fine. I learned that we had been on the island for three days, and the plan was to leave the next day.

Sonny handed me a wooden cup.

"What is this?"

"A sort of beer they're trying to make. It comes from some plant around here."

"A *sort* of beer they're *trying* to make. I don't think so."

"Good choice," Jill said.

"It's fine," Sonny said. "Look it doesn't affect me at all," he stood up and stumbled back into a seated position.

Jill gave him a sour look.

The music stopped, and the man named Frank stood up. He was a strapping sort and wore an orange canvas hunting vest instead of the standard issue camp poncho. Given his short stature and petite frame, I wasn't prepared for what came out of him when he began speaking.

"On their last night with us, I just wanted to wish our new friends good sailing," the deep voice boomed. "May your waters be smooth and your wind friendly, and if you don't find what you are looking for down south, please come back. You are always welcome here."

Sonny, not usually one for words, stood up to reply. It must have been planned that way.

"We just wanted to thank you for all that you've done for us. We could never have fixed the RY without you. And I personally wanted to thank you for the beer and, uh, other stuff." Many laughed, and children whispered questions to their parents or older siblings and were rebuked.

"I've made a lot of friends here," Sonny continued. "And in other circumstances I would stay. I am committed to seeing this through, but you may see me again." The onlookers greeted that statement with cheers.

Frank came over to sit with us and took a seat on a small bench with Sonny. Given his small frame, he fit perfectly well there. Frank had dark hair under his hunting cap, and his thin moustache and pock-marked face reminded me of a porn star from the seventies.

"I hope you are feeling better," Frank said to me, his voice equally imposing close up.

"I am. And thank you so much for your hospitality."

"Your friends have told me much about you and your journey. You've been through quite a lot. I am sure you will make it, and I sincerely hope that you find your family safe and well."

"We know it's a long shot," I responded. "What do you know about what has happened on the main land?"

"Less than you, I think. We came out here right at the beginning. We have no contact with the outside world, and you're the first people we've seen since."

"Do you really think you can make it here?" I asked.

He told me that they had everything they needed. Among their numbers were people skilled and knowledgeable in engineering, construction, survival, hunting, and many other useful disciplines. I wasn't concerned about that.

"What did you do before, Frank?"

"I was a molecular biologist for a major industrial firm. I became disillusioned with corporatism and in researching an alternative, came in contact with some members of this group. Long story short, I was honored to be selected as the leader of the group when the shit hit the fan."

"You must know that it's going to get very cold this winter. I mean it's already snowing here, and it's July."

It turned out that I wasn't telling him anything that he didn't already know. They had surmised the same things we had, and despite the obvious difficulties that lie ahead, they were already locked into their course and simply had to make the best of it.

"The ocean will moderate the climate here," Frank said, "But we are laying away all the resources we can to prepare for the long winter."

"And hopefully the experts were right about global warming," he said.

"I wouldn't hold my breath," I quipped. "As a meteorologist, I know that the only thing we're sure of is that we aren't sure of anything."

"I don't know the consensus was pretty strong. All the experts agreed," Frank said.

"Well, that's what we were told. I'm just not as enamored with experts as everyone else—any experts. Experts agree about all sorts of things that don't turn out to be right. I could give you a list a mile long, but, suffice it to say, there was a time when all the experts agreed that the earth was flat."

Frank laughed. "Touché! I guess we'll find out."

"Indeed we will," I replied. "I'm pretty sure that we have cut our carbon emissions now—a lot! Unfortunately, this isn't a controlled experiment." I pointed toward the sky. "I think that will have a lot more to do with it than CO_2."

Everyone continued talking, but I zoned out and just stared at the fire. I had to admit that even though on some level I envied the people of Gilligan's Island, I longed to be back on Kwaj. If all of this had happened just a few weeks sooner, I would be there with my family right now. I would have had everything—the safety and solace that these people enjoyed along with warm weather and an abundance of food. It had occurred to me early in our trip that we might be able to get our families and go right back out to Kwaj. However, after all that had happened, I knew the odds of us making it were slim.

Come to think of it, I had been so focused on getting back to my family and worrying about their safety, that I hadn't spent much time thinking about what I would actually do once I got there. My friend Sean McMasters popped into my head. His dad had a ranch in the Olympic Mountains not far from where Kate's parents lived. He mentioned to me one time that the ranch was his bug out spot. I didn't think much of it at the time, but I suddenly wondered if he made good on that plan. If we couldn't make a go of it at

Kate's parent's house, maybe we would check that out. I knew for sure that he would welcome us. He was good people as my grandfather used to say.

All that worry made my head hurt. The booming sound of Frank's voice startled me out of thought: "Matt. Are you sure you are ok? You don't look so good."

"I think we should go now," I blurted out.

The group stared at me. Frank finally responded: "That would be suicide without instruments in the dark. These passages are filled with sand bars and rocky reefs that you can only see in daylight."

Jeff and Sonny helped me back to the teepee. Jill came in just before I drifted off with some more herbs.

"Do you really trust that stuff?" I asked.

"They have regular medicines but not really anything that would help you. They insisted that we try, but we don't want to take what they have, especially if it won't help. These natural medicines are as good for you as anything."

Jill held her hand on my forehead and it felt red hot. She was full of life again, a bundle of energy. Surely she still suffered inside, but she had a purpose, and sometimes that's all anyone needs.

"Jill," I whispered. "I think you should stay here."

She stood silently feeling my forehead. Then her fingers searched along my scalp to where the stitches were. She delicately explored the wound with her fingers. She walked to the other side of the teepee to retrieve something and returned. She stuck her finger in a jar and pulled out a dollop of some pine scented salve. She silently rubbed it over my stitches with great tenderness.

I broke the silence: "It's not that we don't…"

"Shhh!" She lamented.

When she was done with the salve, she leaned down and kissed me on the check and hugged me. I hugged back.

She whispered into my ear: "I know what you are doing, so you can just stop it. You and Jeff and Sonny are my only family." And she walked out of the teepee.

. . .

The next morning, Jeff and Sonny woke me early and escorted me to the boat. I insisted that I was fine, but they refused to release my arms. It turned out that it was a good idea, because the path down to the beach was slippery from rain and snow the night before. I nearly fell twice. Rain tapped at the leaves as we walked down the moist forest path, and our breath turned to cloud as we exhaled. The salty air filled my nostrils. It smelled as it had for millennia, a hearty, almost metallic aroma that was neither offensive nor pleasant in and of itself, but was inviting if only because it smelled like life.

As we emerged from the forest, a slight breeze slapped me in the face, but I hardly noticed as I focused on the RY. I couldn't believe my eyes. They had fashioned an entirely new mast out of a tree and restrung the cables and sails. It was a thing of beauty. A knotty-pine mast, and save for the light tan color of the pole, you could hardly tell anything had happened.

Frank strolled up.

"Nice work," Jeff said. "We can't thank you enough. Won't you take some of our supplies? At least Sonny's beer?"

Sonny chuckled nervously.

"No. You will need those things. We have all we need here."

"That is really impressive," I said, pointing to the RY.

"Thank you," he said. "We have excellent artisans among us."

"I'll say! And thank *you*."

"You'll have to take it easy. The wood is fresh and flexible and strong, but it is not seated well. If you overstress it, she could come free."

Jill strolled up, trailed by a half dozen women. The women held trays of freshly prepared foods—gifts for us. Jill's mile-wide smile lit up the beach.

"Guess what I just did," she said gleefully.

"By the look on your face, I'd say you just won the lottery," I said.

"I just delivered number 180!" she said, ignoring me. "A healthy baby girl!"

We all smiled at the thought of new life. We needed good news like that.

"I hope you all watched closely," Frank said to the group of women. "There will be more of those and it's best to learn from a pro."

"Oh go on!" Jill said. "They would have done just fine. It was more of a case of them letting me have the honor."

As we were getting ready to board skiff to take us out to the RY, Frank pulled me aside.

"I wanted to ask you about something you said last night," Frank said, "about the climate here. It sounds like we've both come to the same conclusion about what took place. What is the worst case scenario, meteorologically speaking?"

"We could easily be heading into another ice age," I said. "Our climate is balanced on a razor's edge. That is why, right or wrong, the climatologists were so worried about CO2 and global warming. They talked of a tipping point where we would head into irreversible warming, a sort of feedback loop that we couldn't stop. Well, there is also a tipping point and feedbacks in the other direction. Send up enough crap to block out the sun for an extended period of time, whether by nuclear war, volcano, asteroid impact, or whatever, and it could get real cold, real quick. Build up enough snow on the continents during a prolonged winter where it doesn't melt off in the summer, and then it begins to feed back, and we're off toward snowball earth."

"So if the glaciers come, head south?" Frank asked rhetorically.

"I can't imagine the glaciers coming this close to the ocean. Can you imagine what kind of heat reservoir this ocean is? What worries me is the lack of sun. No sun, no photosynthesis. As a biologist, I don't have to tell you what that would do to the food chain. In the end, it might not matter where you are, but you're starting off at a disadvantage in an already cold place like this. Maybe you'll be fine—you certainly seem to have to smart people around here. I'm just saying."

"I really appreciate your concern and your insight," Frank said.

"It is the least I can do. One more thing to consider: everybody left on earth will eventually figure out what I've just said. It may be hard to find a safe place in the south. If you can make it here until the sun comes out again, you might do really well."

Frank looked out over the bay considering what I had said.

"Now I have a question for you, if it's all right," I said.

"Shoot," Frank said.

"It's something I've always wondered about, and you are the only biologist I've ever known."

Frank stood up a little straighter, squinted his eyes, and tilted his head in order to concentrate on my question. One thing I liked about Frank is that he made whatever you were discussing seem like the most important thing in the world at that moment.

"Since you have only 180 people here, how can you avoid inbreeding down the line? If you were the only people left on the earth, could you repopulate it?"

Frank carefully considered his answer.

I continued before Frank could answer: "I mean, we know that the religious story of creation cannot be true—two people could not have populated the whole world, but what is the optimal number?"

"Yes, of course, it would have been impossible for only two people to populate the whole world," Frank agreed. "And that is not at all consistent with the theory of human evolution. Genetics is very complicated and not my specialty, but I've seen studies that indicate remote Pacific islands, whose populations had been devastated by natural disasters, were able to repopulate from as few as twenty people with few ill effects. In fact, some studies have shown that of the original people that crossed the Bering land bridge and populated North America, the genetic material of only 70 of them can be found in their modern descendants. It doesn't take much genetic diversity to carry on."

"Huh," I grunted, satisfied with the answer.

"Besides," Frank continued with a chuckle, "We might be hillbillies now, but that doesn't mean we fancy our daughters!"

I laughed. By this time, Jill had come back to see what the holdup was. She caught the tail end of our conversation.

"He's very inquisitive," she whispered to Frank, just loud enough to make sure that I could hear it.

"It's perfectly all right," Frank replied smiling. "None of us knows everything, but that doesn't mean we can't try to."

After the goodbyes, one of the island men shuttled us out to the RY and helped us aboard.

As we cast off and began to motor away, I looked ashore. People emerged from the forest and began waving. By the time we got out of earshot, it looked as if the entire community was on the beach. It probably was. That's the kind of people they were.

16

DAY 47 AT SEA, NORTHERN VANCOUVER ISLAND, CANADA (DEAD RECKONED POSITION: 50.7°N, 128.5°W)

The ache in my head seemed to be worsening, but I didn't care much. I just wanted to get there and get it over with—whatever *it* was. I began to have prolonged bouts of nausea and vomiting which worried my shipmates greatly, especially Jill. I blamed it on seasickness, like that which I had experienced when we first set sail. Jill rightly pointed out that after more than a month at sea, only a few days on land shouldn't be enough to cause it to return. After that, someone always seemed to be unable to sleep when I was at the helm, but, curiously, no one had any trouble sleeping when anyone else stood watch. I could have complained, but maybe they were right. I decided instead to just let them fake insomnia in order to hide how much they cared for me.

Sonny and I sat silently staring as we passed mostly uninhabited sections of northern Vancouver Island. It was a calm day by our standards, but cloud continued to envelop the mountains rising up from the beach. The clouds occasionally lifted enough for us to see a crust of snow over the higher elevations. I reckoned the snow level to be no more than a thousand feet—very low given the time of year.

The engineers on Gilligan's Island tried to fix our electronics, but to no avail. As Jeff thought, we would have had to replace nearly the entire system of electrical wiring, and they just didn't have the supplies. So, we were still dead reckoning, but having regained our bearings, we had a good fix on our position.

We weren't making great time due to the abnormally light wind and opposing current, but the new mast and sails were holding up well. The folks of Gilligan's Island had dyed our only remaining sail dark and made us another dark sail, so we could keep them up most of the time without being easily seen. With any luck, we figured it would take no more than three days to reach Whidbey Island. Given what we'd been through thus far, we thought that the odds surely must have favored good luck.

We had passed several outcroppings of buildings, but Sonny and I jumped up to take a close look at the first real town we had seen on the whole trip. The sign above the port indicated the name of the town, which was a long Indian name that I had no chance of pronouncing. Like most towns in this part of the world, it was probably a fishing village. It looked quite nice despite a complete lack of any sign of life. There was no smoke, no lights, and no movement of any kind.

I scanned along the shoreline toward the south and came to the entrance to the town where something gave me a start. I couldn't make out any details from two miles out, but I had no doubt about what it was. A person who had been hanged from a tree rocked slowly back and forth in the breeze. My eyes quickly darted around and found others—six in total—hanging from light poles, trees, and even the welcome sign to the town. I noticed a small sign attached to the victim hanging from the welcome sign, but couldn't read it.

"Do you see that?" I asked Sonny.

"No, what?"

"At the south end of the town—those bodies. Can you read the sign on that one?"

Sonny scanned frantically around the scene and then stopped. "Yep, I see it. I can't make it out. What does it say?"

I rummaged through the drawer below the wheel and found Jeff's sailing scope. I pointed it toward the town and twisted the two-part scope to bring it into focus. It turned out there were others—maybe a dozen—and they all appeared to be men, or were at least dressed like men. The ones hanging closest to the ground looked like they were missing their feet—perhaps chewed off by animals.

I bored in on the sign and tried to hold the scope steady on the rocking boat. I struggled to focus on the letters and then I finally put all the words together. I said it out loud for Sonny's benefit: "Looters and rapists go back!"

"Good for them," he said sincerely.

We sailed for another hour past endless evergreen forests and driftwood littered beaches. Snowcapped mountains jutting up into the overcast became more frequent on the island the further south we moved. Other than the occasional bird, we saw no further sign of life along the coast. It looked just as it had for thousands of years, and during brief moments of detachment from reality, I actually found myself enjoying it.

I picked at the remnants of food from our friends on the island. Suddenly, a whooshing sound behind me gave me a start. Water sprayed over the gunwale and pelted us. The seas were only a few feet and the wind light northwest, so it couldn't have been a breaking wave. Sonny sprang out of a half sleep as the drops hit his face.

"What are you doing?" he asked confusedly.

I had already turned but saw nothing except a vanishing disturbance in the water.

"Porpoises?" I offered.

We had seen many porpoises in Kwaj and knew they existed much further north, but hadn't seen any in weeks.

As we watched, several large mounds of water formed just to our starboard. The mounds continued to grow in the center, and the water around the edges sloughed into the depression until, finally, the huge animals broke through the surface and breached.

Six of them flew out of the water and performed a variety of dives for our entertainment. A torrent of water sprayed over us as the several-ton animals crashed back into the sea. They were not porpoises.

"Killer whales," I said.

They immediately did a second breach for us and made quite a show of it. The closest whale came straight out and went straight back in nose first with very little splash. The next closest whale came out sideways and fell back in on its back, sending a shower of water in all directions. Satisfied that we had seen them, they proceeded to swim alongside of us, surfacing only occasionally to breathe.

I pounded on the window and roused Jeff and Jill. They hurried topside, and we watched the whales play. Their clicks and whistles occasionally pierced the unusually calm quiet weather. We counted a total of ten whales, at least two of which were calves. I thought I recognized one male amongst the pod—males have much larger dorsal fins—but I couldn't be sure. It didn't matter, they were beautiful whatever their sex.

One of the whales seemed particularly interested in us and swam very close by—no more than ten feet off starboard. I reached out to see if she would get close enough that I could touch her. We gazed in amazement as she rolled over on her side and looked right at us with her left eye. She held the pose and stared for a few seconds and then rolled the rest of the way over and disappeared under the boat. The rest of the pod followed her off to our port stern and disappeared.

Tears welled in my eyes. I looked at the others, and they too choked back emotion.

"What have we done?" Sonny said rhetorically, before he turned and went below decks.

Yes, I thought. What have we done, indeed?

17

DAY 51 AT SEA, MOUTH OF BARKLEY SOUND, VANCOUVER ISLAND, CANADA (DEAD RECKONED POSITION: 48.8°N, 125.3°W)

The fog comes
on little cat feet.
It sits looking
over harbor and city
on silent haunches
and then moves on.

-Carl Sandburg

It was Jill's turn to babysit me as I stood watch. The weather remained benign, so we chatted about mostly meaningless things to pass the time. I tried to impress her with things that always fascinated me. I told her about how the sun converts six million tons of hydrogen into helium every second, which is enough to power civilization for hundreds of thousands of years. I pointed out that since electrons orbit the nucleus of every atom at a great distance, solid objects are mostly empty space. She just stared ahead. Such things didn't interest her, which I found interesting in and of itself.

Jeff came topside and silently stepped past us. He stared up at the mast.

"You know what interests me?" she finally asked.

"No. What?" I replied, excited to find out what it was and glad that she was, apparently, listening.

"Evolution."

"Really?" I replied. "So you don't believe in the Biblical account of creation?"

"Pfff!" she exclaimed. "No. The evidence in favor of evolution is overwhelming!"

I hesitated. She brought up the topic, and I wasn't sure where it was going, but I found nearly everything interesting, so I waited.

"I mean some things you have to take as a matter of faith, but that doesn't mean you suspend all critical thinking and ignore huge bodies of scientific evidence," she said.

I nodded in agreement.

"Creation could just be an analogy for the moment when mankind became sentient," she continued. "Couldn't it be that God breathed consciousness into us rather than literal life?"

I thought for a second and decided that wasn't too bad of an idea.

"So what interests you about evolution?" I asked, steering her back to the original topic.

"It's amazing enough that all this diversity evolved from just a few, or maybe one organism," she continued. "But when you think about the complexity of our systems, it's just overwhelming. The brain, for example. Or the eye—it is thought that it evolved from a patch of light sensitive cells."

"I've always thought that seemed absurd," I said.

She looked at me quizzically. "Really?"

I knew that evolution made perfect sense. Natural selection can be seen in action today. But certain aspects of it were just unbelievable. I struggled for how to articulate what I thought about it. Suddenly, I thought of an analogy.

"Let's say I wanted to start the process to grow another arm on our backs a million years from now," I said. "Is there something I could consciously do to bring it about?"

She shook her head in acknowledgement of the obvious.

"So then how can an unconscious process like selection start with a patch of light sensitive cells, evolve that into a ball, connect it to the brain via cords, grow lenses in there, and make it see?"

"I don't know," she said. "But it happened."

"Just because we have eyes, doesn't mean that's how it happened," I said. "I know that's our best theory, but it's just hard to swallow—for me, anyway. As they say, what good is half an eyeball?"

Jill smiled.

"I'm well aware that just because I can't see how it could happen doesn't mean it didn't happen," I continued. "But it's beyond incredible if you ask me though."

Jill seemed like a different person since the last philosophical conversation we'd had. I sensed that she was in a much better place mentally, much less fragile. So I asked her a question that I'd been curious about since the last time we went down this road: "Jill, as a doctor, isn't religious faith a little incompatible with your scientific training? Scientifically, much of religion is absurd."

"Like what?" she asked immediately.

"Jesus rising from the dead, for one. Scientifically speaking, people don't rise from the dead. The flood—there isn't enough water in our entire earth/atmosphere system to submerge all the land masses. Jonah spending three days in the belly of a whale. All the miracles."

"Don't you think a god who could create the universe could temporarily suspend the scientific laws he created in order to accomplish something?" she replied.

"Yes, I do," I replied. "But then I would also have to allow for Santa Claus, the Easter Bunny, and the Tooth Fairy too because, theoretically, God could create all those things."

"That's where faith comes in," she said. "I believe God could and did suspend the laws to accomplish things that were needed in his plan."

After a few moments of thought, I replied: "I don't really understand faith."

"I'll bet you have faith in all sorts of things," she responded.

I shot her a skeptical look. She mentioned that I used satellites in my work and believe that the pictures they send actually are from space, but I don't really know. I get a burger from a restaurant and have faith that it's beef and not dog meat. Really, any understanding or belief in history requires a modicum of faith, according to Jill.

"But I believe in those things because I have no reason to doubt them, which is because they are plausible," I responded. "I am willing to believe things that I don't know for certain about as long as they are plausible. A guy spending three days in the belly of a whale and coming out alive, just isn't plausible. So I have absolutely no reason to believe that. There is no reason for the engineers to lie to me about weather satellites and it is plausible that we sent up those satellites and they're sending down photos."

Jill just nodded.

"Are you feeling better about your faith than last time we talked about this?" I asked.

She nodded.

"I'm glad," I said.

"Since you're on the subject of interests, you know what interests me?" Jeff chimed in as he fiddled with the cables and cleats on the mast. We had forgotten that he was there. He didn't wait for us to respond. "We all know that nothing can escape a black hole, even light. And nothing travels faster than light. So how does gravity act on objects outside the black hole if it cannot escape it?"

Neither Jill nor I responded. That was indeed amazing.

"They say that space is warped around big bodies, like a bowling ball on a trampoline," Jeff continued. "It's hard to imagine how space could be warped. What does that even mean?"

Jill, ignoring Jeff's rhetorical question, settled back into her seat. A serious look came over her, as if deciding how best to say something weighty. I hoped it was more about evolution.

"What are you going to do if no one is home when you get there? Or worse, they're all dead?" she asked.

Over time, my skin had thickened from the inside out, so that such lines of questioning stung less than at first. I studied her expression and it contained not a hint of remorse for having asked such a thing, but her face winced and eyes squinted in painful anticipation of what she expected to hear.

"Jump off a bridge, I guess," I replied. "And I'm not sure that their not being there would be worse than just finding them dead, other than it would give me hope of finding them again. But I'm deathly afraid of what their absence would mean for them."

"What would it mean, necessarily?"

"Nothing necessarily. But it would suggest that they had been captured or at least that they were out there somewhere where they could be captured. I assume capture would be a fate worse than death."

"Maybe not. Maybe they just took up with the neighbors or friends and went off somewhere safe."

"I don't know where that would be, and, anyway, I told Kate to hunker down there with her parents and ride it out."

"Does she always do exactly what you tell her?"

"Rarely."

"Then you don't know. Why don't you just assume the best until you find out otherwise?"

"Human nature."

The last of Vancouver Island scrolled slowly by to port, barely visible. We stayed close to the shore the entire way down the coast, but decided to back off a little as we closed in on civilization.

The wind had remained uncharacteristically calm, and it took us three excruciatingly long days to travel the length of Vancouver Island.

Despite being summer, it was cold enough for snow every night, and then it warmed up enough to change the snow to rain during the day. The snow never accumulated on shore because of the salty air, but the landscape turned white not far above the beach. The gray sky never broke, even when the precipitation stopped.

Jeff continued to stare up at the new mast, its tan wood quickly darkening in the damp sea air.

"It seems to be holding up," he said, turning to us. "We need to discuss our passage through the strait and sound and where our drop points are going to be."

He went to the helm and produced a nautical chart of the Strait of Juan de Fuca and Puget Sound and spread it out before us. The wind lifted the edge he could not control, but Jill grabbed hold and restrained it.

"Obviously we're going through the strait," he said, pointing at the channel between the north Washington Coast and Vancouver Island labeled Strait of Juan de Fuca.

"The narrowest point is at the west entrance to the strait, and it is almost twelve miles," Jeff said. "We should be able to stay out of trouble from the shore at that distance, and it's pretty much uninhabited out there anyway. But that doesn't address what kind of traffic we might run into on the water. There might be all kinds of people streaming out of there. We'll just have to deal with whatever comes up."

"I've been to Port Angeles," I interjected. "You can see all the way to the Canadian side."

"Still, six miles is a helluva distance to be able to see our little boat," Jeff continued. "The first major constriction we come to is Admiralty Inlet, between Port Townsend and Whidbey. It is less than four miles across."

"Luckily, it's also not very inhabited," I said.

"Once we get inside the sound, we're going to need lots of luck. At best, we will never be more than three miles from land on one side or another. We'll try to stay closer to the unpopulated side—whichever that is, west side, mostly, I guess—but we should all keep watch the whole time."

Jeff paused, staring at the map. He rubbed his chin and then looked up.

"And we're starting to run low on fuel," he continued.

"Low on fuel?" questioned Jill.

"I just dumped in the last can this morning. We've been motoring a lot."

"But that still leaves us with a hundred gallons, right?" I asked.

"Yes. We will be fine getting to where we are going, but if we want to go anywhere else, we need to conserve. We'll get at best a hundred and fifty hours out of that which is about six days. You know as well as I do that it can be too calm to sail for days in the Puget Sound."

"I'm sure we can find some gas somewhere," Jill interjected.

"Maybe," Jeff and I replied simultaneously.

I continued the thought: "There is probably a lot of fuel left out there. But if the power is off, and it seems that it is, we will have a hard time getting at it."

We sat in silence for a few minutes, and then Jeff continued: "When we round the south end of Whidbey, it gets really tight."

"South end of Whidbey?" I questioned. "We can't go up the east side. Mukilteo and Everett are right there on the mainland, and they are heavily populated areas. Or were."

"But if we go around the north end and then back around the go south it will take an extra day. Not to mention that Deception Pass if far narrower than the southern route. This is the best way to Langley."

"You can just drop me off at the old Marina north of the Bush Point lighthouse. It's pretty old and rickety, but it's deep enough, and there will hardly be anyone over there."

Jeff slid his finger around the map as he scanned for Bush Point. He found it on the western shore of the island.

"But it's gotta be five, six miles to Langley from there."

"Ten, actually, but I'll hoof it. After coming all this way, I am not going to risk getting us killed before I ever set foot on the damned island!"

"There is one other question," I continued. "How are we supposed to know if Seattle has been nuked?"

"Ah, I think we have that covered," Sonny said as he emerged to join the conversation. He carried a small wooden box with a speaker dangling from the side by wires. He sat beside me with a satisfied look.

"We built this homemade Geiger counter when we were on Gilligan's Island," Jeff said.

"What? How?" I asked confusedly.

"You remember when my phone kept going dead?" Sonny asked.

I nodded.

"Well, it turns out I have one of the test phones for project Tattle-Tale."

"What the hell is project Tattle-Tale?"

Sonny looked at Jeff. Jeff explained that it was a project started by the Department of Homeland Security to fit cell phones with tiny solid state radiation detectors. When the phone detected radiation, it would call the DHS to alert them and then they would track the phone. They were trying to head off a terrorist packing around a dirty bomb.

"I've never heard of it," I said.

"Of course not. They had to keep it under wraps because terrorists wouldn't want to carry around little government Geiger counters, now would they?"

"They were in the testing phase of Project Tattle-Tale," Jeff continued. "And they put the devices in about one out of every hundred new phones. The call back to DHS went unnoticed during normal phone usage. The user could never detect the transmission unless they knew what to look for. But Sonny's phone kept going dead way too soon after being charged, especially when it wasn't being used. I never thought anything about it. But we got to talking with some of the engineers on Gilligan's Island, and we put two and two together.

I lowered my head. "So that means we *were* in the radiation during the ash storm!"

"Yes," interjected Jill. "But it must not have been much of a dose or we would surely know it by now. None of us has any symptoms of radiation poisoning."

"So then you built this thing?" I asked. "What does it have to do with the phone?"

"Well, we couldn't use Sonny's phone as a detector because until it made the connection with the DHS, it wouldn't reset. So we'd never know if it was detecting new radiation or still trying to call on the first detection. The engineers on the island knew what to look for so we took apart the phone, figured out which parts were which, and made our own crude Geiger counter. He motioned to the box on his lap."

"How do you know if it works?" I asked.

He switched it on, adjusted the speaker, and it started making a series of clicks. I became nervous.

"Don't worry," he said. "It's just background radiation. It's normal. We'll know we're heading into radiation when the rate of the clicks increases."

I suddenly felt very lightheaded and weak. My head felt like a shaken compass suddenly righted, the ball rolling around inside, trying to find up. I felt my consciousness began to slip away. Jill and Jeff took hold of my arms.

"You need to take it easy," Jill said. "You've had a very serious head injury. And I don't know about you walking all the way to…"

"I'm fine!" I said as I forcibly freed my arms, determined to remain conscious. "I'm just tired, and I need to lie down."

. . .

DAY 52 AT SEA, ENTRANCE TO THE STRAIT OF JUAN DE FUCA, NORTHWEST WASHINGTON STATE (DEAD RECKONED POSITION: 48.4°N, 124.8°W)

I awakened the next day to yet another pounding headache.

I rolled over and noticed that the boat pitched in a way that I had not experienced before. The boat rolled from side to side, but there was no bow to stern motion—we felt like a boat adrift. Suddenly concerned that something was wrong, I sprung out of my bunk and nearly hit my head on Sonny's bunk. I had to hold onto the counter, not because I was unsteady on the sea—I surely was by then—but because I was still dizzy from having gotten up too fast.

I needed aspirin badly but didn't dare ask for any. They were already suspicious enough of my health. They would insist on going with me when we got to Whidbey, and I couldn't have that. I rummaged quietly around the cabin but found nothing. Then I remembered Jill putting the first aid kit under her bunk near the head and subsequently and discreetly found what I was after.

I downed four of the pills and sat dizzily on the edge of the bunk. Sometimes I could convince myself that I was getting better, until I tried to do anything. I worried that I was dying. What then? Jeff knew where Kate's parent's house was, and I felt confident that he would check it out, even if I died. I considered talking to them all about it, but then they would know for sure that I was ill, and I would become a burden. I absolutely did not want Jeff helping me at the expense of his own family.

I emerged topside in a fog, literally and figuratively. Jeff had put the RY in park, which was some sort of maneuver that forced the sail, hull, and rudder to produce force in opposite directions. So long as the wind and current remained fairly constant, the boat hardly moved. I had never tried it, but I'd seen Jeff do it twice, including this one. So there we sat, stuck in a fog bank. Strangely, that was our first and only encounter with the ubiquitous North Pacific fog on our entire journey. The parking maneuver put us almost head on into the southwest wind, but it was the northwest swell that rolled the boat oddly from starboard to port, which was what I had sensed below.

I found my three shipmates sitting at the helm talking. We were somewhere near the entrance to the strait, but there was no way we could attempt to enter with such low visibility and no instruments. It would have been suicide, and there were doubtlessly many ships on the sea floor below that could attest to the danger.

· · ·

DAY 54 AT SEA, ENTRNACE TO THE STRAIT OF JUAN DE FUCA, NORTHWEST WASHINGTON STATE (DEAD RECKONED POSITION: 48.4°N, 124.8°W)

Two days, several arguments, and about forty secret aspirin later, it began to rain. The wind switched to easterly, and we watched the fog retreat west, like a curtain pulled offshore at the speed of the wind.

No more than three miles to our southeast, the white and orange Cape Flattery Lighthouse stepped out of the mist and stood silent and dark atop the rocky and battered Tatoosh Island. Swells grew into giant breakers that hammered the weathered ocean side bedrock of the island, while much tamer waves lapped at the vegetated shores of the inland side. The island was dotted with no more than a half dozen trees, and save for the gnarled, bushy slopes on the leeward side, only hearty grasses survived among the tattered rock outcroppings. Of the trees that managed to cling to life on the rocky island, most were twisted and bent toward the east, permanently deformed, as if shying knowingly away from millions of years of grizzly weather.

A scant half mile past Tatoosh Island loomed the far northwestern corner of mainland Washington State. I had been there as a child and never forgot the secrets it held. As I stood on the cliffs and looked down upon craggy channels filled with tiny tree-topped islets and crystal clear water and over slung by trees growing straight out of the dripping cliffs, I wondered how many people had ever ventured out that far to witness such beauty. I understood then why God put such treasures at the ends of the earth rather than right in the middle to be trampled upon and ignored.

We passed miles of breathtaking scenery, numb and nearly ambivalent to it. No one stirred as we passed the tiny fishing village of Sekiu where, as a child, I took my first chartered fishing trip with my father. I failed to set the hook on my first bite as I daydreamed about the foreign country of Canada just on the other side, and it got away. I caught a King later, but my father didn't miss another opportunity to remind me to pay attention during the rest of the trip.

We passed Crescent Beach, where, in summers passed, the waters of the protected Crescent Bay almost certainly shimmered beautifully in the fading sunlight as teenagers from Port Angeles lay on blankets on the course, gray sand and had their first kiss. We passed Crescent Lake, a lake so deep and frigid that local legend maintained that the lake was actually connected to the strait through a channel at the bottom. Folklore was that huge sea creatures had been seen in the lake at night and that a subterranean connection to the ocean was the only explanation. We passed the locations of numerous Bigfoot sightings, and we never saw a thing.

We turned our make-shift Geiger counter on only occasionally, to save the batteries. It sampled nothing but background radiation.

We drew ever closer to a place I knew well: Port Angeles. The mountains jutting up in the background reminded me of my friend Sean McMasters and his parent's ranch up there. Last I heard, he was in the military and working toward being in the Special Forces or an Army Ranger or something. If he did indeed bug out to the ranch like he said, he was probably well equipped.

Suddenly we saw the first sign of life—a campfire on the beach. Do we even call them campfires anymore? People weren't out camping, they were surviving. Still, no one stirred.

A tanker had run aground on Ediz Hook Sand Spit, the tiny sliver of sand that enclosed Port Angeles Harbor. It leaned heavily and lifelessly to starboard. A massive, rusty anchor hung motionless, under its own weight, from a hole near the bow. The links in its massive chain looked large enough for a man to walk through. Massive shipping containers, the kind normally filled with useless crap from China, lay on the beach and in various states of submersion in the strait. The contents of the single container that someone had managed to get open lay strewn over the beach.

As we rounded the spit, we came face to face with our first inhabitants. A large motorboat roaring out of Port Angeles Harbor slowed to watch us. We did not have time to pull our weapons or, perhaps subconsciously, we thought better of it. Women and children scattered as men raced to the gunwale and trained their weapons on us. They watched us carefully as they passed not fifty yards in front and then to our port. They finally lowered their weapons when they were safely past and went back to their families. They probably could have taken us over were they so inclined, but they apparently meant us no harm—however, they certainly allotted us no trust. We allowed ourselves to hope that civilization was still civilized; maybe there would be lots of people like us.

Suddenly we were downwind of Port Angeles and got our first whiff of death, North American style. The smell of rotting flesh is as unmistakable as it is indescribable—but once smelled, it is not forgotten. The intensity of the odor built as we moved further downwind of the town.

Sonny brought me out of thought with a tap to the shoulder.

"Here," he said as he handed me a vial of menthol jelly. He mimicked rubbing his finger under his nose as if to demonstrate the procedure. I declined, reasoning that I had better get used to it.

We made it to the town of Sequim just as dark settled over the area. Being that close, I desperately wanted to continue, but it was just too dangerous at night. The wind died down considerably and shifted to the northeast, a direction which should keep the fog at bay. There was definitely a bite to the wind, though, as we anchored on the tip of Sequim's Dungeness Spit. The five mile long sand spit is one of the longest in the world and was said to be growing by more than ten feet per year. We chose that location because it was over two miles from the mainland, afforded a three hundred and sixty degree view for security, and there was only one way in.

I chose first watch that night because I wanted to be fresh as we arrived at my drop-off point the following day. I had been out on that spit before. It was not unusual to be alone out there since Sequim was a town of only about 5,000 people, and the weather, among other things, was certainly not conducive to a sunset walk on the spit. But I found the darkness of Sequim, Port Angeles, and Victoria on the Canadian side unsettling, to say the least. The light from the cities normally bathed the area in a romantic orange glow, but that night was pitch black.

. . .

DAY 55 AT SEA, DUNGEONESS SPIT, SEQUIM, WASHINGTON STATE (DEAD RECKONED POSITION: 48.18°N, 123.09°W)

The wind picked up and rain began to fall toward the end of my watch. By the time I awakened in the morning, it had changed to snow and blanketed our decks with six inches of wet, gray slush. A cold front had passed in the night which broke the low cloud deck and brought out the striking Olympic Mountains to our south. The snow blanketed the town, the surrounding countryside, and the mountains, but it stopped abruptly at the high tide mark on the beach.

Now I knew something was wrong with the climate. Summer snow in Alaska was one thing, but it rarely snowed at sea level in Washington State during the winter, much less in August. A ridiculously cold northwest wind buffeted the decks, eroding the snow at the edges and chopping the strait furiously. If not for the ashen gray nuclear overcast tens of miles above us, it would have been a beautiful winter morning. The mountains jutted up to nearly 8,000 feet and towered over the scene, appearing much closer than normal under the high ceiling. Small lens-shaped clouds capped the peaks. I had not realized how much I missed the mountains until that moment. I felt like I was home.

The days always get shorter in August, but the shortening was accelerating at an alarming rate. We figured there may be no light at all by the beginning of winter. The stratospheric debris was thickening, or at least becoming more uniform. The indistinguishable sun occasionally lightened a portion of the sky on its daily trek, but it never came out, even partially. We wondered what it looked like in places less prone to inclement weather, like deserts. Did the sun come out there, even briefly?

We hurriedly prepared the boat to weigh anchor. I saw movement in my periphery but ignored it—the wind had been moving the snow around on the deck since I awakened. It moved again and caught my attention. I glanced over and jumped as a young boy, maybe seven or eight years old stood on the spit not thirty feet away. His tattered, filthy clothing hung loosely over his emaciated body and flapped in the wind. The skin on his face stretched tightly over his bones. He tucked his mangled left arm up under his armpit like a chicken wing. His right arm extended stiffly in front of him with the hand at its end clamped to a hiking stick. A streamer on the top of the stick fluttered off to his right. He looked like little shaman standing there staring blankly at us.

I yelled to him, but he just stared. This alerted the others and they gathered on deck. The boy's eyes darted among the four of us, and then settled on Jill. At the moment she called to him, he bolted. He sprinted back down the spit toward town, carrying the stick in his right arm like a javelin, its rust colored pointy end forward. Jill lunged toward the rail as if she were going after him. Sonny grabbed her and held on.

"Let me go!" She cried.

"Jill!" Jeff said as he put his hand on her shoulder. "You can't save the world."

"But I can save him!"

"No you can't," I said. "We came here for a reason, and it wasn't to spend half the day chasing a wild boy around Sequim."

"Besides, maybe he's not alone," Sonny weighed in. "Maybe he came out here to lure us into a trap."

Jill began to cry as we pulled up the anchor. The boy had stopped a half-mile down the spit and stood looking back at us.

"He looked like Zach when he was that age," Jill said hoarsely, through the lump in her throat.

18

DAY 55 AT SEA, ADMIRALTY INLET, WASHINGTON STATE (DEAD RECKONED POSITION: 48.16°N, 122.73°W)

We all stood watch as we ventured back into the strait and turned toward Admiralty Inlet. Jeff piloted and watched our makeshift Geiger counter, I scanned starboard, Sonny port, and Jill watched for anyone coming up on our stern.

Despite our fuel problems, we decided to motor, reasoning that a boat under sail presented a much larger and more obvious target than necessary. The RY could have easily gone unnoticed from shore with no sails but would have been visible for miles with several hundred square feet of sails flapping in the wind.

We had not talked about it in detail, but we all thought about it. It was pretty clear that there had not been a major nuclear strike on Seattle, or we surely would have seen some evidence by now. We turned the box on about once an hour, and it clicked normally each time. It was certainly possible that terrorists had set off a small nuclear device or dirty bomb nearby, but they were more likely to choose the major population centers—downtown Seattle, wealthy suburbs like Bellevue, crowded stadiums, or the like —not the places we were going. Such a small scale strike could have gone unnoticed by us.

On the other hand, if a major adversary like China or Russia had struck, they would have gone for the military targets like the nuclear submarine base at Bangor, the Whidbey Island Naval Air Station, or Fort Lewis, and they would have done so with much larger ordnance. We likely would have noticed some sign of that by now, especially if they went for the naval air station, since we were within a few miles of it. Even though a large 100 megaton nuclear warhead would produce noticeable destruction only within the first few miles from the blast itself, we couldn't imagine not seeing some signs, or at least some radiation, assuming our Geiger counter was working correctly.

Of course, except for the poor souls near ground zero, the blast itself wasn't the issue; it was the radioactive fallout. Lethal fallout could spread for tens of miles downwind. Luckily, we were in the climatological downwind location for only one such site: Bangor. We had to take the chance, and if we had any luck at all, the wind would have been from the west or north on D-day, sparing our route entirely. What a queer thought: hoping that the fallout went toward the more populated areas rather than over our intended path. We had our little device, and even though we didn't know for sure if it was working, it was better than nothing. I'm not sure what we would have done if it had started detecting radiation. Turn back?

It took less than three hours to reach Point Wilson, and like so many before it, its lighthouse stood dark and silent. As we rounded Point Wilson, Port Townsend came into view just a couple of miles to the south. I laughed out loud at the sight of it.

The rest of the crew listened intently as I recounted the time I talked my friend, Sean, into jumping off the ferry boat as it approached the dock in Port Townsend, or PT as it was called by the locals.

As best friends, Sean and I had a lot of history, and most of it revolved around me talking him into doing something stupid. I loved to push his buttons, and because of his competitive nature, it worked nearly every time.

One summer day before our senior year in high school, we rode the ferry back from Whidbey Island. As it approached the dock in PT, I began to play on his machismo and told him that there was no way he could jump off the ferry—he'd drown because of the currents, or get caught by the cops, or beat up by the ferry staff—all things that I knew would rile him up. The next thing

I knew (and to the utter dismay of the girls we were with), his shirt and shoes came off, and there was a splash twenty feet below. I timed my ribbing just right, so he actually could make it to the dock. After all, he was one of my best friends, and I didn't want him to die. But beyond that, if he drowned, what would I do to entertain myself? I looked over the rail in time to see him smile, flip me the bird, and then turn and swim for shore. As I knew would be the case, the crew didn't catch him. He was on shore and disappeared into the streets of downtown PT before the boat even docked.

I'll never forget the sight of a soaking wet, half naked teenager in his underwear hurrying gingerly up the barnacle-laden beach toward town. To make matters funnier, when he reached the top of the ladder onto the bulkhead, he mooned us and the rest of the stunned ferry passengers.

Of course, we were questioned, but we just told the crew that we didn't know him. We passed police cars hurrying toward the scene and picked him up outside the high school football stadium a few minutes later.

That sort of competitiveness served him well though. He got a full ride football scholarship to Oregon State in our junior year—practically unheard of back then. Unfortunately for Sean, he never reached his potential academically or athletically. Two weeks after we graduated high school, Sean was hit by a car while training for his first college football season. He died on the way to the hospital, but they were able to bring him back. He was in a coma for two months, and it took him nearly two years to fully recover from the accident. By that time, any thought of playing college football was long gone. Oregon State vowed to honor his scholarship anyway, but he never attended a single class. He went into the military instead—at least somebody still valued his physical skills.

The crew of the RY got a kick out of the story, and it was nice to have something to laugh about.

The PT harbor was quiet, and nothing moved. Small columns of smoke rose from the beaches, but compared to the normal hustle and bustle of the harbor to which I was accustomed, it was a veritable ghost town.

Besides the ferry that normally crisscrossed the harbor, activity on the water generally included sightseeing boats coming and going, fishing vessels bringing in the days catch, ships hauling away various paper products from the PT Paper Company, whose smoke stacks hauntingly spewed no smoke that day—a sight I had never witnessed before. You could almost always see cranes swinging mechanically about as they worked to refurbish warships on Indian Island, a naval base nestled between the Olympic Peninsula and Marrowstone Island to the east. There was always traffic in town or people scattered about in pleasure craft. Something, anything! PT Harbor was like a little San Francisco nestled into a tiny harbor in a secluded portion of northwest Washington. We heard nothing but an eerie silence.

Port Townsend's claim to fame was that it was almost a huge town. Assuming that, as the first safe and significant port between the Pacific Ocean and the vast and productive Puget Sound to the south, legions would flock to the city as the region grew, the city's founders decided to build a big city. I once read on a placard on one of the public docks in PT that it was built for a "large population that never came." I assumed that it failed because of its remoteness. A similar harbor on the east side would have thrived. In fact, one did. It was called Seattle.

With Mount Baker looming to the east, we passed Port Townsend uneventfully and entered the Triangle of Fire. The Triangle of Fire was the impenetrable military triangle formed between Forts Worden and Flagler on the west side of Admiralty Inlet, and Fort Casey on Whidbey Island. The three forts were constructed in the late 1800s to defend the Puget Sound from foreign invaders. They existed in a geologic miracle of sorts—at almost exactly three and a half miles between all the forts and with nearly sixty degree angles at each corner, the triangle of fire was as close to a perfect equilateral triangle as nature could provide.

All three forts were built on bluffs hundreds of feet above the beaches and sported a variety of armaments. The Triangle of Fire so completely discouraged unauthorized entry that none of the forts ever had to fire a shot at an enemy. For reasons similar to those that deterred nineteenth and twentieth century commanders, we worried about entering the military choke point.

Admiralty Inlet remained as the only obstacle between me and my point of disembarkation. Despite its well-earned reputation for giving sailors trouble, Admiralty Inlet remained relatively calm on that day, almost as if in deference to our long, hard voyage. A large quantity of water from the Puget Sound basin flowed through Admiralty Inlet during tidal changes, and in calm waters we might have made the final ten miles between Port Townsend and Bush Point in an hour and a half. But naturally, on that day it took three. It seemed as if literally all the water tried to escape from the Puget Sound at the exact time we were trying to enter it.

We remained alert as we slipped through the narrow channel, our tension growing by the moment. I felt particularly apprehensive, not just fear of the unknown, but a dread of it, as we putted south along Whidbey Island toward my drop off point.

In contrast to the lushly vegetated and comparatively gentle slopes on the west side of Admiralty Inlet, the slopes to the east side on Whidbey Island are barren and stark. From a distance, Whidbey's cliffs look like sand and extend several hundred feet above the beaches and run essentially the length of the island. Upon closer inspection, the cliffs are alternating layers of sand, soil, and rock extending back millions of years—a veritable play land for the geologist. Huge trees of all variety—Douglas Fir, Western Hemlock, Lodgepole and Shore Pine, Western Red Cedar, and even Madrona—teeter on the edge of the cliff. Sometimes—usually after heavy rainstorms—large chunks of the cliffs come down and take the trees with them and a new generation of vegetation takes its rightful place as guardian of the cliffs. The evidence for such calamities is visible intermittently along the beach—as fresh scratches down the cliff face lead to out-of-place mounds of earth and debris resting on an otherwise uniformly smooth beach. It may take decades or centuries for the tide to remove the evidence, but it will, and then more will fall, and it too will be removed.

I started to feel flush as we edged to within a mile of the Bush Point Light, or what used to be a light. It was nothing more than a decrepit old shell of a lighthouse, its light not having worked for as long as I could remember. Rather than standing as a sentry against shipwrecks, it was literally a relic in someone's back yard.

We took turns scanning the beach and surrounding cliffs for any sign of life or more to the point, any sign of trouble. Jeff looked for a long time at our landing point, a dysfunctional old dock attached to what used to be a busy marina. Adjacent to the old marina was a relatively new facility with a boat launch and a new dock designed for small recreational boats rather than larger fishing vessels of decades past. It was in much shallower water and only extended about twenty feet from the shore—not useful for our purposes.

Something like panic crept from my groin up my back and into my brain as Jeff turned on the Geiger Counter. Click, click, click—normal, background radiation.

After a half hour of observation, we made the executive decision to land.

My palms began to sweat and I sensed my consciousness slipping again. "Look!" I exclaimed, with the dual purpose of distracting myself and heading off the coming emotional storm. "I'm not one for long good-byes anyway, but I think we had better say our good-byes now. I am going to get off this boat and scramble for cover as fast as I can, and you guys need to get the hell back out to sea ASAP."

"Agreed," said Jeff, as he approached me.

He extended his right hand which I grasped and shook. We gave each other a half hug with our left arms, and I said to Jeff: "I can't tell you how much I hope all is well with Brenda and the kids."

"You don't have to. It's the same thing I feel for you and Kate. Please be careful. I know we haven't discussed this, but I hope we can come back this way when we get things together. This will probably be safer than Bainbridge."

"You are welcome here any time," I said, sounding obligatory, but fully meaning it.

"You know," I said "I haven't really thought much about what I'm going to do after I find them. If they're all fine, what then? I guess we'll stay around her parents' house as long as it's safe, but I've already been thinking about the next step."

Jeff looked at me with curiosity.

"I told you about my friend Sean. I'd bet my last dollar that he's holed up at his parent's place up on the Olympic Peninsula. And if he is, he'll be well prepared. If all else fails, I'm going to head up there to check it out."

Jeff and Jill all stared at me skeptically. None of us knew what to say or do.

"Let's just say right now that I will try to give you a month to get back to Kate's house, but after that, don't count on me being there."

"Agreed," said Jeff. "One month, starting now."

Jill stood stoically looking at me. I didn't know what to make of it.

"This isn't right," she said. "You are in no condition to go alone."

"I'll be fine," I said.

"Bull shit!" Sonny exclaimed as he walked up behind us, and dropped his backpack.

"What do you think you are doing?" I asked.

"I'm going with you."

"The hell you are!" I said, more sternly than I had spoken to anyone in a long time.

"You need my…"

"No I don't! They do," I said, pointing to Jeff and Jill. "They need you to help get them to the end, wherever that is. This is as far as I need to go. The rest is on me. You've given me more than I could have ever asked for, and I'm not letting you abandon them for me."

"There's nothing you can do to stop me. I'm going."

I grabbed Sonny by the back of the head and pulled him toward me.

"Listen," I said through gritted teeth. "I know this island well. I don't need your help. I don't know what I'll find, but I do know that they need you more than I do. I appreciate what you want to do, but it's not right. You guys go down and get Brenda and the kids and then beat ass back up here. I'll be waiting, and then we'll all be back together. Jeff knows where to go. They can't sail the boat by themselves and protect themselves at the same time. I can walk alone."

I looked at him as a brother might look at his beloved sibling. I let out a sigh, relaxed, and then spoke calmly. "Sonny, seriously, I want you to stay with them more than I want your help. Please don't make this harder than it needs to be."

"But…"

"I'll kick your ass if I have to!" I yelled. "Seriously!" I punched him solidly in the chest.

He almost laughed. "You're in no condition to fight me."

"But I will, and then what condition will I be in? Will I be in a condition to find Kate and the kids? Do you want that on your head?"

Jill began to cry.

"That's it!" I said harshly. "This is bullshit. We don't have time for this. You are not going, and that's final."

Sonny looked at Jeff and then Jill. Neither had any clue what to say or do. Finally, Sonny relented. "Fine."

"Listen," I said, to all of them. "You are the finest people I have ever known. I love you all. You are like family to me. Do what you have to and come back. We need each other. We can get through this, damn it! Let's go." I turned away, partly to avoid bursting into tears.

"Why don't we all go?" Jill asked.

"No way! You can't expect Jeff to put off his…"

"Now wait a minute!" Jeff cut in. "Don't speak for me."

"Shut up! All of you. I almost got us killed in the storm, and there is no way I'm letting you do this. I don't need any of you. Just let me off this fucking boat!"

They all stared at me, stunned and hurt.

"I don't mean that. Come on. We know what the plan was, now let's stick to it. I'm fine. I've thought through every option over the last two months, and this is the only way."

"All right," said Jeff. "But we're going to wait and watch just off shore. If we see any trouble, we're coming back in."

"Fine, but I'll be out of here and up over the ridge in ten minutes. There won't be anything to see."

They all moved in for one last group hug. Jill buried the side of her face in my cheek, and her silent tears trickled down my jaw and onto my neck where they cooled in the wind.

Sonny watched the depth over the bow as Jeff eased the RY up to the old dock. Jill scanned the surrounding homes with the binoculars as I prepared to jump ship. The pilings were still strong and in good shape, but the cracked and weathered decking clung intermittently to the few joists that remained. It didn't look safe at all, but there was no other place to disembark.

We bumped against the dock in a place where no decking existed. Jeff gunned the motor and boat lurched forward to a safer place. I jumped over the side and onto the dock. I felt the boards strain under my weight, and I stumbled forward as my sea legs tried to compensate for a pitch that no longer existed. The weight of my pack counterbalanced my stumble and allowed me to stay on the dock.

I heard Jill yell that they all loved me and to be safe, but I was too focused on my balance to respond. I heard the motor purr heartily as the RY labored back into the waves and away from Whidbey Island. As I looked up, all three of them watched me, focused selflessly not on their own peril, but on mine.

I leaped from board to board without much thought as to whether they would hold. I reached the old building at the beginning of the dock and jumped over to a concrete wall that ran along the edge. I ran the length of the building and jumped.

At 2:06 PM on day 55 I landed on the western shore of Whidbey Island, Washington.

I fell forward on my elbows, and my face hit the sand. I held there for just a moment, digging my fingers into the sand and feeling the earth. In that split second, all my efforts and troubles and pain and fatigue ran through my body and poured onto the beach and vanished. I made it.

19

WHIDBEY ISLAND, WASHINGTON

I stood, and suddenly the stark solitude and my own vulnerability hit me fully. I reached into my jacket and pulled out my pistol. I held it with both hands, close to my shoulder, and pointed up. I sidled up to the building and peered around the corner like some sort of FBI special agent.

I scanned the buildings, and nothing moved. Nothing fluttered in the wind or skipped down the street as might be expected in such a stiff breeze. All loose objects had probably settled into shelter long ago.

With my senses unexpectedly heightened, my ears tuned into the sound of a snaphook on a flagpole halyard banging against its aluminum pole. The hollow sound clanged rhythmically with my heartbeat. Suddenly, I became aware of everything. I heard every sound, felt every vibration, and noticed the slightest movement. I was surprised by the ease with which my body rose to a state of such awareness. Everything felt different and dangerous.

My eyes stopped on a conspicuously small brick building at the end of the boat launch. It had been painted with the ubiquitous tan of the Washington State Parks, and the edges of its aquamarine colored metal roof had already begun the process of oxidation that, without intervention, would unequivocally lead to the building's demise. The building had only two doors, one marked men and the other marked woman. I paused momentarily to consider the oddity of the use of the plural word men and the singular word woman. Between the two doors stood an empty fire extinguisher case, its contents stolen.

Paralyzed by fear and apprehension, I hugged the wall. I noticed placards on the end of the building that cautioned against the use of fireworks and called the user's attention to all manner of plant and animal life that inhabited the park.

Suddenly there was movement in my periphery. I swung the gun around and nearly shot a small crab as it skittered between rocks. I leaned back against the wall and lowered the gun. I breathed deeply, trying to calm myself down. My head throbbed.

I walked along the edge of the old marina building, stopped at the corner, and peered into the parking lot. There were no cars in the lot, and I could see across the way past several houses, where there were also no cars. I saw no sign of life, but I figured that if I had lived there, I wouldn't want anyone to know I was there either.

Between the parking lot and the main road that led away from Bush Point, there stood an old phone booth surrounded by a patch of withering dandelions. The sign across the top said: Whidbey Telecom. The red sheet metal around the bottom of the booth remained intact, but all of the glass had since been removed, probably by rocks. On a whim, I ran to the phone booth, entered and crouched inside.

Cobwebs dangled from every corner of the booth. The phone was an old style coin-operated variety. I picked up the receiver and was stunned to hear a dial tone. I couldn't imagine how the phones were still working with the power so obviously out, but then I remembered that was frequently the case during storms—the telephone companies had their own power generation and energized their own lines. A generator somewhere up the line must still be running, perhaps on its last ounces of fuel. Or maybe things weren't as bad as I had feared.

I hurriedly dialed Kate's Parents' number from memory and heard a few clicks followed by the timeless message:

"We're sorry. Your call can not be completed as dialed. Please check the number and try your call again."

I wondered if I got the number wrong so I dialed the zero for the operator followed by the number for information: same message at both.

I dialed 911 and it said: "All circuits are currently busy. Please try your call again later." Is that really the message they set up for 911, I wondered. In an emergency, I should try my call again later? What if I'm dead later?

I moved back out into the street and scurried to the next house. As I ran fully exposed in the open, I became keenly aware of my lack of training for such a thing. I had no idea how to hold the gun, and I felt very awkward running with it. I tried to mimic the action heroes I'd seen in the movies. What else could I do?

Next to the house, I looked back down Bush Point Road and saw the old light. The path to the light was roped off, and a sign read: "Private beach. No access. Photographs permitted but no trespassing please."

I darted from house to house like a scared mouse. Suddenly, I remembered that an old school friend of Kate's had lived down there. His name was Paul Arondsen, and his family owned a service station on the highway at the top of the hill. Their station, Arondsen Automotive, was the only station in the world, as far as I knew, that still provided full service at the same price as everyone else. Stopping at Arondsen Automotive was like time travel back to the fifties. When you pulled in and ran over the black hose on the ground a loud "ding ding" echoed through the station, and a service boy with a little white cap ran out to help you. "Filler up," I'd say. He'd lean in to look at the gas gauge and say: "Yes sir. What's this, a 78?" The boy scrambled to check your oil, scurried around to sample the pressure in all four tires, and furiously scrubbed the windshield as the numbered wheels on the old pump clicked by. He'd pull a red rag from his pocket to rub off the stubborn bug guts, while looking nervously at the pump. He knew how many gallons every car took—he had to because the old pump would not automatically click off. They wouldn't take tips at Arondsen's, but they never refused the cookies and cakes dropped off by old ladies. If you had time to go inside, there was always something delicious on the counter for the taking. I remember always feeling a little bit of nostalgic sadness as I pulled away.

I approached Paul's house cautiously and walked around back to the garage. I peered through the dirty windows and could make out what looked like an automobile under a cloth but nothing more. I remembered that he restored old cars and thought maybe I could borrow that one.

I went to the house and looked in the back door window. The neighbors were sufficiently far away, so I knocked. After a few seconds, I knocked again. No one answered.

I tested the doorknob and found it unlocked. I cracked the door open and yelled for Paul. Nothing. I hesitated to enter anyone's house unexpectedly. In the current state of affairs, that seemed like a good way to get shot. So I decided to leave well enough alone and went back to the garage. It was locked, but I forced the door open and walked inside. Dust fluttered about as I entered, and some sort of rodent startled me as it ran for cover.

I checked around near the door and workbench and found no keys. He had a great variety of tools which was not surprising given his occupation. The car cover was slightly askew, so I pulled it the rest of the way off and discovered a beautifully restored car. Mint condition. Not a car buff myself, I really didn't know the make and model, but it was not a common car in my experience; definitely some sort of foreign sports car though. I opened the driver side door and got inside. I checked the ignition, glove box, and visor and found no keys. I looked under the seats but still came up empty.

From the driver's seat, I noticed the door at the opposite end of the garage was open. I got out and walked over to investigate. The door had been forced open, and as I came around the right side of the car, I noticed a piece of rubber tubing extending out of the gas tank and lying on the floor.

So much for this car. No gas.

I went back to the house and knocked a few more times. Still no answer, so I decided to go in. The back door opened to the kitchen. As I walked in, I noticed a faint smell of death, which gave me the willies. I yelled hello a few more times, but decided that it was probably in vain.

The small kitchen was tidy, but dust had already accumulated on the surfaces, and the flowery wallpaper had started to peel at the edges and seams. I moved cautiously into the dining room and over to a table where a stack of newspapers sat neatly folded.

I resisted the urge to flip through the papers and instead moved into the living room. Like the kitchen, it was neatly arranged, but cob webs stretched from corners to anything in reach. Photos of Paul's parents adorned the mantle and coffee tables, but I noticed a lack of children or a wife in any of the pictures. As I crossed the room, the smell became worse and seemed to be coming from upstairs. Morbidly curious, I approached the stairs and looked up.

I placed my foot on the first wooden step, and as my weight shifted forward, it creaked and groaned loudly. The hairs on my neck stood up, and I withdrew my foot. Out of fearful habit, I looked behind me and around the room. I yelled out again, and still no one answered. I put aside my fears and climbed the stairs. I had to force myself to ignore the clicking and popping and creaking of the old staircase as I ascended.

The smell increased exponentially as I reached the top of the stairs and moved down the hallway toward a closed bedroom door. Whatever or whomever created that smell was clearly in that bedroom—the other two were empty. I found the door unlocked and slowly opened it. I winced as the hinges creaked like in an old horror movie. I stepped inside, and the unmistakably raw and sharp smell of death hit me, like a sharp spike boring into my sinuses. My eyes began to water, and something like pain rose behind them. I pulled my jacket up over my mouth and nose. It hardly helped.

The old, small bedroom appeared to be the room of his childhood. Why he hadn't moved into the master bedroom, I could not say. In the center of the far wall, a bed stood in front of the primary window. Cobwebs stretched from the ceiling and window corners to the bed posts and onto the corpse lying in the bed. Dust floated by in the air, illuminated by the filtered light.

The staircase suddenly popped behind me, and the sound echoed through the room. I froze, unable to turn to look. The old staircase rebounding from my weight, I hoped. I listened for a few seconds, and nothing happened.

I focused again on the gruesome body. I could not recognize the caved-in face, but it was almost certainly Paul. Something grew on it that reminded me of a chia pet. Suddenly, struck by a fear that I could not name, my testicles pulled up inside me. My hair stood on end again.

Why should I be afraid of a dead body? Every ounce of reason in me suggested that there was nothing there but a lump of rotting flesh. Why should I be any more wary of what lies there than a side of beef in a butcher shop? Perhaps it was what C.S. Lewis called the fear or dread of the numinous, which is not a fear of an object like a corpse but the fear that the numinous may exist. Most of us can live in denial of anything numinous. But if the corpse were to suddenly move, we would be confronted with the reality that such a thing can happen. Suddenly, it would be possible that all the noises you heard as a child really were monsters after all.

Curiously, only a human corpse inflicts such dread. If I happened upon a dead elk, my fear would be limited to the predator that may be nearby and not a worry that it would get up.

I ignored the terror and choked back my last meal and approached the thing. Even upon close up inspection, I could not identify it. My urge was to poke it to verify that it would not move, but I refrained. I went to the closet and pulled out a blanket and draped it over him. A spider scurried back up along a strand of web into the corner from which it had originated.

I looked around the room for anything useful and found his wallet on the chest of drawers. It contained Paul's identification and over $1,000 in cash, which I took, thinking that he wouldn't need it any more. Of course, neither would I, but I didn't know that then, and old habits die hard. I flipped open his cell phone, and it was dead. I considered for a moment that I should say something, but then I decided that I did not know what to say except: "Good bye friend." I feared this would not be the last time I gave someone their last rights. I took his keys and left the room.

I bounded down the stairs two at a time and hustled back through the living room. With the house cleared, I stopped briefly to scan the papers on the dining room table. I picked up the top paper, which was dated about three days after we left Kwaj, the day Paul apparently stopped getting the paper. The headline read: Virus Spreading Rapidly. Tens of Millions Feared Dead. Tip of Iceberg?

I scanned the headlines since they generally told the whole story: Suicide bombers continue to target hospitals; Explosive filled truck rams Houston MTF (Mobile Treatment Facility), detonates; 28 Daycare Centers targeted across nation, hundreds of children murdered; EU Imposes 24-Hr Curfew Over Europe; Bank run triggers lockdown; major interstate fuel lines hit, OPEC stops production, gas to $40!; Societal collapse? President considers martial law; Dow Zero?; China Takes Taiwan In Bloodbath, Says Japan Next; Peacekeepers Leave Africa, Blood Flows, Aid Stops; and on and on it went. One particular article several papers into the stack caught my attention, so I read into it:

Salt Lake City, UT: Extremely low humidity coupled with hot winds and tinder dry forests created the perfect conditions for the latest terrorist strike across the western U.S. on Sunday. Armed with flame throwers, terrorists drove along interstates, highways, and rural roads setting fire to millions of acres of forest across six western states.

Further down the stack another headline described the result: 100 million acres burned, 17 towns destroyed, more threatened.

I kept reading, and it just kept getting worse. The virus spread without restraint and was determined to have been purposely engineered by terrorists. Communication was next to impossible. Commerce stopped. Grocery stores emptied. Israel bombed Iranian Nuclear Facilities. Wildfires raged out of control across the west, and there was no relief in sight. India and Pakistan squared off. Lawlessness prevailed, and the government was helpless to stem the tide. For the first time in its history, "the United States of America, indeed the entire civilized world, teetered on the brink of total collapse" said one editorial.

I suddenly realized that the behavior of all of the world, outside my own little sphere, was as unpredictable as the weather and just as potentially malevolent.

A crashing sound shook the entire house and startled me back to the present. I involuntarily dropped to my knees. Something crashed through the living room window and sent me sprawling for cover from the shattering glass. I cowered in the corner of the dining room. The sound died down as the shards of glass came to rest, and then all was quiet. I peered cautiously around the wall into the living room. A giant tree branch lay motionless, wedged through the window frame and against the floor. I crept to the window and peered through. Nothing moved.

Satisfied that the falling tree had been a natural occurrence, I returned to the table and dug through the remaining papers looking for anything positive. I found one headline: Leaders Ponder Future Of Regional Light Rail. On the margin a small headline told of how the Mariners had swept the NY Yankees and were then in first place in the American League West. A small story toward the bottom of page one said: Experts Warn of Danger Of

Bioterrorism. The paper was dated before Kate and the kids even left Kwaj, which got me moving again.

On my way back through the kitchen, I checked the cupboards for food. A variety of canned goods lined the shelves, but I already had all I could carry. I pocketed a couple of granola bars and chugged a room temperature bottle of water. I opened the refrigerator, and due to the smell, quickly closed it again. The perishables were so far past their shelf lives that they probably would have smelled even if the refrigerator still had power.

Back in the garage, I tried the keys in the vehicle. It turned over a few times and then sat dead. As I suspected, the gas gauge sat on E. I glanced around for a gas can, but obviously any gas cans would have been easier targets than the gas in the car's tank. I wondered why they took the gas but left the car.

The garage contained the usual supplies: camping stove, tent, tools, a broom, a rake—stuff that could be found in most garages—things I thought I could probably use but couldn't carry. Then I noticed an old bicycle hanging from the rafters. I found a step ladder and lifted the bike down. The tires were flat. I rummaged around and located a tire pump and re-inflated the tires.

It suddenly occurred to me that Paul's house had not been rummaged, and, on a whim, I ran back inside. I looked through all the closets, behind picture frames, and under rugs. I finally found a small, portable safe in the closet of the room that served as his office. It was not a gun safe, and I didn't really even know if Paul had owned a gun, but it was worth a try in my estimation.

I took the safe back down to the garage, found a pry bar, hammer, and chisel and spent a few minutes ruining, but not opening, the locking mechanism. I was sure I would never regret having another firearm or more ammunition or money, but it was no use.

I jumped on the bike and road cautiously out into the street. I peddled up the hill as fast as I could, thinking that speed would reduce my chances of being seen, which, in hindsight, was probably about as logical as running through a rainstorm to avoid some of the drops or driving faster to get to a service station before you run out of gas—as if time, not miles, were the enemy. I reached the top of the hill just as the tires went flat again. I cursed myself for not bringing the pump. My legs felt like lead and my head began a new round of pounding, so I jettisoned the bike.

I paused to look out over the water. From atop the hill, I could see the RY motoring south through the channel. I fished out my binoculars. Sonny had Jeff's scope and swept back and forth in my direction. Jill looked through binoculars and seemed to be staring right at me. I waved and she didn't respond. They were only a half mile off shore, but it might as well have been a million—I was a needle in a haystack now. I watched as Jill lowered the binoculars and sat down. She put her head in her hands.

I had never felt so alone nor so terrified.

I set out on foot. The road wound along through the trees, the tops of which, at times, completely closed in overhead and obscured the sky. I stayed close to the ditch and listened for any sound—in particular, the sound of automobiles. I encountered few houses along the first few miles of Bush Point Road, and I approached the ones I did warily. It slowed my progress greatly, but I spent time observing each house before I passed.

In the long stretches between houses I thought of many things, but mostly I thought of my children. I didn't truly appreciate the predicament we were in at that time, but it was clear enough that our lives would never be the same. At a time when women were breaking the glass ceilings all around them, even in the good old boys world of politics, I wondered if my daughters had lost their chance to change the world. I wondered if my son would have the chance to fulfill his dream of playing football. I wondered if any of them would have the chance to go to college or even high school. I wondered if any of them were still alive. Despite the fatigue, the dizziness, the headache, my pace quickened at such thoughts.

The trees quickly thinned and then disappeared as Bush Point Road passed Mutiny Bay. The clearing was wonderful for the homeowners seeking a view of the bay, but bad for a traveler trying to pass undetected. Even though it slowed me down, I decided to walk in the ditches as much as possible because I could see everything from the surface of the road and, therefore, everything could see me on it.

My thoughts went to Kate. What had she gone through in these months? What had she seen? Had she and her parents been able to protect the children? If she was still alive, had she given me up for dead? If so, had she taken another lover for protection, or worse, for love? The thought sickened me. I desperately wanted to hold her, or more to the point, to have her hold me. It had been such a long journey, and I was so tired.

My thoughts suddenly came to present as the reality of my worsening symptoms hit home. As a man suddenly becomes aware of his heartbeat when he feels the slightest pain in his chest, I became aware that I was not well. It was a similar to the resignation one feels when it dawns on him that he's had way too much to drink and that the last two drinks probably aren't even in his bloodstream yet: loss of control imminent, mitigation unknown.

I felt the back of my head, and just as a tongue easily detects the slightest abnormality in the mouth, so did my hand detect the increased swelling, the tenderness, and the dampness of blood. In a wisp of thought, I wondered if maybe I should have let Sonny come with me. I knew the RY was gone and out of reach. I began to panic at the thought of dying alone.

Despite the desperate urge to press on, I had to rest. I intended to lie down for just a minute, but it must have been longer than that—much longer.

20

WHIDBEY ISLAND, WA

As I approached Kate's parent's house from along the beach, I couldn't believe my eyes. Light flooded the house, and smoke rose lazily from the chimney. Kate talked gaily on the phone while her dad sat in his usual chair, watching the Seahawks game. A fully decorated Christmas tree sat in the corner, surrounded by gifts. Waves lapped at the beach, and the sun warmed my skin as I stood there in bewilderment.

I ran to the sliding door and threw it open.

Kate smiled and held up a finger to stall me and then told her caller that she had to go because "he just walked in." Her dad did not even turn to look.

"Well, it took you long enough!" she said. "Where have you been?"

"Where have I been?" I exclaimed. "I've been sailing across the Pacific for the last two months."

She threw her arms around me and gave me the hug and kiss I had longed for. "That's absurd," she said.

"Kids, come out here!" she yelled over my shoulder. "Your dad is here."

The kids! Soothing waves of relief washed over me. I felt as if I floated in the air.

"Daddy!" they screamed running to me and gathering for their hugs.

I suddenly felt the sensation of falling as a strong, sharp pain rose in the back of my head.

"I need something for my head," I told Kate.

"Oh don't be silly," she said. "There's nothing wrong with you. Look!"

She turned and pointed at the mirror. The entire back of my skull was missing. I touched the back of my head, and it felt like cold tofu. I ran my fingers over the ridges of my soft, spongy brain. My fingers began to pick at it. I couldn't control them. Walnut size bits of brain dislodged and dropped into my hand.

Kate's dad turned to look at me. He had no face, bleached white bones stared back at me. "Dinner at eighteen hunnerd?" he asked as his bony lower jaw moved mechanically.

I looked at Kate as panic washed over me.

"See?" She said. "Everything is fine."

"No, really," I said. Kate and the kids began to fade from my vision. I desperately tried to hold the image. Confusion and fear turned to dread.

"Mommy! What's wrong with him?" one of the kids asked. I didn't recognize the voice through the black.

"I told you. It's his head."

It wasn't Kate's voice. The voice was deeper, frightened, frightening. The sounds of their voices echoed as if they were talking through a culvert, but gradually the reflections of sound coalesced as my mind focused.

"Is he going to be all right?" the child asked.

"I don't know."

I sensed the wetness on the back of my head—like a cold patch of drool on a pillow. I opened my eyes and flickering firelight cast picket-fence-like shadows on the wall next to me. Somewhere a door opened, there was a rustling, and then a dull thud like firewood being dropped echoed through the structure.

I quietly tried to move and found that I was tied down. I wriggled against my restraints, and the apparatus upon which I was lying shifted, causing the floor to creak. The people immediately became silent, leaving the irregular crackling of the fire as the only discernible sound.

"Get your brother," the woman whispered.

A pitter-patter of footsteps, and then a distant door opened and closed again.

I heard a turn and click of a knob on a much nearer door. A plane of firelight slowly opened up and spread across the blanket over me. I closed my eyes and tried desperately not to blink.

Realizing that the woman was alone, I began to fight against the restraints and the pain in my head. Light spilled into the room as the woman rushed in with a lantern.

"Please don't do that!" she pleaded. Her long, dirty, frazzled hair made her look like a witch in the light of the lantern.

I managed to get one leg free just as a teenage boy entered the room and pointed a shotgun at my face. "Don't move!" he yelled.

I froze.

"Where am I? What are you doing to me?" I asked as a younger boy entered.

"Oh, I don't know," the woman said in a tone of voice that was part guilty cry and part remorseful whine. She grabbed the younger boy and rushed out.

The older boy stood there and studied me for some time. A handsome boy of maybe seventeen with fine hair clinging in patches to his tightly stretched facial skin—his meager attempt at a beard. I smelled in him more fear than hate.

"Well?" I asked.

The woman rushed in and pushed down the barrel of the shotgun.

"Mother!" exclaimed the boy.

"Stop it! We can't hold him here like this. I'm going to untie him and let him go."

The boy protested that I could be dangerous, that maybe I was one of them.

"I'm not going to hurt anyone," I said. "I promise. I just want to get out of here."

She untied my legs first.

"You're sure you're not going to try anything?" she asked.

"Try anything? What have I ever done to make you think I'd try something?"

"Nothing. It's just, well, you know."

"No I don't, really. By the way, where am I?"

"What do you mean?" asked the older boy.

"I mean, last thing I remember I was walking along the road, and the next thing I know I'm here."

"No, I mean what do you mean you don't know?"

I explained to them why I didn't know what they were talking about, how I had been at sea for two months, out of contact. I pleaded again for the woman to finish untying me.

"We found you in the ditch," said the woman. "We brought you here in hopes that…" her voice trailed off. "Oh, I don't know what we expected."

"You needed help, and you thought maybe I'd help you. Is that it?"

She nodded remorsefully.

"You thought tying me up and holding me prisoner would put you in my good graces?"

"No. No. We… We just don't know what to do," said the woman. "We couldn't just leave you there to die, and we couldn't trust you."

Apparently satisfied at my sincerity, she untied my hands. The older boy remained vigilant but kept the gun lowered. I sat up and rubbed the tightness out of my wrists and flexed my muscles.

"How bad is it?" I asked. "I mean out there." I pointed randomly, having no sense of direction but knowing which way was out.

"Ok, you're free. Now get out!" said the boy.

"Jimmy!" snapped his mother. "He seems ok. Come into the kitchen," she said.

"Mother, I don't think that's…"

She raised her finger, and he stopped talking immediately.

Still feeling light-headed, I walked gingerly out into what she called the kitchen in what appeared to be in a barn. Dust kicked up off the dirt floor as she walked and the ribbed wall of uncovered studs provided little barrier to the cold. An old wood stove sat in the corner with firewood stacked next to it and a pot on top. The blackened wood stove looked as if its fire burned on the outside, and its flue extended through a rough hole cut in the roof.

The younger boy skittered over to a built-in ladder, vaulted up the rungs with monkey-like dexterity, and peered back down over the edge. Jimmy leaned against a chair and watched me suspiciously but he held the shotgun pointed toward the ground. The woman immediately set about to filling a coffee pot and placing it on the stove.

"All we have is warm water—no coffee," she said, embarrassed.

"That will be fine," I said.

"What has been going on around here?" I pressed.

"Well, see for yourself," she said indignantly, motioning about the room. "This is what it has come to. We're living in our barn. A few weeks ago, my husband went out to look for food and get some help. He hasn't come back yet, but we're still expecting him at any moment." She glanced at the little boy and then looked at Jimmy in much the same manner she might have in order to silently forbid him from casting any doubt on Santa Claus.

"A few days later, *they* showed up."

"They?" I questioned.

"Yes, the zombies. That's just what we call them since they have no souls. But they're not real zombies, you know, actual living dead like in the movies. They go around capturing and killing people and God knows what else."

"Luckily, we were out here working when they showed up and were able to slip into the woods before they found us. They looted our house and then burned it down. Look, see?" She opened a sliding window in the barn, and it was dark out.

"Well, you could see it across the way if it were light out."

I glanced at the wood stove again.

"They haven't been back, probably because we're way out here and they think there's nothing left."

"So there is only one band of them?" I asked.

"We don't know. It's the only one we've ever seen. One band could rule this whole island, you know? There were at least twenty of them."

"So what else is out there? What else has happened?"

She sighed. "I don't even know where to begin. It all started when this virus began to spread around the world."

"Yes, yes, I know about that. I know everything up to the point where someone set off the e-bomb. Oh, and I know that there was a nuclear war. Were there any strikes around here?"

She explained that they never saw any evidence of nuclear strikes around there. Her husband, Dan, was a line repairman for Whidbey Island Power, and he made the same assumption we had when the skies clouded up for good. It was bad at first, but the real trouble came after the e-bomb. The lights went out, and people packed up and headed off to God knows where. Police drove up and down the roads telling people to stay in their houses and that Marshall Law had been declared. They heard that the military took over on the mainland. Most people, including them, became afraid to go out because of the virus, the police, and because of what might happen next. They just hunkered down on their property to wait it out. They had been hunting and fishing, but it wasn't enough. When they ran out of food, Dan had to go out for help. He left and never returned.

"Speaking of which, do you want something to eat?" she asked. "I was fixin' to cook up the rabbit that Jimmy caught before you woke up."

"No, I'm fine," I lied. I was actually starving but didn't have the heart to take any of their food. "I have some food in my pack," I said. "You're welcome to some."

"Oh we couldn't," the woman started.

"Mom!" cried Jimmy.

"Well, maybe just something for the kids. I'm all right."

"Your backpack is outside," yelled the little boy.

"Go get it, Kevin," said Jimmy. Kevin raced down the ladder and out the door.

"So, you don't know anything about the shape the country's in?" I asked.

"No," she said. "Once the power went out, nothing worked any more. We haven't seen anybody alive since the zombies—until now. And it sounds like you don't know anything either, so I guess we're all in the same pot."

Kevin returned with my backpack.

"Listen," I said. "What time is it?"

"You see a clock around here?" asked Jimmy sarcastically.

"Sun went down about two hours ago," said the woman as she frowned at Jimmy.

I remembered my solar powered watch and pulled up my sleeve to find an empty wrist. I looked at Jimmy accusingly, but Kevin looked toward the ground and kicked at the dirt.

"Kevin?" queried his mother.

He reached into his pocket and pulled out my watch. He handed it to me without looking up.

"I'll deal with you later," said his mother.

"But I thought he was de..."

"Never mind," she snapped.

My watch said 8:30 pm.

"Listen, I have to go find my family over near Langley, so I can't help you now. But..."

Kevin howled: "See, I told you he wouldn't help!"

"No, no, no. You didn't let me finish. I will try to come back here when I find out about my family. I will really try, but I can't promise anything. I don't know what's going to happen—only that I intend to try. But if something better comes along, don't wait for me."

"You don't have to," the woman began a controlled sob.

"I know I don't, but I'm not sure how many good people are left. You seem like good people. What is your name, anyway?"

"My name is Karen, Karen Blackman. This is Jimmy, she said pointing to the older boy. And this is Kevin."

I told them my name. "I am glad to meet you. I just wish it were under better circumstances."

"We do too," said Karen. "We're really sorry about tying you up, but we just didn't…"

"I know," I cut in. "I understand. I'd have probably done the same thing in your shoes."

I opened my pack, pulled out three of the MREs I had taken from the boat, and placed them on the table.

"Just add hot water," I said.

"No really," said Karen. "Two is enough."

"No it isn't. I don't need them. I still have two days' worth for myself and my family. Please just take them."

I also took the granola bars I stole from Paul's house from my pocket and placed them on the counter. I took out my knife and picked up a slick piece of wood. I scratched the address to Paul's house on the board.

"This is the address to an old friend of mine. He's dead, but he's got a couple of weeks' worth of food in his cupboard if you can get over there. It's only a couple of miles, down at Bush Point. I didn't see anybody along the way, so if you stay off the road, it should be pretty safe."

Jimmy propped the gun against the wall and came over to me. His face softened, and he extended his hand.

"Thank you, mister," he said. "Thank you so much. I'll go over there tomorrow."

"Don't mention it," I said. "And, you know, you don't have to be afraid of everyone. We're not all bad people."

He smiled apprehensively and then nodded.

Kevin ran up and hugged my leg.

"How old are you?" I asked.

He held up four fingers and said: "Five."

"Do you know how to tell time?" I asked.

"Yep, when the sun goes down it's time for bed."

"You'll learn," I said as I stuck my watch into his hand.

I turned to leave.

"I should look at your head," Karen said. "I'll put the boys to bed and look at your head. I feel like it's the least I can do." She ran her finger down the collar of her blouse and hooked it on the first clasped button. Jimmy looked away, embarrassed. Kevin stared at us oblivious. "You shouldn't go out at night," she continued. "Just stay the night and I'll get you fixed up....for all your trouble."

My left thumb instinctively traveled to the inside of my ring finger and began working the gold ring over. "You don't have to," I said, pretending to have missed the overture. "You really don't. I will come back if I can—to help you."

I opened the door and stepped out.

"I hope you will," she said, as she closed the door.

21

WHIDBEY ISLAND, WA

I walked carefully through the dark and found the road. Once on the pavement, the going became easier. I'd heard that people who lose one of their senses experience compensatory increases in the others but had never experienced it. However, practically blind due to the pitch blackness, I felt as if I had super hearing. I noticed many things I might have never heard before: the clicking of a single bug deep in the bushes, a dog barking miles away, a slight increase in the wind coming through the trees. I had no idea until that night, that you could actually *hear* rain changing to snow—the tapping sound of the drops became more intermittent and hollow as flakes began to outnumber them. Once the change to snow was complete, all sound dulled and faded except the ticking of snowflakes hitting the shell of my coat. As a meteorologist and attentive observer, you might think I would have noticed that before.

Normally, it gets lighter out when it snows at night. Snow is a very effective reflector of light and usually amplifies any ambient light. But in the virtual absence of light, the opposite can be true, and the heavy snow allowed me to experience total blindness firsthand. I didn't care for it. Afraid of bumping into something, I walked slowly and carefully down the road. I came to sense the crown of the pavement and managed to stay roughly in the middle of the road thanks to that single practice of civil engineering.

Just as I began to feel comfortable and increased my stride, I ran into something solid. Luckily, I hit it just right and only bloodied up my shin before falling onto the hood of what turned out to be a car. I felt my way along the vehicle and then to an attached trailer. The combination smelled faintly of cheap barbeque.

I trudged on through the growing cushion of snow, which froze my feet but helped my knees. The snow came down harder and began to make a sound discernible over the ticking on my jacket and crunch of snow under my feet. The wind picked up, whipping the fat, stinging flakes into my face and up under my hood. I veered to the ditch and felt along for an evergreen tree. I found one and tugged at one of the branches, but it wouldn't come loose. Dragging it probably wouldn't cover my tracks anyway.

Light came earlier than usual because of the snow cover. I reached highway 525 and turned right toward Freeland. Now able to see and given the increased danger of travelling on the main north-south route of the island, I kept mostly to the shoulder and close to the safety of the woods. To conceal my tracks, I walked in the ditch when practical.

I crested a hill, and just on the other side, a road led off to the left. My heart skipped as I noticed a man standing motionless next to the stop sign. I dropped to a squat and drew my gun. My right hand shook as I held the pistol, so I slowly reached over with my left hand and steadied it. Butterflies raged inside me.

"Hey!" I yelled. "Hello?"

The man just stood there. I yelled at him again, but he ignored me.

I stood up and approached carefully, my trembling gun hand trained on him. I got within about ten feet of him and finally noticed snow on his hatless head. Then I saw the rope around his waist and around the sign pole.

I walked up to him and pushed his arm and touched the hole in his forehead. He felt like fossilized wood. His feet and legs had been gnawed at, post-mortem judging by the lack of blood. Severe exposure made him look ancient, but he couldn't have been more than twenty five. He stared straight ahead, a ghostly statue guarding the intersection. I don't know why I tried to close his eyelids, but they wouldn't move.

My curiosity exhausted, I walked on, keeping my gun drawn until safely out of sight.

The snow fell more heavily as I walked. There was a burst of snow that dumped an inch very quickly, then the snow stopped and the wind picked up from the south. Within an hour or so, the snow began melting from the road. While it had been light enough to see for two hours, it hadn't made it out of twilight. By late morning, the snow completely melted off the road, so I went back to walking on the pavement in an effort to dry out my feet.

I stopped and filled my canteen with snow and placed it under my coat. I didn't care much for the foul water that resulted, but it didn't seem to harm me. I walked on.

I reached the top of another hill just in time to see a vehicle coming over the next hill toward me, lights still on. I scrambled into the bushes to wait for it to pass. It crossed my mind to flag the vehicle down and see if they knew anything. But I was afraid they knew too much, so I stayed put.

About a half mile before it got to me, the vehicle stopped. I could see that it was some sort of van—like one of those hotel shuttles. There is a hotel still operating? A man got out and opened the hood of the vehicle and looked inside.

Damn it! They're broken down. Now I'll have to walk through the woods—and quietly. That was just what I didn't need. I decided to get closer so I could see what they were doing.

Just then a small person, perhaps a woman, came out of the door and began running up the road. Her long hair whipped as she ran, and her adequate bosoms flopped violently under the threadbare undergarments she wore. The man under the hood raised a large stick and pointed it at her. I saw a flash and then a puff of smoke. The woman dropped into a heap in the road. A couple of seconds later, the crack of the rifle reached me and echoed through the woods. I slipped deeper into the forest and started picking my way south, quietly.

It took me half an hour to travel the half mile to the van in the thick underbrush, and another fifteen minutes to close the final hundred yards on my belly. I passed the heap in the road and stopped to take a look. Definitely a woman and not well cared for—and shot in the back, to boot. Her head was turned toward me and her eyes stared.

I quietly moved to approximately even with the front of the van. I saw seven other women sitting on my side of the van, sullen and fearful. The other woman was probably better off heaped in the road than still in the van. I didn't recognize any of them, which would have been a relief, except that that is like being glad that a tornado struck your neighbor's house instead of yours.

The women sat obediently, staring straight ahead, apparently without much thought of going the same route as their dead counterpart now cooling in the road, a hundred feet to the north.

I looked back down the road at the dead girl and then at the girls in the van. I thought about my wife and daughters and fought against the moistening of my eyes. The hairs on the back of my neck stood up and my balls crawled again as I realized what I must do.

The only sounds were of the man tinkering in the engine compartment and his labored breathing. Then he suddenly seemed pleased with himself. He stepped down, backed away from the van, and went around and got back inside. Remorse crept over me. He tried the ignition, and it started. He got back out and came around to close the hood.

I drew my gun, ejected the magazine and looked inside—still full of bullets. I don't know why I would have thought otherwise. I replaced the magazine and quietly pulled back the slide and looked down inside as a bullet shifted upward and into the barrel. I had never fired at a human being. In fact, the only shots I'd fired in years were a couple of practice shots from the RY. I was skeptical whether I could even hit him. But even if I missed, he'd duck for cover, and I could easily outrun that fat slob. I'd never have been able to live with myself if I didn't try.

I lifted the gun, braced it with my left hand, and drew a bead on his chest. I knew not to go for the head except a point blank range—too small a target and much higher chance of missing. With the rifle in his left hand, he reached up and grabbed the hood with his right, exposing his chest to me fully. I lined up the sights and squeezed the trigger.

The gun kicked much less than I expected, but the sound stunned me. All external sounds ceased as a loud ringing rose in my ears. The spent shell casing tumbled end-for-end in front of me and passed slowly through my field of view.

The fabric of his overalls tore open just under his armpit. He slumped forward and then staggered backward in slow motion and fell to the ground on his back. His arms flew over his head as the rifle cart-wheeled just out of his reach. A red circle formed on the side of his chest and then grew and then began to drip onto the pavement.

My first thought as time sped back up was that the women could be restrained in the van. I slipped further under cover and waited to see what they did. If they couldn't get out, I'd have to think of something. A woman stood and looked out the front. She turned and said something to the others. Then they all stood.

One woman came to the front and then stepped out of the van and approached the still man. He reached lamely for the rifle, but she grabbed it. All the women poured out of the van and surrounded him. I scanned nervously through the faces—unfamiliar all. One woman jumped on the man, grabbing him around the neck, choking him. They all began yelling and kicking him like wild animals. They tore at his face and spit on him. Finally, the woman with the rifle yelled: "That's enough!"

The women all stepped back. The woman stepped over to him and placed the muzzle of the gun to his forehead. She pulled the trigger, and all the women jumped as half the man's head vaporized and stained the street red.

The women began looking around. One pointed to the bullet hole, and then they turned in my direction. I bolted. Fear set in and I ran with everything I had. Branches slapped at my head, poking and scratching my face, and the gray snow whipped into my eyes as I dashed blindly through the forest. Then I heard yelling. "Wait!" They shouted. "Thank you!" shouted another one. I dropped back to a walking speed, panting. They wouldn't come for me. And now they were free, their destiny back in their own hands, for what it was worth. More importantly, they weren't my problem anymore.

I stopped to rest against a tree. My hands trembled as I thought of what I had just done. Killing a man is much more shocking than I would have imagined. I vowed to avoid doing that again at all costs.

Within an hour, I had Freeland in sight, just across an isthmus. The strip of land was about a half mile long, most of its length barely wide enough for the highway. Driftwood logs lay scattered throughout the strips of tall sea grass that lined both shoulders. Sand sloped down from the grass to the water's edge.

I waited and watched nervously for a few minutes. Nothing moved. The lone house on the other side showed no sign of life. The only other way around would have added ten miles to my walk. I might have walked on the beach to limit my conspicuity, but I decided that the less amount of time spent on that exposed cape the better. So, I took off running down the pavement.

Maybe it was shorter than I remembered, because I reached the half-way point in just a few minutes. That's when a bright, orange truck squealed around the corner and onto the road in front of me. Without breaking stride, I veered onto the shoulder and dove into the weeds. I scrambled lower on the slope and settled down amongst the grass. I tried to pull sand over me, but I had nowhere near enough time to bury myself as the truck rumbled down the road. At the last moment I took off my back pack and tossed it into the weeds behind me. I took out my gun and checked it. Safety off.

The high pitch squeak of brakes pierced the air as the truck decelerated in my vicinity.

"Who's in 'ere?" came a voice from the truck as it ambled in close.

The truck stopped, and the doors opened.

As always, they could have been good people or bad. Intuition told me that it was likely the latter. I nuzzled further down into the grass—a snake couldn't have gotten lower. I listened as boots clicked on pavement and then gravel crunched under the men's feet. They stopped at the edge of the grass.

"Come on up outta there."

I struggled for an idea. I calculated the odds of each of my limited options. Scenes from action movies flashed through my head. Start shooting and hope to get three of them before they got me? I knew it wouldn't turn out like that. Run? I had no valid option.

"Don't shoot," I said.

"We ain't got no guns."

I slid one knee under me and edged up to where I could see. All three men held guns pointed in my direction. I quickly ducked back down and cursed. The men laughed.

"Come up outta there or we'll just open up on ya."

I nestled my gun back into the waistband in the small of my back and stood up, hands in the air. I pleaded with them not to shoot. They ordered me up to the road, and I complied. All three had long, ratty hair and beards and were dressed in filthy work clothes. They looked like hobos. They ordered me down to the pavement, and the man to my right moved in and patted me down. He quickly located my gun and relieved me of it. At that moment, I knew I was dead.

"Stand up."

"Please don't kill me," I pleaded again.

I heard two distinct clicks as the man to my left repositioned himself to get a better angle. I closed my eyes.

"Come on! What's the point of killing me?"

"Less fuckers eating what food's left," the man to my left said.

"What the fuck you want yer life for in this shit hole?" the man in the middle asked.

"Just do."

He chuckled. "How 'bout that fellas. Everybody begs and gives us some bullshit about God or they got money or a poor Granny counting on 'em for medicine or whatnot. But I believe this son of a bitch. He just said it straight out."

I opened my eyes. He had lowered his gun and was scratching his beard. I wondered what lived in that beard.

"Awright. Let's see how much you want to live. Take off 'em clothes."

I stood dumbfounded. I was prepared to do anything to stay alive and get to my family, but I honestly had never dreamed it would be *that*.

"Go on, bitch, get 'em off," the man on the left said. "And 'em boots too."

I undressed and threw my clothes over to them as directed. I stood buck naked and barefoot in the road.

"Look, he's cold," the man on the right said, pointing his gun at my crotch.

The man in the middle picked up my clothes. I heard a muffled sound from the truck. The man on the left grunted and scampered over to the truck. I climbed up on the wheel of the gigantic, brand-spanking-new, four-by-four pickup. The gaudy, metallic-orange color of the truck stood out like a sore thumb in the gray, dank scene. "I told you to shut…" he paused, raised his rifle and slammed it down into the bed of the truck. The butt of the gun made a dull sound like tenderizing hammer striking a steak. "…the fuck…" he raised it and slammed down again "…up, you damned chink!"

The other two all laughed and then moved toward the truck. "I can't believe that shit," one of the men said as they piled in. The driver flipped off me as they drove off in the direction they had been travelling. "Have a nice day!" one of them said as they pulled away. They all laughed at my predicament.

I began walking slowly down the road. As soon as the truck was gone, I scrambled back to the beach to find my backpack. The sharp blades in the waist deep grass cut at everything they touched. I located my pack and took off running at full speed toward Freeland—this time on the beach.

I hadn't run a hundred yards before the adrenaline in my blood began to decrease and anguish overcame me. I sobbed uncontrollably as I ran. I scrambled carelessly up to the first house I came to. I ran around behind the house and hid in some bushes and cradled my backpack.

When I had gathered myself and realized how cold I was, I took out the only other set of clothes I had. Unfortunately, I had no other shoes. After I dressed, I stood up and cautiously looked in the window of the house. I quickly knelt back down. Defenseless and petrified, I struggled to summon the courage to do something.

The hopelessness of my situation settled over me like a darkness. To my recollection, I hadn't had a prayer answered in my life, and even though I hadn't attempted to talk to God in thirty years, the thought crossed my mind. I thought about Jill. Despite my skepticism, I decided it couldn't hurt.

"Ok, I don't know if you are even there, and if you are, you know that I've hated you since my mom died. I still hate you. What do you expect, right? Look around! Nothing but misery!" I paused, suppressing my anger. "I don't know what you want from me, so I give up. I'm fucked, ok? If this is what you wanted, you win! I don't have any shoes, no way to protect myself, and everybody is out to get me. You've probably killed the rest of my family, and if so, I'll be coming to see you as soon as I find out. I have nothing left. I quit. So if you are really there, really a God, and give a half a shit about me, now would be one hell of a time to prove it."

Nothing happened.

The outburst did make me feel better, and I was able to move again. I decided against searching the house for shoes and went back out to the highway.

The Freeland Convenience Store was the first building of the town on highway 525. I approached the store carefully, but it was obviously deserted. I stepped carefully over broken glass and up to the side door. It was intact and locked. I sneaked around front and peered through the broken glass. Deserted and torn to hell. It literally looked like a tornado had gone through.

I moved to the front door, and instead of stepping through the broken door, I opened it. My heart nearly stopped as the doorbell chimed. "Shit!" I yelled, then ducked, then looked around, embarrassed. I bent down and looked at the chime. It was mechanical.

I walked quickly through the store, preferring not to linger. I found nothing much useful: some liquid soap, various toiletries, and nudie magazines. My eyes locked on to a pair of boots on a shelf toward the back of the store. The black rubber boots with the red rims and rubber pull-on handles were at least a size too small, but my feet went in, and anything was better than going barefoot amidst a sea of sharp objects. I had better get out of here, I thought, and headed for the nearest door.

22

TOWN OF FREELAND, WHIDBEY ISLAND, WA

"To believe in God is impossible - to not believe in Him is absurd" -Voltaire

I stepped to the side door and looked out the window in the direction from which I had come and saw nothing—all clear. I tried the door again, but it remained locked. Why wouldn't it be?

I walked to the front door and was startled by a man walking down the road from my left. I froze and desperately hoped for him walk on by. He paused at the gas pump, lifted the nozzle, and squeezed. Nothing happened. He sniffed the spout, and, apparently discouraged, dropped the nozzle to the ground and turned and came toward the store.

Startling him inside the store could have gotten me shot, so I stepped through the broken glass of the door and said: "hello." He jumped and scrambled back a few steps and began fumbling with his overcoat.

"Hey, hey, hey!" I yelled, holding up my arms. "I'm not armed."

"Jesus! You scared the hell out of me," he said, relaxing a bit.

"Sorry about that. I'm heading that way, and I wonder if you could tell me what is up there."

We both kept our distance.

"Nothing," he said. "Same as here."

"What is that way?" he asked, pointing to where he deduced I had come from.

"Same."

"Ok, then. I'll be seeing you," he began to walk away.

"Wait, where are you going?"

He stopped and looked back at me.

"Don't know," he said, finally.

We stood there awkwardly, neither of us knowing what to say.

He finally broke the silence. "All I know is that there ain't nothing back there worth seeing."

"You're just walking for no reason?"

"I guess," he said. "I'll see what I find."

He turned and faced me squarely. He let out a sigh and began to rub his forehead, as if kneading some thought that had come forward or to ward off a headache.

"I mean," he continued, "what am I supposed to do? Go into a church and pray? Settle down and make a life? Find another wife?"

I had no reply.

I can't say why, but I felt at ease with him. God knows, I had every reason in the world to be suspicious of people, but my intuition told me that he was probably all right. Maybe I just felt better being in the company of someone whose first intention, apparently, wasn't to harm me. I still didn't want him to know exactly where I was going, but I gave him the gist of my story.

He reciprocated by telling me more about what had happened while I was at sea. There hadn't been any nuclear attacks around Seattle, but he did hear of some back east. Terrorists continued to terrorize, but the Red Plague did most of the killing. In his estimation, most people were dead. The cities were horrible. Those who weren't dead and decaying in the streets lived like rats. The worst imaginable situation had come to pass. Finally, having had enough of his home town, he simply left and began to walk—just hoping for something better. At least that's what he told me.

"My name is Joe," he said as he extended his hand.

I looked at his hand and hesitated.

"It's ok. I haven't had any direct contact with anyone for over a month. If we don't have it by now, we probably won't get it."

I introduced myself and then said: "If it's all the same to you, I won't take the chance."

"What if it's not all the same to me?" he asked, chuckling nervously.

"Then I guess you'll feel slighted because I still won't chance it."

His face straightened.

"Fair enough," he said as he lowered his hand and straightened his overcoat.

"Is there anything to eat in there?" he asked, motioning to the convenience store.

I considered offering an exchange of what food I had for any sort of weapon. But I had already given away too much when I told him I wasn't armed. He had either forgotten that I said that or didn't realize that he had the upper hand. I decided not to push my luck.

"I didn't see any," I said. "But I wasn't really looking for food."

"I'm starving," he said. "Haven't eaten since yesterday morning. I got chased out of Clinton before I had the chance to look around. And I don't want to go up to any of these houses."

Suddenly, I felt the urge to get away from there, but I was paralyzed by fear. Even though I didn't know Joe from Adam, I felt safer in his company than not.

"So if you weren't looking for food, maybe you've got some to spare?" he asked.

Here we go, I thought. This is the part where Joe takes my remaining belongings. Maybe he'll just shoot me and get it over with. Of course, I didn't actually know if he was armed. I decided not to go down without a fight either way.

"I've got to save what I have," I said.

"Maybe I should just take it," Joe said. He slid back his jacket to reveal a huge silver gun in his waistband. "You said you weren't armed."

I froze. A million thoughts raced through my head simultaneously. He is only a few feet away. I'm bigger than him, but can I get control of him before he gets his gun out? Gouge out his eyes? A punch to the throat is pretty effective. No, I should just go straight for the gun.

Joe laughed. "I'm just messing with you. I'm not one of them."

I must have been holding my breath because I let out a tremendous sigh and suddenly felt light headed.

"Hey, take it easy," Joe said, reaching for my arm to steady me. "I was just kidding."

"I'm ok. I've just been through a lot."

"I'll remember to go easy on the jokes," Joe said, studying me. "I think I'll look around in the store."

He walked to the front door and pushed it open. Broken glass fell out of the door and onto the floor. The mechanical doorbell chimed and gave him a start. I followed Joe into the store and watched as he rifled around in a pile of debris in the corner. He came up with a miniature can of franks and beans. He set the can down on the floor, took out his gun and slammed the can with its butt. The can split at the seam between the side and top. He squeezed the can as far open as it would go and poured its contents into his mouth and swallowed it in one try.

"Delicious!" he exclaimed as he threw the empty can on the floor.

"And good for you too," I replied sarcastically.

He walked to the next aisle and grabbed a small bottle of liquid hand soap off the floor and stuck it into his pocket.

"What were you looking for in here?" he asked.

I showed him my new boots.

"Nice," he said.

He stood thinking for a moment and then with a confused look asked: "How did you lose your shoes?"

I told him of my mugging.

"Damn," he said. "That sucks. I saw those fuckers driving around, real dumb shits."

Noticing my embarrassment, Joe said: "Hey, I was hiding and they didn't see me. It could have happened to any of us."

We continued walking around the store and poking at the trash.

"Ho....ly......shit!" Joe exclaimed as he ignored the "employees only" placard and walked into the manager's office. "How did they miss this?"

He threw a stainless wire shelf out of his way, reached down, and held up a pint of Jack Daniels.

"Now we are in business," he said, bouncing out of the office.

His genuine smile told me that he had found a modicum of happiness that had eluded him for a long time. He hurriedly twisted off the cap and smelled the mouth of the bottle, deeply inhaling the aroma from the liquor, and then took a drink. Then he offered it to me.

"I don't really like Bourbon," I said.

"Good, because Jack Daniels isn't technically bourbon. It's whiskey," he said, shoving the bottle into my hand. He went behind the counter and continued his rummaging. "Not a cigarette in sight," he mumbled.

I decided that my frayed nerves could use some calming. I took a sip of the whiskey and thoroughly enjoyed the taste. I had forgotten how smooth it was and didn't realize how much I needed a drink of something, anything, at that point. I took another, larger pull. It's amazing how hard liquor can begin to calm one's nerves immediately.

"Whoa, there! Save some for me," Joe said, laughing.

I stepped behind the counter with Joe as he fiddled with the till. He lifted the drawer inside and found nothing. Disgusted, he pushed the entire appliance off the counter, and it clanged to the floor. He picked up a nudie magazine, thumbed through a couple of pages, and then threw it to the floor. "Garbage!" he exclaimed. He picked up a Sudoku magazine and seemed pleased as he stuck it in his pocket.

Suddenly a low rumble materialized and became louder by the second. The floor vibrated and shook the building; some glass dropped out of the front door. Just then a light shined through the front window, illuminating the store.

"Damn!" yelled Joe, as he pulled me back into the office. We peered around the corner. I recognized the orange hood of the truck, and my heart sunk.

"That's them, huh?" Joe asked.

I nodded.

Equipped with a heavy metal door that opened out, the office obviously served as a safe room for the employees. In fact, the store's safe sat cracked and empty in the corner. The room afforded easy access from the cashier area but couldn't be seen from the outside. Joe quietly shut the door and locked the dead bolts.

"You seriously don't have a gun?" Joe whispered.

"They've got it," I said, embarrassed.

I jumped as Joe grabbed my hand and slid something cold into it.

"My extra nine," he said. "Do you know how to use it?"

I told him that I did. It felt good to have a small amount of my own destiny back in my hand.

At least two of the men came inside and began rummaging around. We sat listening silently, and while the men didn't speak, they made quite a ruckus.

"Here's a desk," said one of them.

The distinctive sound of metal scraping against concrete echoed through the store as the men slid the desk.

"Fuck! It's not here. I told you we shouldn't have killed him until we checked it out."

Finally, one of them tested the handle on the office door.

"Hey, maybe this is where they kept it," said the man.

"So check it out, you idiot!" yelled the other from across the store.

"The door is locked."

"So break it in."

The door rattled but didn't budge as the man put his weight into it.

"It's a pretty stout door, he yelled back across the store."

"Get out of the way," said the other man.

The door handle rattled again which was followed by a larger thud against the door. It held.

"The door opens out," said one of them, finally realizing the obvious.

"Get the winch," said one of the men.

More commotion followed as the men brought in the winch cable from the truck and wrapped it around the door handle. We heard a twang as the cable became taut, and then the door handle groaned and shot out of the door. We heard breaking glass as the cable and door handle whipped around the store before finally coming to rest.

Fingers poked through the hole and pulled at the door, but it didn't budge.

"God damn it, it's still locked somehow!"

"Reach in there and see if you can find the locks."

A hand squeezed through the hole and felt around. It unlocked the first dead bolt but couldn't reach any more. The door still wouldn't move. An eye peered through the hole but couldn't see through the darkness inside.

"How the hell can this door be locked from the inside? Is there another way...."

"Oh shit!" exclaimed the man as they both scrambled away from the door.

"Who's in there?" asked one of the men.

"Open the door and come out!" exclaimed the other.

We didn't make a sound.

"Ok, let's blow the door off," said one of the men, his boots clicking on the floor as he headed for the truck.

Joe finally spoke: "Stop! There are six of us in here, and we are all armed. This will be your only chance to leave us alone, or we'll come out shooting."

The men laughed.

"Yeah right," said one. "We're real scare't."

Joe stuck his gun through the hole and fired. The deafening explosion and blinding flash inside that little room stunned me. For a few seconds, I was completely deaf. My hearing quickly returned, mixed with a loud, sharp ringing.

"Do you believe me now, you son's a bitches?" Joe yelled.

"No, we think it's just you. If you do that again, we'll blow this whole god damned place up."

"Listen," said Joe. "This place is solid concrete and this door is solid steel. You can't get in here unless we want you too."

"We'll burn you out. Smoke you out. Something."

"Just tell us what you want."

"We want in there."

"We were already looking around in here before we closed the door and there is nothing in here," I said.

"Ok, so there are two of you. Big deal. Let's hear from the other four."

"Fine, there are only two of us," said Joe. "But that's all the more reason for us not to come out. Look just leave us here, give us ten minutes to get away and then you can have whatever it is you want."

"Yeah, sure, and then you make off with the gold," said one of the men.

"Shut up, you moron!"

The men were suddenly quiet due to the man's accidental revelation.

"There is no gold in here," I said. "We looked around. Nothing."

"Yes there is. The owner told us so."

"Why would he do that?"

"Let's just say he felt like it!"

The men all laughed again.

I thought about the guy in the back of the pickup during my first encounter with them.

"The safe was smashed open, and there is nothing in there," said Joe.

"Under the desk," he said. "There is another safe in the floor. There is shit load of gold in there, we've got the combo, and we want it."

"So just give us the combination and we'll take out the gold and give it to you," said Joe. "You can leave and we go our separate ways."

The men whispered to each other and then finally agreed.

Joe pointed out that we couldn't see to open the safe. One of the men pushed a lighter through the hole in the door, and it dropped to the floor.

"Now step back," I said. "If I see so much as a finger near the hole when he opens the safe, I'll blow it off."

They all backed up.

Joe moved the desk as I covered the hole with a piece of trash I found on the floor.

"Ok, I'm at the safe," said Joe. "Read me the numbers."

One of the men read the numbers off as Joe spun the dial.

Joe opened the safe and it did, indeed, contain a large amount of gold, perhaps forty or fifty pieces. It also held thousands in cash, which, apparently, didn't interest the goons, or they didn't know about it. Joe collected the coins and began to feed them through the hole. The attractive ring of each coin hitting the floor echoed through the store, and as multiple rings and echoes mingled, the room came alive like a sort of random bell choir.

"Wait a minute," I said. Joe stopped and the symphony rang to an end. "Once they've got what they want, what keeps them from blowing us up anyway?"

"Nothing, except that they don't have any explosives."

"What makes you say that?"

"They wouldn't have agreed to this if they did. It would have been safer just to blow us up and collect the coins themselves. If I'm wrong, we'll just have to shoot our way out of this, which is what we would have had to do anyway. Dolts like these three weren't going to go away without the gold."

"We can hear everything you are saying," said one of them.

"I know," said Joe. "So now you know your choices. When you've got all the gold, just leave, or we will try to shoot our way out of this. You know we are armed. Some of you won't make it out of here. Which of you will it be? Who wants to die here today?"

The men didn't say anything.

"And one more thing, you fucking idiots. You took some clothes, shoes, and a gun off a friend of mine a little while ago. Get it all and bring in here or nothing comes out of this hole except the barrel of my gun."

The men still stood silently.

"Move!" Joe barked, loud enough that it even startled me.

"Go get his shit," one of the men directed.

They did as Joe ordered and he fed the rest of the coins out through the hole. Joe's plan worked. Once they had the gold, the men simply walked out and drove away.

"Do you really think they are gone?" I asked after a minute.

"They're gone. Too stupid to do otherwise. They had no way to anticipate what we were going to do, so it was easier for them to just leave."

Joe slowly opened the door and cautiously walked out. I followed. The store was deserted, the truck gone. I collected my stuff and handed Joe back his extra gun.

"You have no idea how it feels to get this stuff back, Joe."

Joe smiled. Then he closed the door to the office, reached up inside, and locked one of the deadbolts again.

I shot him a puzzled look.

"When they come back they'll think we're still in there. It will keep them busy for hours."

We laughed.

We slipped out the front door and ran around back into the woods. We stopped so I could put on my clothes. We could still see the store through the trees, and just a few minutes later, the truck returned, this time with more men.

"Maybe one of them has a brain this time," said Joe.

"Yeah, maybe."

"We better get going," he said. "There's always a chance they could figure it out."

"We?" I asked.

"Mind if I tag along? I don't have anything better to do."

I would have preferred to say no, but I liked Joe, and he saved my ass.

"It would be my pleasure," I said.

I started down a trail, and Joe followed. He held out the pint to me, and this time, I took it willingly.

"Good thing it's not bourbon," he said as we walked off into the woods.

• • •

We walked silently through the woods as dusk settled over the area. We happened upon a trail heading in our general direction. We took it and picked up speed.

Joe took the last swig of Jack and pitched the empty pint into bushes along the trail. I had consumed about a third of the pint and marveled as I had many times at how alcohol could warm a person from within—a sensation that I facetiously referred to as internal combustion in my drinking days. I recalled with a smile that the frequency and volume with which I made that reference both rose in direct proportion to the amount of alcohol consumed. I had no idea why alcohol warmed me, but I knew that thermodynamically speaking, the phenomenon made no sense.

We had been a half hour on the trail, and just as I was about to ask Joe his opinion about the warming effects of alcohol, a bright flash lit up the forest from behind us.

I turned and began counting. "Lightning?" I questioned.

The flash was followed by the sound of a gigantic explosion ten seconds later. Even with all the force- and sound-deadening forest between us and the explosion, we sensed a significant concussion. A large cloud of smoke, illuminated from below by the distinctive orange glow of fire, billowed up from the general direction of the convenience store.

"Good God!" I exclaimed.

"How long do you think they tried to talk us out of there before they decided to blow it?" Joe asked.

"The good thing is that the ruse worked, so they won't come looking for us."

"I hope they did the world a favor and blew themselves up in the process!" Joe said.

We walked on through the increasing cold.

After another half hour, darkness swallowed us whole, which made the going very difficult. Sense of direction faded in the ink black night, and the danger of trudging on blindly through the forest hit home when I nearly took out an eye on a low-hanging branch.

I groped the ground and gathered all the leaves and needles I could reach into a pile, flattened it, and laid down on it. Joe foraged around some feet away. He lit the lighter we got from the morons and then applied the flame to the small pile of dry duff he had assembled. The pile caught fire, smoked, and then went out. He tried again, this time holding the lighter to the pile until it was fully burning. He grimaced and pulled his hand quickly away and stuck his thumb in his mouth.

"Look, another gift from our loving creator," Joe said, angrily holding his thumb out for me to see.

"I know how you feel," I said.

The fire lit the scene just enough for Joe and I to find some small dry twigs and more litter for the fire. It wasn't much, provided little heat, and we had nothing to cook on it, but I could feel the rise in my spirit solely from the token sign of life.

I felt so tired—more so emotionally than physically. The experiences of the last few days had rattled me to the core. Everything I thought I knew was being tested. Until Joe came along, I thought humanity was gone from the world.

"So are you an atheist?" I asked bluntly.

"I hate that word."

"Why?"

"We already have a word for people who don't believe in Santa Claus and trolls and unicorns," he said. "Adult." He poked at the fire and then looked up. "Why do we need a special word for people who don't believe in other fantasies like God?"

He waited for my reply, but I didn't have anything to add.

"Do you believe in God?" Joe finally continued.

"Kind of. No, not really," I stammered. "Until today, that is. Maybe."

"You found God in this mess?" Joe asked.

At the depths of despair, it seemed as if I had finally had a prayer answered. I didn't know how else to explain it. Now less embarrassed to admit such a thing as I had ever been, I told Joe exactly what happened. I expected him to laugh.

"I think that is the best reason for believing in God that I've ever heard," Joe said. "I wish I had a reason like that. Sometimes I think it would be easier if I just believed all that bullshit."

. . .

We awakened just as the darkness eroded into a milky dawn. It used to be that dawn looked different from sunset, perhaps because of the temperature difference between morning and evening or perhaps because our perceptions were different at different times of day. Maybe it was just as simple as the light hitting objects from opposite sides in morning and evening. But I could not objectively say if it was getting dark or getting light. Dawn and sunset were identical—indistinguishably cold and monochrome.

We stood quietly and urinated. Out of habit, Joe kicked some dirt onto the cold, black smudge of last night's fire. We began to walk. Some while later, we emerged onto a road that ran north-south. I recognized the road but could not name it. We turned right and immediately had to climb over a tree that had fallen across the road.

It suddenly occurred to me that killing a human being felt much differently than I imagined. While I didn't feel any remorse for having shot the fat man the day before, I felt different as a person. I couldn't name the feeling other than to call it something like loneliness.

"I killed a man yesterday," I blurted out.

Joe turned his head and studied my expression. "How do you feel about that?"

"He deserved it," I replied.

"I already assumed he deserved it. I asked how you feel about it."

Joe was unusually perceptive.

"I feel weird," I admitted.

"You're still stuck in the old paradigm," he said. "There is no law here now. Right and wrong have become much more subjective."

"You sound like a relativist. There has got to be some objective right and wrong."

"Name something that is always and everywhere wrong," Joe said.

"Well, the guy that I killed was keeping a bunch of women as sex slaves. That's wrong."

"Not always and everywhere," Joe said.

"What?" I exclaimed.

"Many societies throughout history have kept slaves, including sex slaves. It wasn't considered wrong by them."

"That is absurd. Of course, it was wrong!"

"Hold on," Joe countered. "Don't react; just think about it for a second. Where does that notion come from? What makes it an objective truth? The law? God? Those are your laws, your God. Different cultures have different laws and gods."

I could think of nothing to say.

"Who decides what is right and wrong, right here, right now?" Joe asked.

"We do," I replied.

"Exactly," Joe said, smiling. "I just hope we were raised right."

At the top of the very next rise, we came to within view of Mary's. Mary's was one of those wonderful, local hole-in-the-wall diners. Some people ate at national chain restaurants because you always knew what you would get and it always tasted the same. The rest of us ate at holes in the wall like Mary's because you never knew what you would get and it never tasted the same.

I had met Mary once and eaten at Mary's dozens of times, but I did not know her. The locals all knew Mary. Mary had to have been coming up on 80 years old, but last I knew, she still worked in that restaurant as she had been doing for the previous 65 years. She started out washing dishes and worked her way up until she could finally buy out the previous owner—I think his name was Dick and I think it was called Dick's back then—and change the name to make it her own.

Mary had employees for sure: cooks, dishwashers, other waitresses. But even at her age, Mary insisted on waiting tables during every meal, seven days a week. "The regulars are my family," she would say, "and I'd be doing this for my family anyway, if I had one." She must have put in sixteen hour days in order to work three meals a day and manage the business itself. But that was her way, and I figured her as the kind of person who could imagine no other life for herself.

As we stood at the top of the hill observing Mary's, I thought about the last time I'd eaten there. Mary was slight but had a gigantic head of unnatural red hair—thin and sparse, but always poofed up. Her wrinkled, withered skin hung from her face and arms like gathered curtains. I watched her as she carried the entire meal for a table of eight in one trip—plates stacked carefully one on the other and wedged between fingers with bulging knuckles—and wondered how many times she'd made the same trip. How many plates had she lost before she could do that? She probably required multiple trips to serve large parties in her early career, but gradually built up her strength and balance, plate by plate, until she finally reached the height of her career and could do it all at once. The Michael Jordan of waitresses. What pride she must have felt at having mastered what none of her other staff—some less than a quarter of her age—could do.

After enough time had elapsed, we moved down the hill toward Mary's. As we neared, I noticed some faint yellow light spilling from a window. We walked up to the small building and peered carefully through the old, wavy glass. A candle flickered on the counter. Everything inside looked in order.

"Do you think we should go in?" Joe asked.

"I don't know."

Just then, movement inside startled us. A withered, old hairless Chihuahua of a woman shuffled slowly about. She ran bulging knuckles through the few remaining strands of poofed-up red hair. Gravity continued its relentless work on Mary's sagging skin. Her sallow eyes, however, glinted with the last remaining sign of life within her.

"What the hell is that?" asked Joe.

"It's Mary," I said, motioning to the sign. "I think it's ok. She looks harmless. Everybody eats here. She might know something."

Joe pushed open the door, and the bell jingled which gave her a start. She quickly regained herself as we came through the door. "Hello," Joe and I said in unison.

"Come on in and sit down anywhere you like," she whistled from a puckered and toothless mouth. "Except table four. That's reserved."

We looked to our left and saw the 'Reserved' placard on table four.

"Are, are you open?" asked Joe.

"Why sure! We're open every day of the week here at Mary's."

Joe and I looked at each other and shrugged while Mary stared at us intently. Although the worst had passed, the stale smell of rotting food and cigarette smoke wafted through the room.

"Well, then. Where will you sit?" she gummed.

"I guess we'll sit at the counter," I offered.

"That will be fine. Keeps me from walking so far."

Joe and I took seats in the middle of the long counter, near the candle.

"Can I get you some coffee?" Mary asked, even though she had already turned over both cups and placed them on their saucers.

"Sure, but we don't have any money to pay," I said.

"We'll worry about that later," Mary said, chuckling.

She grabbed a clear pot with the orange handle and pretended to dispense coffee into Joe's filthy cup.

I put my hand over my cup. "I'll take regular," I said, motioning to the pot with the brown handle sitting on the coffee machine. Mary switched pots and pretended to dispense caffeinated coffee into my filthy cup.

Joe and I looked at each other again. Joe circled his finger around his temple to signal that she was crazy. I nodded. We smiled and began to pretend to drink from the cups.

"So what's kicking Mary?" I asked in an upbeat voice, attempting to play along and change the tone of the conversation. "Do you remember me?"

"Of course!" she lied. "Will you have your usual?"

"Naturally! And may I say you are looking as beautiful as ever?" I said.

"Now Jim Lambert! If I didn't know your wife, I'd think you were trying to pick me up!" she exclaimed.

"You keep that between us, huh Mary?" I said.

"And for your friend here?"

"Uh, I'll have what he's having," Joe said.

"In a jiff!" Mary said as she wrote out the ticket, clipped it to the wheel, and spun it back into the kitchen.

She turned and faced us and placed her gnarled, knuckled hands on the counter to balance herself. I was afraid she'd fall and instinctively reached toward her. So did Joe. She caught herself without our help.

"Well, then. I guess I had better go back into the kitchen and see what's taking so long," she said.

Joe began to rise. "Why don't you let me check? You stay here and rest."

"Nonsense!" she scolded as she waved Joe off.

Joe sat back down.

She shuffled to the end of the counter and around the corner toward the kitchen.

Joe and I waited. Nothing needed to be said. Mary was obviously off her rocker. She either didn't know or didn't care that anything had happened. How she stayed alive in that restaurant was anybody's guess. But there would have been no point in saying anything to her. We couldn't help her. She had spent her entire life in that restaurant and was obviously quite content to spend the rest of it there too—however little remained. Even if we had tried to help her, she probably would have died ten minutes after leaving the restaurant. She was better off there than anywhere, and the best thing we could do for her, as fellow human beings, was to play along.

She placed two plates onto the service bar and shouted: "Order up!" She emerged from the kitchen and served the dirty plates to us.

We pretended to eat, and she pretended to tend to other business.

"Say, Mary?"

"Yes Jim."

"Do you get many customers anymore?" I asked, faking a mouth full of food.

She looked at me, puzzled.

I cleared my throat. "This economy, I mean."

"Well, Sunday's are our busiest day. But it varies. Not so much, no. But personally, I'm busier than ever."

"That's good," Joe said.

"What are you up today, Jim?"

"Well, I'm off to Langley to get the truck fixed, and Joe here, he's riding along."

"I didn't hear your truck pull up."

"How could you have through all this noise," I asked. I winked and smiled and motioned around, despite the silence.

Mary smiled.

"Have you seen Carol lately?" Joe asked, making up the name. He must have thought that everyone knows someone named Carol—especially someone who would have been exposed to as many people as Mary.

"Why no. How do you know Carol?"

"She's my mother."

"You don't say. What did you say your name was?"

"Joe."

"Of course! I think I remember Carol mentioning you."

"Anyway, tell her that I said hi when she comes in again, won't you Mary?"

"Of course I will."

"And tell her I'm back in town for good."

Mary suddenly had a twinkle in her eye—a purpose. To wait for Carol, whoever she was, and to give her an important message from her son.

"Of course, I'll be happy to," she gummed, less articulate than before.

Sensing that we were finished, Mary offered us desert. We declined.

Her mouth relaxed from smile to neutral as she folded the check and placed it in front of us.

"Will you take a credit card?" I asked.

"Nope! Machine's busted!" She pointed off into a dark corner where a broken credit card machine must have sat collecting dust.

"Well, I guess we'll be paying in cash then." Joe and I pretended to fish for our wallets.

"Now, you go on, Jim Lambert! Your money's no good here. I just appreciate your coming in," she said, as she sighed.

I remembered the money I had taken from Paul's house. I reached into my coat pocket and pulled out a hundred dollar bill. I put it on the counter.

"Keep the change," I said.

"I'm not taking your..."

"I insist," I said.

As we made for the door, Mary repeated: "I just appreciate your coming in. Please come again." She meant it.

She cleared our dishes and placed our check and the hundred dollar bill amongst the other receipts.

As we passed by the front windows, Mary leaned back against the counter and stared at the candle.

Joe and I walked along quietly. It grew colder, and a light rain began to fall. I couldn't see much of the sky through the canopy of trees, but had I been able to, I probably would have seen the clouds lowering in advance of another storm. My apprehension grew the closer I got to the house. Less than an hour away then by my reckoning, I increased the pace.

We approached a bend in the road, and blackened woods on the far side of the curve caught our eye. We hustled to the corner and stopped at the edge of a small gully. About ten feet below sat a blackened car upside down. Blackened ground surrounded the car and a burn scar extended away from the road as far as we could see into the woods.

Joe looked back up the road. "See those skid marks?"

I looked back and saw two sets of skid marks—one set stopped at the edge of the pavement and the other extended across the shoulder to where we stood and off into the gully.

"This car was run off the road," Joe said.

We picked our way carefully down the bank to the vehicle and peered in. The stench was overwhelming. Nausea burned in me as I recognized the blackened remains of people still buckled into their seats. Two adult-sized people remained strapped into the front seats and two smaller humans were buckled in back. A little black lump of melted remains sat slumped on the ceiling of the car, just below an infant car seat.

Joe stepped to the front of the car and dry heaved.

I sat back against the wet ground and fought back tears. "At least it was probably quick," I said to no one in particular.

Joe stood upright and looked intently at something behind the car. "Uh, Matt? Take a look at this."

I moved around behind the car and found Joe kneeling next to another body—this one not black, but a normal looking male leaning against a tree. He slumped to his left and the left half of his head was gone. A gun lay next to his right hand.

Joe rolled the body over and retrieved a wallet from its back pocket. He flipped through the contents and then threw it on the ground. "Christ," he said and walked away.

I picked up the wallet and studied the driver's license. Jeremy Peterson, age 33, from Raleigh, North Carolina. I found a common access card assigned to him by the Whidbey Island Naval Air Station. I flipped through his photos. There were photos of a beautiful teenage girl in a cheerleading uniform, school photos of young twin boys, and an infant girl. There was also a wedding photo of him and a stunning redhead.

I wiped the tears on my sleeve and stood up. I threw his wallet into his lap, sighed heavily, and turned to leave. I stopped and retrieved the gun from his dead hand—a big, shiny, silver gun—and shoved it into my waistband. I scaled the bank back to the road.

I caught back up to Joe.

"What are we going to do?" he said.

"I don't know," I replied.

We walked on in silence.

It crossed my mind to turn the gun on myself. One of those involuntary thoughts that seemed to come from nowhere. But contained within the fact that I still had a gun was the suggestion that I should carry on to the end. I had at least some inkling that prayers could be answered now. Maybe it was all coincidence—Joe, the exact kind of person I needed, coming along just when I needed him. But what if not? No, I had to go on if for no other reason than when I found them all gone or dead, I could end it knowing that there was no further reason to live, nothing else I could do on this dreadful planet, just like Jeremy Peterson. Suddenly I remembered that I had never actually asked for the very thing I wanted most. God knows I had hoped, but perhaps there was a difference. I dared not take that chance.

"Ok, so I still don't know if you are there, but I am willing to take the chance after all that has happened. I still hate you, and I still give up. But I need Kate and my children to be ok. I need them. I don't know how I'll care for them, but if you are there and can do this, I will figure it out. I don't expect an answer since I've never heard one before. But we'll see what happens. At least I need to know what happened to them. That won't give me a reason to live, but at least I can put a bullet in my head, hoping to see them on the other side. Maybe I'll see you, for all I know, and then I can tell you what I think about putting us through all this."

I didn't say those things out loud, but somehow it made me feel better to articulate them to myself. Then doubt crept back in, and I felt ridiculous.

"Do you think it is wrong to keep sex slaves?" I asked Joe as we ambled along.

"Yes," he replied.

"I don't understand how people can behave like that."

"Hunger," Joe replied.

"That fat bastard I killed yesterday wasn't hungry," I said.

"Maybe not for food," Joe retorted.

"Whoever ran those people off the road back there wasn't looking for food," I said.

"What made people ever behave?" I continued.

Joe explained his theory that, at some point during our evolution, a few people found it easier and more beneficial to get along with each other than to oppose one another. It came to be considered good or moral to treat each other in a certain way.

"Then," he said, "Certain moral beings noticed that not everyone was behaving this way. They had to come up with some way to make them all toe the line. They invented gods and devils and heaven and hell to scare everyone into good behavior."

"So you think morality came first and then religion." I stated rather than asked.

"Yes. I believe religion was simply man's attempt to make everyone conform," Joe said.

"But what makes two heathens like us behave?"

"The ironic thing is," Joe replied "The religious types try to behave out of fear that the great watcher is watching, whereas you and I behave because we know that they were right in the first place: it is just better to get along. So, I ask you: who is really moral, the ones who behave out of fear, or you and me, who behave just because it's right?"

I thought about that as we walked along. Then my mind wandered to a different subject.

"You know what my worst fear is, Joe?" I asked. "That what seems most likely is actually true—that, like a candle, we die and then, poof, we're done. And I'll never get to find out the answers I've always wanted to know."

"If there is a god and you could ask him one question, what would it be?" Joe asked.

"What is outside this universe?" I responded immediately.

"Not one of the usual questions like what was the purpose?" Joe asked.

"No, by the time you get to God, the answers to most of the big questions will already be obvious," I said.

Joe smiled. "You are a surprising person," he said. "I'd ask him what we were supposed to have learned from little babies suffering. And then I'd tell him what he can do with that answer."

We reached a fork in the road. One path circled back around toward Holmes Harbour and, although circuitously, from whence we had come, while the other made directly for Shadow Point and my family. I had thought long and hard about a request I was about to make of Joe, and I knew this was the best and last place to make it. Any further and Joe would have to backtrack, which wasn't that big of a deal, but truth be told, I felt a strong desire to be alone when I discovered whatever I was to discover at Shadow Point.

Joe and I stopped and looked back and forth down the east-west oriented road.

"It's right, right?" Joe asked.

I indicated that it was.

"What's the matter then?"

"Listen Joe. There is something I have to ask you."

"Shoot," Joe said.

"You remember when we first met, you asked me what else you should be doing besides walking around aimlessly?"

"Of course. And you think you know what I should be doing?"

"I made a promise to some people, and I don't think I can keep it. But I think you might be able to."

23

TOWN OF LANGLEY, WHIDBEY ISLAND, WA

Having parted ways with Joe, I suddenly felt very alone. Whidbey Island started to seem more like a morgue than a quiet tourist island. The thing about Whidbey Island is that it gets spookier as you go east. The west side is weathered and beaten from the incessant parade of Pacific storms, and while it has plenty of vegetation, it tends to be sparse in places, which makes the west side seem lighter. The east side, by contrast, is densely vegetated and overgrown. It seems dark because, in the afternoon, it is. The beach upon which Kate's parents lived was called Shadow Beach precisely because, as an east-facing beach with high cliffs, it came into shadow in the early afternoon and remained that way until dark. The mornings were nice and warm, but the afternoons and evenings were shadowy and cool, exacerbated by the afternoon north wind that frequented the area during the summer months.

Less than a half hour after leaving Joe, I came within sight of Langley, WA. I didn't need to go down into the town as the road to Shadow Beach passed by on a bluff above. I stopped for a moment at the overlook and scanned the town for any activity. A few overturned cars sat rusting in the middle of Main Street. The windows of many buildings had been broken out. One building—a restaurant, if memory served—had burned to the ground. A huge fishing boat remained perched in dry-dock on the beach down below town.

Langley always struck me as odd. It was a town of over 5,000 residents, but I found no reason for its existence. It sat next to the water but seemed to ignore it. It was the only tourist town I had ever been to that seemed oblivious to the one thing that might have attracted tourists. Not one of the beach side restaurants actually faced the water. Buildings blocked the entire shoreline from the rest of the town. Stairs that led down to the water and the so-called waterfront below looked like more of an afterthought than a planned attraction. A single, poorly maintained dirt road provided the only vehicle access to the beach, and even that led only to a dilapidated marina. Langley couldn't claim to be a gateway to anything, a ferry from the mainland didn't terminate there, the town effectively blocked its only view, it lacked a great waterfront, and it wasn't even at a crossroads. There simply wasn't much there. Yet it existed.

I noticed heaps in the road—bodies I guessed. Then a flash of movement in an alley, which vanished before I could lock onto it. Someone was down there; time to move on.

I had but a mile left, and I knew it would be a spooky walk. Within a few minutes, I entered what the kids called "the tunnel." Whenever we drove the road north of town to Shadow Beach, the kids talked about the tunnel. Less affected by the warm, drying late afternoon sun, that part of the island stayed moist, and virtually everything grew there. Competition for sunlight was fierce, and as a result, the ground rarely got any of it. Pines towered above, and species such as alder and madrona, complete with its constantly peeling red bark, over slung and enclosed the roadway. Branches tangled and twisted their way across the road, except for a small square, perhaps ten feet on a side, through which trucks passed. Even at the top of the day in the height of summer, that road was dark, moist, and mossy.

A chill leapt up my spine as I passed a dripping ceramic driveway sentry. Covered in green slime, the little troll's eyes peered out from under the hood of its raincoat and followed me as I passed. How the driveway's owner could have enjoyed this greeting every time he returned home eluded me.

Close then, I began to run. I crested the last rise and saw them not fifty yards in front of me. It stopped me cold in my tracks. Six of them stood over a corpse in the road, their mouths dripping with blood. They ripped and tore at the flesh of the thing, fighting amongst themselves for the best morsels. One of them stopped and stared blankly in my direction, chewing and oblivious to my presence.

I pulled out my gun and tried to recount how many bullets were left. I had additional ammunition in my pack, but there would be no time to reload once they noticed me. And there would be no sneaking past them. They could not be fooled, eluded, or outran. I had to scare them off or kill them all. It was them or me, one on six.

Frozen, I didn't know how to proceed. I doubted whether I could hit one from fifty yards and I didn't dare waste any of the bullets left in the clip, so I decided to walk straight up to them. I hadn't made three steps when they heard me, or smelled me, or sensed me. Whatever it was, they all turned simultaneously and began walking toward me.

God damn it! I've come five thousand fucking miles and I'm going to be killed within a mile of the house. I struggled to remember how many bullets my gun held. It was a Glock-19, I thought, so does that mean it had 19 bullets in the clip? My mind reeled as I remembered bits of conversations about magazines versus clips and bullets versus cartridges. I felt for Jeremy Peterson's gun and noted its position in my belt.

Oh, hell! This is it. I stood up straight and quieted my mind and controlled my breathing and heart rate. Just shoot and if you run out of bullets then fight with your hands. I'm not going to die in this damned street by a pack of wild dogs!

I raised my gun and aimed at the leader. At 20 yards, I decided it was close enough, and I fired. I hit it. It fell in the road and flailed, trying to get back up. It finally laid still. The others recoiled from the gunshot and stopped to look at the leader. The two taking up the rear suddenly scampered into the woods, but the other three tore out after me. I fired as rapidly as possible at the approaching menace. Within the first half-dozen shots, two of the three fell and struggled in the road. I took a bead on the final predator and fired repeatedly. Finally, within a few feet of me the last dog whimpered and fell to the pavement as my gun began to click harmlessly.

I dropped to my knees and gasped for breath as my hearted pounded in my chest.

Suddenly, I remembered the other two dogs and snapped back to the present. I wiped the tears from my vision with the back of my hand and pulled out Jeremy's gun. Thinking better of trusting my life to an unfamiliar gun, I ripped off my pack, fished out the other magazine and clicked it into my gun. I pulled back the slider to chamber a round, stood up, and held it out in front of me. I kept my eyes ahead as I shoved Jeremy's gun into my pack and slipped the pack back on.

I scanned the woods as I edged down the road. The dog closest to me clung to life with shallow, raspy breaths. I decided not to waste another bullet on it. The next two lay still in the road, and the fourth followed me with its eyes, the rest of its body paralyzed and useless. I stopped at it and considered its pink, foaming mouth. A sudden shutter ran up my spine.

I walked up to the twisted heap of flesh, organ, and bone in the road. It bore no resemblance to anything in my experience. It surely wasn't human, but the steam that rose from it indicated it had been alive in the not too distant past. Maybe it had been one of the pack. Or maybe the poor creature just happened by only to be ambushed. With a little different timing, I could have been that meal.

Keeping a wary eye on the woods and my ears peeled to my rear, I jogged the rest of the length of the road and turned onto Shadow Beach Lane. Just as I entered the road, I heard a gunshot echo through the woods from the direction of Shadow Beach. The road wound down another half mile before hair-pinning back toward Kate's parent's house. With urgency, I instead took a shortcut sprinting over a cliff.

I bounded recklessly down the hill, fearing that I had come all that way only to have gunshots end my family minutes before I got there. I saw some movement and stopped in a small clearing just above the beach.

The child was on one knee, flipping rocks over and poking at the sand. At least from my vantage point it appeared to be a child. He held a shotgun in one hand. I slowly moved closer, careful not to give away my position. He wore dirty blue jeans, and a tear down one side revealed a gaunt white leg. His filthy, red hooded sweatshirt stood in stark contrast to the cobalt water of the bay and the dreary, gunmetal sky. Could that be my boy? He was a little skinny, but that would not have been a surprise after all that time, and he was about the right age.

A single flake of snow fell somewhere between us and interrupted my gaze.

He stood up and threw a rock into the cold, still water. It tumbled end for end through the air and pierced the surface without creating a splash. Ripples spread out in perfect circles and upon reaching some predetermined distance, vanished back into the tranquil water. He took a handful of pebbles and whirled around, spraying them across the water. He crouched down and paused as if to study the sound of the stones tearing into the water. Maybe he imagined himself firing an automatic weapon or ducking for cover as bullets pierced the water around him. Must be a boy. He spun as he finished the throw and I caught a glimpse of the side of his face. Obscured by long, sandy blond hair that protruded from under his hood, I could not identify it.

Right color hair.

He walked a little to the right, and, even from a distance, I could hear the sound of gravel crunching underfoot through the still air. He turned over a larger stone and pounced on something like a cat on a mouse. He picked it up and studied it for a moment, flipped it over several times, and then put it in his mouth.

There was a sudden disturbance in the water; a strange linear ripple emanating from left of the boy's position straight out into the bay—too straight to be natural. He scrambled toward the origin of the disturbance, set down the gun, and grabbed a fishing pole from among the weeds. The pole heaved forward as the boy struggled against the creature on the other end. Each time he pulled a streak in the water appeared as the line tightened, then as he relaxed and reeled, the line slipped back under the surface. A fisherman's worst enemy poked its head up through the water and looked curiously at the boy. Then the seal disappeared back under the surface.

It was not long before the boy dragged the flapping prize onto the beach, silver flashes piercing the monochrome scene as the fish flipped from side to side. The fish writhed and jerked, and its gills heaved mightily in and out as it struggled for oxygen. The boy grabbed a large rock, and with a swift, sharp chop, ended the commotion.

Suddenly, I heard rapid footfalls behind me. As I dove down into the weeds, my knee landed square on a twig and the snap of it cut into the cold air like a firecracker. I heard a skidding sound as the person came to an abrupt stop and cautiously listened for more sound. I held my breath. After a few tense seconds, the footsteps resumed, and the figure ran past me down toward the water. I slowly lifted myself up and peered down toward the bay. It was another child about the same size as the first one, but with much broader shoulders—likely another boy. He was also armed and carried something furry by the legs. He set down his rifle and dropped the creature on the beach.

I saw a brief glint of steel as the first boy took out a knife and began cleaning the fish. He plunged the knife into the fish's underside and in one clean motion, opened the cavity from the anus to the jaw line. He ripped out the innards and dropped them on the beach and then, as if thinking better of it, scooped up most of the mess and tossed it into the water. With a scooped hand, he shoveled water onto the beach and washed much of the remaining evidence from the scene. It was either a small silver or a very small King Salmon, but food either way.

Good for them. Well done.

The spectacle suddenly made me aware of my own building hunger. He slit the skin from head to tail along the spine, peeled down the skin revealing the pink flesh. A few more cuts and he had several small boneless salmon fillets. He cleaned the fish just as I had taught my son to do it when he was old enough to safely handle a knife. The other boy moved in and after a brief, barely audible disagreement, they began eating.

A shrill screech poured out from the forest behind me. An emaciated crow flew over me and swooped down over the boys, searching for leftovers. It landed about ten feet from the boys and hopped toward their days catch. One of the boys edged over toward the guns, while the other picked up a tiny bit of the entrails and offered it to the bird. The bird got about as near as a bird will get, and the boy lunged forward but missed. Millions of years have taught birds just how close they can get to potential predators. After a while, the only birds left are the ones that know how close is close enough.

The bird flew off toward me in a fit, shrieking loudly. As the bird approached, its eyes locked onto me, and it let out another series of caws and began circling over me. My hair stood on end and my pulse quickened. I heard pellets spray into the forest behind me and then I heard the shotgun blast.

"Don't shoot!" I yelled. "Charlie, is that you?"

I felt around for any kind of projectile, and my hand landed on the freshly broken twig. I hurled it toward the fowl, and it flew off. When I stood up, the boys were gone.

I closed the remaining distance to the beach in what seemed like a tenth of a second. I arrived just in time to see the boys rounding the peninsula about a quarter mile down the beach. I yelled out, but they kept running. Then I set out after them.

I reached the first house on the beach. It had been burned. As I passed houses, I caught whiffs of death. I followed the tracks in the sand until one set peeled off and went up toward a house about four houses north of Kate's parents. I suddenly took notice of my carelessness—both of the boys were armed, and thought they were being chased. I also had no idea who else might still be living down there. My awareness regained and my gun still drawn, I sprinted for the beginning of the bulkhead, which stood taller than me and provided some cover.

I edged along the bulkhead until I arrived in front of Kate's parent's house. The house was dark, its windows broken out. Dread spread over me like a cold wind.

A light mixture of rain and snow began. The wind suddenly gusted from the south, dragged down from above by the onset of precipitation. The rush of air funneled into my hood and inflated my jacket with a chill.

I peered up over the bulkhead, and nothing moved.

To get to the stairs, I had to walk through the ankle-deep water of the incoming tide. Frigid water topped my boots and squeezed into my socks and trickled down my ankles and into the soles. My shoes made a squishing sound as I cautiously climbed the stairs one by one.

I got to the top and yelled: "Charlie! Are you in there?"

There was no response.

I scampered up to the sliding door and looked in through the broken glass. My heart sank as I cringed at what might have taken place there. In addition to the sliding door, most of the windows had been shattered. Debris was strewn about, furniture overturned, the cupboards open and empty. The door on the other side of the kitchen banged shut in the wind and gave me a start.

My eyes gravitated to a well-worn path through the rubbish to the back of the house.

I stepped into the house and called for Charlie again. Still no answer. I walked slowly through the house with all sort of wild, horrible thoughts pulsing through my head. Every closet and room in the house had been rummaged except for one—the closet door at the end of the hallway.

"Charlie! It's your dad. Don't shoot." I didn't hear a sound.

I walked slowly to the end of the hall and tapped on the door. "Charlie, are you in there? Don't shoot. It's me, Dad."

I grasped the handle, twisted, and pulled. The door squeaked open.

The boys screamed and pushed their feet against the floor in an effort to get further back into the small closet. I recognized the other boy immediately. It was Tommy, Charlie's friend from down the beach. Both guns pointed a gun at me.

"Don't shoot," I said, quietly and calmly. "It's me, Charlie, your Dad."

Tommy sat terrified, the gun trembling in his hands.

Charlie stared at me with eyes like saucers. His gun dropped to the floor.

I knelt in the closet door and asked Tommy to give me the gun. He handed it over.

I held out my hand to Charlie, and he took it and stood. He reached his hands out to my face and touched it. His fingers ran over my beard, a feature he'd never seen on his father. His eyes locked on mine. He didn't even blink. Tears welled up in his eyes.

"Is it really you?" he asked.

"Yes," I said, my voice beginning to crack.

He looked far worse than I had dared to imagine, but, at the same time, he was the most beautiful thing I had ever seen.

He stepped forward and threw his arms around me and clenched tightly. I returned the hug with my right arm and reached out to Tommy with my left.

"Are you all right?" I asked to Tommy.

He sat stunned and confused.

I grabbed Tommy by the arm and pulled him to us and hugged him too. Charlie and Tommy sobbed in my arms.

"I thought you were dead," Charlie said.

"I told you I would come," I said.

"I know, but it took so long. I thought you died."

After a moment of joy, caution kicked back in. I checked the boys over and other than being dangerously thin, filthy, and terrified, they seemed ok.

I asked Charlie where his mother and the girls were. My stomach tightened as Charlie looked to the floor.

"Whatever has happened is not your fault. Just tell me where they are."

"They are around back."

"Show me."

My legs grew weak, and I could barely walk as we headed to the back door. I began to perspire at the thought of what I was likely to encounter next—nearly my worst fear.

We walked down the sidewalk and rounded the corner when I saw two mounds in the yard. Both mounds had make-shift crosses, and there was a third cross stuck in the grass next to the mounds.

"No, no, no..." I muttered through building tears as I ran to the graves.

"Daddy, no! Over here!" Charlie said, stopping me cold. He pointed to the side of the house.

I ran to his side, and he began to remove firewood from the side of the house near the foundation. I began to claw at the pile. An old vent into the crawlspace beneath the house revealed itself, chipped away at the sides to the approximate size of a man.

I dropped to my knees and peered into the black hole. Were they buried under here?

"Do you have a light?" I yelled to the boys as I tried to wriggle into the hole.

I pushed myself back out and demanded to know what was down there.

"Mommy and Kelly," Charlie said matter-of-factly as he jumped in the hole.

I heard someone speak faintly from within: "Who's there?"

I forced myself back into the hole behind Charlie. From behind a rock, Charlie produced a beer bottle filled with what looked like gasoline. A wick stuck out from the throat. He struck a match and lit the wick. Yellow light flooded into the crawlspace. It had been dug out on all sides to make space for people, dirt piled up against the foundation in every direction.

I saw the face of Kelly, my oldest daughter, emaciated, pale, and sickly—nearly a zombie and much worse than Charlie or Tommy.

"Who is it? Charlie, is that you?"

"Honey? It's Daddy."

She sat back, stunned. I wriggled myself through the hole and fell into the dirt.

"Daddy?" She muttered, like an automaton. She sat and stared straight ahead.

I peered further in and saw a figure lying in the dirt covered by filthy blankets. I scrambled over and hugged my daughter, but she pulled away. I slid over to the figure and rolled it over. It was Kate. Alive!

I shined the light on her and my heart immediately sank. Her jaw hung open and drool dripped from the corner of her mouth. Scarred over sores covered her face. Her eyes darted about—the only movement in her otherwise immobile body. Her head rolled back to its original place, looking away from me but struggling to turn back.

I suddenly doubted that this was even my Kate. Was the beautiful, confident, bright-eyed woman that I loved still inside this dying shell?

I couldn't speak as a lump formed in my throat. I struggled for what to do. Thoughts rushed from dialing 911 to dragging her to the hospital to rushing out to find Jill.

I held her head back up and looked in her eyes. I saw the pain and the struggle. Then I saw the glint. Although her body had been ravaged and was near death, her eyes told me more in that instant than an hour long conversation could have. She was still there, and she knew I was here now.

Charlie scrambled over to her and put his hands on both sides of her face and put his nose right up to hers and said: "Mamma, it's Daddy, see! I told you!"—as if he had communicated with her a million times in that exact way. I held her and Charlie and pulled Kelly to us.

"What happened to her?" I asked to no one in particular.

"She got sick," replied Charlie. "She got the flu, but she lived. She went to sleep for two weeks, and when she woke up, she never moved again. Except her eyes. And she breathes."

"How have you kept her alive?" I asked.

"We give her water and mashed up food. Sometimes she chokes, but it goes in."

A sense of pride and awe flooded through me.

"We've got to get her out of here," I said as I began to pick her up.

"No!" cried Charlie. "She doesn't like to move. It hurts."

I looked at her and began to cry again. Her eyes softened, and a tear rolled down one cheek. I carefully put my arms around her again and held her. "I don't know what to do for you," I said.

A whoosh of air came out of her mouth as she struggled to speak.

"What?" I asked. "What should I do?"

I leaned down and placed my ear against her lips.

"Nuh" she said as all the air rushed out of her lungs. She struggled to reinflate her lungs and then continued: "hing."

I looked at her puzzled. She gasped for another breath and tried again: "Nuh-hing." It wasn't speech but rather sounds forced out by sheer willpower.

I nodded.

Relief spread across her eyes. She closed her eyes and managed to raise the corners of her mouth ever so slightly. Her lungs rattled, and she involuntarily jerked with a deep, wet cough.

She opened her eyes again and tears streamed out.

I wanted her to finish the sentence from the last time we spoke on the phone. I knew she couldn't.

"I love you too," I said.

I didn't know if she could feel much, but I pulled the filthy blankets up around her neck—I knew how she hated being cold. I kissed her on the lips and then the cheek, and then I held my face to hers. My face felt hot against her cold skin, and I willed the heat out of my body and into hers.

She coughed and struggled for breath. She sighed and relaxed, and I knew.

"I'm here now. It's ok."

She looked at Charlie and then to Kelly. I pulled them in and laid each one next to her. They snuggled up to her without hesitation, as they surely had on many cold, scary nights.

I rested myself across her and the children and laid my head down on her chest, careful not to cause her any more discomfort.

Her breathing grew shallow and intermittent. I wondered how long she had been fighting for breath. I laid there for a few minutes listening to her heart beat. It gradually slowed. A bitter hatred began to bubble up from somewhere within me, but I fought it back.

Charlie and Kelly began to cry. "Mommy, no," Charlie whispered. I pulled them both tighter to their mother.

"This is what she wants," I told them.

Every fiber in my body wanted to do something, to drag her from the hole and rush her to the hospital, the rush her to where I thought Jill and Jeff and Sonny were. I fought against the feeling, because there was no help. There was nothing to do but hold her.

The time between her breaths lengthened unbearably. Finally, she exhaled for the last time. I sobbed uncontrollably on her chest as I listened to her heart slow, thump-thump…..thump-thump………..thump-----thump………and then it stopped.

Part of me died with her. I held the love of my life for a few more seconds, and then panic washed over me.

"Where is Elaine?" I demanded. Visions of the red plague, vans, orange trucks, and guys in overalls skipped frantically across my mind. I jumped as I saw motion to my side. Tommy, still staring into the hole, repositioned himself.

"She's in the yard," said Charlie, unemotionally, still lying next to his mother.

Another part of me died. I sat back and struggled against another outburst as my mind reeled. It was too much to deal with at one time. I felt like I was going to explode. I struggled to catch my breath in a frantic attempt to hold it together for Charlie and Kelly.

"And Grandma and Grandpa?" I asked.

"Grandpa died in a shootout," said Charlie. "He's next to Elaine. Grandma got sick and left and never came back. She said she didn't want to get us sick. I followed her to the top of the hill, but she cried and told me to get away and threw rocks at me."

"You found her and buried her?"

"No, but she's dead. I put up the cross so she could be next to Grandpa."

I grabbed the children and held them again, Charlie returning the hug, Kelly ambivalent, imperceptibly trying to free herself.

I fought the urge to give up. I had no idea what to do. Kate was gone, and now there was no one to help me figure things out. I was the only adult, and two children depended entirely on me. The crushing weight of responsibility bore down on me. Two months of emotion and doubt and anguish boiled to the surface all at once. Only half of my prayer had been answered, but that was more than I honestly expected. The pull of despair and the push of hope battled for my mind, and it was up to me—and only me—to decide the winner.

24

SHADOW BEACH, WHIDBEY ISLAND, WA

I buried the love of my life next to her parents and our beloved daughter. As I shoveled dirt back into the hole, I felt ironically grateful to have been the one to do it. The hole was for her, but I could have easily laid down in it myself and never got out. But in that hole, I got my closure and found some resolve.

I stood up straight, back aching, dirty, sweaty, and cold and stared defiantly into an ambivalent world. It would have been easier to give into fate, but I had half of my life back, which was half more than I had dared to hope for. What I had already been through was nothing. This was the purpose. It was time to man up.

"Where is mommy?" Charlie asked suddenly.

I had half expected such a question eventually, but its frankness startled me, nonetheless. I leaned on my shovel and looked at him.

"What do you mean?" I asked, stalling. "I just buried her."

He picked a carrot out of his MRE and threw it angrily onto the grass.

"No! I mean is she in Heaven?"

I swallowed hard. It was tempting to fall back on mankind's crutch and just say yes. I found myself sympathizing with millions of our ancestors who, when faced with such a dilemma, chose the soothing path of hope over the painful trail of truth.

"You know I would never lie to you, don't you?" I asked, sitting down next to him.

Charlie nodded.

"This is one of those things that I don't know for sure. But I will tell you this: if there is a Heaven, no one belongs there more than your mother."

"But what do you think?" he asked, unsatisfied.

"I think that as long as you remember her, how she smiled and how much she loved you, and as long as you make her proud by doing the things that she told you were right, she will always be right here," I said as I placed my hand over his heart. "She will always be part of you."

Charlie lowered his head.

"You know, Charlie, sometimes when you feel bad or you're scared or you don't know what to do, if you just pay attention, you might be able to feel her. I don't know what happens after people die, but wherever she is, if there is any way she can help you, she will. Do you believe that?"

Charlie nodded.

I hugged him and then leaned back to think. Kelly continued to work quietly on the MRE I had given her. I asked her what she thought, and she ignored me.

"Did you bury Grandpa and Elaine by yourselves?" I asked.

"No, Tommy helped," Charlie responded.

"Where is Tommy?"

"He went home."

Charlie explained that Tommy lived with his grandmother a few houses down. I remembered that she was very old, possibly an invalid. Tommy's grandmother was sick, according to Charlie, but not like the others—just a cough. That worried me.

I considered the three crosses they had built. Made of driftwood, each cross had a name scrawled across the cross beam—or at least the name Charlie and Kelly assigned to each person: Elaine, Gramma, Grampa. They also scratched out a number which represented their best guess as to the person's age. They got Elaine right but wrote 80 on both Grandma and

Grandpa's crosses—about 15 years high on both. I reckoned that kids always guessed high on the ages of adults.

Not particularly religious, Kate and I had never taken the kids to church. Yet, they thought to place crosses on the graves, which I would have found curious if not for the conversation we'd just had.

"Why did you put crosses on the graves?" I asked.

"So God can find them…when he comes looking," responded Charlie.

"Do you think God will come looking?" I asked.

"Tommy does."

I remembered that Tommy's family had been religious, and I suddenly knew where Charlie had gotten his new interest in God and Heaven. I asked if he wanted to put a cross on his mother's grave.

"It's cold," Charlie said. "Can't we do that tomorrow?"

"No, now," said Kelly.

They were the first real words she'd spoken since I arrived.

"Me and Tommy dig the holes, and Kelly makes the crosses," said Charlie.

"Ok, honey. Do you want to help me pick out the wood?"

She nodded.

I carried Kelly down the beach piggyback, as I had done many times. She selected two pieces of driftwood which were much larger than the others. I carried Kelly and one piece of wood back while Charlie carried the other piece.

On the way back, I suddenly got a strong case of the willies. I stopped and scanned the houses along the beach. I felt like we were being watched but nothing moved. I shrugged it off to circumstance and continued on.

Kelly showed me how to etch the names and numbers into the wood with a shell. Charlie got a nail and rock and secured the two pieces together and beat it into the soft mound of dirt over their mother's grave.

By the time we finished, darkness had settled across the land and spilled out over the water. A light rain resumed. The sound of much larger drops echoed from the forest creating the audible illusion of two different rain rates.

I took the children inside the house and cleaned them up. I washed their clothes in the bay and dressed them in some of mine while theirs dried. I selected the driest firewood and built a fire in the fireplace. Then I dragged three mattresses into the living room and made them up with the least dirty of the blankets and linen.

"We have to go back down in the hole," Charlie said.

"I'm here now," I said. "And we're not going to live like animals anymore."

Charlie looked away, embarrassed, and I immediately regretted the remark.

"Come here," I said to them both.

"I am so proud of both of you, staying alive this whole time, finding food, caring for your mother, and doing hard things like burying your sister and grandparents. I don't know how you did it, but you two are like grownups. In fact, you are more grown up than a lot of grownups I know."

This gave Charlie a boost. Kelly continued to stare blankly at me.

"Look, you two did the best you could, and I am very proud. But I am here now, and I will protect you. If anyone comes around to harm you, I will kill them. Do you understand? I won't let anything happen to you again. We have to be careful, but we are not going to be afraid of everything. We are not going to hide in the corner. Do you understand?"

Charlie nodded. I'm not sure Kelly heard me.

"But what are we going to do?" Charlie asked. "They will come back."

"Who?"

"The bad guys."

"What bad guys?"

Charlie described the looters and their big, bright, orange truck. He told me that they went through the houses looking for food and guns. He said that they sometimes teased people or stole them. He said that it had been weeks since they had last come, but surely they'd be back once all the low hanging fruit on the island had been harvested.

"I hope they don't come back," I said. "But if they do, I won't let them hurt you. Besides, we won't be here long."

"Where are we going?"

"I'll explain that later. For now, we are going to stay and wait for some friends to come here. When they do, we'll go with them."

"What friends?"

"You'll find out."

"Why won't you tell me who it is?"

I resisted getting his hopes up. Truth be told: I shouldn't have gotten my own hopes up. I couldn't know whether Jeff had found any of his family alive and if he hadn't, whether he could have found the strength to continue on. Would I have sailed back up here to find him if I had nothing left? I thought back to my moment in the grave. At least he had Sonny and Jill.

"I don't want you to get your hopes up. You'll find out if they come."

"If they come?"

Charlie looked into my eyes and must have understood what I meant because he dropped his line of questioning.

"Can Tommy come with us?"

"Tommy!" I exclaimed. I had forgotten about him. I needed to check on him and his grandmother.

"Are you two all right here by yourselves for a minute? I want to check on Tommy."

Charlie and Kelly shook their heads in unison. Kelly began to shake.

"Ok, you can come with me."

"Tommy won't let you in if you don't know the special knock anyway."

"Of course he wouldn't. Why didn't I think of that?" I said, smiling.

I motioned for Charlie to follow me into a back room. Kelly sat rocking on the floor.

"What happened to Kelly?" I asked.

Charlie looked down in embarrassment again. I reassured him again that none of it was his fault.

"The bad guys came," he said. "They teased her."

"What do you mean 'teased her?'" I asked, suddenly more concerned about the meaning of the word "teased."

"I don't know. Tommy said they was teasing her."

"How does Tommy know?"

"He's the one that came back from hunting and found them teasing her. He shot at them, and they ran out to their orange truck and took off. That's when we dug the hole under the house—to hide."

A sharp anger rose in my belly.

"Did they tease mommy or Elaine?" I asked. Part of me didn't really want to know the answer. Since they were both already out of their misery, the answer could do nothing but hurt me. But another part of me had to know the truth.

"I don't know," Charlie replied. "Mommy and Elaine were here though, so I think so."

Another part of me died. I had to fight to mask my anger in front of Charlie. I felt like I couldn't breathe and I started to shake.

"How long ago was this?" I asked with a trembling voice.

"Long time. Just after it got cloudy."

"And they didn't come back?"

"They came back the next day," Charlie said.

My blood began to boil.

"But they got run off?" Charlie continued, chasing me out.

"By Tommy again?"

"Nope, up on the hill, before they came down. Shooting and stuff. It sounded like Cowboys and Indians. They were shooting and hollering like Indians all day. Tommy and I dug the hole in the basement and got in."

I was puzzled by the cowboys and Indians thing, but who knows what kids imagine when they're scared?

Charlie and I walked down the street toward Tommy's while Kelly rode piggyback. The rain had turned to snow but, to my relief, was not yet sticking on the pavement. The falling snow deadened all sound except for the tapping of large, melted drops falling from the trees in the woods next to the road. My flashlight barely cut into the eerie, quiet darkness.

The feeling of being watched came back. I tried to look around, but it was too dark to see. I felt for my gun and was relieved when I had hold of it.

After about eight houses, Charlie stopped at a fence, swung part of it to the side, and stepped through the resulting hole. I lowered Kelly to the ground and helped her through the hole and then followed. Charlie crossed the yard and stopped in front of a small window in the basement. He knocked three times fast and then waited. He knocked three times fast again. Then he knocked three times slowly and loudly. A light flickered behind the window and then it cracked open.

"Charlie?"

"Yeah. My Dad's here and we're coming down. Don't shoot."

"I won't," Tommy whispered.

We walked through the front door, and like every other structure I had entered since landing, it had been ransacked. But unlike the others, it had been cleaned up again. Large stains on the carpet in the living room suggested prior savagery. A salty breeze wafted in through the missing front windows.

We descended the stairs and found Tommy waiting in front of a shelf askew to the wall. Behind the shelf, the wall opened into a hidden room. Faint light flickered inside.

I grabbed Tommy and hugged him tightly. He hugged back, unsure of what was going on. He was already a hero, and I vowed to protect him like my own.

"Tommy, how is your grandmother?" I asked.

"She's ok. She'll be fine. She's sleeping," he said nervously.

"Can I see her?"

Tommy glanced into the room, then back at me, and then back to the floor.

"I don't know. She don't like company."

I had only met his grandmother in passing at the beach. Charlie and Tommy had been friends for years and were practically inseparable during the summers when Charlie visited. The few times I'd seen his grandmother she had always been nice, and I sensed that she liked me.

"I think it will be all right Tommy. I just want to see if she needs some help."

"Ok," Tommy said reluctantly as he stepped aside.

I instructed Charlie and Kelly to wait outside and then wedged into the dank, moist room. The cinder block walls enclosed a space barely large enough for two beds and a table. A bucket sat alone in a corner. The room smelled of sickness.

I approached his grandmother and immediately heard the rattle of her shallow breaths. The skin on her face had drawn tight from dehydration. She struggled for breath through her agape mouth. I reluctantly placed the inside of my wrist across her sweaty forehead. She was on fire and quite near the end. My best guess was pneumonia. At her age and with no possibility of medical attention, whatever the illness, it was going to be fatal.

"How long has she been like this?"

"A couple of days," Tommy said.

"Tommy?" I said, intentionally furrowing my brow.

Tommy kicked hesitantly at the dirt.

"I need to know. It's ok."

"Maybe a week….or two," he said quietly. "But she only started sweating yesterday!" he exclaimed, before I had a chance to speak.

I noticed a prescription bottle on the floor next to the bed. I picked it up and shook it. Pills rattled around inside. I turned the bottle toward the candlelight and read the label: amoxicillin. The expiration date was eighteen months ago. I pushed down and twisted off the cap. Only five capsules remained.

"She can't take those no more," Tommy said. "She only chokes."

"Can she take water?"

"Yes."

"We can open these capsules and put it in the water. She'll get it then."

"I'll get some water," Tommy said, buoyed by the new development.

"Tommy," I said.

He stopped at the door. There was no longer any point in sugar coating things with children. The world was different, and they knew it.

"You've got to know that she is very sick," I said. "This probably won't work."

"I know," he said as he turned and slipped through the door.

After we administered a few ounces of water laced with the powder from two amoxicillin capsules, I left Tommy to tend to his grandmother. I felt confident that what she had was no longer catching; otherwise, I would have forced Tommy to come with us.

• • •

I awoke at first light, and for the briefest of moments, I hadn't a care in the world. No matter what the situation, sleep is an anesthetic and the fog of waking a brief, lovely narcotic.

Then I felt two bags of bones wedged in on either side of me and reality returned with a blunt force. A knot formed in my stomach as I considered the plan of the day. I had to find food, develop some basic defenses, and prepare for a journey that we would be taking whether or not the RY and its crew ever returned. If we had to walk, I would give the children a couple of weeks to build strength, but the trip might still kill them. Something would eventually kill us all if we stayed, so I set my mind on the only alternative that gave us a chance.

I arose to find several inches of snow outside which didn't please me. The children slept peacefully, I let them sleep and went out to survey my first project for the day. I grabbed an axe and headed up to where the road curved and began to climb the hill. About a quarter mile up the hill I found the perfect spot. Several medium sized trees grew close to the road on both sides. The banks rose sharply from the edge of the pavement to create a bottleneck in the road.

The feeling of being watched had been with me since I left the house, but it suddenly became overwhelming. I jumped and drew my gun as a heard a sound in the woods on the other side of the road. Because of its density and darkness, the forest in the Pacific Northwest could always be spooky, but this was different. I crossed over the road to investigate. I followed a natural animal path about twenty yards up the trail to where I thought the sound had come from. There were no prints in the light snow cover, so it was impossible that anyone had been there. Understandably, my mind was starting to play tricks on me.

"Is there somebody out there?" I yelled. "I am armed and not afraid to use it." I listened but no one replied. In fact, the forest was silent.

The feeling left me, so I returned to the bottleneck in the road. I chose a tree at random and began to chop. I found the going easy through the soft, wet wood and kept at it. Before long I had felled a half-dozen eight- to ten-inch-thick trees across the road, but I remained unsatisfied. A big truck could have pushed those trees out of the way. Then I selected the biggest tree I thought I could manage—a nice sixteen-inch thick hemlock—and tried to decide how best to make it fall where I wanted.

Felling a big tree in a particular spot isn't as easy as most people think. Having grown up in the Pacific Northwest, I knew a little about chopping down trees. I eye-balled up the tree, and it was fairly straight, so it didn't provide me with any insight as to which way it naturally wanted to fall. I walked back down to the house and dug around in my father-in-law's garage and found two wedges in a drawer. I couldn't imagine what I'd need more than one wedge for, so I selected the thickest one and went back to the tree. I began chopping a wedge out of the side of the tree in the direction I wanted it to fall. I chopped out a pie-shaped piece roughly one-third of the tree's diameter.

Now, the bases of big trees tend to kick quite unpredictably when they fall. There are lots of physics involved and little of it is easily discerned just by looking at the tree. It depends on the weight distribution through the tree, its dimensions, what it strikes on the way down, and chaos. There it is again: chaos. Just as the butterfly spawns the typhoon, random processes, interactions, and torques will affect the path of the falling tree. My only escape route was downhill, and I couldn't chop left-handed. I had to chop on the uphill side and escape downhill, past the tree, just as it began to go. I considered for a moment abandoning that tree for the danger, but trees take time to fall and I figured I could get downhill pretty quickly.

I began to chop out the back side of the tree, about six inches above the center of the wedge I took out on the fall side. After I had opened a pretty good gash in the backside, I put in the metal wedge and began to pound it in. I pounded the wedge all the way in, and the tree never moved. I cursed myself for not realizing that the metal wedge was supposed to keep the tree from pinching down on a chainsaw and not to tip over the tree by pounding. Now I had a wedge in the way, so I couldn't chop any more.

I considered whether to try to get the wedge out but decided instead to go back for the other wedge. I pounded the other wedge in below the first wedge. About half way in, I heard a loud crack and ran down the hill. The tree held. I waited a half minute and went back up and pounded some more. I became discouraged when the wedge was nearly all the way in. Just when I was about to quit and go to a nonexistent plan-B, the tree snapped at me again and began to shake. I scrambled out of the way, and the giant tree thrashed amongst its neighbors as it descended through the trees. It bounced off the opposite bank with a loud, dull thud, and the ground under my feet vibrated. A series of lesser thuds and vibrations followed as it settled into its final resting place. A brief shutter of fear rattled through me from the violent spectacle.

The tree came to rest in a perfect position, wedged in between trees on both sides of the road and suspended about a foot off the ground. I felt confident that no vehicles could get into the neighborhood without making a lot of noise.

The children were still asleep when I returned. I rebuilt the fire and started to cook up three of the MREs—two biscuits and gravy and one Salisbury steak. After the three meals I had given to the Blackmans, the ones we ate the previous day, the two I gave to Tommy, and the three I prepared that morning, we only had nineteen left. Nineteen meals for a walk that might take a week or more. I suddenly wished I hadn't used the three that morning.

I had to find other food to eat while we waited. After breakfast, I explained my plan for the day to the children. I could tell by Kelly's expression that she didn't like it.

"I'm just going out to check the beach houses, honey. I set up a barricade at the bottom of the hill. Nobody can get in here. If you see anybody or anything that scares you, you just have to pull this rope." I had hooked up a rope to a small bell on the roof. A sort of panic bell.

Kelly sat silently rocking back and forth.

"Honey, I need to search for food."

Silence, rocking.

I sat down beside her and put my arm around her. I considered telling her not to smile which always made her smile, but thought better of it.

"I wish you would tell me what's wrong," I said. "I can't help you if I don't know what's the matter."

She didn't respond.

"I heard about the bad guys," I said.

A pained look spread across her face. She tried to fight it, but the tears suddenly burst through. I held her tight and rocked with her.

"Honey, I am so sorry I wasn't here to stop that. But I am here now and I will die before I let anyone hurt you again. Ok."

The crying ebbed, and she looked up and nodded.

I really would have been hobbled if I had to take her with me on my neighborhood search, but after two months of not knowing if she were dead or alive, and after all that she'd been through, how could I have left her, even for a moment? And what about my recent strange feelings? I suppressed those thoughts and decided that she was safer there in the house than with me. I didn't know what I would find out there, and there was no choice. I had already boarded up the broken windows, so I locked the doors and told Kelly to ring the bell for any reason.

I checked on Tommy and his grandmother. Her fever seemed less to me; otherwise, she hadn't changed much, despite the two additional doses of amoxicillin that Tommy had given her. There were only two pills left. Then I noticed that her breaths were more spaced out—maybe eight to ten seconds between them—and still through a gaping mouth, like a fish out of water. That was bad. It was only a matter of time.

On my way out of the house, I noticed what had eluded me in the darkness of the previous night: two crosses on mounds in Tommy's yard as well. I thought about the millions of crosses that had probably been erected the world over by then.

After the snow had melted, I sent the boys out fishing again since they seemed good at it. Fish would be helpful, but we couldn't live on protein alone. We needed energy—carbohydrates. I realized why they were all so skinny—not because of a lack of food but because they'd been living almost exclusively on fish. In essence, they had been doing the low carbohydrate diet. It obviously worked as a weight-loss diet, but it was just slow starvation.

I started my search at the far end of the beach. I kept my pistol at the ready at all times. The boys told me that, except for us and an imaginary friend they called little bear, the beach was deserted. But I suspected different and took no chances. The first house I checked was an old cabin. Since the family did not inhabit it year-round, it did not have a lot of the amenities normally found in the houses at Shadow Beach. It had been ransacked, nevertheless. I found a can of green beans on a high shelf, but no other food. I left the house and placed the green beans in the wheel barrow I had so optimistically brought with me, and pushed it to the next house.

I found nothing in the second or third houses except a lot of damage and a general lack of valuable items. In fact, I hadn't seen one television set or computer in any house I'd been in since my friend Paul's.

I entered the fourth house with some trepidation since its residents were—had been—friends of ours. Every house on the beach was known by the last name of the family who originally owned it—not its current occupant, but its original owner. A family named Spencer could move into the Brown's house, but it would remain the Brown's house. The fourth house was known as the Hellenberg house. Our friends, the Hellenbergs, were a beautiful family of four. Eric, the man of the house, was an airline pilot for Alaska Airlines and Jenny, his wife, was a flight attendant. Their two young daughters, Amy and Kathryn, were beautiful children. So beautiful, in fact, that they modeled clothes for department store catalogues. My trepidation was well founded as I was greeted just inside the door by a grizzly scene, and an even worse smell.

Two adult bodies laid on the living room floor in an advanced stage of decomposition. They were so far gone that I could not tell the sex of the victims—not that I wanted to get close anyway. I instinctively held my gun out in front of me as I moved through the house—which seems ridiculous in hindsight, but you can't fight instinct. I quickly searched the kitchen and found nothing of use.

I should have left it at that, but I did not. I moved down the hall and found two small bodies in one of the children's room. I suddenly felt light headed and nauseas and began to leave when I noticed a foot in the doorway of the master bedroom. I took a quick look and saw the rest of an adult body, bound and gagged, decomposing at the foot of the bed. It wore navy blue pants with a stripe up the side of the leg. Eric. My eyes moved up to the bed. A nude, unmistakably female corpse was melting into the bed, its bones still tied to it. I vomited on the floor. Tears began to stream down my face as I ran toward the door. I only hoped that it hadn't gone on long.

Suddenly, I heard the panic bell in the distance.

I tore out of the Hellenbergs and burst onto the road. I ran with every ounce of energy I had toward the house. My heart thumped in my chest as the bell continued to ring. I scrambled around the corner into the yard and nearly fell in the gravel. I gained speed as I approached the house and flung my weight into the door. The locks gave way and I tumbled into the house, gun drawn.

I waved my gun around the house. Kelly sat in the middle of the room crying and pulling on the rope.

I rushed over to her. "What's the matter?"

"I'm scared."

Suddenly very rattled, I picked her up and headed for the boys' fishing spot. When I arrived, the boys dropped their poles and raced over to me. They had caught one small fish but also had a chunk of some sort of dark flesh. It looked like a large chicken thigh, but its size and dark skin were not fowl-like. I thought maybe it was a chunk of seal leftover from a shark or whale attack that washed up on the beach. They said they had eaten some of it before. I told them that they shouldn't eat dead things they find on the beach, but they boisterously informed me that it had been given to them by little bear. I didn't argue with them about their imaginary friend, since I questioned even my own sanity at that point.

"Boys, look," I said. "Have you searched any of the houses for food?"

"No, we're scared to go in any of them."

"Are there any that haven't been broken in to?"

"Yes, the Mercer house," said Tommy.

"Which one is that?"

"Three houses from the end," he pointed to the end opposite that of which I had just been.

"Come with me. I don't think we should split up any more."

We proceeded to the Mercer house. It was locked up tight, just as the boys had indicated. The Mercer house and the two further down were walk-ins. Nothing but a narrow sidewalk along the bulkhead connected them to civilization, which served as a reasonable explanation as to why they had not been touched.

"Are you boys sure there is no one here?"

"The Mercer's were on vacation when the Red Plague started," Tommy said. "I never saw them again."

We knocked on the door anyway. No answer. We walked around and looked in the windows. There was no sign of anyone or anything unusual. I knocked on the large beach side window. Nothing moved.

I went around to a side door. I put Kelly down and kicked the door firmly near the knob. It popped right open. Once again, a storm front of death stench blew out of the door. By that point, I had gotten somewhat used to it, but I was also tired of what it meant: that nothing but dead people would be found. This time, however, there were other familiar odors mixed in, but I couldn't unravel the smells to identify them.

I resigned myself to the facts, steeled myself against what I would find, and entered, restricting the children to the outside. The door accessed the kitchen, and I noticed that, while the house had not been gone through, there were numerous piles of feces on the floor. The unusual odors materialized in my mind as urine and feces—probably cat. I stepped carefully around the piles and opened one of the cupboard doors. Boxes of food neatly lined the shelves and my heart jumped. I opened the next cupboard, and it was filled with canned goods.

I moved excitedly into the darkened pantry where I stepped on something squishy and nearly fell. I heard a dull pop, and what followed can only be described as the most horrific smell that exists. A decaying body puts out a fair amount of odor, but what most people don't know is that the vast majority remains trapped within. If you leave it alone, it stinks, but if you meddle with it, the smell could gag a maggot, as my grandfather used to say. The only good news was that the smell came from Smiley, the Mercer's cat, and not one of the Mercers. The bad news is that my shoes were never the same.

After I disposed of the cat and opened the doors for a while, we took four wheel barrows full of boxed and canned food out of the Mercer house. I also went through their closets and found a pair of hiking boots for me—a little tight but doable—and a pair of boys sneakers that were too big for Charlie. I gave them to Tommy. I checked the two houses further down, and they were also undisturbed. I found several more cupboards full of food but decided to get it all later.

The four of us enjoyed a dinner of Au Gratin potatoes, green beans, and salmon—not a bad meal after the end of the world. I forced them to throw away the seal though. The children ate all they were served which struck me odd, since those were three items that my children wouldn't have touched just a few months prior. Even children eventually discover that when you are hungry—really hungry—any food always tastes better than no food.

We were startled awake in the middle of the night by a banging at the door. I couldn't make out the muffled yelling through the solid front door and thick-glassed storm door. I retrieved my gun and flashlight and scrambled to the door. Standing aside of the door, I shined the light through. Tommy peered back with tears streaming down his face.

I opened the door, and he raced into my arms.

"What is it?"

"It's Grandma! She won't move!"

Charlie and Kelly were also awakened by the commotion, so the four of us made the dreadful walk to Tommy's house. Indeed, his grandmother had died in her sleep. We broke the frosty ground in the darkness and fog and buried her. Then we went back to bed—this time, Tommy stayed with us.

Now I had three children.

The next day, the boys helped me rig up an alarm at the top of the hill while Kelly watched, or at least looked at us. Shortly into our project, I got the feeling again. I had the urge to go looking, but didn't want to spook the children. I casually kept an eye out but never saw a thing. The feeling wasn't as frightening as before. The stream made me aware but wasn't telling me to be wary.

We found a long rubber bladder, filled it with water, laid it across the road, and covered it with leaves. We loosely stoppered the valve in the end of the bladder so that the water wouldn't run out. We fished the neighborhood rope swing to the top of the hill, tied a large boulder to it, and secured it to a tree with a double metal ring and upside down pin. We tethered the boulder to another line which ran from the top to a pole at the bottom. We fastened the bell from Tommy's neighbor's sailboat onto the pole. Finally, we attached a bucket to the bottom of the pin and set the bladder valve inside the bucket.

The boys jumped on the bladder to test the system. The stopper popped out which filled the bucket with water. The bucket pulled the pin, setting the boulder free. It careened along the guide wire and smashed into the bell. The force of the heavy boulder drove the edge of the bell about two inches into the pole and it stuck there, hardly making a sound. We pried the bell free and placed it on the side of the pole, refilled the bladders, and tested it again. This time, the sound was so loud that I was afraid we would attract attention clear down in Langley.

We reset the alarm and went back down to the beach. The alarm would definitely alert us of any approaching vehicles, but it would do nothing about an intruder on foot unless he walked down the road and happened to step on the bladder with enough force to dislodge the stopper. A single intruder, I could deal with. A car full of thugs, we'd need to hide.

We spent the next week alone at the beach, fishing, eating, and building our strength. Twice the boys came back with food from the little bear—a ling cod and a Dungeness crab, both of which are deep water creatures—which smelled fresh, so we ate them. I honestly had no idea what to say about this imaginary little bear friend, but it grew more worrisome. I was sure that these were just things washing up on the beach, although, somehow, I never found any of it myself.

The weather grew ever colder, and the days continued to shorten. On the fourth day of that week, it snowed over a foot. On the fifth day, the snow hadn't melted a bit, and the wind came up from the north. The salt spray began to freeze on the deck and the windows. That meant the temperature was well down in the twenties. I also realized that the freezing temperatures meant an end to our alarm's effectiveness. Despite the fact that a car could probably no longer get down the road, we spent the fifth day re-tooling the alarm. We tied a rope to the pin and stretched it across the road, just below the surface of the snow.

When the wind hadn't abated on the sixth day and it began to snow again, I grew very worried. We couldn't fish, and the salmon run was waning. I had hoped to lay in a lot of salmon while they were around, but so much for that. We hadn't had any meat for days, and we were getting too far into our supplies already.

Worse yet, there was no way we could make the walk I had planned through a foot of snow and near blizzard conditions. It would have been bad enough in good weather, but in winter weather, it would have been the end of all of us. But to stay there also meant likely death—an agonizing, slow, painful death from starvation. We had plenty of wood to burn for heat—we had tons of wood, in fact, considering all the houses around us—but we had all the food there was and I calculated it would last us less than two months. We'd run out in the dead of winter.

It snowed through the entire seventh day. The children sat inside and read and played games. I almost got the feeling they were happy. I continued to worry.

On the eighth day, the wind switched to the south, and it warmed up and rained. The heavy rain on top of almost two feet of snow made a terrible mess of things, but the combination of salty air, wind, and warm rain ate into the snow quickly. It blew and rained all day and melted the snow down to only a few inches by day's end.

I was never so glad to see the rain in my life. As a meteorologist, I should have known that, despite the lack of sun, the Pacific was still quite warm and the wind would eventually switch. But my tendency was to worry—about things as they were, but more so about things as I feared them to be.

On the ninth day, the snow melted off entirely, and it became warmer than I had experienced in over a month. Not since I was out in the middle of the Pacific had it been that warm—the cheap thermometer on the fence read 74F at the day's zenith. The sky was still dark and gunmetal gray, but the south wind brought in much deserved comfort. I spent some time fishing with the boys and noticed that they used a homemade lure. It turned out that little bear had shown them how to make it. I let it go.

We caught only two small bullheads in three hours. We had never considered eating the bullheads before. But with the salmon run apparently over, we wouldn't have considered throwing them back. We needed the protein.

Having been skunked, I gave up and sent the boys to check on Kelly. Although she was ok being alone in the house since we'd installed the alarm, we'd been gone a while.

I nonchalantly combed the beach and woods along the shore. I hoped that a varmint would pop out of the woods and give me an easy meal or that I would find something washed up like as boys had. I neared the point where I would eat beach-kill if it didn't stink.

I nearly came out of my skin when someone paddled around the corner in a canoe, not fifty yards in front of me. Out of habit I ducked down, but there was no hiding on the barren beach. The woods were only about twenty five feet away, but surely I had already been seen. The man stared at me and continued to paddle straight in my direction.

As I knelt frozen, the only sound I heard was the glop of the paddle entering the water and the sprinkling of water as it moved forward for the next iteration. I watched cautiously as the canoe, a green one like you get from a sports store, lurched quietly through the water toward me. I slowly reached to the back of my waistband and slid my hand over my gun. It relaxed me.

The canoeist had long black hair and tan skin and wore a flannel shirt and wool ski hat. As he approached, I noticed him to be of some age. His wrinkled face showed no hint of aggression, but his flat nose, dark complexion, and slender face were unmistakably American Indian in origin.

Perceiving no threat, I stood up but kept my hand near my gun.

The man paddled up to the beach right where I was standing. He placed an oar flat against the water and coasted to a stop, not five feet from shore. He just stared at me.

I stared back.

He looked me up and down as I continued to evaluate him.

It startled me when he reached into the canoe. I tightened my grip on my gun. He brought out a black object and threw it at me. It landed at my feet. I kicked at the thing and examined it without bending down. It looked like a large chicken thigh but with black skin. He reached down, selected another one, and threw it on the beach. Together, they must have been five pounds of meat. My stomach growled as I lowered my empty gun hand to my side.

We stared at each other.

I nodded.

He nodded back.

He placed one oar in the water and pulled back with great force, turning the canoe completely around with one stroke. Then he paddled off. I watched dumbfounded as he rounded the bend and disappeared.

The boys clamored up behind me. They stood quietly watching me watch the horizon. Finally, Charlie bent down and picked up the seal flesh.

"You saw Little Bear," he said.

"Yes, I did," I said through a lump in my throat.

I left the boys to their fishing and returned to the house. A panic washed over me when I found the living room empty. I ran around back and found Kelly sitting at her mother's grave crying.

I sat next to her and put my arm around her.

She ran both her hands through the fresh dirt. She picked up some dirt and brought it to her face and smelled it. She got up onto her knees and laid her head down on the mound.

"We all miss her sweetie," I said.

Kelly sat back and looked at me with dirt smudges across the bridge of her nose. For the first time, she really looked at me. I could tell there was someone there again. She blinked, and her eyelids pinched off a few tears. She laid her head against my chest.

"Are you ever going to talk to me again?" I asked.

"Yes," she whispered.

On the tenth day, I sat on the deck and watched the children play. Then I spotted it. A boat, approaching—a dark boat with quite a few people on board. Fearing the worst, I commanded the children inside. I wished I had binoculars. I wanted to watch, but I couldn't risk being seen, as if we hadn't been seen already. I put out the fire in the fireplace, but it was almost certainly too late. We had prepared for being spotted. We scrambled back into the hole in the foundation and pulled some of the dying plants in over the cover and waited.

After a tense half hour or so in the crawlspace, our alarm went off. I couldn't imagine why the boat people had gone up the hill unless they had some particular place in mind to go. Certainly, they were now aware of the

DEAD RECKONING

alarm, but I hoped that they hadn't dismantled our roadblock. I also hoped it meant that they hadn't seen us after all.

I never heard them land on the beach or pass by the house. I decided to continue to wait and listen. Hours passed. Agonizing hours. I thought I heard something several times, but I couldn't be sure, and I certainly had no idea what was going on outside. We waited quietly and listened. Tommy spoke first.

"Maybe they went by," he whispered.

"I'm not sure," I said. "I don't hear a thing."

"Should we check it out?" Tommy asked.

"I will. You all stay here."

"No!" whimpered Charlie. "Don't go."

"I will be careful."

I quietly pulled back the cover and moved the plants aside. It was getting dark out.

I gave Tommy back his gun and cocked my own and began to emerge from the crawlspace.

I edged down the sidewalk that ran along the house toward the beach. My senses piqued just as they had the moment I set foot on the island. I realized that I had unwittingly let my guard down over those last days, and I cursed myself for it. I tiptoed along the sidewalk and neared the deck.

A lone gunshot rang out from down the beach or up in the woods, I couldn't tell. I dove for cover.

Knowing that the children would be scared, I went back to the crawlspace.

I poked my head in.

"What happened?" Tommy asked.

"It wasn't me," I whispered. "It was somewhere down the beach to the north. Or maybe up in the woods."

"I'm going to check it out."

"Daddy, I'm really scared," said Charlie.

"Me too, buddy."

"I'll be back as soon as I find out what is going on."

I went back down the sidewalk along the house and peered around the corner, over the deck toward the water. To my surprise, the boat I had seen earlier bobbed up and down in the surf, right in front of the house. In the darkness of dusk, I couldn't make out any name on the side. It didn't help that the boat was also dark in color—like camouflage. Nothing moved on the boat, but I couldn't risk being out in the open so close to the unknown craft.

I worked my way back along the sidewalk and then slipped in behind the neighbor's house. I walked behind several houses and then emerged back on the beach side. With enough space between me and the boat, I moved to the edge of the beach and peered north along the waterline. I saw several men crouched down behind the bulkhead about four houses further down.

A shot echoed through the woods. The sound echoed too much to determine its origin, but the flash seemed to come from somewhere up the hill.

Then the men on the beach returned fire. Several flashes lit up the beach. I noticed something familiar about one of the men—something about the way he stood.

I moved very quietly another house down and went beach side to take another look. I couldn't see anything in the dark.

One of the men flicked a lighter to life and lit a cigarette. The light briefly illuminated the man in question. The way he leaned against the bulkhead was familiar as was the way he braced himself against the breeze when he shifted position.

I turned back toward the boat to take a more careful look. I still couldn't see it. I turned and worked my way back to the house. Once at the edge of the deck, I looked at the boat. That was when I noticed the hand-carved mast.

Suddenly, I realized who the man was on the beach. I ran back between the houses and got right up on them before I emerged at the beach. I was less than twenty yards from the men. I had no idea who the other two were. I considered how to make my presence known without getting my head blown off. What if I were wrong about the man? But I knew that posture.

I felt a hand on my shoulder.

I whirled noisily and pointed my gun at the visitor.

"Dad!" Charlie said, much too loudly.

"Shhh!"

Tommy was right behind him.

"I thought I told you two to stay," I said.

I turned back to the men on the beach, who were already under cover and out of my line of sight.

"Who's there?" one of the men said.

I took a chance and said: "Jeff, it's me. Matt."

"It's him," I heard Jeff say. "Don't shoot."

"Are you sure?" asked one of the men.

"How else did he know my name? Take it easy."

"Are you all right?" Jeff asked.

"Yes, fine."

"Stay put," one of the other men said. "We've got hostiles on the hill."

"Roger that," I said, slipping into military-ese.

"Do you know anything about them yet?"

"Nope. We saw them up on the hill when we pulled up. They saw us, and we've been standing off ever since. They just fired at us a few minutes ago."

"How many?"

"I saw four, maybe more. Only two separate muzzle flashes though."

"Didn't you hear the racket they made coming down?"

"Yeah, that was our alarm."

"No shit! I'd say it worked. They probably heard that in Seattle!"

"What are we going to do?"

"Wait them…"

Someone yelled from up on the hill.

"Did he just say my name?" I asked Jeff.

"Sounded like it."

"Is that you? It's me Joe! I've got the Blackmans with me."

"Oh my God!" I said.

"Yes, Joe, it's me," I yelled back. "Is it just the four of you?"

"Yes."

"Come on down. Be careful of the barricade at the bottom of the hill."

"How do you know there aren't other people with them?" one of the men asked. "Could be a trap, a Trojan horse."

"Joe's a smart guy," I said. "He'd have figured out a way to let us know. Besides, I don't think he would have brought anyone else here."

Charlie, Tommy, and I jumped down onto the beach and joined Jeff and the two men.

Jeff grabbed Charlie and hugged him.

"I'm so glad to see you. And who's this?" he asked, pointing at Tommy.

"This is Tommy. He lives down here. He's with us now."

"Good, we can use all the men we can get," Jeff said.

Tommy stood up straighter as if to re-affirm that he was, indeed, a man.

I stepped forward and extended my hand to the first of the unknown men.

"Dean Collins, Brenda's brother," the man said, shaking my hand and nearly crushing it. The first thing I noticed about Dean was his square head and shoulders. He was short and stout.

The other man stepped forward and took my hand.

"Josh Collins. Brenda's better brother."

Dean slugged Josh firmly in the shoulder. The solid punch knocked his tall, skinny frame back a couple of steps.

"How are Brenda and the girls?" I asked Jeff tentatively.

"They're fine," he said. He looked at Charlie and then sheepishly toward me. He raised his eyebrows in a sort of nonverbal question.

"Kelly is back at the house. It's just the four of us now."

Jeff performed the squinted smile one might make when experiencing a sharp pain—it was the facial gesture of condolence. It's next to impossible to know how to behave in the presence of an adult who has just lost a dear member of his family much less a child like Charlie. Jeff did well.

"Let's go back to the RY," Jeff said.

"We'll go escort your visitors," Dean said while motioning to his brother.

As we walked down the beach, Jeff hooted toward the boat.

Heads popped out from below decks.

"It's ok," he said.

Three adults and two children spilled onto the deck. I thought I knew who those people might be. A plank of wood lowered to the beach and people filed down, their arms held wide for balance.

Within seconds, Jill and Sonny had me in an embrace. Brenda grabbed Charlie and bear hugged him. Brenda had lost a lot of weight since I'd seen her last. She was always cute but could have been described as pudgy before. She was positively slender as she held Charlie. At only 5'2", Brenda was dwarfed by Charlie now.

"We're so glad to see you!" exclaimed Brenda.

Tommy and the Riggins girls stood quietly by, unsure of what to do.

While Brenda held Charlie, she looked at me and mouthed the word "Kate."

Tears welled in my eyes. I pursed my lips against the emotion and shook my head. Tears welled in her eyes as she mouthed "the girls."

Shit, I exclaimed. I broke free from Jill and Sonny, leapt over the bulkhead, and ran around back to the crawl space. Everyone followed.

I scrambled inside and found Kelly crying and rocking back and forth.

"We're ok, honey. Charlie and Tommy are fine. We're all fine."

Kelly wrapped her arms around me.

"There are two people here to see you," I said.

She looked out through the hole curiously.

I pulled her out as Jeff's girls screamed and yelled happily: "Kelly!"

Kelly smiled for the first time since I had returned.

Brenda's brothers escorted Joe and the Blackmans to the house. I introduced everyone to everyone else. And our group suddenly grew to sixteen.

We all exchanged stories of our experiences since my disembarkation at Bush Point. It turned out that the rest of the RY's trip was uneventful. Just as expected, Brenda's brothers had protected her and the girls, and they were hardly the worse for the wear when Jeff arrived. They spent time repairing the RY and outfitting it for whatever voyage lay ahead.

We had talked through a number of different plans, and finally settled on going to see if my friend, Sean McMasters, was indeed holed up in the mountains near Port Angeles as I suspected. I was fairly certain of three things: If he had survived the Red Plague, he would be there; he'd be better prepared than anyone else; he would welcome us. Backup plans included coming back to Shadow Beach and trying to make it there, sailing back up to Gilligan's Island, and taking one of the thousands of sea-worthy boats that must be still around and trying to get back to Kwaj.

The children listened for a while but eventually peeled off into their groups to play. The Blackman boys hit it off right away with Charlie and Tommy, and the girls immediately became inseparable again. The adults were a little more guarded at first, but we also quickly formed into a collegial group. With their military training, Brenda's brothers immediately tried to take charge and lead our group. Joe resisted that notion outright, and Jeff had already earned the allegiance of Sonny, Jill, and I. So no true leader immediately emerged. That was all right, though, since we had proved that leadership by committee could be made to work. I think everyone was truly impressed that we made it all the way across the Pacific against such odds. It earned us quite a bit of credibility.

We decided to leave for Port Angeles the next day. We sat silently watching the children play and contemplating what lie ahead.

Charlie rubbed his eyes, sneezed, and then coughed.

Are you all right, I asked.

Everyone turned to look at him.

"Yes," he said.

25

SHADOW BEACH/LANGLEY, WHIDBEY ISLAND, WA

Despite my assurances, Josh and Dean insisted on standing watch overnight. I admit that I got my first good night's sleep in a long time knowing that someone else was on the lookout for bad guys.

Yet, I awakened to one of my worst fears: a wheezing sound coming from my little boy's chest. A bead of sweat rolled down his forehead as I leaned in to listen. I pressed my wrist against his head and felt his cool, clammy skin. I unzipped his sleeping bag and ran my hand over his chest. His heart thumped quickly inside, and his feverish body warmed my hand.

I quietly awakened Jill and told her what I had found. She crawled over to him and placed her head against his chest and listened. She squinted as if trying to focus on something.

Jill got up and walked out to Dean who was sitting outside on second watch. He nodded and spit something on the ground. Then he got up, looked around, and walked up the plank into the RY.

Jill came back over to Charlie and me and sat down.

"Should we do something to bring down his fever?" I asked.

"I'm not sure yet."

Dean set the first aid kit down next to us and went back to his post. Jill fished out a thermometer, lifted Charlie's shirt and arm, and placed it in his armpit. He shifted and whined softly, as if annoyed, and then went back to sleep.

After a minute, Jill removed the thermometer and reported the results: one hundred and two degrees.

"That's high," I said.

"Not really," Jill contradicted.

"I stashed away some children's ibuprofen," I said. "I'll go get it."

Jill grabbed my arm.

"We don't want to bring his fever down," she said.

"Why not?"

"We get fevers for a reason, and it's to fight the infection."

"But you know how uncomfortable a fever is."

"Yes, and the effort to make us comfortable has been one of the biggest failures of modern medicine. We defeat all sorts of important natural defenses against disease by masking symptoms. We stop coughs that are designed to rid our lungs of fluid. We cover up pains that are designed to force us to stop using joints so they can heal. We stop diarrhea which is supposed to flush poisons from our intestines. And we reduce fevers that are one of our best natural defenses against infections."

"But you can't let a fever get too high, right?"

"Right, but 102 isn't too high. If it gets much over 103 we'll have to do something, but this is actually good for him. A person won't die until it gets up around 106."

"106, really?" I asked. "Hell, most of the time I wished I were dead with a fever of even a hundred."

"Viruses and bacteria don't like it either," Jill pointed out. "102 or 103 won't kill you, but it will kill many invaders."

"I see. Just the same, shouldn't we at least start him on antibiotics?"

"If it's a virus, it won't do any good. And it could do some harm. Antibiotics aren't that easy on your system, you know?"

"Yeah, I know. It kills the good bacteria in your intestines."

"Among other things," Jill said.

"I'm just worried that he has what Tommy's grandmother had."

"I thought you said it was pneumonia?"

"Yeah, but I don't know for sure."

"Yeah," Jill said to no one in particular. "Let's just see how he does today before we jump to any conclusions."

I couldn't bear to go through this again. Jill sat there next to Charlie and stroked his arm. I was so glad that Jill was back with us again. She leaned over and rested her head against my shoulder.

"It makes it worse, you know?" I whispered.

"What does?"

"Having them back."

"What, the worry?" Jill asked.

"Yes. I had resigned myself to them being gone. If something happened to either of them now, I, I don't know. I couldn't go on."

Jill took my hand and said: "We won't let that happen."

"The problem is: we don't have that much control anymore," I lamented.

• • •

As a group, we decided not to leave with Charlie being sick. The wind was generally from the west, and that meant fairly benign weather, at least in the short term. When the wind backed to the south, it meant an approaching storm, and when it veered north, it usually meant cold and sometimes snowy weather.

Despite the high overcast, we could still see that old bell-weather, Mount Rainier. And since Mount Rainier remained uncapped—that is, its top was not obscured by clouds—it was unlikely to rain in the next twenty four hours. Unlike so many old wives' or farmer's tales, the one about a cap on Mount Rainier actually had a basis in science. When Mount Rainier's top became obscured by clouds it meant that moist flow off the ocean had developed, which almost always preceded rain by about twenty four hours.

So we stayed put and continued final preparations for our journey.

Charlie's health declined at such a pace throughout the day that, by dark, I was preparing to head out to look for some strong antibiotics. We had the garden variety stuff like Amoxicillin, Penicillin, and Erythromycin, but that wasn't good enough for me. Jill feared that Charlie had pneumonia and, despite her assurances that pneumonia was normally caused by bacteria easily treated with such broad-spectrum drugs, I wanted the real stuff, just in case. We started him on Amoxicillin, but I planned to take no chances.

"I'm sure the pharmacies have all been cleaned out," Brenda pleaded with me.

"Maybe, but what should I do, wait until it's too late? If I go now, maybe I can find something before it's too late."

"Or maybe you'll get yourself killed," Jill said.

"I'm not going to do anything stupid. But I'm also not going to sit here and watch my son die."

I looked around to make sure Tommy wasn't within earshot.

"It was too late when I got to Tommy's grandmother, but she carried on for a week or more. Charlie is healthier than her, and maybe he can beat it, or maybe the Amox will work, but I'm not going to find out too late that it's too late."

"You saw the stores," Joe said. "What are the odds there will be anything left in a pharmacy?"

"Not good," I said, as I picked up my backpack and slung it over my shoulder.

It was as useless for them to try to talk me out of going as it was for me to try to talk Jeff and Sonny out of coming with me. So we set off to check out the closest pharmacy, Langley Drug.

We covered the five miles to Langley in a couple of hours and arrived there at what I reckoned to be around midnight. We surely could have gone faster, but we walked the road in darkness and only occasionally switched on our flashlights on to verify our course. As we walked in silence, I thought back to the dogs I had encountered as well as the figure I saw down in Langley as I passed by. When we passed the spot of my dog attack, many of the carcasses were gone. It made for a hell of a story anyway. Our walk was entirely uneventful, but I spent most of it tensely fretting over what I would do if we couldn't find any antibiotics.

We knew we were getting close when the smell came up. We split up as we edged inside the city limits, Jeff and Sonny on one side of the street and me on the other.

Langley Drug was one of many shops that lined Main Street in downtown Langley. By my recollection, it was the fifth store on the south side after we passed Second Street. Glass occasionally crunched under foot as we moved slowly along the street. I accidentally kicked a bottle as I walked, but we otherwise made little noise. We were getting good at stealth.

We all stopped when we heard a sound in the distance. The sound came from the bluff above Langley, and it grew louder as we listened. Then headlights came over the hill and began to descend into the town.

I joined Jeff and Sonny and we ducked into a gutted-out building. The vehicle pulled onto the main street and idled along, music blaring. The men laughed and carried on. Finally, the unmistakable orange truck stopped several buildings down and the men got out. I peered around the corner and watched them walk toward a building on the other side of the street. Anger surged through my veins.

"Oh no," Jeff whispered. I had told Jeff and Sonny about my encounters with those three, but they didn't know it all—Jill and Brenda were the only ones who knew about all of my suspicions.

They entered the building. Fear and doubt crept up on me just as my anger reached a rolling boil. My emotions battled for a few seconds, and, finally, anger won. I stepped out and began walking toward the building.

"What are you doing?" whispered Sonny nervously.

I kept walking. I pulled out my gun and pulled back the slider to chamber a round. I knew the clip was full. Jeff and Sonny scrambled up behind me and grabbed me.

"Matt, you got your stuff back. It's water under the bridge. This isn't worth it," Jeff pleaded.

I stopped. "That's not the half of it," I said, my eyes boring into Jeff's.

Whether Jeff and Sonny truly understood at that moment or not, they stopped trying to stop me.

The truck continued to rumble in the roadway as I walked by. Country music blared from the stereo. The men thrashed around noisily inside the building, oblivious to the approaching menace. They'd obviously had the run of the island for too long.

I got to the front of the building and looked in. The men rummaged through the CDs of the small music store. There were no weapons in their hands. The truck's headlights shined from behind me into the building. I had all the advantages: the light, the element of surprise, and most importantly, just cause.

I raised my gun and stepped into the building. Glass crunched under my foot, and they all turned.

"If any of you move you are dead," I said.

The men shielded their eyes from the light behind me.

"Who the fuck are you?" asked one of them.

"Hey man. Take it easy," said another. "We're just looking for tunes."

I walked to within five feet of the men. There was no doubt that they were the guys—Tommy described the truck to a tee. Sonny and Jeff followed in behind, weapons drawn.

"I don't give a fuck about this store," I said. I turned to illuminate my face.

"Hey, we were just screwing with you, dude," one of them said. "We gave you your shit back."

"I don't give a fuck about that either," I said. "I know you assholes have been down to Shadow Beach. I just want to know which one of you raped my wife and daughters."

The dread that spread across all of their faces told me everything I needed to know.

"You mother fuckers," I heard Jeff whisper under his breath. He attempted to push past me, but I stopped him with my left arm.

"I'll take care of this," I said calmly.

The last drop of fear drained from my body and left only anger. There wasn't a single cell in my body that didn't want those guys to suffer terribly. I had no idea if one of the guys was the main culprit, but as far as I cared, they all represented the same thing. I chose at random and pointed the gun at the man on my left.

"Admit it and I won't kill you," I lied.

"Fuck no, man. I didn't do sh…" I pulled the trigger and shot him in the face. Blood and bone and tissue sprayed all of the shelves behind him and on the man in next to him. The man in the middle jumped up to run, and I shot him in the back. He sprawled out on the floor.

"Jesus!" I heard Sonny say under his breath behind me. Neither Sonny nor Jeff moved.

I turned to the last guy. He trembled and held up his hands.

"It was all them," he said. "I tried to stop them."

I recognized him as the one who took my clothes back on the road.

"Stand up and take off your clothes," I said.

He did as I demanded. I pointed my gun at his naked crotch and told him to beg for his life. He began to beg, and I pulled the trigger. He stumbled backward a few steps, dropped to his knees, and looked down at the hole in his groin. Blood poured out. The nine millimeter is a small bullet, and it didn't have the effect I intended—much of his manhood remained intact.

I walked right up to him and put the gun to his forehead. I leaned down, my face just inches from his.

"Why would you do that to women, girls?" I asked. "They never did a thing to you. What about all the others? How many were there?"

"I never did nothing," he said.

"You either did it, or you let them do it," I replied. "How many more were there?"

He froze in fear.

"How many!" I screamed, my angry spit spraying onto his face.

"Fuck you," he said calmly, resigned to his fate. "That's just how it is now."

My mind flashed to the beach community on Vancouver Island. I stepped back and told Jeff and Sonny to cover them until I returned. I ran to the truck and searched it. Amongst the general filth in the cab, there was a variety of firearms, a couple of gold coins, and some cans of food. I rummaged around and came upon a girl's flip-flop, a dirty and worn outline of a little foot in its middle. I angrily threw it from the cab.

I stepped out and looked in the bed. Dark stains covered the rusty metal floor of the bed, but I found what I was after: a length of rope. I tied a noose as I re-entered the music store. The man pleaded for Sonny and Jeff to stop me.

"Shut the fuck up," Jeff said.

I pushed past Sonny and Jeff and went over to the other man on the floor. He struggled in pain as I placed the noose around his neck. I pulled on the loose end and flipped him over. I dragged him kicking from the store. I dropped him in the street next to a light pole and went back in for the other one.

"You are fucked in the head," the last man said.

"I'm fucked in the head?" I questioned indignantly. "You pillage and loot and rape innocent women and children, and I'm fucked in the head?"

I grabbed the man by the hair and began to drag him out. He grabbed my legs and tried to fight. While still holding him by the hair, I lifted my left leg and brought it down full force on his left arm. I felt the bone snap as he screamed out in pain. I dragged him out in the street and positioned him next to the other man.

"I want you to watch this," I said.

I threw the rope over the light pole and raised the man up until he could no longer touch the ground. He kicked and squirmed as blood and spit foamed from his mouth. He tried to grab the rope above his head and pull himself up. It was no use. He trained his bulging eyes on me and I saw the terror. I dragged the last man over in front of him.

"Watch!" I yelled as I grabbed his hair and forced him to look. I held him there as the man struggled. It took about two minutes but finally he twitched for the last time.

I cut the remainder off the first rope and began to tie another noose. The man screamed at me as I placed it around his neck and dragged him over to the pole.

I leaned down to his ear and whispered: "How does it feel, you piece of shit?"

I waited for a response, and none came. I punched him in the face, and he grunted and struggled as blood trickled from his nose. Then I grabbed his broken arm and twisted. He screamed in pain and nearly fainted. I slapped him back to reality.

"He was for my wife and daughters," I said, pointing to the man swinging slowly from the light pole. "You are for all the other women."

"I'll see you in hell!" he screamed.

"There has to be a different hell for people like you," I replied.

I looked over the Jeff and Sonny. They stared in shocked silence. My anger began to drain away. Having had all the suffering I could stand, I took out my gun and shot the man in the back of the head. He fell dead on the street. Then I strung him up the pole and tied it off. The rope creaked as he swung back and forth.

"I should have let him hang too," I said as I passed Sonny and Jeff on my way back into the store. "But I'm not like them." They didn't say a word.

Jeff and Sonny dragged the third man out of the store and strung him up as I fashioned a sign that read "this is what happens to rapists in this town." I held the sign to the chest of the man in the middle and plunged his own knife through the sign and into his chest.

It was done—revenge had been exacted. I had expected to feel some closure, but I felt nothing.

Sonny checked their clothes for useful items while Jeff and I went to the truck. Music still blared from the stereo. The lights and noise made me suddenly self-conscious, so I walked around to the driver's side and killed the lights and ignition.

I used my flashlight to collect all the firearms, ammunition, and other useful items from the truck and piled them in the street. Sonny took two handguns and a hunting knife off the men and added them to the pile.

"How are we going to carry all this stuff?" Jeff asked.

"We could take their truck," Sonny offered.

"There are a lot more animals in this pack," I said. "I don't want that truck anywhere near Shadow Beach when they come looking for these three."

We turned our attention back to the task at hand. I walked over to Langley Drug and swept the store with my flashlight. All that remained of the front windows of Langley Drug was a small triangle of glass with the letter L on it. The aisles were oriented lengthwise in the narrow store allowing us to see all the way to the back. Debris was everywhere, but there were no bodies inside.

Langley Drug was one of many businesses in Langley that were owned by the Rajcik family. The Rajciks were Russians that had immigrated to the United States less than a generation earlier. They established businesses on Whidbey Island, mostly in Langley, and were thought to have been involved with the Russian mafia before coming to America. They were nice people, but had a bit of a mysterious side which only fueled people's suspicions of them. Nevertheless, within just a few years, they owned half of Langley, and so all people could really do was to try to get along with them.

I stepped through the broken window into Langley Drug whilst Sonny and Jeff covered the front. As with every other place I had been, the store had been savaged. Everything not edible or intoxicating was smashed on the floor, and all that remained upright were the shelves too heavy to move.

I clicked on my flashlight and scanned the floor for anything useful as I moved down the aisle toward the back. I moved quietly but quickly to the pharmacy. The metal security fence over the "submit prescriptions here" window had been forced open. I crawled through and to my surprise, there were many prescription medications strewn across the floor. I saw bottles of injectable insulin, heart medications, and pills for male sexual dysfunction. Sonny and Jeff came in behind me and went right to picking through the medications.

"Look at this," said Sonny.

He held up a box with the word Oxycodone on the side.

"Empty," he commented.

"I think that's all they were after," I said. "The painkillers. See, here's some more amoxicillin."

"Yep," Jeff said. "Vicodin, empty."

"Hey guys!" Sonny exclaimed. "Here is something. Cipro!"

"How much is there?" I asked.

"A whole big assed bottle!"

"Ok," I said. "Let's get out of here."

"Wait a minute," Jeff said. "Grab as much of these other antibiotics as you can."

I began filling my backpack with anything that sounded familiar. Jeff and Sonny did the same.

"As long as we don't need a tooth pulled we'll be fine," Sonny said. "Everything else you can think of is still here."

Jeff moved further back into the shelves of medications. His light flicked about as he scanned the products.

"Hey, look at this."

Jeff held up a huge ring of keys.

"It says Langley Motors on it."

"The people who owned this drug store also owned a car dealership here," I explained.

"We can't take their truck," Jeff said. "But I don't think anybody's going to miss one of these."

"Yeah. I'm getting tired of walking," agreed Sonny.

We gathered up all the pharmaceuticals we could hold and made for the back door. Since the back door entered directly into the pharmacy, it was solid steel and dead-bolted. Jeff unbolted the door and kicked it, and it swung open to the alley behind the row of stores. A Cadillac Escalade sat vandalized in the alley. The windows were broken out, and the body was severely dented. The interior smelled of alcohol. The gas door had been pried and was severely mangled, but it had thwarted the gasoline thieves.

"I suppose it still has gas," I said to Sonny.

"I guess there were so many targets that if it didn't give up easily, they moved on," Sonny replied.

"These keys are mostly for Fords and Dodges," Jeff said. "There are only a few Beamer keys on here and, oh yeah, only two Cadillac keys." Jeff jumped into the driver's seat and tried the first key. Nothing happened. Jeff inserted the second key and turned it and the dash board lit up.

"You've got to be kidding me," Sonny said, racing around to the passenger door.

Jeff started the Escalade and music poured out of the speakers, bass thumping.

Sonny began to pump his head in rhythm, smiling. I let the armload of drugs I had fall through the window into the back seat and I climbed in.

Jeff turned down the stereo.

"No point in drawing more attention to ourselves than we already have."

"If there is anybody else here, they know we're here now," I said.

"Screw it!" said Jeff. "Let's see them stop us."

Jeff put the SUV in gear and gunned it down the alley. We rounded the corner and covered the half block to Main Street in a split second. We drove back up to the truck and loaded all the other supplies we had gathered into the Escalade. We piled back in. Jeff slammed it in reverse and gunned it. We screamed down the street backwards and then Jeff attempted one of those rolling U-turn maneuvers we'd seen in the movies. It didn't go as planned and we ended up crashing backwards through one of the store fronts.

"Oops!" Jeff yelled.

He put it in drive and tore out of the store, dragging debris all the way. We screeched back onto the street, and Jeff floored it up Main Street. The headlights suddenly illuminated two vandalized cars blocking the exit to town.

"Hold on!" yelled Jeff.

He stomped on the accelerator again, and we plowed into the parked cars, hurtling them off into the ditches. The impact barely fazed the Caddy.

We screamed out of town and turned onto a straightaway that extended almost all the way to Shadow Beach. Jeff opened it up, and within a few seconds, we were careening down the road a hundred and ten miles an hour. The wind poured through the broken out windows, and it felt exhilarating.

Just as we approached the end of the straightaway, a raccoon jumped out in front of us. Out of habit, Jeff turned slightly and avoided it, but he could not avoid the deer that had stepped out into the road right in front of us. We smashed into the deer at about eighty miles per hour and sent it sprawling thirty or forty yards down the road. We came to a stop just before we ran over it again.

The deer lay lifeless in the road, blood pooling near its head. The Cadillac sat idling in the road with its only unbroken headlight on the deer.

We got out of the SUV to look at the damage. We heard a rustling in the brush and immediately crouched down for cover.

Two spotted fawns came bounding awkwardly out of the thicket, and seemingly oblivious to our presence, walked over and stood by their mother.

I began to feel sick as one of the fawns licked the blood from its mother's head. The other knelt down on her front elbows and began nuzzling at her mother's belly.

Paralyzed with sadness for what seemed like an eternity, we stood speechless. I was the first to act. I drew my handgun and pulled back the hammer. The click caused the fawns to look up. Jeff followed suit, slowly, so as not to scare them off. As they stared at the headlights, we put them out of the misery that we had caused them.

We dragged the fawns off into the ditch and wrestled the deer onto the hood of the Cadillac. We drove to the log across Shadow Beach Road and walked the rest of the way to the house.

When we got back, Jill said she thought Charlie's fever was beginning to break. Maybe Charlie was starting to win the battle, or maybe the antibiotics had started to work. I was glad either way.

The adrenaline long gone, sadness settled over me. I had no specific remorse for what I had done, but just a general feeling of sadness that the guy was right: that's just how it is now.

I awoke the next morning with Brenda sitting next to me. I pretended to still be asleep as she grabbed my hand and looked at my scabby, blood-crusted knuckles. She began to cry as she stroked my hand. She leaned over and kissed my cheek for an uncomfortably long period of time and then got up. I heard Kelly walk in and ask Brenda what was wrong. "Nothing, honey. Everything is going to be just fine," Brenda said.

Brenda's brothers collected the stuff from the Caddy and slaughtered the deer we killed. We ate venison that day and thanked our lucky stars for what we had. I knew Jeff spilled the secret to Brenda, as spouses will do, but we never discussed the men in town or the fawns with the group. The world was different and not everything needed to be discussed.

26

SHADOW BEACH/PORT ANGELES, WA

"If you want a happy ending, that depends, of course, on where you stop your story." -Orson Welles.

It was very painful to leave my wife and daughter at Shadow Beach, knowing I may never return. Deep down I knew that they weren't really there at all. Those were just shells in the ground, but, yet, that gravesite represented half of my life. It was the same feeling I had when they left on vacation, only no place on the calendar marked their return. I struggled by the graves for some time, before the other half of my life helped me to summon the courage to walk away. If it hadn't been for them, I think I would have sat there with Kate and Elaine until I died.

It took half the day to sail back to Port Angeles. We found a small, secluded inlet and anchored the RY inside. It didn't offer much protection, but Sonny, Jeff, and his brothers-in-law had done a good job painting the RY black which helped it blend in. There was nothing around there on land, and it would have been hard to spot the RY from the open water with the sails down. And it was the best we could do.

The target spot was fifteen miles inland by my recollection. A small group of adults could make at least two or three miles an hour, and as such we could get close by nightfall. We would camp until daybreak, check out Sean's place, and be back to the RY by mid-morning the next day no matter what we found.

A large group would be slower, and the children would drag us down considerably. As obvious as it was that there would be no sense in taking everyone with us, it was a hard sell—especially to the children. Nevertheless, sometimes adults have to make hard decisions, and we decided that the traveling party would consist of me, Sonny, and Josh.

Since it was my plan and only I knew the way, I had to go. I trusted Sonny with my life, and Josh's military training and understanding of tactical operations could come in handy. So they were both natural choices. That left Joe, Jeff, Dean, and Jimmy to protect the women and children on the RY until we returned.

We took minimal supplies—two MREs each, weapons and ammo, and canteens. Water would not be an issue, but we needed something to treat it in. We didn't even bother with sleeping arrangements. We needed to travel lightly and quickly.

The mountains loomed in the background, each distinct set taller than its predecessor and gradually decreasing in clarity—different shades of blue all. First the crystal clear ridge that rose from the water to the main plateau and then the hazy but still distinct foothills with their top most, snow-covered trees rimming the ridge like jagged saw teeth. Taking up the rear were the distant snow-capped peaks. They were still distinct against the overcast skies, but lacked detail when compared to the features in the foreground.

We crossed over the highway west of town. We considered walking straight down the highway for several miles, and while that would have shaved an hour off our trip, it would have taken us straight through town. I knew the back roads, so we opted to stay out of sight as much as possible.

We crossed a surprisingly traversable stretch of forest. Due to the moist, mild climate of the Pacific Northwest, most of the forest was impenetrable, choked with thorny and stinging underbrush that would have been the envy of any tropical jungle. But the stretch we happened upon was mostly pine and fir, and the needle fall prohibited much undergrowth. We had to duck under branches often, but we walked along most of the time on a soft, cushioned needle bed—a nice reprieve for our feet and knees.

After a few hours, we emerged from the forest into a clear cut. It was the first time I had ever appreciated that deplorable logging technique. We walked for a couple of miles over and around stumps and brush piles.

Finally, we climbed over a ridge, and the Elwha river valley opened up before us. The Elwha is the main river that empties snowmelt from the Olympic Mountains into the Strait of Juan De Fuca. It cuts a deep gorge through the foothills, but about ten miles upstream the gorge opens into one of the most beautiful valleys in the world. The federal government owned much of the valley, but private citizens—politicians' friends, mostly—had snapped up a few of the tracts. We were heading for one of the private tracts.

We followed a forest service road that snaked along the river. It softened the hike through the gorge a bit, but it had grown over to a surprising degree in such a short time. I savored the thick smell of pine, a nostalgic smell from my youth in woods just like those.

When night fell we camped very close to the creek at a turnout in the road. The rumble of the creek was a change from the sound of the sea. But, after almost two months on the RV, I doubted I could have slept much in complete silence anyway.

That part of western Washington abounded with dry firewood for two reasons: first, it was in the rain shadow of the mountains; second, what rain did fall tended to be light and was quickly absorbed by the thick canopy above, leaving any wind fall to dry on the ground below. Unfortunately, we couldn't take advantage of the abundance since a fire would have been very conspicuous.

Josh insisted on taking first watch, and I was to take second followed by Sonny on third. I fell asleep shortly into my watch and thus never awakened

Sonny. Sonny's morning wink let me know that he woke up first, and Josh was none the wiser.

It took us a couple of hours to traverse the length of the gorge. By the time we neared the end, the rain began. It fell lightly at first and then came down hard. We saw nothing unusual along the way, although it could be said that, by that time, it was unusual to see nothing unusual. Despite the thick overcast and rain, the gorge remained as beautiful as ever. The gorge was only a mile wide for most of its length, and shear walls jutted up at its edges. I thought it made the place pretty defensible, and I smiled at the thought.

We reached a major decision point three hours after daybreak. We could continue along the road or shave two hours off the trip with a short cut. The narrow dirt trail shortcut hugged a cliff and intersected the road just a half-mile along. The paved road looped around for at least three or four miles just to reach the same spot. The gorge loomed below, and while I had hiked the trail before, I remembered it to be dicey in spots—even when dry. Surely the pouring rain would make it worse. However, we were already behind schedule, so we chose the short cut.

We ambled carefully along the slick, muddy trail. What was a steep vegetated slope at first, turned into a vertical rock wall both above and below us within a few hundred yards. Josh led as we picked our way past miniature waterfalls that had formed in the heavy rain. Bits of the earth had washed out along the downhill edge of the trail. Roots stuck out of the uphill side, and we had to swing precariously out over the abyss to get by them.

About half-way across the short cut, some rocks came loose and tumbled down from above. Josh didn't see what was coming, but Sonny did. He pushed Josh out of the way just in time. The rocks cracked and snapped against the bank above our heads and then fell silently for a few seconds below us before shattering on the gorge bottom. I peered down and saw millions of shards of rock at the bottom—that was hardly the first rockslide there. I looked warily above and then caught up with Sonny and Josh.

We rounded a corner and saw the paved road a hundred yards ahead. The terrain flattened out into a meadow in less than fifty yards. We hurried along the trail to reach safety. I watched the rhythmic movement of Sonny's feet as I kept my eyes on the trail in front of me. Sonny stepped oddly on a rock with his left foot, and in the attempt to catch his balance, he overcorrected, and his right foot slipped out from under him. He tumbled toward the edge of the cliff and clawed for purchase. I dropped to my knees and tried to grab him, but I missed. Sonny went slowly over the curved edge of the cliff, and Josh and I were powerless to stop him.

We heard the thuds of Sonny bouncing off the cliff through the driving rain. I stood numbly and looked over the cliff.

We could not see where Sonny had landed. We called for him, but he didn't respond. We moved forward into the clearing where the slope was much gentler. I scaled lower and then worked my way back along the edge of the gorge, Josh right on my tail. I shimmied along a ledge and around a bank of rock when I spotted him. He was flat on his back, his left leg bent awkwardly behind him. We continued along the ledge and reached a place just above the rock ledge upon which Sonny landed.

"Sonny!" I yelled.

He did not respond.

"Lower me down."

"It's got to be ten feet," countered Josh.

"I can't jump that far, but maybe if you lower me a few feet, it won't be such a jump."

Josh grabbed my arms, and I slipped feet first over the ledge. When Josh had lowered me as far as he could, I told him to let go. I tumbled against the rock wall, landed awkwardly on me feet, and then fell backwards, nearly slipping over the edge. I caught myself and scrambled over to Sonny.

I immediately checked his pulse: strong and steady. Breathing: fine. I slapped lightly at Sonny's cheeks, telling him to wake up. No response. Sonny's leg was bent behind him, and his thigh elbowed about half way between his hip and knee. A sharp piece of bone poked through his pants.

"Shit," I muttered. "He broke his leg."

"Damn it!" came the response from above.

"Help me down."

I stood and reached up as Josh slid over the edge. I grabbed his feet and lowered him until I could no longer support his weight. I let go, and he landed gracefully on his feet.

With Josh by my side, I retrieved my knife from my pocket and cut Sonny's pants open. His leg bulged terribly.

"Jesus," said Josh. "Look how much it's swollen already."

I pushed at Sonny's leg, and it was spongy. I depressed the skin next to the bone, and blood shot out in a spurt. When I let go, it slowed to a trickle.

"God damn it. I don't think it's swelling. It's bleeding inside. Do you think he nicked the artery – the femoral artery?"

Blood began to force through the opening and run down his leg.

"I'd say so. Now what the fuck are we going to do?" asked Josh.

"Look at how big it is. What does the human body have, eight pints?"

"I think so."

"There has got to be a couple of pints already, just in his leg."

I ripped Sonny's pants wide open, trimmed off the fabric of the leg, and began to cut strips.

"Here. Tie this together to make a tourniquet."

Josh did as I asked and then wrapped the fabric around Sonny's upper thigh. When we moved his leg, then skin near the bone tore from the pressure and blood gushed out. I put my hand over the wound in a lame attempt to stop the blood flow, and the skin tore long and deep, like a hardboiled egg squished between two fingers. Blood roared from the wound, so I stuck my finger inside Sonny's leg. Blood ran over my hand and wrist. It felt warm and thick, like sticky motor oil.

"Tighten the tourniquet."

"It's as tight as I can get it!" exclaimed Josh.

The tourniquet wasn't working at all. I felt the pulsating, warm gushes on my fingers and realized that Sonny was in deep trouble. I felt panic rising inside me and began to feel flush and nauseas.

"He's going to die right here on this rock if we don't stop this," I said.

I pressed hard on the wound, and Josh cranked on the tourniquet again, this time with everything he had. The blood slowed a little. Rivulets of water shot off the bank above and washed some of the blood from his leg.

"Get into my backpack and get the first aid kit."

I tried to slip one arm out of the strap, but it wouldn't bend that way.

"Cut the fucking thing off. I can't let go."

Josh cut through the strap and began to rifle through my backpack.

"I'm going to cut into his leg. We've got to find that artery and fix it."

"The fuck you are! What do you think you are, a trauma surgeon? If he's not dead now, he will be when you do that."

Unable to find my kit, Josh upended my backpack and dumped the contents onto the rocks. He rifled through my stuff and then stopped on something.

"Jesus! You've got Celox! Josh said as he ripped open the pouch.

"Move your hand!"

Josh ripped open the pouch and poured the powder on the hole in Sonny's leg. He pushed it down into the hole with his finger and then poured more on and packed it around the bone.

"What is it?" I asked.

"Coagulant. We used this shit in the field in Iraq. Where the hell did you get it?"

"A good friend," I said, thinking of Bill. "I didn't even know what it was."

Josh wrapped more of the fabric strips around Sonny's leg and tied them tightly. I found the first aid kit and gave him some gauze which he wrapped around the wound.

"That'll slow the bleeding, anyway," Josh offered.

"Now all we need is a life flight out of here. We just delayed the inevitable."

"Let's get him out of here," Josh said.

"If we move him, it may make it worse. Maybe we take out the rest of the artery, and he bleeds out before we ever get him off this ledge."

"Well, then let's get out of here. We've got to find help."

"I think you should stay, Josh. I'm the only one that knows where to go and somebody's got to watch over Sonny."

"What good am I here?"

"You can build a fire, keep him warm."

"Then you fall off a cliff and we're done," Josh said.

"Maybe you're right. Let's bundle him up. It shouldn't be much further. We'll come right back if we don't find anything." In reality, I began to resign myself to the idea that Sonny was as good as dead anyway.

It was further than I thought. It took almost an hour to reach the end of the gorge where we caught our first glimpse of the Valley of the Gods, as I called it. Only a god was big enough to occupy such a place.

Just as I began to wonder if we shouldn't start being careful of other people again, a strange sensation of falling came over me, momentary weightlessness and then a painful collision with the ground. Josh disappeared first, but it did not register until my shoulder dug into the earth. The only thing that saved my shoulder bones from certain shatter was a bed of pine needles and leaves.

I felt the barrel of a gun poking my rib cage. A hand ran quickly up and down my legs, inside and out, around my waist and fished out my gun, then continued over my torso.

Out of the corner of my eye, I saw the black leather boots and the bottom few inches of the pant legs of the man that held Josh down. He wore camouflaged fatigues, old style, green and black, not the light weight brown and browner fatigues that had become all the rage in the age of desert wars.

"Base. Over."

I could not hear a response.

"Two of the three in custody. Males. Over."

He paused, apparently to listening to the reply.

"Stand by."

My captor rolled me over. The barrel of his gun was now directly over my heart. He wore a camouflaged hood with a clear plastic mask covering his face. In the twilight and shade of the forest, his pearly white eyes were the only recognizable feature on his face. A little foam microphone like the ones that the skinny, fake-boobed, charlatans wore on MTV, pressed against the inside of his mask.

"What is your name?"

I told him my name, which he repeated back into the microphone, labeling me adult one.

"What are you doing here?"

"I'm looking for someone who used to live here. Sean McMasters."

"Base. Adult one claims to be looking for a Sean McMasters."

I still couldn't hear what was being said on the other end.

"I don't have any ID," I said, before he could ask the question.

"Negative ID. Over."

"Look," I said. "If McMasters is here, just tell him it's me and he shouldn't be jumping off ferries."

He looked puzzled, like a man who saw something familiar but couldn't quite place it. He repeated what I said back to base.

"Copy," he said. "Standing by."

The soldiers helped us to our feet.

"What's going on?" I asked.

"Standby," the soldier said. "Remain where you are."

A minute passed as everyone stood in silence. All the men were dressed in military fatigues, hoods, and masks and carried automatic weapons.

Vehicles rumbled in the distance and then grew closer. They stopped, and we heard doors open and close. Men beat through the underbrush and emerged. A man held up a flashlight and pointed it at me.

"Jesus H. Christ! Is that you? Lower your weapons, men."

It sounded like McMasters, but because of the light in my eyes and the mask he wore I couldn't tell. He lifted his mask and turned the flashlight on himself; it was him. He did not look a day older than the last time I saw him.

"Any chance you've got the plague?" Sean asked.

"No," I said.

Sean removed his hood and mask entirely, ignoring the protest of his comrade.

"Fellas," he said. "This is the sum-bitch I was telling you about. Got me to do all kinds of crazy shit, back in the day."

He bear hugged me. I tried to return the gesture, but any number of pieces of equipment strapped to his person dug into me.

"I see you figured where I'd be, huh? Where have you been? What did…," he trailed off. "You look like shit. Oh, what the hell's the matter with me? Are you all right?"

I rubbed my forehead and eyes with both hands and exhaled loudly. I choked back tears of relief and squeaked: "We've had a rough time."

"Where's your third party?"

"Third what?" I asked, dazed.

"There were three of you coming up the canyon before we lost sight of you."

"Oh! Damn!" Josh and I yelled in unison. "Sonny!"

"He fell down a cliff. Broken leg, badly hurt. We've got to get to him."

I began to run back through the brush when one of the men grabbed me.

"Sir," said the soldier, his mask still drawn. "We'll drive," he pointed off in the direction of the vehicles.

"Mount up!" Sean shouted to everyone and no one in particular. Like machines suddenly switched on, the men fanned out to escort Josh and me into a waiting vehicle just through the brush.

Sean piled in next to me and asked where Sonny went down. I told him about the short cut and explained the injuries. The driver clicked down his night vision goggles, and we raced off into the settling blackness at a healthy speed, headlights unnervingly off.

As we bumped along down the valley again, Sean spoke into his mic:

"Get a medic down to point seven, he said. One casualty, broken leg, possible mortal injuries. And bring Phillips. Sounds like we may need to make a remote extraction."

"Affirmative."

"Negative. We've already got a security detail."

Sean was apparently done with his orders.

"Sean," I said. "There's more. A lot more."

"What is it?"

I explained the situation with our families on the RY.

"Copy that," he said slowly, as if considering something.

"Sit tight. We'll get you back to base and fixed up. I'll muster the team, and we'll make the rescue."

Sean put his arm around me.

"I'm glad to see you man," he said. "And I'm damned glad you are ok. Don't worry, we have some of the finest men there are. We'll get 'em back here just fine."

. . .

Sean's men had Sonny out of that canyon, and we were all on our way to base camp in less than fifteen minutes. The medic complimented us on our first aid. He made no promises, but he assured us that the best field surgeons that government money could buy were in that camp. He told me that they'd seen much worse. Of that, I had no doubt.

While Sean put together his team, the medic checked Josh and me over. He poked and prodded and pronounced us without the plague and in generally good condition.

When Sean returned, I refused his offer to remain at base camp. So did Josh.

The rain had stopped as we headed back out into the night. We piled back into what I now recognized to be Humvees.

"Tell me again which alcove they are located in," said Sean.

"It's the one about three miles east of town just off Highway 101."

I sensed we were heading east and didn't recognize the road, so I questioned Sean about it:

"So we're not going straight down?" I asked. "I don't know this road."

"No, we can't. Not safe. If we came straight down the road, someone might catch on that we are up here. We'll go east, drop down on the highway about ten miles out and then back track."

"I see, so anybody sees you coming, they'll think you came in from the metro area?"

"Exactly. Then we'll high tail it back that way and they will think we're gone. Anonymity is the prime directive, remember? You didn't tell anyone about my plan, did you?"

"No," I said. "Just the people we're with."

"Good man."

On the ride down, I questioned Sean about his outpost:

"So, how about all this?" I started. "How many of you are there?"

"About two hundred," said Sean. "We started with ninety-nine of my closest friends—mostly military. We've almost doubled our ranks since then."

"How?"

"We send out scouts looking for people. Everyone who lived in the valley is with us now, and we've gathered quite a few new citizens from the towns below. Sequim and P.A."

P.A. was the local abbreviation for Port Angeles.

"How....uh....why?"

"We need all the people we can get if we want to survive. I mean we could have just holed up here, us guys, and then what? In ten, fifteen, twenty years, we'd all be dead and for what? It's grim out there as far as we can tell, and we want to maintain our species. We monitor the towns and the Strait. Sometimes we watch people for days."

"So that's how you knew there were three of us."

"Yep, we watched you all the way up. In fact, my men probably saw your boat come in. It's kind of unusual to see many boats these days, but as long as you don't bother us, we just watch."

"Anyway, after we watch people we approach potential targets and make them an offer they can't refuse."

"What offer?"

"Do you want to live in a safe, harmonious community? We can offer you protection, food, shelter, medical care. All we ask for in return is your effort. Provide us with whatever you are good at. Oh, and if you agree, you cannot leave. Ever."

"Cannot leave?"

"That's right. We can't risk anyone knowing we are here. We've expended considerable effort maintaining operational security and secrecy, and we aren't going to give it up for a minute. No one has ever left here once they see what we have to offer. Not yet, anyway. But we will take steps to ensure that no one can leave and compromise our security—if it comes to that."

Both Josh and I understood his meaning, and, suddenly, the place started to close in. But we knew what the world was like outside that valley and knew we'd get over the sudden feeling of imprisonment.

"Have people refused?" asked Josh.

"Yes, many."

"And then what?"

"Nothing."

"Nothing?" I asked.

"Yeah, we never bring them here first. We approach them in the theater—I mean, out there—and give them the ultimatum. If they refuse, they can be on their way to whatever fate awaits them."

"How do you decide whom to approach," I asked.

"As I said, we watch the towns. We look for women and children first since women are extremely useful and children are generally harmless. Plus, women and children are the most desperate and most likely to agree, especially once they realize we aren't like the rest out there. We also look for men who appear to be decent. You know, trying to care for families, not doing the usual things we find men doing out there." Sean looked disturbed, as if he suddenly remembered something horrible.

"What do men do out there?" asked Josh.

Sean hesitated as he considered his answer. I could have answered that question myself.

"Not good things, as you might imagine. Anarchy rules, and that means deep-seated emotion can flow unchecked. Just last month we were watching a building in P.A. that we thought had women inside. As my scouts surveilled the building, some men hustled several girls outside into the cold. They were buck naked and looked as if they weren't more than fifteen. They then duct taped the girls to light poles by their hair and started spraying them with hoses. Mind you, it was cold, like now. After a few minutes of that, two of the men grabbed the legs of one of the girls and held her so that the third man could rape her. Having seen enough of that, my men took them down."

"You were close enough to shoot them?" I asked.

"My scouts are all sniper trained. They could kill a man at a mile out, and no one would ever know they were there."

I stared out into the black for a few seconds and then said to no one in particular: "Is that all we are, just a bunch of thugs and rapists?" Brutality was pretty much all I had seen since I set foot back in "civilization." I had started to fear that, deep down, we all really were just animals. Eat, screw, and torment others was, apparently, all that most of the scumbags left cared about.

Sean broke my train of thought. "When all anyone thinks about is their next meal or their next orgasm, they'll do some pretty short-sighted things. I guess they see men as a threat to be eliminated and women as useful items to be collected and used. But that's not how we think. We are taking the long view."

"So what happened to the girls down there?" Josh cut in.

"They are with us now. Nice girls—three sisters. And their mother too. The men had abducted the whole family, killed the father and held the women in that building. They'd been there several days when we stepped in. They don't talk about what happened, but it's not hard to guess."

I thought about all the women in my life. The only ones who had escaped that fate, as far as I knew, were Brenda and her daughters.

"A fourth man was still inside the building," Sean continued. "He came out after we took down the other three. We immediately snuffed him out and moved in. The girls were terrified at first, of course, and we found their mother inside—equally terrified. Once we calmed them down and explained the situation to them, they gladly came with us. They've been in camp ever since and are quite helpful."

I thought about the women in the van back on state route 525 on Whidbey. I hoped they had fared as well, but I feared not. I reminded myself that I couldn't save the world.

"That is not an isolated incident," I said. "Trust me."

Sean nodded. "I think we're just the most sensitive to the plight of the women. Plenty of men are being killed and tortured too. Cannibalism is starting. It's only going to get worse, I think."

I lowered my head into my hands. Sean put his hand on my shoulder.

"I think there are a fair amount of us out there too," Sean consoled. "We've been in contact with some not too far from here. It'll be ok, eventually."

"So what's the rest of your plan?" asked Josh. Even though he was still a little sore from the takedown, I could tell he was warming up to Sean and his men. They were just his sort of thing.

"Well, we're starting over, right up there. Sean motioned back up the hill."

"We've got food for years and water is never an issue in these parts. We have enough fuel to keep our generators running through the winter."

It suddenly dawned on me that they had power, but I never heard any generators running at all.

"We've already got our engineers working on geothermal power for when the fuel runs out."

"Geothermal?" I questioned.

"Yep. Remember the hot springs?" He said. "How long did it take us to learn not to go in there drunk?" Sean laughed. I felt like smiling, but didn't.

"Anyway, it's an unlimited source, and it doesn't depend on anything else," he continued.

"What about wind?" Josh asked.

"Too conspicuous," countered Sean. "A wind turbine big enough for our needs would attract attention. It would be visible for miles."

"How about hydro on the river?"

"It will be frozen solid this winter and may take years to thaw. We can't count on running water for a while. We'll work on that when it becomes available again. In the meantime, the spring will provide what we need. We are already setting up another village closer to the spring. It will be a long winter, and our sources tell us that it will probably last a couple of years. But we plan to come out the other side, and then we are home free."

"How about defenses?" asked Josh.

"There is only one way into this valley and you found it. We could defend that entrance from the Red Army if we needed to. And you can help," Sean said, pointing to Josh.

Josh sat up a little straighter in his seat.

"We monitor the canyon and the surrounding towns and countryside twenty-four seven. You've been introduced to our men. Nobody is going to breach our perimeter."

Josh and I nodded.

"It looks like you've thought of everything," I said.

"Surely not!" Sean countered. "But every person we bring on thinks of something new and we get that much closer."

I asked Sean what had gone on around the world. I knew he would know better than anyone.

"It's bad," he said. "Everybody started shooting at everybody else and it just went downhill from there. We didn't get nuked up here, but other parts of the country were hit hard: Cheyenne Mountain, DC, all the silos in Montana and the Dakotas. We're out of business. It's not just us either, the whole world is dark. We bombed ourselves back to the Stone Age. I'll fill you in later, but whatever you've heard, it's worse than that."

We suddenly burst from the woods and squealed out onto highway 101, westbound.

A few quiet miles later, we came to a stop in front of the alcove.

The night was as dark as ever, and thick trees obscured the water. I stepped out of the Humvee and walked through the strip of woods to the water's edge. I gave the pre-arranged signal of three short whistles, two short whistles, and one long whistle. No reply.

The quiet night should have permitted them to hear the signal. Maybe they heard the vehicles approach and were scared. I signaled again, this time as loud as I could whistle. Still no response.

Sean crept up and stood next to me.

"I'll have to walk around the shore and get closer," I told him. "They're anchored over there." I pointed toward the left.

Sean and I walked along the shore, and I repeated the signal several more times.

"Damn!" I lamented under my breath.

"Maybe they moved to the other side," I whispered to Sean.

Sean sighed.

"Hold on a sec."

Sean spoke into his mic: "Team, need location on the boat in the bay. Over."

"Sorry sir, can't see through the foliage," came the reply.

"Shit."

"I don't like to use any light when I'm out at night," Sean said. "But we can briefly light up the bay to see where they are."

We crept through the trees and knelt down behind a log near the water's edge.

"Get down over there," Sean whispered as he motioned to his left. "I doubt anyone is out here, but if someone is going to shoot, they'll shoot at the light. It's best not to be behind it."

He crawled about ten feet to my right and set his light up on the log.

"I'll scan the bay, you look," he said.

"Copy," I said.

He switched on the light and started to scan the bay.

He swept back and forth across the several-hundred-yard-wide bay. Nothing. The RY was gone.

"It's not there," I said.

"Are you sure this is the right one?" he asked. "There are dozens of these."

"I'm sure," I said, dejected.

"Secure the perimeter," Sean said into his radio. "We need to have a look around."

On cue, motors started, and vehicles rolled out.

In a minute, the reply came back: "perimeter secure."

"Can you see the bay now?" he asked into the radio.

"Roger. Empty," the soldier said, anticipating Sean's next question.

Sean flipped on his light and stood up. He began to scan the ground. He ordered two other men to do the same. Three lights pierced the darkness scanning the ground around the bay for clues.

It took less than five minutes for one of them to find something. Half a dozen of us closed in for a look.

Sean motioned to one of the men. "What do you think?"

"Two out, five in."

"In or out first?"

"Look at these ones," the man said, motioning to a particular set of tracks. "The inbounds overlay these outbounds. Outbound first."

"They're all different," Sean said. "Do you have seven individuals?"

"Affirmative."

"All men, right?"

"Affirmative."

"Three heavy, over 200, the rest lighter."

"He can tell all that from these tracks?" I asked Sean.

"That's his specialty."

"So what does this tell us?"

"Two men came out of the water first. Both men were under 200 pounds. They were walking. Seven men went back into the water later. Three ran, four walked in. We can't tell in what order. We know they were men from the gate and depth and style of the imprint. So, I would guess that two of your party came out of the water from the boat, were sighted, and ran back in. They were followed by five others. That is presumably why they are not here now. We have to assume your people have been captured."

"How do we even know these are our people?" Josh asked.

"The tracks were laid down after the rain and since the last tide change. This happened within the last 5 hours."

My heart sank.

Sean nodded to two of the men, and they scampered back up to the Humvees. The two other men continued scanning the beach with flashlights.

A minute later, the two scanners returned and reported finding no other tracks.

A loud whistle came from a small ridge above the bay.

"Up here!"

When we arrived, the soldier extended his hand and showed us three shell casings. He then shined his light to the ground and illuminated two sets of tire tracks in the sod.

"Trucks?" asked Sean.

"Roger."

"Any more footprints?"

"Negative. The sod is too solid. Looks like our five below weren't alone. They were just the boarding party. Two vehicles makes our adversary at least seven individuals."

"Is it them?"

"Think so. Tracks are consistent with their vehicle."

The radio crackled to life: "Lookouts reported movement on the water toward P.A.," the voice on the other end reported. "An hour and forty five minutes ago. No direct visual. Too dark."

"Copy. Roust VanDyke and give him a Sit Report. Tell him to scramble four combat units and meet us at point 14, a.s.a.p."

"Copy."

The radio went dead, and Sean hustled me back to his Humvee.

Speeding down the highway with no headlights in pitch black darkness is very disorienting. An eerie green glow emanated from the night vision goggles worn by the driver and front seat passenger. The other men, including Sean, checked and rechecked their equipment.

"What did he mean by no direct visual?" I asked.

"From our distant vantage point up on the bluffs over town, we can't directly see much in town in this darkness. With NVG, we can detect movement on the water and sometimes make out the type of vessel from that distance, but that's about it."

"So we don't know where the boat went exactly? Or even if it was the RY?"

"No, but who else was it? We have a pretty good idea where it went though."

"Where?"

"Pier 3. For the last two weeks, we've been monitoring a group set up there. About ten individuals. Until lately they'd just been the typical assholes—treasure hunters, we call them. You know, pillaging the town for its valuables. Opportunists, not violent. Real pussies. But they abducted two passers-by the day before last, and that's usually the sign that they've turned the corner from being assholes to being pieces of shit. We've been planning to take them out, but on our terms. Tonight they get taken out on their terms."

The radio barked: "Four to one, target located. Pier 3. Visuals on five hostiles. No visual on victims."

"Copy," Sean said. "Hang tight."

"How did they see it?" I asked.

"They're already on site."

"They came straight into town?"

"No. There is a way out to the west also. Much shorter. My men don't waste any time."

"So how do you not give yourselves away riding into town in vehicles like this?"

"This is the first time we've been into town by vehicle. We've always gone in on foot."

"Sorry to bring you into this," I lamented.

"We would have neutralized this situation even if I didn't know you."

"But you wouldn't have rolled right into town, guns blazing."

"Probably not."

"Thanks. I just hope none of your guys get hurt."

"Any of these guys would lay down their life for any of us. That now includes you and your family. But don't worry about that. We won't be getting hurt. These fuckers will never know what hit them."

"I imagine," I said.

"McMasters, this is VanDyke," the radio said. "In position and ready. No news."

"Copy," Sean said. "Use your judgment. We're within 20."

"Use your judgment?" I questioned.

"Every one of these men is either fully capable of leading teams like this or already has. Each has my tacit approval to act if he deems it necessary to secure the objective. We act as a team, and I lead the team, but I trust every one of them with my life. These are the best soldiers in the world, and if anyone can get your family out safe and sound, they can."

"How many are we looking for?" Sean asked.

Sean smiled and chuckled as I counted on my fingers.

"Thirteen," I said.

"Thirteen?" Sean questioned. "Not including the three of you?"

I nodded.

"Adults versus children?"

I went to my fingers again.

"Six adults, seven children."

Sean keyed his mic. "Be advised we are looking for thirteen individuals. Six adults, seven children."

"Copy thirteen, six by seven," came the reply from the voice I began to recognize as VanDyke.

Suddenly the soldier behind us stood up, opened a hatch in the roof, and with the wind suddenly whistling by, he manned a gun mounted on top. Darkened buildings started rolling by outside the windows.

"Here, you'll need these." Sean handed me a pair of NVG.

I had used NVG to take night time weather observations back on Kwaj. But these were different. I slipped them onto my head and flipped down the goggles, but nothing happened. Anticipating my trouble, Sean reached over and switched them on. He guided my hand to an adjustment and twisted, showing me how to operate it. Everything came into focus and turned green. The technology was incredible. I could see better with NVG at night than with my own eyes during the day.

We squealed around a corner and into an alley and then onto another main road. We swerved to avoid two mangled vehicles in the road.

That smell appeared again.

"How do you know they don't have lookouts that see us coming?" I asked.

"Too stupid. We've been watching them. Remember? We know their habits."

We skidded to a stop in front of a building. The sign on the front said Ocean Treasures. Some sort of touristy curio shop. Ransacked.

"Follow me," Sean said to me. "And be quiet."

I got out of the vehicle and saw three other Humvees already there with at least a dozen men fully outfitted in army fatigues and all variety of gear.

Sean made a litany of hand signals and then as quietly as church mice, the men scattered in every direction.

Sean motioned me to follow him, and we entered the building and bounded up the stairs.

On the roof, we encountered a man positioned at the edge of the roof, his rifle trained on the marina. I saw the RY as plain as day. A man paced the deck, rifle in hand.

Sean introduced me to VanDyke.

"Sit tight," Sean said. "I'll be right back."

"Can you hit him from here?" I whispered to VanDyke.

VanDyke laughed quietly.

"Sir, this is a M82A3, 50 cal, silenced, range 1800 meters. I have 22 years of experience as a sniper. We are at 147 meters. It is not a question of whether I can hit him, but which eye socket I would like the bullet to enter and where I want him to land afterward. A 50 cal to the head will knock him back two to four meters and I want him to land quietly in the bay, behind the boat."

Sean scrambled up behind us.

"Team one is go," he said to VanDyke. "You know what to do."

VanDyke nodded.

It occurred to me that every one of those guys knew what the plan was without even talking about it.

Sean motioned for me to come with him.

We ran several blocks toward the pier. Sean pulled me aside.

"You are only here in case we need to differentiate between victim and perpetrator. Anything else and you will be getting in the way. Every man knows what the other will do, and every angle and every ass is covered. You are a variable that could compromise the mission. Stay on my ass. Understood?"

"Of course."

Sean reached up to my NVG and hit another switch.

"There is an earpiece," he said.

I placed it in my ear and suddenly heard lots of radio traffic.

"Update status. A?"

"Can take out. Not ideal."

"B?"

"Got em."

"C?"

"Got em."

"That's minus three now, looking for seven inside."

We ran to within one block of the pier. I could now see the RY and the dead man walking on deck. He had no idea how close he was to death. VanDyke had told me, that at 854 meters per second, the bullet would explode in his brain before it even registered the muzzle flash he just saw.

Sean handed me a device shaped like a pen.

"What is this?"

"Laser pointer. If I tell you to light up a hostile, use that. But for Christ's sake, don't light up the wrong person. The person you light up probably dies. There is no room for error."

Sean spoke into his mic.

"Status. Team one?"

"Go."

"Team two?"

"Go."

"Team three?"

"Go."

"Snipers? "

"Go."

I peered around the corner, having no idea what to expect next.

"Stay on my ass," Sean said sternly.

"On my mark, Sean said into his mic. Three, two, one, mark."

The head of the man on the RY exploded, and he disappeared behind the boat, out of sight. As he did, his finger involuntarily pulled the trigger, and one shot echoed through the night. The man was already dead, but sometimes gravity, momentum, or just bad luck can cause even a dead finger to depress the trigger.

"Damn it!" exclaimed Sean.

"Go, go, go, go!" Sean yelled as he grabbed my jacket and dragged me along toward the pier.

Two more muffled shots rang out as we ran.

The radio spoke: "Minus two. Five left."

We arrived at the pier simultaneously with several of Sean's men. He motioned to them, and one by one they poured into the building.

We waited.

More shots rang from within the building.

"Perimeter and external zone secured," a man barked through the radio.

"Snipers?" Sean spoke into his mic.

"All clear. Five down," came the response from VanDyke.

I could hardly understand how calm these men sounded.

"They're confined to one room," said another voice. "I've got visual. Four hostiles, armed, holding hostages. Fourteen hostages, seven adults, seven children."

"That's wrong," I said. "One extra adult."

"Are you sure?"

I thought again through the roster.

"Yes."

"Standby," Sean said. "One of the hostiles is among the hostages."

"Come on."

We scrambled into the building.

We got to the area where they were being held. It was some sort of processing facility for seafood. The room, littered with dozens of gray plastic crates, was entirely concrete and stunk of fish. Cables with hooks and pulleys hung from the metal rafters. Four men with guns crouched behind some of the hostages. Charlie, Brenda, Dean, and Jeff and Brenda's daughter Penny were all being held at gunpoint; the cowards using them as shields. Jill sat in a side group with Joe, Karen, and the rest of the kids, facing away from us. Some guy had his arm around Jill.

"We're leaving out the back door and taking off on the sailboat," said one of the men.

"You're not going anywhere!" yelled Sean. "You are surrounded. Your only chance to live is to let the hostages go and drop your guns."

"Which one is the fifth? Sean asked me. "Light him up."

I peered over the waist high wall in front of me. I held down the button on the laser and shined it on the man's back. Certain Sean had seen it, I clicked it off.

Sean whispered into his mic: "Did somebody get the mark?"

I watched as one of Sean's men subtly adjusted his aim. I watched his lips move as he whispered into his mic. "Got him."

Sean leaned in to me. "Is that it?" he asked. "All the rest are your people?"

"I looked again."

"Yes."

Sean stepped out from behind cover into the door way, his handgun extended in front of him.

Four of Sean's men did the same thing.

Fear washed over the faces of the bad guys when they finally saw what they were really up against.

"This is your final chance," Sean said.

"We will kill these hostages," one man said.

"Do I look like I'm fucking around?" yelled Sean. "Your only chance to live is if they live. Step back and drop your weapons. All of you, or you all die."

"I will count to three and then you die."

"One."

Bang! Five guns went off simultaneously. On cue, each of the villains fell to the floor, and their hostages dropped, unharmed, from their suddenly dead hands.

My heart jumped as I scanned the room.

Everyone sat stunned, but fine.

"Mission accomplished," Sean said into his mic. "Stand down."

The men shouldered their weapons, scrambled to the perpetrators to secure the guns, and began checking the hostages.

I stood up and looked over the group. Charlie and Kelly locked eyes with me. They jumped to their feet and ran into my arms. I collapsed to the floor and held them.

It was finally over.

27

20 YEARS LATER – NEAR WHAT USED TO BE KNOWN AS PORT ANGELES, WASHINGTON STATE

"In the midst of this chopping sea of civilized life, such are the clouds and storms and quicksands and thousand-and-one items to be allowed for, that a man has to live, if he would not founder and go to the bottom and not make his port at all, by dead reckoning, and he must be a great calculator indeed who succeeds." – Henry David Thoreau, *Walden*

My grandchildren often ask me to tell them stories of how things were before the red plague and the wars—the great reset, as we've come to call it. Kids find comfort in stories about the past from old people. At least they did when I was a child. As I didn't have to walk to school shoeless, through waist-deep snow, and uphill both ways, I was better off than the generations that went before me. At least that's how my grandfather told it. It seems to me that children must find solace in the belief that life perpetually improves.

Some would say it didn't turn out that way for our children, but I don't know. Sure, there isn't any cable television, no professional sports teams or singers to idolize, and no internet. You can't drive down to a store that sells every imaginable product, and every cold you get these days could, ultimately, be your death. It takes work to eat—we have to find, grow, or kill our food. We have electricity, but it takes a lot of effort to keep it going. If I fall and break my neck, there is no trauma hospital to go to. We can't fly all over the world just because we want to.

All those things are true, and if convenience and the ability to occupy your abundant idle time with trash are the tests, then, by all means, our children are worse off than we were before the great reset.

I try to see our cup as half full, though. There is a benefit to figuring out what you want to know instead of just looking it up on the internet. Children these days can find their way to a fishing hole without GPS. Since there is no television and we have to work for our food, no one is fat anymore. Our kids entertain themselves like we used to: by playing games, reading, or creating. We spend a lot of time outside where we belong. The innocence of childhood exists again.

One of my favorite things is that books are back in style. Children don't find reading quaint or boring anymore. I maintain that books were the greatest invention of the whole of civilization before the reset. Books facilitated all other grand inventions. For with books, one can pick up where someone else left off and turn his ideas into an invention that changes the world. Without books, we likely would not have had advances in medicine, engineering, physics, or mathematics. Would Einstein have achieved all that he did if he first had to sit down and invent the calculus? Maybe. After all, he was a genius, but I'm skeptical. No, I believe we would not have had a civilization so advanced without the written word—it is just that simple. Since, unlike the internet, books are still here along with all the knowledge they contain, I am vindicated. One day we can perhaps rebuild what we once had.

Thankfully, we collected a great number of books to keep with us after the reset. The children marvel at the telling of classics like Tom Sawyer, The Grapes of Wrath, and Moby Dick. Ironically, they envy the likes of Tom Sawyer with all the conveniences of his day and the grand times he had traveling about. They dream of being free like Tom. When I read it as a child,

I imagined Tom Sawyer as rather regrettable, better off than, say, Oliver Twist, only because he was in America.

Unfortunately, by the time of the reset I was in the minority in my regard for books. Everyone believed the internet would last forever, and so the printed word gradually fell out in favor of electronic means of information storage. What no one seemed to grasp back then was that as we became an electronic society, our entire civilization began to hinge on the availability of a single thing: electricity.

At the beginning of the twenty-first century, nobody could imagine life without electricity nor could they grasp the reality that once removed, our newly formed, high-tech civilization would cease to exist, instantly. Thus, the events of that time were almost exclusively recorded by electronic means and are, at this time, lost, perhaps forever. Lifetimes of work, stored in so many bits and bytes on servers in other states or on other continents, up and vanished overnight. Some of the authors and architects of the internet achieved great things in their lives. In the end, it hardly mattered.

Losing so many of our loved ones during the reset was very painful. That billions of people suffered so needlessly is heartbreaking. But now, every task in our day has meaning. I know and care about everyone here and would trust them with my life. We don't spend 51 weeks of the year waiting for the one week of vacation so we can go outside. We know where our food came from and what's in it. Ironically, many people before the great reset longed for much of what we have after it.

About the world outside our domain, I don't know much more than I knew twenty years ago. In the first few years after the reset, I heard many stories of the times before, which were utterly false—out of ignorance, embellishment, or malfeasance, I do not know. I heard a story about how we had colonized the moon before the reset, and all its inhabitants were unaffected by the disaster, and that they are almost certainly preparing to come down and rescue us—to bring back technology, medicine, industry, civilization. I wondered if the storyteller was trying to start a new religion. Another storyteller claimed that the whole thing was done to us by our own government. I asked him why such a necessarily sociopathic government would wipe itself out too. He didn't answer. All those stories make for great talk at our community fires on Saturday nights, though.

We don't know how many people are left in the world, but it seems the plague and violence that followed cut a wide swath through humanity twenty years ago. An ambivalent and brutal natural world took over from there and nearly finished the job, far as we can tell. The towns around us are all empty now. We haven't gone into a major city for a long time—Seattle is quite a trip without cars and interstates, and what would be the point? We kept in touch with some other groups via the radios until they stopped answering—their chilling tales told us all we needed to know. We haven't seen another soul in ten years. For all we know now, we are all that's left.

However, there are still faint signs of the old civilization. Nothing puts a charge in the children like seeing a satellite fly over at night. On clear nights, they'll stay up for hours scanning the sky for any sign of movement. Logically, we know that satellites were built to be autonomous and that they most likely continue on their robotic, solar-powered journey, executing computer code, collecting data, and beaming it down to a world that is decades past being able to receive it. But we suppose it is possible someone still controls them.

In twenty years, our group has grown to the size of a small town. We've gotten past living hand-to-mouth, and some sense of order and civilization has returned. At first, it felt almost pointless to bother—to what could we aspire? But then it occurred to us that maybe it was never really so different before the reset. To what more could we aspire simply by virtue of having cable television, a smart phone, and high speed internet?

The point of life remains the same: it is what you think it is. The meaning of life is intrinsic, what goes on outside is of little consequence. One needs only to look to a child to prove it: a child doesn't want for purpose. I find meaning in my family, good books, and contemplation. Others find meaning in spirituality, building great structures, or helping others. Still others find meaning in living in spite of the apparent meaninglessness of it all. Hell, somebody might find their life perfectly meaningful by staring at a rock. None of that is different.

Whatever the case, there is no map to lead the way or instruments to guide us to our purpose, and there never were. We plod along, each of us, sure only of where we've been and how long we've been at it. Much like our trip across the Pacific, the journey through life could be summed up, then as now, by just two words:

Dead Reckoning.

ABOUT THE AUTHOR

Tom Wright has a bachelor's degree in Atmospheric Science from the University of Washington and has been a professional meteorologist since 1995. He grew up on Vashon Island, WA and graduated from Vashon High School in 1987.

Since graduating from college, he's lived and worked in Pennsylvania, Montana, Kansas, and Oregon where he currently lives with his wife and two children.

He also spent six years living and working as a contractor for the U.S. Department of Defense on Kwajalein Island in the Republic of the Marshall Islands, where the storyline of Dead Reckoning begins. In fact, the concept for Dead Reckoning was born over beers one evening at Emon Beach on Kwajalein. Tom has been to most of the locations in Dead Reckoning, including Wake Island.

Tom spent three years as an Incident Meteorologist for the National Weather Service, predicting the weather for firefighting efforts on wildfires. That job took him to amazing places like Yellowstone and Glacier National Park, Grand Canyon, and Gila National Forest. He has been interviewed for numerous national radio and television news programs and was featured in a three-part series on wildfire on The Weather Channel.

Tom is a life-long fan of Seattle sports teams—especially his beloved Seahawks—has coached youth sports through his life, and is currently the special teams coach for the Rogue River High School football team.

Dead Reckoning is the culmination of Tom's love for weather, writing, and apocalyptic literature. He blogs about science and weather at theweatherguru.com.